Maximizing Jordan

A NOVEL

Lewis Banks

Quill Mountain Publishing

Jacksonville, FLORIDA

ISBN 13: 9780991609703
ISBN 10: 0991609700
Library of Congress Control Number: 2014934075
Quill Mountain Publishing, Jacksonville, FL

Cover designed by: Nessgraphica
Printed in the U.S.A

DEDICATION

This book is dedicated to my ultimate fan, my mother Dolores as well as the rest of my family; blood and extended. And for all of you women who find yourself as a Jordan or Daria, this one is for you. And for all of you men and women who are looking for true love, this one is for you too! Enjoy the ride of this novel.

ACKNOWLEDGEMENTS

There have been many people along the way on my journey to releasing *Maximizing Jordan*. I would like to acknowledge them. Some of them are professionals, other authors, family, friends, and classmates. This book has seen the expansion of that circle to include college professors, clergy, and the very fabric of nature itself.

I would like to acknowledge my friend and fellow author L.A "Leslie Esdaile" Banks who provided me with her valuable insight. Sadly Leslie passed away before this release, RIP. My pastor friend Larry Coleman for whom words cannot describe what he did for me. I am a writer today because of his spiritual guidance during my wilderness time. I want to thank my editor Barbara Cronie for the speed and thoroughness of her editing. Barbara you are great. I also want to acknowledge some of the finest people and writers in Barbara Cronie's The Writers' Colony in Delray Beach, Florida. The Writers' Colony helped me become a better writer by providing great feedback out of the love for words. I'll never forget the Writers' Colony. I also want to thank Dr. Diane Chandler at Regent University who taught a class that galvanized my purpose, my ministry, and my spiritual formation. Dr. Patricia Mercier, Regent University, thank you for your wise counsel in helping me to answer a pivotal about which way I wanted to go with some story language.

I want to thank my CSU Marauder family; many of my characters were woven from the personality quilt of so many friends and classmates. My sands, Mike Brown, Calvin Collins, and Mark Rendleman, are my brothers for life. I want to thank Melanie Ridgeway who honored me by allowing me to use her name for one of my characters, although Melanie is real and her character is fictitious, I'll never forget writing an entire chapter on a flight from Miami, and then discussing it and laughing about that chapter with Melanie while waiting to catch another flight at Atlanta Hartsfield-Jackson International Airport. Mel thanks for keeping it real.

I want to thank my focus group for your input as I wrote. They are many, but I will name a few; Mel, Bev, Vivian, Alitash, Deborah, Bridgett, LA., Mark, Johnna, Melinda, Adrienne, S. Ray, Joy, My Regent University family, and so many others who know who they are.

I want to acknowledge and thank my family, children, and friends who have always been there to support and encourage me; my parents Mel & Dolores, Sonny Sherry, Veta, Carmen, Alex, Gabrielle, Irie, Fred, Val, Cherita, Darrell, Hank, Shaun, James, Carlos, Ariana, Adrian, Johnna, Jackie, Bev, Mike, Dawn, Ora, Anthony Woods, Gwen, Joe, Henry, Dr. Louis Baptiste, Hannah, Linda, Judy, Pam, Perry, Thomas, Phyllis, Theo, Joe, Mark, Mike, Tom, David, Diane.

I want to give a very special thanks to my everything Patricia "Trish" who spent many mornings, afternoons, nights, weeks and weekends reading, editing, and listening to my ever changing perfectionist ways of telling this story. Your advice and ever listening ear kept me from getting out of hand. Much love! We are an awesome team, get ready for round three. And to all the other friends and family too numerous to name, or my memory too bad to recall…thank you!

Chapter 1

THE LIGHT

You've got to be kidding me. Another damn red light! It seems like every traffic light turns red just before I make it to the intersection. I guess our tax dollars don't pay for synchronizing these stupid lights. This is going to be another one of those long drives home, I thought. I was driving my best friend Marcus Harris home from a black tie charity event. Marcus is a handsome guy with a medium chocolate skin tone, athletically built, and stands about six feet two inches tall. He has dark brown eyes and keeps a short, almost bald haircut. He is a great guy who tries to be such a ladies' man. I departed from my thoughts and broke my silence.

"Marcus, why are we going home alone and wasting these pristine tuxes?"

"Max, no, I'm not going home. You're going to your broken home. I'm going to call up a honey and work this tux to the hilt."

"That's cold, Marcus, why don't you just stab me in the heart now?"

"In fact, I'll drop you off at home and you can let me drive your Lexus so I can have the honies jumpin' through the window trying to get at a brotha. I'm an exquisitely manicured brother in a black tailored tux, smelling good, and driving a black, big boy Lexus. The ladies will be hoppin' and you know what'll be droppin'."

"You're a tramp!" I replied bursting his bubble.

Marcus and I had attended a gala held at the Ritz Carlton, a swanky event with corporate power players and contributors to community causes. The women were absolutely gorgeous in their evening dresses that looked like they were designed around their well-sculpted curves.

1

The night was almost perfect except for getting caught by all these doggone red lights. I was annoyed with the traffic lights but kept my cool about it.

We just continued driving home and talking on this warm summer night. There was a glowing white full moon, so bright it made the night brighter. Every star in the universe seemed to drift across the horizon. There was a feeling in the air tonight that seemed to say that everything was going great.

Marcus has been my best friend since the third grade. Our close bond makes many people think we're brothers. We've always had each other's back. He was the best man at my wedding. He knows all of my secrets, my indiscretions, and has always kept the confidence of my personal business. He is so loyal to our friendship that I don't think he would disclose my business even if he was served with a court order.

Attending black tie events with me landed Marcus his corporate pilot job. He flies one of those nice customized private jets that you see the rich and famous traveling in. I introduced him to an executive, who knew another executive, who was looking for a new pilot to fly their corporate jet. At times I affectionately throw that back in his face when I need to talk him into going with me when he doesn't want to. I push the guilt trip onto Marcus until he breaks and gives in to me. I know I'm a manipulator, but Marcus is my best friend and doesn't really mind, even though he sometimes whines about it.

My wife Gina used to attend these events with me until her increasing insecurity got the better of her one day. I remember talking to Naomi, the new general counsel for our division at work, when Gina walked up and said, "And what trick is this you're screwing now?"

Naomi, a short and slender Asian woman is quite gorgeous. Her jet black hair was neatly slicked back leading to a single ponytail that fell just below her shoulder blades. It didn't look like a single strand of her hair was out of place. Naomi is so sweet and soft spoken, not normally characteristic of an attorney.

I was mortified and wanted to crawl underneath the carpet. If that wasn't bad enough, before I could pick my face up off the floor in shame, Gina threw her glass of champagne in my face.

Naomi, shocked, turned as red as a cardinal. I know she must have wondered how I could be so accomplished professionally and yet be married to a woman who just displayed such vile behavior. I dared not turn my head around to see who else saw that spectacle. I was confident that everyone in the room including the valets parking the cars outside saw that humiliating episode.

Outside of work, social events are not supposed to be considered work, but they really are extensions of the office. Many neophytes in corporate America mistakenly think work events and outside work social gatherings are different. The rookies let their guard down and shun proper decorum. The consequence of their naïveté has caused many promising careers to crash and burn. I certainly knew better.

Needless to say, that was Gina's final curtain call with me at office events or charity functions. As Gina exited the room at my insistent urging, she hurled one last parting piece of venom at me in front of the entire room.

"Max, it isn't bad enough that you are screwing these American tricks, now you're going international with Asian tramps too!" Nothing could have been further from the truth—Naomi and I were just colleagues and nothing else, but she was an innocent victim of Gina's tirades.

My embarrassment was only exceeded by Naomi's shock. I wondered if my company had an embarrassment leave of absence that I could take. I asked myself how in the world I was ever going to be able to face anyone at work or in the community after that disaster.

When I saw Naomi again, I hung my head apologetically. Naomi said that she may have done the same thing if she had too much to drink and saw her good looking husband talking to a new woman in a sexy dress. I think we both knew Gina wasn't drunk, but Naomi allowed me to save face and I appreciated her reaction as a true professional. Naomi mercifully changed the subject, thank God. We went on to the business at hand and never spoke of it again.

Thinking back on that episode, I happily sighed that long gone are the days of taking Gina with me to public events. The world is a small place. You see many of the same people at different charity events. I bet they are happy that my sidekick Marcus comes with me now instead of Gina. This was another Gina-less night of Marcus and me hanging out for charity.

This wonderful night was drawing to an uneventful close. My boy and I had kicked it and had a good time as usual. The flesh had been sufficiently pressed. All of the required networking was done. Marcus tried to swoon as many single ladies as he could, unsuccessfully I might add. He was right, I was returning to my broken home. I dreaded it too.

Marcus broke our momentary silence. "Max, how long are you going to hang in there with Gina before you call it quits?"

"I don't know. I can't take much more," I replied in exasperation.

"What's keeping you there?"

"Hell, I don't know. More bad choices in my personal life I guess. Man, I kept hoping we'd turn the corner and things would get better. I don't know what it is with the women I've been with. I thought Gina was the one. I've tried to be loyal to my marriage and hang in there. I just want a woman who will be down with me like four flat tires. As corny as this might sound, I would just love to find that one true love that I can build something with. This has turned out to be a disaster and more wasted time. Can a brotha find the real thing?"

"What cha gonna do then playa?" Marcus asked as if he knew the answer but was looking for me to give it to him.

"That is the $64,000 question isn't it? Thank God Daria has always been there for me since undergrad. If I didn't have her in my life, I would've jumped off a cliff by now."

"Thank God! Max, God ain't got nothing to do with it. You need to find something else to claim the Lord for, but you and Daria ain't it, Maxi-Max." Marcus replied busting my Daria rationalization bubble as only he could.

"Why do you have to piss all over my Daria thing? If you weren't my boy, I'd make your plane crash, just like you're trying to crash me and Daria now." I fired back, letting him know he got me.

"Max, we're more like brothers than friends so I'm gonna keep it real with you. You and Daria have been playing friends and having an emotional affair without the sex. Personally, I don't see the fun in that. Daria has been waiting for you over fifteen years since we graduated. You have her strung out like a Max-addicted crack-head. You all walk the line, but don't cross it. Basically the two of you are playing with fire while hoping you don't get burned. I think both of you are holding a lit match while wearing gasoline drawers."

"Listen to you, junior Socrates, trying to dispense advice that you don't believe yourself," I said reminding him of his own misdeeds.

"I am not trying to be the All-American family man like you. I'm a dog and proud of it. I don't want love. I want a cheap thrill. I want a "7-11" babe. You, on the other hand, need to release Daria from her emotional nun-hood, waiting on the Max arrival that will never come," Marcus said with a degree of truth that I hate him for speaking.

"Marcus, you are so stupid. What is a "7-11" babe?" I asked.

"A quick, low maintenance woman who runs into the 7-11 store, shops and runs out. She gets it to go. That's a 7-11 babe," Marcus replied shamelessly.

"Boy, you need Jesus!" I snapped.

"Max, you are the smartest guy I know, with damn near a genius IQ. You're a brilliant businessman, but your personal life is out of control and you can't get it right with women. What the hell is wrong with you? You haven't been with a sane woman since college. Gina is just another in a long line of Maxwell Dean's love misfires."

Before I could respond to Marcus' comment, I saw something out of the corner of my eye that redirected my attention away from him.

"Marcus, look at this guy on my side. He's trying to walk up to the car on the sneak tip."

"Yeah, there's one coming up on my side too. Man this doesn't look good. Run the light Max. Let's get outta here!" Marcus shouted with a sense of panic in his voice.

I punched the accelerator. The Lexus' big engine responded with the horsepower it was known for. The tires screeched. I heard a pop that sounded like my new car was backfiring. I didn't see anything because I was making sure I didn't hit another car as I ran the red light.

"Oh shit," I heard Marcus say with sheer terror emanating from his mouth.

About that time, I felt something hot on my back. It felt like scalding hot water or coffee. I didn't remember Marcus having a cup of coffee in his hand. I didn't think he spilled anything on me. Then it felt like something sharp stuck me in my side, in the middle of my left rib cage.

I glanced over at Marcus. It looked like he could have hit his head when I punched the accelerator. He was wincing in pain. My breathing picked up like I had been running. My limbs trembled from a sudden infusion of adrenalin dispatched by my brain to keep pace with this unfolding crisis.

"Max, they're shooting at us. I'm hit!" Marcus screamed out in utter panic.

Right about then my leg started going numb. I couldn't feel my foot pressing the accelerator. In all of the commotion, I never heard any gun shots or saw any muzzle flashes. I started losing control of the car. Everything was happening so fast but it felt like things started moving in slow motion. I'm not even certain I really processed what Marcus just said. It was like I heard him, but I didn't hear him.

I woke up to this void in time like I was either in a dream or coming out of one. I thought Marcus was with me, and now he's not. "Sir, what is your name?" I heard someone say.

Who is he talking to? I wondered. Come to think about it, who is this dude and where are we? This has to be a dream because I can't see anything.

Then another man sounding excited said, "I need a type and cross, and get me that portable x-ray in here stat!"

And yet a third man said, "Put the other guy over there and get some additional people down here now!" There was panic in his voice. *Why couldn't I see anyone?* I wondered.

The people speaking were like sound bites fading in and out. I didn't see anyone. Nothing anyone said registered in my mind or made sense. As the sounds were fading out, I heard a lady's high pitched voice say, "We're losing him!"

It all felt like a dream. It didn't seem real. I had no idea what was going on. It was as though I went to the theater and walked in on the middle of the movie. The scene was being played out, but I wasn't sure what was going on or who the characters were. At that point, I didn't even remember seeing the people, but I heard the conversations.

"His driver's license says Maxwell Dean," I heard a different woman's voice say.

They're talking about me, I thought. Right at that point the darkness and picture-less landscape of my mind turned bright white. My grandmother who is deceased appeared just as I remembered her the last time I saw her, alive and healthy.

"Max, you have to do it right," she exclaimed in her sweet grandma advice-giving voice.

I thought, *Now I know I'm dreaming because my grandmother (Nanna as we called her) has been gone since 1977.*

"Max, you've been doing it all wrong, you have to get it right this time," Nanna repeated.

"What do you mean Nanna? What didn't I do right?" I asked my angelically soft-faced grandmother whose image was slightly out of focus.

Nanna faded out as quickly as she came in and so did my slight understanding of what she said. I thought that was the strangest dream. I dismissed it quickly. Then some guy in what looked like an all white bathrobe waved good-bye to me and said, "I'll see you later."

I thought, *Who was that guy and how did he know me. I didn't know him. In fact, I didn't really see his face. I only saw his silhouette.*

I recall waking up in a hospital bed with my eyes trying to adjust to the brightly lit room. My nose quickly picked up that sterile hospital smell. I was surrounded by institutional white walls. It seemed like I was hooked up to every machine in the hospital. They were making a concert of various low volume noises. An IV was in my arm and a clamp on my finger. My lips felt dry and parched. I couldn't move. What was going on? I had no idea why I needed all of this stuff.

I vaguely saw Marcus sitting at my bedside. He got up and came towards me, saying something like, "Max you're alright, you're gonna be alright!" Voice trembling, "Look at my boy, laying here like six foot five inches of shot up beige brilliance. Wake up Max. I am going to kill those little bastards for chopping you down like a tree with their bullets. You just wake up and they will get theirs, I promise."

I had no idea what happened to me and why I was in this hospital bed. I felt a little drugged up. I couldn't keep my eyes open. I heard Marcus calling for a nurse as I drifted off to sleep.

The next morning I woke up to Marcus looking at me with a big grin on his face. He seemed so happy to see me awake. Man was I hungry! I wanted to eat something soon and hospital food was not gonna do it for me. My main concern was what the heck I was doing here in the first place. The last thing I remembered was a feeling of heat coming over me when we were in the car.

"Marcus, what happened to me man?" I asked still feeling a little groggy.

He looked at me with concern. "We both got shot by two teenagers who were attempting to carjack us on our way home from the charity event. You passed out at the wheel and lost control of the car. We ran into a tree. Dude, your car was totaled."

"What do you mean we? I am in the hospital and you are walking around. What's wrong with this picture? Where is your wound?" I said, crinkling my eyebrows, dumbfounded by Marcus' apparent healthiness.

"I was treated and released. The bullet went clean through my arm."

"But you don't even look hurt?" I said still puzzled.

"Max, you were shot three times and have been in a coma for three weeks. It was touch and go for a while. Do you remember that?" his facial expression was sad and he looked like he was starting to cry.

I thanked God that I was still alive, but I also had a bunch of questions in my head. I didn't remember being shot. I was trying to replay the incident in my mind. Was I really out of it that long? What about my job? Had anyone told my parents? I knew my family must have freaked out. Questions, questions, I had nothing but questions.

"Where is Gina? Has she come by?" I quizzed Marcus.

"She came by a couple of times to see you right after it happened. I haven't seen her since the first couple of days after you were hospitalized," he acted like he was apologizing for Gina's sparse visits.

There was no mistaking where Gina and I stood now. Not coming by the hospital to see me often while I was in a coma was about as telling as it gets. You discover people's true character when things aren't their best. I lost precious time that I couldn't get back. Things happened for a reason and it was my duty to figure out why this had happened to me. But first, I needed some really good hot food. I was starving.

"Did they catch the boys that shot us?" I questioned Marcus.

"They did. Max, they were only thirteen and fourteen years old. There were some eyewitnesses who saw the whole thing go down. Thank God for that." Marcus sighed.

"What the hell is going on in this world? These kids just don't seem to care about anything and apparently not my life either," I said disgustingly.

"A lot of people have been by to see you, Pike and Sarae, your boss, some of your co-workers, and that sexy little Geisha girl Naomi. Your family was here for a week and then your brother and sister had to go back to work. Then there were the usual cast of characters, Mason and Mel. Your mom just went back home for a minute. I know she'll be sick that she wasn't here when you woke up. Daria came in here and fell apart. She was hysterical right as Gina walked in."

"Oh boy, I know that was drama," I cracked.

"Yep, and Gina told her, 'Leave trick'." Marcus replied smirking.

"I can count on Gina to act like that—at least she is predictable. I'm glad I was still in a coma when those two met."

"You know Daria is classy. Although Daria was crying, she bit her tongue and left without a confrontation. Have you even noticed all of the cards and plants that people sent you? It looks like a botanical garden up in this joint." Marcus said changing the subject as though my health couldn't take the stress.

"Marcus, I didn't even ask how you are. Are you okay?" I asked, thinking about my boy's health.

"That shit hurt three weeks ago, but I'm fine now. They had us in the same emergency room for a while until they sent you up to surgery. Man you had blood coming from everywhere. At one point they did something to you and blood just poured out of your side onto the floor. One time it seemed like there were about twenty people working on you," Marcus solemnly said, shaking his head.

I continued listening to Marcus' story with disbelief and horror. I could only imagine what was happening then. I must have been unconscious because I didn't feel a thing or remember any of that. I had all sorts of thoughts ravaging my brain, but I kept quiet as Marcus continued horrifying me with the events of that night. "Your heart stopped. I thought you were gone. They shocked you with those paddle things and got your heart back. I started yelling that they had to save my boy. I told the doctor not to let you die. I said, "He is my brother." After that they took you away; your side of the ER looked like a bloody war zone. There was a pool of your blood on the floor. There were gauze and bandages soaked with blood lying everywhere. I wasn't sure if I'd see you alive again," Marcus' voice crackled a little bit.

"Damn man, that sounds like it was crazy," shaking my head in disbelief.

"When the doctor came back from your surgery, he told us that one bullet entered your back, hit the collar bone and ricocheted into your lung. The second bullet went between your ribs into the abdomen. They had to remove your spleen because one bullet fragmented and did too much damage. The third bullet went just atop the ear and grazed your left eyebrow. The doctor had such a solemn expression on his face I told him don't tell me he's dead because I won't make it. If he had said that, I think I would've jumped up and kicked his ass! " Marcus said in his animated way.

"So you were ready to go full blown ghetto up in the hospital?" masking my own anxiety about hearing the events of that day.

"Max, you know how we roll beige boy, I ain't lettin' nobody mess wit ma boy."

Marcus' eyes were watering as he choked up. That was my boy and I would have done the same thing if it were him. I can only imagine what he must have felt. Heck, I'm trippin' just listenin' to him. The third bullet got to me just knowing how close it was to my head. If that one had hit me flush, I think I wouldn't be here now.

I extended my hand out to Marcus to shake his hand, or give him "the man grip" as we call it. As I grabbed his hand, I pulled him down to me. With our man grip getting tighter, I put my other arm around him and patted his back. Giving my boy a man hug with tears streaming down my face, I whispered, "I'm glad you're alive. You are my best friend, my brother, and I couldn't bear to lose you. Thanks for staying with me man, I love you brother."

Marcus couldn't help breaking down then. As we continued hugging, finally celebrating surviving the ordeal, he cried like an inconsolable baby. Then he sniffled and said, "Max, they shot you down like a dog in the street. My heart broke seeing you like that and not knowing whether I would still have my boy at the end of the day."

I have never seen Marcus breakdown like this. I've never broken down like this in front of him either. But the joy of my first daylight since the shooting was more than either of us could emotionally contain. They say best friends will ride and die for each other—we nearly did. We came face to face with death and survived. Here we were two grown men hugging each other and crying like two little school children. I didn't care who saw us.

Marcus was crying and trying to speak through the tears and sniffling the dreaded crying snot when he finally got it out, "Max, you know I'm straight, but I love you too man."

I gave him a tighter dude hug and attempted to increase my weak grip, "I know brother, friends to the end."

We were already tight and rock solid friends, but in the moment of our shared tragedy, we cemented our bond for a lifetime. I looked up at the ceiling of my hospital room and thanked God for giving me a friend like Marcus.

Just then the doctor walked into my room and asked Marcus to step out of the room while they checked me out and ran some tests. I knew they wanted to know if I suffered any brain damage. Marcus was more than willing to leave rather than let other people see him crying.

We were tight, but men still have a problem crying in front of other men, even a doctor.

Weeks had passed and I was about to be discharged. It was four weeks of grueling, intense therapy and rehabilitation. After being bed-ridden so long, I had to train my leg muscles to walk again. A couple of times I developed infections, fevers, and other complications from my injuries. One time I fell going to the bathroom and tore my stitches open. There were moments when I thought I was never going to leave the hospital. I cursed my shooters at every painful setback. All together, I was in the hospital almost two months. I had never been in the hos-pital that long before. And it was even harder to believe I was in there for being shot. It was just plain old disbelief.

When my long awaited discharge came, Nurse Rionelli wheeled me to the exit. It was hospital policy to take you to your car via wheelchair. I had to call Marcus to pick me up because I couldn't reach Gina. I was glad to see Marcus pulled up to the front of the hospital. He went in to the hospital with me and was with me when I came out. That's why he's my boy. "Max, I have to tell you that Gina said to let one of your tricks pick you up." *I guess that explains why I couldn't reach her,* I thought.

"Man, I'm not even trying to deal with that, let's go," I said just wanting to leave the hospital and not deal with Gina at this particular time.

During our ride home Marcus caught me up on what I missed while I was in the hospital. When we arrived at my house, I could tell he didn't want to come in to experience the drama.

"Max, can you make it in alright on your own?"

"Yeah, man. I feel you punk. But I don't blame you, I have to do the drama, you don't."

"You know it boy. Holla at you later." Marcus laughed as he drove off peeling rubber like he was getting away from the scene of the crime.

Coward, but a smart coward, I thought. As I stepped inside the house and closed the door behind me, Gina's scornful eyes greeted me.

Although it was probably just my imagination, the house looked different. I had been away from the house on long business trips before, but being away in the hospital for about eight weeks made me feel sorta like a stranger this time. Things were rearranged. It made me think Gina was preparing for me to die. It felt like my return interrupted her plans.

"Hi Gina."

"Who brought you home, your co-partner in crime?" Gina sarcastically asked.

"I understand that while I was in a coma, you didn't visit me at the hospital much. Why?"

"When I came to see you, Daria was there. You had enough women around and didn't need me," Gina said hatefully as she turned her head away, full of attitude.

"You know it wasn't like that. I was in a coma. How was I going to control who came by to visit me?"

"Exactly, you didn't know, so you didn't miss me," Gina replied with ice cold sarcasm that signaled she was completely devoid of even a modicum of care.

"Marcus told me that it was friends from school, work, and church. They were just concerned and stopped by to show support."

"Max, let's not front. This thing between us is over and has been for quite a while. I didn't want you to lose your life, but beyond that, my place wasn't there among your harem. I didn't want to walk into Daria or some other woman like her, crying over you like she was your wife. You were covered," Gina said putting one hand on the counter and the other on her hip.

"You know it wasn't like that."

"Max, baby you are fine now, so we can pick up where we left off… on our road to divorce."

With that volley of indifference, Gina left the room. I wasn't sure if I disagreed with her indifference. The shooting wasn't going to make us get back together, so why should she act as if we were in love. But still, I expected some compassion. I couldn't decide if she hated me or was just numb. Anyway, I was grateful the bitter exchange was short. I wasn't up for another long Gina-tirade after just getting home from months in the hospital. The vibe in the house was just as I left it before the shooting—arctic cold.

Two weeks later I walked into the DA's office to meet with the prosecutor who was handling the case of my assailants. Their inner offices looked real official and intimidating with the huge bronze seal of the District Attorney's Office on the back wall as you entered the office. Two brown and white marble columns reached up to the ceiling from the brown and white marble floor. The receptionist's desk was a beautiful Brazilian cherry wood with two flags on each side of it; one for the state of Florida, and the other the U.S. flag. The official pictures of the DA and the Mayor hung on the white walls. What's up with all of the institutional white walls?

In walked this tall, gorgeous-looking woman who could easily pass for a runway model. She had to be about five-foot-eight or five-foot-nine inches tall with smooth butterscotch-colored skin wrapped around a petite frame. Her face was slender with a defined jaw line. Her beige pantsuit was so fly. Her silk ginger top was as understated and classy as her simple white gold jewelry. The tips of her dark brown pumps protruded out past the inch and a half cuffed pants. Her suit fit her so well, not too tight and not too baggy—definitely not off the rack. Her dark brown hair was about shoulder length and exquisitely styled. As she walked directly towards me, I wondered who she was.

"Hello Mr. Dean, my name is Collette Hawthorne. I am the Assistant District Attorney assigned to prosecute the two juveniles who shot you. I am sorry for what happened to you. I can assure you that they will get just punishment for their crimes against you," as she reached to shake my hand and then walk me to the nearby conference room.

Oh hell naw! I knew this fine thing was not the prosecutor. She was way too beautiful to have a vicious prosecutor's streak to her. I hoped she had more than just good looks and not just a pretty airhead. Dumb or not, right now I was enjoying the view. I looked at her ring finger to see if she was married. No ring. Maybe there could be an after the case meeting between Max and Ms. Hawthorne. Okay Max, stay focused, bring it back to business, boy, I thought.

I put my gawking on hold for the time being and replied, "I didn't really see them good. Things were moving so fast and seemed unreal that I didn't even know they were shooting at us. My adrenalin was so high that I didn't know I had been shot until I woke up from a coma three weeks later."

"I'm glad to see you up and around. How are you doing? You've been out of the hospital... what six or eight weeks now?" Collette asked.

"I'm getting along okay now. It's been about two months since I was released from the hospital."

"A lot has happened since then—preliminary legal work. Now we are going to trial and I need you there. Will you be alright with facing them?" she asked, getting right down to business.

"I don't know how good of a witness I can be, given how little I saw," I replied, disappointed that I couldn't be more helpful.

"That's okay. We were fortunate to have reliable eyewitnesses who clearly saw the whole thing. I want you to testify about what happened to you and the injuries you sustained in the attack. I want the jury to see and feel your pain. Marcus is going to testify to seeing your heart stop in the ER. We want the jury to see the magnitude of their crime. The fact that you both were gunned down leaving a charity event in tuxedos will play well to the jury," Collette replied, suggesting she had a no-nonsense plan of attack.

"Ms. Hawthorne..." I began and paused as though I wanted her to confirm that was her name.

"Call me Collette, please," she replied, showing her softer side to me.

"Collette, what about the two kids? What kind of kids are they?"

"Mr. Dean..." She said pausing as I did.

"And please call me Max," I said reciprocating the okay to be informal.

"Well, Max, they have been in and out of trouble in the last couple of years. Until now they hadn't been caught for anything more serious than truancy and petty shoplifting. They both came from single family homes without fathers. I'm not excusing what they did, but by most accounts they were just misguided youths," Collette replied in total control of this case.

"What a shame. What a waste. What is wrong with these kids today?" I shook my head trying to understand what's going on in their heads.

"I am going to prosecute these kids. Make no mistake about that. I am sick of this out of control youth crime and violence. I don't care about how bad their backgrounds were, or the fact that their fathers weren't around, that is no excuse. They moved up to the big leagues with this crime, and they're going to get big time for upgrading their criminal portfolio. You ready to do this?" she sternly asked, showing her prosecutor's grit.

Collette and I met for about two hours going over evidence and eyewitness statements. She questioned me about everything I could remember—my job, education, and much more. At times it seemed like she was writing an autobiography rather than preparing for trial. I must admit, she wasn't just a pretty face in a suit, the girl was good. Hell, I was beginning to feel sorry for the two boys. They didn't stand a chance. I wouldn't ever want to be on the other side of the law facing Collette.

The D.A. kept my bloody tux and had the bullet holes identified. They had pictures of me and my wounds taken when I was in the coma. Man, I looked jacked up. I saw the pictures of my totaled car and the tree that I hit. The air bags deployed on impact with the tree. It looked like the paramedics used the "Jaws of Life" to open my driver's side door. The steering wheel and the top of my car were cut off. I guess it was easier to extricate me from the car with no roof. Seeing all of that started getting to me. It brought me back to that night. I saw how close I came to losing my life. Damn those two kids. *Burn 'em for the rest of their lives*, I thought as anger welled up inside of me.

A few weeks after I met with Collette, the trial began. The trial hadn't been going on too long before she called to set up a meeting with me. The defense had requested a plea deal. The defendants' attorney said they would plead guilty if they could be sentenced under juvenile guidelines and receive counseling. Collette wanted to know how I felt about it.

"Collette, why are they willing to plead the case now?" I asked.

"Max, they're looking for a lifeline. I suspect their attorney has convinced them that their fate will be sealed with a jury verdict. The combination of the strong eyewitnesses, the pictures of the car wreckage and your wounds, coupled with your and Marcus' testimony has the jury on the edge of their seats ready to convict. Did you see the jury's faces when they saw the photos?" Collette confidently asked as if she already smelled victory within her reach.

"I wasn't looking at them. I couldn't get past the image of the life I almost lost at the hands of these two little sociopathic degenerate hoodlums."

"Well, I did. The jury had the same feeling. It's my job to read the expression on the jury's faces. Some jurors looked disgusted and others were ready to cry. On the inside they were outraged. Your case touched them. You are a decent hardworking guy who was gunned down after being charitable to the community. The jury saw you and thought that could be one of them. They aren't so willing to release these miniature terrorists back into their community. People are tired of being afraid. In your case the evidence against these boys is indisputable."

My first thought was to throw their butts away for life since they almost took mine. In fact, technically, they did kill me since I temporarily died in the emergency room. All I could think about was the expressions on the faces of the two juveniles in court. It looked like they really didn't care that I almost died. Come to think about it, I'm not even sure if they knew how to feel anything for anyone else. No, they should go down for the count. On some inner level I felt like they should be electrocuted.

I thought about the day I was shot. For some reason I remembered seeing my grandmother and what she said. This thought made no sense. But something inside of me said let it go and move on with my life. Why was I so conflicted? It should have been easy to want the maximum punishment for the two sociopaths that shot me and Marcus just to get my car. I thought, *It was just a stupid car for Christ sake!* A senselessness crime.

Their crime cost me time out of my life. Time I would never get back. *Ignore the other voice and just send them away for as long as possible,* I thought. I told myself it's okay to hate them. No one would blame me. I wished we could've sent their parents away with them for not supervising these little gun-toting monsters. Their absentee fathers should be tracked and publicly stoned in the street like back in the biblical days. Maybe if they hadn't abandoned their sons, this might not have happened. This should have been easy. All I had to do was tell Collette to hang them. The jury was ready to hang'em. I just had to put the lever in their hands.

"Max, say the word and I will reject their plea offer out of respect for you as the victim of the crime? If you say no, they will go down as adults and you'll be getting your retirement before they see the outside of prison walls. I'll get them convicted without even breaking a sweat. What do you want to do?" Collette asked with a determined stare just waiting for me to give her any sign to take them down.

I stood there frozen by her expression. I couldn't get any words out of my mouth. The entire incident flashed before my eyes in an instant. I saw Nanna again telling me I had to get it right this time. I didn't move a muscle—I couldn't. I just stood there in an almost catatonic stare at Collette.

Collette looked at me as if something were wrong, "Max, Max, Max?"

Chapter 2

DOG DAYS

Labor Day just passed signaling the time was nearly at hand for my annual college homecoming. Like most people, I returned to work attempting to get back into it after a holiday weekend. The only thing separating me from most of them was my thoughts of the approaching homecoming. Homecoming is more like a family reunion than an official college event. Thoughts about a gathering among college friends were momentarily interrupted by painful memories of this same time last year. This time last year, I was meeting with a D.A. regarding the fate of my two would-be assassins. *Max, you gotta let it go,* I desperately tried to convince myself.

I knew the time was at hand for homecoming and I couldn't escape it. You could set your watch by Tuesday after Labor Day. Telephones blew up and e-mail traffic went into hyper drive. People tried to determine who was going to homecoming. Various groups, clicks, and friends set up hospitality suites, massive eating spreads, and drinking layouts that could rival most bars.

Some people sought opportunities to rekindle old flames. Some wanted to know how many kids you have. It was always interesting to see how much larger some classmates had gotten since our malnourished dormitory days. Guys were huddling up to relive the glory days of the past. The stories of old campus prowess increased in size and some new ones developed, counting on the hope of faltering memories. The women are on fashion alert, stalking the outfits of other women. Some women looked for any reason to hate on another woman. Those types were easy to spot; it's the ones who were the same way in college. Some things never change. The sensitivities of the haters were heightened as they scoured the homecoming landscape to see which women became baby-making family lineage re-populaters, and which women had disgustingly retained their same slim college figure. We guys were so simple; we just wanted to recall the wildest party, our drunkest moment, and see what the girls we frolicked with back in college looked like today. Shallow I know, but we weren't very deep that way. It always seemed like the drunkest wildest person on campus was now a Congressman or Corporate CEO. God help our country!

I had a new story—the "shot" person. I missed last year's reunion because of the trial. This year, holding high anxiety, I feared the constant drag of suffocating pity or intrusive curiosity that would turn into endless rounds of interrogations. I would be forced to incessantly relive what I wanted to forget. I am not putting myself through that torture. Max is staying home. At least with Gina, it would be the usual and familiar torment, having nothing to do with the shooting. I was torturing myself just thinking about all of this madness. Where was Marcus when I needed him? *Maybe I should call Daria.*

It was 10:00 a.m. eastern time and my phone rang as it has for so many years at this same time. For the moment my agony was interrupted by this phone call. I was perched behind my big wooden mahogany desk staring down at mountains of paper, reports, and projects. There were even more piles on the credenza behind my desk. To finish all of this work I needed to become a warrior like one of the ancient Chinese Samurai pictured on my office wall. This phone call provided me with a much needed break from my paper chase. Even before I looked at the caller–id I knew who was calling. I picked up the phone without my usual corporate greeting.

"Hey Mason, what's up? What do you want?" I questioned as if I didn't know he was gonna quiz me about going to the reunion again.

I knew it was Mason because he had a tradition of calling me at 10:00 a.m. the next workday after Labor Day. He always wonders how I know it's him. Mason is shorter than Marcus and me, slightly more portly and darker in complexion. Mason's nickname is "Dark Ark." I got the dark part, but I never really understood the "Ark" part other than the rhyme. Mason's bald head and small hoop earring in his right ear give him an opposing presence. A shirtless Mason with his portly body looks like a black genie. He is a loyal friend and fun to hang around with.

"Max, how did you know it was me?".

"What, besides the caller id?" I replied as if to say *duh.*

"Well, never mind that, are you coming?"

"I always know it's you. No one else stalks me but you."

"Man, can you believe it's been over a year since you were in the hospital with bullet holes in you, fighting for your life?" Mason just had to go there.

This is exactly what I'm talking about. Not more than two or three sentences into a conversation and up comes the shooting. Mason is one of my other closest buddies, so he gets a pass, but I know this is what's in store for me if I go to homecoming.

"Yeah, it is pretty hard to believe. Who would have ever thought?" I replied with calm patience.

"Max, it's been almost a year and a half since the shooting. You need to come back and be around your friends and people who love you. Man, don't let those little bastards keep you from living your life. Everybody keeps asking about you. They miss you, bruh, we all do," he said, pleading his case.

"Mase, it's been hard to get back in the saddle. It took me almost a year to be okay with getting back into a car. I wanted to take the bus everywhere I went, and even that was tough. Last month, I drove for the first time since the shooting and darn near had a panic attack. Besides, I'm not ready to face a thousand questions."

Mason listened so closely that I wondered if he was still on the phone. I didn't know why I said what I just did. I guess maybe I was either too tired or too scared to continue living within my own fear. Maybe I needed to unfairly drag someone else into my mental madness. What was he going to say, shut up? I got what I was looking for—an ear.

"They should have executed both of those little bastards for what they did," Mason exploded disgustingly. "You can't let them kill your spirit. I know you're better than that. My boy ain't going out like that!"

"Mase, at times the pain was so unbearable, it brought me to tears. The constant pain dragged me down into depression—pain from the gun shots, pain from the surgery, pain of being exhausted from so many sleepless nights, and the pain from being scared. Once I contemplated suicide. You are the first person I ever admitted that to, and I don't know why the words just came out of my mouth now."

"You don't still feel that way do you?"

I could feel Mason venturing back and forth between outrage and compassion. This had to be a shock. He's never seen me unsure of myself. I always oozed confidence. Now I had been reduced to a terrified, tall 6'5" little man.

"No, I'm not suicidal, but I'm not me anymore. The shooting changed me and I just can't find the old Max. I feel violated. I've seen violence before, but I remained an unemotional spectator watching it on the news. I never thought something like that could happen to me," I said perhaps trying to convince the both of us.

"Max, this crap is pissing me off all over again," Mason angrily shouted.

"I'm not trying to get you worked up again." I quickly replied trying to stave off Mason's hatred for the two young shooters.

"I had no idea they screwed you up like this. You know I'm in law enforcement. Say the word and I'll make sure they feel some pain, even in prison." Mason angrily retorted.

I knew if I said the word he would do it. I think Mason knew everyone in law enforcement. Thinking how badly they screwed me up, inflicting pain on the boys tempted me. But what would that gain? It would jeopardize Mason's job and could lead him to the same place as the junior wannabe killers. I wouldn't let him do that. Thank God, I still had enough of me left not to commission Mason to put a hit on my assailants.

We sat on the phone in a momentary silence. We're at an impasse of uncertainty about what to do next. I think Mason was waiting for me to say hurt'em. I wanted to change the subject, but I was locked into having this conversation—getting reeled in like a fish on a hook.

"Mase, I haven't had sex since the shooting."

"What?" Mason screamed in the phone.

Where in the world did that come from Max? I asked myself. That came out of my mouth like someone else was saying it. Admitting to not having sex violated the man code. This would be considered a major violation. Saying it was unthinkable. Any other time he would have called me something like "dusty dong." Mason would have sung his other song, "Maxi-Max, begging Benny, don't get any!" But this time my boy was three quarters pissed, wanting to do bodily harm to my assailants.

I continued with my out-of-the-blue confession, "I never thought it was even possible to go for more than a week without hitting some booty—let alone for eighteen months. I'm not even sure if my manhood works anymore. I have been so stressed out and mentally broken; the plug was pulled on my action. Man, I haven't even had the desire for sex. If I didn't know any better, I could have sworn they blew off my baby maker."

"Boy, I will buy you a hooker! They specialize in fixing your problem with little Max. Those women have some mad skills."

We both laughed. This was truly a new Max coming out. It didn't feel like I had control over him, or what was coming out of my mouth. Something was pulling me into this abyss like a tractor beam from an old Star Trek episode. I was a basket case. How could I go to the reunion like this?

Mason read my mind when he said, "Max, you need homecoming now more than ever."

Secretly I knew he was right, but I wasn't ready. But if I did go, could I be around that many people and not see carjackers around every corner?

"Mase, I have to go to Asia for a meeting. My boss thinks it'll be productive if I'm there. My company has been so good and understanding with me. I'm going because I owe them that. I will consider homecoming when I get back. No promises."

"Whatever, just have yo scared butt back here for reunion," Mason said in his usual overly hyped tone.

"Alright, I'll try."

"Okay, don't get back in time and see what you'll get! I will be at the airport when you get back. I'll slap the handcuffs on you and embarrass you in front of everybody. Then I'll make sure you get audited by the IRS for the next 600 years."

"I know your crazy ass would do something like that.

"Man, don't temp me or I will have SWAT, the Secret Service, drug-sniffing dogs, and even frogmen waiting for you boy," Mason bellowed.

"I won't put that craziness past your ol' sick self. Mason, don't have your boys put food in my luggage again like last time. The dogs sniffed my bags like I was the drug cartel or something. That last dog peed on my Italian leather suitcase. Man that was a $1,200 leather suitcase that I bought in Italy."

"I know you didn't pay that for it. You probably beat 'em down to $50," trying to lessen the severity of their prank.

"That's not the point. I didn't buy it to be a fire hydrant for the canine cops. Ya'll need to take those flea bags outside and let'em pee on a hub cap or a telephone pole. The dog ruined my baggage."

Mason laughed, "How long are you going to hold that over my head? My boys said they were sorry after they finished laughing for an hour. Man, you know that dog was old and had bladder problems."

We both laughed until our sides hurt. Mason made me virtually prick my finger and sign my promise in blood to be at the reunion. I knew he just wanted to get me out among friends so they could begin putting me back together.

It was almost lunchtime when I got e-mail from Daria. She and I dated seriously in college. Many people thought we were going to get married before I surprised everyone and got engaged to Jillian. Jillian and I were together for six years. She was sweet and we had a strong relationship for a while. Taking our relationship to marriage was based more on my need to rescue Jillian from her bad childhood and home life than it was for true love. I suppose both Jillian and I got married for the wrong reasons because it was destined from the start to fail.

Besides, we were both so young and had no idea what we were doing. It took my good friend Melonee Ridgeway, who we just call Mel, to hip me to my crusader madness. I didn't know whatever possessed me to think I was Jillian's savior. I went on with my unresolved issues and married Gina four years later.

Gina, now she was a true twelve on a scale of one to ten. She looked so good. She was finer than frog hair and her trunk wasn't too heavy. The way she smiled at me melted me from the inside out. Standing just five feet three inches tall, she was still a pillar of beauty with a genuine niceness. In the early days we were inseparable. I was so smitten with Gina that I would have walked backwards down Interstate 95 with a party hat on my head and a kazoo in my mouth just to be with her.

We were like best friends before we got married. I did everything for her. I liked shopping for her more than I did for myself. She had the sexiest body. I bought her designer clothes just because they adorned her body so well. Her hair was long and full, perfectly curled and styled. It would have made even the finest magazine models jealous.

When I first met Gina, she had just got out of a bad relationship and was living at home with her mom and sister. Her dad wasn't in the picture; he had left their home when she was in high school. I loved Gina so much that I'm certain I overlooked many things that came up later—the kind of things that cause any relationship or marriage to fail.

I was so happy at home with her that it transcended into my happiness at work. I was on the corporate fast track; getting promoted and traveling the world. My success turned into more time away from her. Although I was well compensated for that sacrifice, the damage to my marriage became evident.

Gina and I tried for years to have children. We were unsuccessful despite doing everything that every doctor, fertility specialist, book, and magazine article instructed us to do. That failure began to chip away at our marriage. Gina became more and more insecure. She thought I was seeking another woman who could bear my child. As a man I can only imagine how that must infringe on a woman's sense of adequacy.

Gina used to yell at me, "Don't come up in this house with another woman's baby just because I can't give you one yet." She was obsessed with trying to have a baby. She had her ovulation schedule down pat. It felt as though thirty seconds after she started ovulating, I was summoned to do the deed.

I remember one time when Gina called me while I was in Japan and demanded that I fly back home because she was ovulating. When I told her I couldn't, she wanted to immediately leave for the airport and fly to Japan. Since there were only first class tickets available, the airfare alone would have been over $3,000. When I told her that wouldn't work, she hurled more expletives at me than a drunk without alcohol.

Another time we had sex for so long I thought I heard my member fracture. She brought all of the testosterone enhancing food she could find to bed. She brought steak, chicken, oysters, black bean soup, broccoli and cabbage. I gagged trying to eat the oysters.

"I will feel it when I conceive," she told me desperately stalking hope.

She was ready with supplements when the friction became unbearable. Gina wasn't going to stop until the Lord Himself parted her eggs like the Red Sea and let my baby seekers do their duty. After many hours of going at it and feeling like I needed to take off my love maker and replace it with a spare, he quit on me. Gina was so desperate she even suggested we get some cocaine to help with my stamina.

I didn't need drugs. I needed a break from her invasion. The suggestion of drug-assisted sex was an affront to my manhood. When I said no to Gina's suggestion of drugs, she said I couldn't deliver because I'd been with another woman. "You'd have more to give me if you weren't giving it to those other tramps." Her accusations desperately sought any way for me to shoulder the blame. I wanted to strike back asserting my fertile strength, but I remained sensitive. I tried to shift the blame to me to make her feel better even though the doctors said I was fine. Gina started drinking for a brief time and went through a mild case of depression about her lack of fertility. Then she just stopped caring. All my successes became reminders of her child bearing failure. Our marriage was rapidly going downhill.

Even though our marriage had its good and bad points, I always had Daria to turn to. She and I never crossed the line after I got married. My pastor once preached about relationships like Daria and me.

He called it an emotional affair, which was more dangerous than a sexual affair because it involved matters of the heart. I didn't think it was wrong because we weren't having sex. I rationalized what we were doing and convinced myself if Gina didn't know and we weren't having sex, then there was no harm.

Daria probably felt she had me first and didn't care what Gina thought. Our friendship required few words. We just knew where each other was and what we needed. Logically, Daria should have been Mrs. Dean. I have no real answer why she wasn't, she just wasn't. In a crazy sort of way being platonic worked for us.

I opened up Daria's email with those pleasant thoughts of her.

From: DariaR

To: MaxD

Subject: Reunion

Max,

Are you coming this year? Has Mason already threatened you again? I bet if you knew he was going to become an officer and pull tricks on you like the dog thing, you probably would have let him get a beat down when you guys were pledging the frat together. I miss you. I wish I could take care of you. I know how tense things are between you and Gina. If she doesn't want to care for you, I will. I respect your marriage and will stay in my place. This is the part about being the other woman in your life that I hate. What's up for this year Mr. Dean? Please come, I'll be there with Lisa, but waiting on you.

Later, D

Lisa and Daria have been friends since freshman year in college. Lisa is tall and quirky. She looks like a bookworm. I think Lisa is ashamed of her height because she walks a little slouched over. Worse than that is girlfriend's hair. Lisa isn't one of those hair-obsessed women. Her hair, or wig as I call it, definitely needs to get done. She has a fierce kitchen on the back of her neck, and I don't think relaxer or a straitening comb will help that, maybe clippers are the solution.

Lisa is a true friend to both Daria and me, but sistah girl needs a makeover, bad. Lisa often commented that Daria and I should get married and be done with it. She thinks we're on the delayed marriage program and sowing our oats with other people. I guess she thinks she's Dr. Ruth. I replied back.

From: MaxD
To: DariaR
Subject: RE Reunion

Lisa is a sexually frustrated man hater. Didn't she eat her last man? Rumor has it that she ran him away, and he's still running. I just went through this with Mason. I'm not up to it this year. Besides, everyone is just going to ask me about the shooting and stare at me like I'm a mannequin on display at Macys.

Maxi Max
From: DariaR
To: MaxD
Subject: RE Reunion

Maxwell Dean, you know if you don't make it I'm coming to your house and dragging you out— Gina or no Gina. Homecoming is our time. I love yo ol' tired half-busted up butt. You know you're wrong about Lisa. Have you heard from Marcus? Is he coming? What about Pike, have you heard from him?

D

Pike is another one of my boys whom I hung out with in college. Some called me, Marcus, Mason, and Pike the four musketeers. Pike was never a real ladies' man. Sarae hooked and married him early on in college and never let her man go. Although we always teased Pike about being whooped, the truth was that he got the best girl in college. I didn't blame him for that one. Any half smart man would have latched onto Sarae and never let her go.

My boys and Sarae have been there through Daria's and my ups and downs. We were like a family in college and it still remains that way. No matter what happened between Daria and me, my friends still liked and respected her. Sarae was always the grounded one of the bunch, never judgmental, and always understanding. She was truly one of God's angels on earth. I think if Pike had messed up with her, we all would have beaten him.

From: MaxD
To: DariaR
Subject: RE Reunion

Daria you must have nothing else to do, except interrogate me.

What about your crew, are they all going to homecoming? Marcus called from the cockpit of his jet telling me I needed to be at the reunion. He asked me if I wanted to come and fly with him. Why is everyone trying to get me out of the house and up walking like I still need physical therapy? All of you mother hens need to stop it and get off me.

That boy is having too much fun with his new pilot job. He makes six figures being a "Corporate Sky Cap." He hates when I call him that. He keeps saying "Don't hate the player; hate the game." I hate that little urban colloquialism. That saying is so played out and tired. Besides, he has no game.

Tell your friend Kenya that Marcus said this year he wants to liberate her from her sexual solitude. She needs to give it to somebody, as up-tight as she is. P.S. I will be in Asia next week.

I'm out,
Maxi Max

Kenya didn't go to school with us. She was one of Daria's post college girlfriends. Kenya wasn't gorgeous but had a really cute face and a whole lot of butt. Marcus liked her. Kenya was a tad bit too much woman for me. She was nice enough but Kenya always seemed so wound up. Much of her conversation was man bashing. Call me stupid or something, but maybe Kenya was so wound up because she didn't have a man. She probably didn't have a man because we pick up on her man-eater attitude. She reminded me of a Black Widow spider who would eat her mate. Someone needed to take Kenya and relieve her bound up tension. Marcus wanted to be the Black Widow's victim.

From: DariaR
To: MaxD
Subject: RE Reunion

Tell Marcus that Kenya is not uptight; she's just a little special. He's a big freak. Max, please come, we haven't seen you in a while. I would be lying if I said I wasn't worried about you. There is nothing that we have to do at the reunion except hang out. I want my old Max back. You don't have to talk to anyone other than me. We can just hang out in your hotel room if you want. Now that being said, don't make me show up at your front door. That'll send Gina over the edge again like she did when I came to the hospital. She'll cut me if I come over. Baby, just come to me and Dar will make it better...please!

Later,
Dar

I was definitely feeling the pressure to attend the reunion. Maybe I did need to go so I could get out of this funk that I'm in. I knew hooking up with Daria would be great as always. To tell the truth, I just wasn't feeling it. Daria would be fine if we just held each other and talked all night. I didn't know if my fragile state of mind could handle it. Boy, I'm my own worst enemy right now. I just don't know what to do. I could come up with a work-related excuse. That was it, a perfect reason for not going. *Great idea Max*," I told myself.

Chapter 3

REUNION

"I would have thought you'd be over the good ol' college days by now. Which skank are you planning on hooking up with? I know all of your college retards think something's wrong with me. They're wondering why I haven't sired the great Maxwell Dean an heir to his dysfunctional college throne. A successor to the frat pack," Gina said totally blowing her lid.

As soon as I told Gina that I decided to attend homecoming, she started in on me. I knew this would eventually lead to me and other women and babies. I wished I hadn't told her. Gina didn't care what I did. It wouldn't bother her if I left the house and didn't return for a month. I could go and not tell her anything, and that would be fine by her. I would have done that if my mom hadn't instilled in me early on in my life, that two wrongs don't make a right. Mom would say, "The Bible says don't trade evil for evil." It could have also said, "Don't treat Gina like Gina treats you."

I knew better than to respond to Gina, but I stupidly did anyway. "It's not like that Gina. Nobody says that about you. In fact it never comes up."

"Just because they don't say it to your face doesn't mean they aren't saying it when you're not around. Especially those baby factory sorority skeezers. I bet they can smell sex and get pregnant. I bet babies shoot out of them like missiles since those tramps are so used to having their legs open all of the time. They don't deserve to have babies since I'm

31

sure they're more interested in whoring than being mothers. I know I am the butt of their jokes."

"Gina, please don't start this again. You are just being paranoid," I agitatedly replied.

"Just go. Get out. In fact why don't you drive?" Gina shot way below the belt with that parting blow. She knew how difficult it had been for me to get in a car since the shooting. Gina's inner demons made her say the vilest things imaginable. I felt like saying something back to hurt her down to her core. I bet she wouldn't like it if I told her that her womb was dried up and as lifeless as the Great Salt Flats.

I thought, *Yeah, I'll drive alright, and run your butt over, how bout that?* I wanted to hurl that painful insult at her, but something in my gut wouldn't let me stoop that low. I just headed for the door feeling partly like a weak spineless man. On the other hand, I acted like the man my mom raised. Swallowing my pride and taking Gina's heart- piercing insults was a bitter pill of true manhood that I had to endure "to do the right thing" mom and Nanna always said.

In just a few hours I'd be terrified by the crowds at homecoming. The alternative was to stay at home with the evil one. I had heard people say, "It's better to deal with the devil that you do know versus the one you don't." Whoever said that obviously never met Gina. Well, I know that Lucifer is at home, and therefore I'm going to homecoming. *I'm out*, I told myself as I left the house.

After I arrived at homecoming, I did the right thing and called Gina. "Hey baby, I made it."

"What does that mean to me?" I heard a click and then the dial tone.

I thought my cell phone dropped the call. I redialed her and said, "Hello?"

There was another pause of silence when I realized that Gina hung up on me again. *This is some real bull crap*, I thought.

"She hung up on you again? Max, when is enough, enough?" Marcus questioned.

"Man, I'm almost there," I said exhausted with the Gina wars.

I needed this reunion of friends if nothing else for a break from the King Cobra at home. Marcus and I sat at the bar of the Four Seasons Hotel having a drink of premium XO cognac and smoking Montecristo Cuban cigars. I brought the cigars back from Europe (not completely legal I might add). That was one of my new things that helped me cope. I'd found an affinity for XO cognac and Cuban cigars.

I was so uncomfortable being in a place that I'd been coming to for many years since college. Between being stressed out from battling with Gina, and being around so many people after the shooting, I was about to implode.

"Lighten up Max! You look like you're ready to make a dash for the door any minute. I got your back," Marcus blurted out, correctly sensing my uneasiness.

"I'm sorry man, but I can't shake these jitters. I always feel like something's about to happen. Maybe I need another drink," trying to force myself to stop trembling like a frightened little puppy.

"You know we're all boys so don't get mad. Mason told me about your year and a half layoff. You don't need a drink. You need some woman to loosen you up sexually. She needs to just take it. I need to get Daria to do you in a major way," Marcus exclaimed as if sex was the antidote to all problems.

"Daria was right, you are a freak," I replied, humoring my boy's ego as if being a freak was a badge of honor.

"Thank you. I'll own that. When is Daria coming in? Man, I don't know what the hell you did to her back in college. You shouldn't have maximized her. She waits for you to be single like a woman waiting on her man to return home from the war. Even if she gets married to another man, her husband will never measure up to her Max."

"I'm not hittin' on Daria. We don't have that kind of relationship," I protested.

"You oughta," Marcus replied.

"That's your style playa, not mine."

Marcus continued, "I think it was the night back in our jacked up apartment when she was begging you to sleep with her. That did the trick. Me and Pat had to tell you to just go ahead and give her some loving just so we could get some sleep. I still can't believe that you boned her in the same room where we were. That was nasty. Man we were so close we could smell yawls' sex. We weren't even trying to look at you two's sex-capades. Besides, you two looked like the mating of the wildebeest.

"Whatever, hater! That was back in college. We were young and dumb back then. I am definitely not that person today. Hopefully, Daria will be here within the next hour or so. She only has a short drive to get here. Daria told me she would never stop loving me. You know Daria and I are still tight, but these days I'm not feeling anything for anyone."

"Max, when was the last time you talked to Ms. Melonee Ridgeway?" Marcus asked in a silly way.

"I talked to my girl Mel last week."

"Is she coming?" Marcus pressed.

"Yeah, she should be here sometime today."

"Mel is one of the coolest babes around, but the girl can curse like a sailor," Marcus replied stating an obvious fact with admiration at the same time.

"Yep, I tell her all the time to dial it down a bit, but you know she's rough around the edges like that. If she wasn't my home girl, she'd probably already have cut me by now," I said smiling at the thought of one of my best female friends.

"If I didn't already know her, I'd swear she's a hood rat."

"Marcus you ain't ever lied. Mel is my girl and I love her to death just like I know you do too."

"True dat Max. What about Gina, how are y'all doing these days? Any better?"

I knew Marcus always checked to see which way we were going with our marriage. He was sometimes protective of me like some old mother hen. But he was my boy and gonna lookout for me.

"Not even! This marriage is over and has been for a long time. I have tried and tried to make it work, but I cannot scale Gina's wall of pain. Her pain became a hatred for me that is so deep there is not even a crack for light to get through. Marcus, man she's trippin all the time. Since the shooting I haven't desired sex which is making her even more insecure. She thinks I'm not doing it because I don't want to get her pregnant. Everything boils down to her not having a baby," I disgustingly responded.

"Damn!"

"Marcus, man, I feel like I don't have a life partner anymore. My life with Gina is relegated to being a sperm donor. If it's not about getting her pregnant, she's not interested. It feels like I am growing both personally and professionally, but she isn't. I don't think she even wants to. It's like her maternal void made her check out on the will to live," I bellowed back with anguish.

"Come on Max. For real?"

"Nah man, I can't figure when or why she stopped living. Between the constant baby pressure, the insecurity, and vile epithets hurled at me daily—I'm worn out. That weight is dragging me down and killing me," I said, exhaling in exhaustion.

"Bruh, you are a hard standard to live up to. Maybe she drowned trying to live up to the great Maxwell Dean. I'm sure the baby thing is breaking her."

You of all people know I'm not pretentious like that. I'm not trippin about the baby issue."

"I know you're not, but your success might be making her feel insecure. Maybe she sees you succeeding with your role in the house and she's failing with hers," Marcus replied with his usual insightfulness.

"She's always accusing me of cheating so you might be right," I conceded.

"Max, your game is lethal. I don't know if any woman can hold up under that weight. If I were a woman, I wouldn't want to try to measure up to your overachiever ass. And for the record, you are cheating on her. Did you forget about Daria?"

"If you were a woman, I wouldn't date yo ol' crusty ugly ass! Daria and I aren't having sex, so it's not cheating—we're just tight," I fired back.

"Max 'Houdini' Dean is quenching his thirst on some more hater-aid. I'm not judging you, but you are married to Gina Dean and hanging on to Daria Ross. If you can't see that Daria still loves you and is hanging around to be the next Mrs. Dean, then you are as blind as Ray Charles. You keep hanging on to Daria like she is your relationship failure lifeline. It's like you don't want her but you can't let her go. She is your safety net against being alone. Daria is just as bad. She is waiting on you like you are the second coming. You and Daria both know you're playing with fire. You two keep just enough distance from the fire not to get burned. What is that, dummy?" Marcus laughed at our verbal banter.

I picked up the name "Houdini" from my fraternity while pledging. They called me "Houdini" because I could always get out of the most impossible situations just like the master escape artist Harry Houdini. Not to mention, I would disappear all the time. Frat names are very common in undergrad. Some of them are quite funny. There are names for guys like Rug, Ox, Elephant Man, FUBAR (F'ed Up Beyond All Recognition), Fish, Hump, and Jim Slob. I knew a girl in a sorority who was called "Vulture" because she walked kind of slouched over. Then there were other girls with names like Mouse, Goggles because of her thick eye-glasses, Think Tank, Chicken, and Bubbles for her bubble butt.

Marcus Harris, my guy, was a Kappa whose line name was "Hump." Even though he and I were in different frats, everyone knew how close we were. Many people said that we favored each other. We are about the same height and size, although I am a little bit taller and bigger. They called him "Hump" because he tried to hump on girls since we were kids. Marcus has been a mannish sex hound his entire life.

Mason Reed and I pledged the frat together. We called him "Straw-Boss." I think they called Mason "Straw-Boss" because of the Wizard of Oz character the straw man (Scarecrow). They also didn't think Mason had any heart just like the tin man. They were very wrong. Mason was nothing but heart and turned out to be the frat brother I was closest to. He was always the comical jokester of our pledge line.

Daria was not in a sorority, but she helped me a lot while I was pledging. Daria's five feet six inch frame is the tallest of any woman I had ever been involved with. The last time I remembered shopping with her, she was about a size eight. Daria's short curly hair was tapered on the back and sides. Her hair style was a stark contrast to Lisa's jacked-up wig.

Daria stepped into the bar wearing a camel brown herringbone pantsuit, power blue shirt with a white collar, and white French cuffs. She was stunning. My girl Daria was gorgeous. Any guy would desire her, especially looking like that. Daria had a one track mind during homecoming weekends, and that was for me. She was wearing my favorite perfume, women's Fendi. Whenever I smelled that fragrance, Daria came to mind. Daria smiled from ear to ear and looked excited to see me. I knew I was excited to see her. No matter what happened, I could always count on Daria to make me feel better.

Daria greeted us with a hug and said, "What's up guys?"

"What's up Daria?" Marcus said as happy to see her as I was.

"Hey Marcus," she replied with that award winning smile of hers.

"Hey Dar, what's up? It took you long enough to get here," I playfully fired at her.

"Nice to see you too, Max."

"I was about to leave and go back home. You know I didn't want to come in the first place," I replied, trying to make Daria feel a little bad.

"Don't get your panties in a bunch, Max. The Dar is here now. It's gonna be alright baby."

"Daria, let's go find Mel 'Sistah Soldier the Revolutionary' Ridgeway for reinforcements cause your boy is so jittery he's about to jump out of his skin," Marcus sarcastically joked cutting his eye and nodding his head towards me.

We sat at the bar and talked like we never missed a beat since our last reunion together. Even though Marcus and Daria were a couple of my best friends, I could tell neither wanted to bring up anything about the shooting. I enjoyed their polite discretion. I wanted to avoid the subject if at all possible. I wondered who would break the harmony and be the first to bring up the shooting. I was safe for now and that worked for me.

The three of us smoked some cigars and drank cognac together before we headed up to the Crown Plaza for the homecoming festivities. I enjoyed good cognac and was hoping it wasn't going to fail me. My anxiety was peaking and I needed Mr. Remy Martin XO to take off the edge.

"Max, I just need you to hold me tight all night," Daria playfully said, trying to get a rise out of Marcus.

"Baby, you know you own the Maxi-Max. Mistress you can have whatever you want. Dominate me Dar," I replied, feeding into her attempts to get a rise out of Marcus.

"What is this dominatrix stuff? Y'all ain't nothin but freaks and I ain't even trying to hear this from you two since I'm by myself," Marcus gruffly replied.

Daria said, "Shut up Hump, I know you're not talking with your ho'n ass."

Marcus and Daria went at it as they usually did when we got together. To a stranger, it appeared like they didn't like each other. But we were all really good friends. Marcus would never let anyone harm Daria.

"You got me all wrong girl," Marcus replied.

With that said, we all left for the Crown Plaza. When we got there, we went up to the eleventh floor to the main hospitality suite. I walked in and saw an old friend.

"What's up, Sid?" I greeted.

"What's up Max? Where are the rest of your Sands?" Your "Sands" were the guys you pledged your fraternity with and the term was coined from the notion that you crossed the bearing sands together.

"Boss is in another hospitality suite. The Grad and Smoke should be here later," I replied.

As we were just standing there talking, I saw these two women across the room. It seemed like they were in a casual conversation. I'd never seen them before. Maybe they came to the university after I graduated. I thought the Yak (Cognac) and the Cuban cigar had me feeling so nice that I couldn't remember them. Daria was across the room talking to some of her girls.

One of the two women looked nice, but I couldn't tell anything about her body through her blue business suit. She had light brown skin and couldn't be taller than five foot one, if she was that tall. I could tell she was petite, but her suit deceptively concealed any particulars. Her hair style was corporate conservative. There was something different about this woman. She had a mysterious allure about her. By my first impression she wasn't drop dead gorgeous, but rather curiously attractive. I couldn't decide if I wanted to say something to her or just blow off my mild curiosity. I was either going to talk to her or run out of this ever crowding suite like a retreating dog with his tail tucked between his legs.

What the heck? I walked over to the mystery woman. "Hello there Missy my name is Maxwell."

She smiled and coyly said, "Hi, my name is Jordan and not Missy, Buster."

"Touché. Can I buy you some dinner?" I asked as if I were serious, pressing forward with my playful antics.

"I don't know, can you? Is it safe, Mr. _____?" she asked.

"It's Dean, but please call me Max. And what follows Jordan might I be so bold as to inquire?"

"I'm not so sure if you've earned the right to know that yet. But I'll take a chance on you. Anders, its Jordan Anders. And, yes, Mr. Dean, you may buy me dinner if I don't have to be the dessert. So what do you have in mind?" Jordan playfully accommodated me with a shy smile.

I walked over to the hors d'oeuvres table. "Right here, I had it brought in just for you."

Jordan looked at me with shock and surprise. I know that isn't what she expected. She laughed at my quick and witty sense of humor—a real trooper, going along with my antics. As Jordan started to pick up the food in equally bird sized portions, I said, "I know you can eat more than that, so don't even try being prissy."

Jordan looked at my plate which I loaded up with chicken wings, laughed and said, "Oh, what should I do load it up with flesh like you?"

"Absolutely," I snapped back.

"Cannibal!" she charged.

I loaded up her little plate with the same chicken wings.

"No you didn't. What's next, a prank call to the animal rights people to report me?" Jordan sarcastically replied.

Daria was still on the other side of the hospitality suite talking to friends and people she knew. I knew Daria's eyes would be periodically tracking me, not from insecurity, but hoping to see me cut loose with my boys like the old days. Daria appreciated the entire college reunion thing in a way that Gina never would. Daria knew what it was and what it wasn't. Daria never crowded me or acted possessive. Given how withdrawn I had been over the last year, she knew another woman was the furthest thing from my mind.

Mason walked in and gave me the frat's grip while staring at Jordan. "What's up with my Sands, Maxwell 'The Corporate Giant' Dean?"

"Don't start Mason," I said smiling at him.

"Who is this fine specimen of a woman?" Mason asked while staring at Jordan. "Jordan, this is my Sands, the not so funny Mason."

Jordan replied, "Nice to meet you. This is my friend Casey." she said turning and motioning towards Casey.

Mason and I stood there talking with Jordan and Casey. Jordan and I left the conversation with Mason and Casey and started talking about what we did for a living.

"I'm an IT Implementation Manager for Zane Bock Consulting," Jordan replied.

"What's that?"

"I travel to customer's sites worldwide and help them to install new system software and hardware packages." Jordan replied.

"And what do you do Giant Max?" Jordan asked.

"Please don't humor Mason. I am Director of International Operations for Boltz One Corporation."

It felt like Jordan and I talked for hours. We spoke about our extensive international travels. We swapped our war stories. I was completely drawn in by this interesting lady. Her conversation was bringing life back to my tattered existence. It was as if the sun was starting to shine through an overcast day. I almost forgot I was here with Daria.

Some other people came into the room. I turned away from the conversation with Jordan, and greeted them. Since we were all common friends, Mason turned away to speak to the new arrivals as well. I overheard Casey trying to talk softly to Jordan. She must have thought we were totally distracted while we conversed with the new-comers, but I overheard Casey say, "Girl, what are you doing. Are you trying to get with him?"

I faintly heard Jordan say, "Sshh! Hell yeah!"

I wanted to stay and hear more about Jordan's interest in me, but I was getting pulled away as the suite started getting more crowded.

"Jordan, can you two excuse me for one moment?" I said as I walked away to speak to another frat brother who had just entered the suite.

I wasn't sure how I felt about Jordan wanting to get with me. I wasn't there mentally. Even if I was, little Max wasn't. He hadn't desired a woman in a long time. As I walked away, I heard Jordan say to Casey, "That brother is fine."

I must admit there was something different about Jordan that peaked my interest. I wouldn't act on it because I was here with Daria. I wouldn't disrespect Daria like that. This is Daria's self proclaimed time. Besides, I always have fun with Daria. After some brief catch-up conversation with people coming into the suite, Mason and I made it back to Jordan and Casey.

"Maxwell, did you line up all of your women for tonight?" Jordan sarcastically asked.

"No, but the friends that I came here with are ready to leave. They're becoming impatient with me."

Jordan looked disappointed by my impending departure, but replied, "I live up in Jacksonville and I come through West Palm Beach all of the time. Do you have a business card?"

"Yeah, here, and do you have one for me?" I replied, wanting to reconnect with Jordan.

"No, but since I have yours, we'll just have to see what I might do with it someday. Maybe I'll see you again, Mr. Dean," Jordan retorted with a devilish smirk on her face.

Jordan turned and jutted her head towards Daria and said, "You are with that lady aren't you?"

"Why do you say that?" I asked giving myself away with the question.

"She's been hawking you while you've been over here talking to me."

"We are all together. We hang out like this every year," I replied defensively.

"Well, I don't want to get you in any trouble, Mr. Lover Man," Jordan quipped.

"I am not going to get in any trouble, Ms. Anders."

About that same time Jordan indicated they were leaving as well. We exchanged pleasantries and parted in different directions. Our eyes met in approval of each other as Jordan and Casey got on the elevator. I wondered if I was going to see her again. I wondered what would have happened if I was at the reunion by myself. I guess I would have to rely on either fate or my charm since I didn't have a way to contact her. Oh well, I would still be with my ol' faithful Daria and that was a good thing.

The first night of the reunion had been great. People reconnected and caught up on one another's lives. This was my first reunion since the shooting. Many of my friends and classmates heard about it and expressed concern. Some of them were so angry with the two boys that they felt like I should have asked for the death penalty. Each time someone asked what sentence they received, I changed the subject. Going down that road was the last thing I wanted to do. I was pleasantly surprised how well the first day turned out.

It was 2:00 a.m. and I was just getting to my hotel room with Daria close on my hip. After showering, we both flopped down on the suite's sofa in exhaustion. We recanted the night's events. We laughed about events of the night and some of the people who were acting like they were back in college.

In a moment of silence Daria said, "That girl in the business suit was interested in you."

"What makes you say that?" I asked remembering that Jordan asked the same of Daria.

Daria looked at me like she couldn't believe I asked her that. "Because she was all up in your face, hanging onto your every word."

"How did you see all that, because I didn't?"

Daria crooked her eye at me and replied, "Steve Wonder could've seen that." Frowning, I fired back, "Paranoid?"

"I'm not paranoid. I'm a woman and I know how we are. She wants you, but she can't have you because you are all mine—Right?" Daria asked, waiting for me to confirm that she and I are still solid.

"Right."

"Max, don't "right" me. I almost lost you to violence for nearly two years. I don't know what I would've done if I had lost you. I accepted losing you to Gina, but this is our sacred thing. I don't ask any questions when you are at home or work. All I ask from you is your respect during this one weekend out of the year."

"Daria, you know I'm your Maxi-Max now and always."

"Max, don't play me. I know where I stand with you and Gina, but I'm not going to be second to anyone else. Don't make me cut one of these heffas!"

"Now you're sounding like Mel," I joked with her.

"Yeah, I am, so don't make me act like her too," Daria said not able to keep a straight face.

I know my relationship with Daria is playing with fire. I've always found a way to rationalize it to a point where I found no wrong with it. There is a familiarity with Daria. I suppose she was the constant in my life over the years going back to college. Daria didn't put demands on me or ask me for much other than this one weekend. That was only to share time, closeness, and friendship. I was more than glad to give her that; after all, she really is a beautiful person inside and out.

On Sunday the reunion concluded as nicely as it started. I didn't see Jordan or Casey again and wondered if Jordan stayed for the entire reunion. It was good seeing old faces again and it was a great departure from Gina. The weekend ended just as it began, with Daria. She and I had breakfast Sunday morning before returning home. We had our usual good time talking about things that happened over the weekend.

Before Daria and I parted ways for our respective homes, she said, "I hate you Max, because you make me love you and I know I can't have you. I hate leaving what we have. I don't get sex from you, I get intimacy. Most men don't understand a woman's desire for intimacy, but you get it. That's why our friendship is so special. That's why we can sleep on a couch all night without sex and still enjoy each other. You make me feel safe, secure, and special. Max, you really get it, which is why you've always had me. You know me like no other man ever has," Daria said, attempting a serious moment with her adorable puppy dog eyes that I actually appreciated.

"You hate that I whooped it on you back in college and have you hooked like a crack-head ever since," I said, breaking up this serious moment.

"You are so stupid, but I love you. Let's talk later in the week, after you and your boys finish lying about all the women you all got this weekend," Daria replied smiling.

"Alright Daria. Later babe."

"Drive carefully, Max. You know I worry about you in cars now," Daria said hugging me.

With that we ceremoniously pecked lips and parted. As Daria drove away, I could see tears in her eyes. Daria was my rock and always would be. Was I betraying her with my thoughts about Jordan? I went from a self imposed exile to adding Jordan into my confusion. *Max, what are you doing*, I asked myself?

Chapter 4

THE PLAN

"You need to be quarantined after your homecoming weekend brothel," Gina yelled picking up right where she left off before homecoming.

I just got home and walked in the front door. It was as if Gina had been waiting there for me since I left. She was locked and loaded, and ready for a fight. Gina had on grey sweat pants and a slightly tattered shirt like she was ready to throw down on me.

"Gina, please don't start this again," I begged, still exhausted from the exchange before I left for homecoming.

Gina froze in her tracks and stopped ranting. She motioned me to come towards her. She had a forgiving look on her face revealing a partial smile like she was just playing with me. I thought she was going to apologize. She was looking kind of sexy standing in the foyer in her little ghetto get-up. She extended her hand out towards mine. I smiled as she displayed a little coy expression on her face. As I reached out, Gina pulled me into her and hugged me ever so nicely. My heart turned to mush. Gina's loving gesture wiped away my defensive posture. I lowered my guard to feel the love. Maybe today was the day our marriage would turn the corner. Maybe, just maybe, we might start putting us back together and return to the old days when we were hot for each other.

"Baby, I'm sorry," Gina softly said as she hugged me pressing her head against my chest.

"Honey we can work through this together if we just show each other some more love. I'm ready to do what is necessary to get us back," I said momentarily pulling away to look into her beautiful eyes.

"I'm sorry too. I'm sorry those little bastards didn't shoot your foul ass up like Sonny in the Godfather. They should've gotten life for missing. What is there to work on, Max? Who wants your ol' shot up half of a man ass? You haven't been able to function since you got shot. I guess they did me a favor. Now I won't have to take in your polluted fluids in fear of producing a child who would be a constant reminder of you. It would be just my luck the baby would look like you, and then I would have to give him up for adoption or leave him at a fire station. That's how much you disgust me. I want to have nothing to do with you. At least now I can say I didn't have a child with you because they blew your balls off and rendered you impotent," Gina said, hurling out the most putrid insults ever.

Gina had to be in so much pain for her heart to be that cold and vile. Until now I gave her the benefit of the doubt. I kept telling myself that it wasn't her, it was the maternal void fueled by our empty nest. They were excuses. A cold evil crawled up into Gina and that's what became of her. I couldn't take it anymore. She crossed the line venturing into inhumane territory. I looked into Gina's eyes as she embraced me and showed me love. Then she went stone cold running a dagger into my heart. In war, this was being up close and personal when you made the kill so you could hear their heart stop as life slipped away. Clearly Gina wanted to experience this phenomenon when she stabbed me in the heart with her words. She wrinkled her eyebrows and scowled as she looked at me as if she was trying to look through me.

"Gina, that was pure evil," I said, pulling away still stunned by her repugnant scorn.

As I walked away, she continued pushing the knife in deeper saying, "Oh baby, that was just the appetizer. I have more where that came from. You're sorry, you wasted piece of life, I can't stand you. If I were a man, I'd whoop your trifling ass. Why don't you just die and quit depriving the world of valuable oxygen that you're wasting with your worthless ass life," smiling as if she was proud of her ranting.

This was headed nowhere. I was too stunned to respond. Gina ran me over with a truck, and now she wanted me to stick around while she put it in reverse to drive back over me. Everything I felt for her left in an instant. Her brow wrinkled. Her eyes turned cold and empty like the blackness of outer space at night. For a minute I expected her voice to become deep while she spun her head around like the demon-possessed girl in the Exorcist. If that happens, forget the holy water, I'm jetting with a quickness.

"Gina, I am so out of here. I don't even know who you are anymore. You can't sink any lower than right now. You want the fight that I'm not going to give you today."

"Coward, I knew you weren't a man. That's exactly why I can't have a baby. Run! Go back to your tramps. I hate you!" Gina screamed as if she was using a megaphone to bring her hatred up from her diaphragm.

I went into our bedroom and grabbed some clothes. I was going to check into a hotel and process what just happened. If nothing else I would get some peace. If I didn't leave, I knew this would go on all night.

As I started walking towards the front door, Gina started towards me like she wanted to grab me so I couldn't leave. This was all I needed. Would she turn violent? The police will arrest a man in a minute if they suspect domestic violence. In most cases they should because there are some angry foul brothers in the world. My mother and sisters taught me better. Hitting women will never be Max's legacy under any circumstances.

I turned to Gina and pointed my finger at her. I waved my finger from side to side motioning no-no. I think she saw something in my eyes that halted her in her tracks. Sockless, in loafers, wearing jeans and a polo shirt, I opened the door and started to walk out of the house, not caring when I'd return.

"Don't forget to take your condoms. That's right, your stuff doesn't work anymore Mr. Limp...," I heard Gina taking her final blow.

I think people living on the next block could hear the earth-shattering boom of my slamming the door in Gina's face. The last thing

I heard Gina say was "limp" as I tried to make the door come off the hinges when I slammed it shut.

I stayed at the hotel for a week before life returned to normal post homecoming weekend. I was back into work's daily grind. Jordan emailed me two weeks later. Initially I missed Jordan's message because I was so busy with work that I had little time to read emails.

I was surprised to see her email message because I didn't think I'd hear from her. I just figured it was one of those chance meetings—one of those things that either happens in the moment or is lost forever in time. I had chalked it up to that and put Jordan out of my mind. My life was already complicated enough.

Jordan's email resurrected the dead:

It was nice to meet you Max. If you are ever up around the Jacksonville area, look me up. Here is all of my contact information. By the way, I called Hertz in Geneva, Switzerland and told them that you were coming back. I said they should look out for you, because you aren't a very good driver and you beat up European truck drivers.

Regards, Jordan.

I was so surprised she remembered my telling her that story. I was involved in an accident on my way to Milan, Italy's Malpensa Airport. Not only was my car semi-totaled, but I got into a physical altercation with the truck driver who caused the accident. It wasn't a fight, but it could have been one. Thank God cooler heads prevailed. When I arrived at the airport's car rental check-in, my car was barely drivable with shards of broken glass from the windshield all over me and the car. The hood of the car had a long tear down the passenger's side where I ran into the back of his semi trailer. The passenger side of my Fiat Lancia went underneath the left rear of the trailer. The dashboard fell onto the steering wheel as I exited the car. The Hertz check-in attendant bucked his eyes wide open, raised his eyebrows, and rubbed his forehead like he was completely astonished and said, "It's destroyed." He looked at me in utter disbelief that I returned the car in this condition. The attendant whose name tag said 'V. Maggioni' looked like he was trying to figure out if he should say anything more. I think he was as lost for words as I was. I gave him the keys and turned away walking towards the car rental counter inside the terminal. I laughed quietly as I walked away. That was a funny scene—a story for the grandchildren one day.

I typed my reply to Jordan's email saying,

Ms. Anders, you know that was not my fault because that trucker ran into my rental car then attacked me. I had to defend myself, plus he was bigger than me. Max.

Jordan replied,

Max he was more round than you, but he looked like he was only 5 feet tall, ha ha. I have attached a picture of me so you will not forget this sassy little J'Ville girl every time you go to a flesh table. Can I call you after lunch today at about 2:30 p.m.?

JA

I replied,

What's this JA signature stuff, are you undercover now? Yes, you can call me at 2:30. By the way JA, what if I don't want to wait until I happen to be in Jacksonville to look you up? I know that I am up in St. Augustine a lot to meet for our twice a month Director's meeting. It would be nice to see you again and continue swapping war stories about our traveling,

MD.

The picture Jordan emailed me of herself was incredible. I didn't know all of that body was hiding underneath her ultra conservative, blue business suit. She was sitting on the front porch of her house in some high cut jean shorts. Her burnt-orange colored strapless halter top wrapped around what looked like firm breasts. What an inviting picture, but to what is left to be seen.

I told myself, *Max this is trouble in the making. You overheard her telling Casey that she wanted to get with you during homecoming weekend. You know what her agenda is about, well at least one part of it. Max, don't be naïve or stupid.*

After what Gina did a few weeks ago, why should I care what happens? She made it clear that she didn't want me. All I knew was Jordan erased some of my inhibitions during our short meeting. Lord knows I could use some civilized conversation. So why not get with Jordan? I wouldn't sleep with her. There wasn't any chance of that happening since little Max was still on his extended hiatus.

Jordan's light complexion is what some folks would refer to as "high yellow." Her legs were very nice and shapely and looked as though there wasn't a mark on them, not even a blemish. Her calf muscles looked taut, with a defined athletic bulge like she was a runner. "How did I miss all of that at homecoming?" I thought. Jordan had great overall muscle definition. My girl was ripped.

She was definitely interested in me for more than just a casual business acquaintance. Sending me a picture like this crystallized her desire. It screamed, "Explore me." Jordan was seducing me through a jpeg photo. This must be the calling card for dating in the 21st century. *I'm out of touch, I conceded. Max ol' boy, this is fire and you are walking straight into the flames.*

Why would I walk down this road when I know what she wants, even if I don't want the same thing? I continued cross examining myself with a barrage of questions I wasn't entirely convinced I wanted answered.

A closer inspection of Jordan's picture revealed a more telling secret. I noticed the ring on her left hand. I couldn't recall seeing a ring on her finger at homecoming. I wondered if she forgot that it was on there when she emailed me the picture. I was floored. Was she married? I hoped not. Even though I planned for nothing more than a growing friendship between us, I wasn't ready to take on any more relationship drama. I had my hands full with Gina. And like Marcus said, Daria was in waiting. My inner voice told me this was trouble. It was 2:30 p.m. when my phone rang and I wondered if it was Jordan calling as promised.

"Hello, this is Maxwell Dean."

"Hi, Maxwell, this is Jordan Anders, did I catch you at a bad time?"

"No, Ms. Jordan Anders, I was expecting your call. I cancelled the rest of my scheduled meetings today just so I wouldn't have any interruptions when a woman as important as Ms. Anders called. So I'm yours for as long as you want me."

She quipped, "You didn't cancel anything you big liar, but it sounds good. Which do you like to be called, Maxwell or Max?"

I replied, in my 16th century English accent, "Whichever one you wish me lady, but my friends call me Max. Are you seeking my friendship?"

"Well Max, it would be nice to be friends with a man who is more full of shit than me."

We both laughed hard. We were wading in BS up to our necks and knew it, which made it even funnier.

"Max, was that your wife or your girlfriend with you in the hospitality suite? I didn't think she was your wife the way you were trying to mack on me?" Jordan questioned as if she was trying to confirm just how far she could go with me.

"No, Jordan, it was neither. She is just a very dear friend who went to school with us back in the day. And for your information, I was not trying to mack you. Wishful thinking though. I was enjoying the conversation, but you on the other hand were sweating me awful hard."

She snapped back quickly, "I ain't gonna perpetrate. I was checking you out tuff, but I wouldn't say that I was sweating you. I liked what I saw. Is there anything wrong with a woman saying that, or are you still living in the Stone Age?"

"No, Jordan, I'm not a caveman."

"At least I can admit it, Mr. Dean. If that girl wasn't your woman, then I know there was something going on between the two of you that night. I know because I'm a woman. I saw how she looked while we talked. Women's intuition."

"I received the picture you sent by email, and was...aaaah," I said pausing.

Jordan interrupted me, "Spit it out Max, come on you can do it. I hope you don't do this when you're negotiating business deals?"

"I see we have jokes today. I was just looking for the optimal word to say that would capture the essence of my viewing experience."

"Now that sounds like an international businessman—smooth, quick, and full of crap, but good and confident crap when he puts it out there. I like that in a man. You get ten points for controlled arrogance," Jordan playfully replied.

"That's not arrogance, controlled or otherwise. True enough it is BS, but you have to admit that it was quick and good BS," I fired back, smiling through the whole thing as though she could see my pearly whites over the phone.

Jordan surprised me with her response. "Are you as quick with your mouth in everything?"

I nearly choked, swallowing saliva, and gasping in surprise at the same time. Knowing that question had a sexual overtone, I replied, "Quick in what I need to be quick, and controlled in others. By the way the picture was great. I didn't know you packed it like that under your ultra-conservative miss prissy business suit."

"I didn't want to go there dressed like some hootchie. Besides, I only show it to the one I want to see it. Did you like what you saw?" Jordan asked as if she knew what the answer would be.

"Not much, but it was alright," I wisecracked.

"Now you have jokes. Should I take it back and give it to someone else?" Jordan retorted.

"I'm not saying all that."

"Now that we have done the email thing, and this phone sparring thing, there is something I need to tell you. You may never want to speak to me again afterwards and I will understand," Jordan paused.

"What?"

She hesitated then with a less confident and cracking voice, "Max, I'm engaged."

"I can't say that I'm surprised. So, what are you doing with me? Being engaged is the time when you are supposed to be the most in love. Why are you sowing your oats with me?"

"No silly, you are my booty call." Jordan momentarily paused and then continued, "I'm just kidding, Maxwell Dean. Things are pretty confusing at the moment. I am enjoying your calming demeanor and sincere conversation. It's quite sweet actually."

I had to give her some points for honesty if there was ever such a thing in this type of situation. But honest in what…telling me the truth about lying to her man? Maybe her being engaged was a good thing… because it will keep her feelings for me in check. Jordan's engagement should keep us from the dangers of going too far.

"I wondered if you forgot that you had the ring on when you sent me the picture," I said, trying to figure out Jordan's intensions.

"I knew it was there, but I wanted to get your response when you saw it. I figured that if you started ducking my phone calls and not replying to my emails, I would have my answer. Do you still want to talk to me?"

"Yeah Jordan, I still want to talk to you, however, I need to be honest with you. I don't want to get caught up in any drama with you and your man. That's how people get killed. I have had one too many near-death experiences already," I replied, thinking about my getting shot twice.

"My fiancé Kyle is not the kind of guy who would kill you or anyone for that matter." Jordan continued, "I am engaged, but Kyle and I aren't getting along. I love him, but to tell you the truth he really pressured me and put me on the spot in front of everyone by asking me to marry him. I said yes because everyone was staring down my throat and I felt like I had to say yes, or face insurmountable ridicule. That's not what I wanted to do. I wasn't ready for that then. He and I needed to talk about it first. That moment would be joy for most women, but it made me hate him instead."

"That's old world thinking and I know you are smarter than that. You could have said no and he would've had to deal with it. He might have gotten egg on his face, but it's unfair to him and yourself to say yes, when you feel no," I said, counseling her as if I was some kind of relationship expert.

"I know. I've been kicking myself and Kyle since he proposed. I should have said no, because I wasn't ready to say yes. He surprised me by putting the ring on my finger in public, and then I cursed his ass out when we were in private. I told Kyle he shouldn't have proposed to me in front of everyone when we hadn't even discussed it." She had tension in her voice that suggested she was still harboring anger.

"Wow, that's deep," I replied.

Jordan jumped back in saying, "Before I saw you at the hospitality suite, I was pissed at Kyle. I was planning to leave him. I packed up some stuff and went to homecoming with Casey who went to your school. I just left without giving Kyle any explanation. So Max, there won't be any drama," she explained.

"To the contrary, that sounds like nothing but drama. So, was I just a diversion to your home life troubles? I can't say that I'm a rebound because you are still in your relationship. We have nothing invested right now and can walk away without any hurt feelings," I replied with some level of rigidity in my voice.

"Max, I promise there won't be any drama. Besides, Kyle is not like that. He is such a sweet guy. He isn't a strong man. Actually, I have trouble being stronger and possessing more testosterone than my man. I wish he had more backbone. No woman really respects a weak man." Her voice broke from frustration and trepidation.

Jordan added another telling bomb when she said, "Kyle got with me right after I broke up from my previous boyfriend. I told him then that I didn't have feelings for him the way he did for me. Kyle was a good friend to me when I was feeling down from my other relationship. He pursued me until I said what the heck, Kyle is nice and I might be able to grow into him. He accepted that and my initial back and forth with Ivan until we were completely over."

"That sounds messy. It seems like Kyle was so desperate that he sat around while you dibbled and dabbled with your ex. I don't know how you can even respect him for that. Kyle seems worse than a backup plan," Shaking my head in disbelief. I paused for a couple of seconds and then continued, "Jordan I have something to tell you as well."

"The woman who was with you at the hospitality suite was your woman wasn't she?" Jordan asked.

"Can I get it out, Ms. Impatient? No, she isn't my woman, but I am married. My wife and I have begun talking about getting a divorce. I think she hates me with a passion and wants me out of the house."

Sounding puzzled Jordan asked, "Why? What did you do? Has Max been a bad boy? Did she catch you dipping your pen into the company ink?"

"No, none of that."

"I bet it has something to do with your homecoming escort. What was her name?"

"Her name is Daria. As a matter of fact it does have something to do with Daria, but not what you think. My friendship with Daria has been a source of irritation to my wife."

"Max, I can see why she would have a problem with your quote/un-quote, friend Daria." Jordan said sucking her teeth as if she were saying right, friend my foot. Jordan continued, "She is cute and most wives would have a problem with her being close to their husbands. What, you couldn't see that?"

"No, I didn't really think it would be a problem since Gina knows that Daria and I have been friends since college."

"Clueless, you men are absolutely clueless. I only saw her around you once and I can tell that Daria has serious feelings for you. If I were your wife, she would be public enemy number one. She would have to be banned. If I left her around you too long, she would eventually work you into her stuff." Jordan announced this obviously having had experience with reeling in men, just like me.

"And how do you know that, Ms. Anders?"

"Well, Mr. Corporate Genius, first, I am a woman. Second, I know women and we are scandalous, and third, because I thought about that possibility too. Can you handle that Donald Trump Jr.?" Jordan fired back boldly.

"Whatever, Jordan. Getting back to the matter at hand, my wife sent me to homecoming powered with hateful insults. We are over and I'm exiting my marriage, whereas, you on the other hand, are engaged at the moment and getting married. So, I now pose the same question to you, do you ever want to speak to me again?"

"Hell yes!" Jordan emphatically declared. "I am relieved because I thought you might not want to see me again, and I am so attracted to you. Oops, I shouldn't have said that, but it is out there now and we are grown adults. I'm not taking it back and I don't want to lose my new buddy. What else did you like about the picture, nasty boy? I sort of look fat in that picture but that is my favorite coffee cup," Jordan quipped sarcastically.

"I liked the entire picture including those shorts. Who took the picture? And I must confess I was looking at several things, but I assure you it wasn't your coffee cup."

"Does it matter who took the picture if you liked it? But since you asked, it was him…my fiancé, okay?"

"It is fine with me. I was just curious. Since as you say, we are both grown adults."

I was thinking, I bet Kyle wouldn't be too happy if he knew I had this picture. I bet when Kyle took that picture he never thought the picture he took of Jordan in shorts with her legs open would be given to another man. I know I'd be pissed if it was the other way around. My moral compass should have kicked in with that realization. Since I knew nothing was going on between us, I convinced myself the picture was innocent. I didn't know how we men can lie to ourselves with such a straight face? One word—denial.

"When are you coming through West Palm Beach on your way somewhere?" I asked.

"Why Max, would you like to see me again?"

"Yes, to have some dinner and some more of your arrogant conversation," I said laughing.

"Well, Mr. Corporate BS-er, I would be delighted to have some more conversation with you, arrogant or otherwise. I would be happy to see you again because I have been thinking about you ever since the homecoming weekend. I think we clicked right from the start." Jordan paused, and then hesitantly said, "I don't know how I could possibly be ready to get married when I am thinking about you like I am."

"My marriage appears to be headed for the big D. Gina and I just can't get past some tough issues. What are you doing with me if you love Kyle and are contemplating marriage?" I fired back challenging her to make sense about what she was doing with me.

Through the deafening silence over the phone I could feel Jordan struggling with the answer to that question. She was repeating her same behavior with Kyle and Ivan. Now I was the fish on the stupid hook. I was just like one of those storm chasers in that movie Twister; if I got too close to the tornado I'd get sucked up by it and destroyed. Like those who flirt with disaster, which one would I become—harmlessly watching from a safe distance or sucked up and destroyed? *Do the right thing Max*, I cautioned myself.

"I really don't have a good answer that makes any sense," Jordan finally conceded.

"You will have to figure that one out before you jump the broom. You still are going to get married, aren't you?"

"I don't really know. My head says, yes, but my heart has a lot of questions," she replied sounding confused.

I could tell by Jordan's voice and answers that she was truly struggling with her and Kyle's relationship. My intrusion into their mix would only exacerbate her confusion.

"Don't let me be the distraction to you finding the answer. I mean that. I am just a new friend with troubles of my own. I'm not trying to add to yours or mine," I replied in all sincerity.

"I will be coming through West Palm Beach in about two weeks on my way to Dallas for a training conference. Let me try to work some things out where I can stay there for a day or two before flying to Dallas. I could stand for a friendly face and some laughter," Jordan said, moving completely past my advice.

Even though my mind was telling me "danger," I told myself, I have this under control. Okay Max, you're playing with fire. Two emotionally wounded people hooking up is a recipe for disaster. There is still time to keep this thing with Jordan as a phone/email friendship. Don't ignore the sexy picture you fool.

"Then let's do it," I enthusiastically told Jordan.

Something inside me said... *You just walked off a cliff.* Another part of me said... *This could be good for you.*

"Max, I gotta go to a meeting. I'll firm up my arrival date so we can set something up. Take care okay? Bye."

"Go do your thing, warrior woman. I'll holla."

Weeks went by. Jordan and I talked on the phone for hours each day. We got closer by sharing more personal things about ourselves. We often spoke about our cravings for the intimacy that was barren in our respective relationships. Those cravings weren't necessarily for each other, but for a fulfilling relationship. We escalated our innuendos towards one another. It was playful and non-committal where either of us could pull out and there wouldn't be any hard feelings.

We talked about our previous relationships and why we couldn't seem to find the right one. Listening to Jordan, I discovered she was as lost and confused as I am. If I could say anything to her fiancé, I'd tell him to run away and don't look back. He was in store for an emotional blood bath with Jordan.

My day was finally drawing to a close. I was packing some files in my briefcase to take home when my phone rang.

"Hello, Max, this is Jordan. I will be getting in on November 18 on Delta at 6:45 p.m. I booked a room at the Ritz Carlton. Would you be able to pick me up, or should I look for a shuttle? If you have something going on or a late meeting, I don't mind taking the shuttle."

"You don't have to take the shuttle; I'll pick you up at baggage claim. I'll be waiting curb side."

"I don't expect anything because I know you have a home situation. I'm not expecting you to stay out late with me. I don't want to cause you any more problems. I will be happy just to see you again."

With Jordan's concern and understanding, I knew she wouldn't put any demands on me. This was going to be a stress-free hookup. This was going to be easy, perhaps too easy. In my mind I debated whether I was going to play it cool or act like an out-of-control butthole and stay out way too late.

Not sure of which I'd be, I said, "Don't worry about that, we'll work it out by the time you get here." I could hear Jordan exhale as she reaffirmed, "It's up to you, Max, but I'm just saying I know the deal and it's really alright either way."

"I know, but I have to run right now. So I will talk to you later."

"Alright, see you later, Maximax."

As I hung up I told myself that not only was I going off a cliff with Jordan, but I might be setting myself a blaze as I went over the edge.

Chapter 5

DANGEROUS LIAISON

I couldn't believe two weeks went by so fast. As I sat in my SUV waiting on Jordan to exit the terminal, I wondered if someone Gina knew would see Jordan getting into my vehicle and tell Gina. Why did I care? Gina hated me anyway. Our marriage was over so it didn't matter if someone saw us, I thought. I was still nervous nonetheless. I didn't know why. I had no intention of doing anything with Jordan. I asked myself what seemed like a thousand times if I was cheating and wrong for having her fly in to hang out with me.

I looked up and saw Jordan walking towards me. Her coco-colored sweater and jeans snugly traversed her body like they were a second layer of skin. It was an age defying picture. This girl's body could challenge the fidelity of even the most devoted and faithful husband, let alone one in a broken home. With my rickety marriage, my resistance could be in serious jeopardy, but it was too late to turn around now.

"Hey Jordan, you are finally here," I said smiling.

"Max, I am finally in Palm Beach," she gasped, handing me her carry-on bag.

We began one of those impersonal hugs where no middle parts touched. Then she pulled her body up to mine and gave me a real hug. Her embrace tightened as she announced, "I missed you, buster."

"The Ritz Carlton is real close which should take us about ten minutes to get there."

As we got into my new black Lincoln Navigator, Jordan said, "This is a boat. It's huge."

Before I could stop myself from being completely corny, I said, "The Love Boat."

"I hope that wasn't your best Mack Daddy line or something," she replied, acknowledging I struck out on the comment.

"Clean up your mind, Jordan. I wasn't trying to Mack you," I replied trying to deflect my idiot comment.

I thought that comment was so retro and weak. I wanted to stab myself in the forehead for saying something so lame. Dude, you negotiate mega deals and that's the best you can do? Shut up, Max, before you have to remove another shoe from your mouth. This could be a long night if I didn't change the direction of my weak conversational gaffes.

Jordan leaned all the way over to my side of the truck and gave me a passionate but respectable kiss. I didn't expect that, and I didn't quite know how to refuse it or if I even really wanted to. Her lips felt so soft and moist—like jellied candies, unlike some women's lips that are hard and boney feeling. She didn't have bad breath. There is nothing more unattractive than a woman with bad, funky, stank, singe-your-eyebrows breath. Her kiss was juicy and tasted like peppermint.

Jordan pulled back and gave me this goo-goo-eyed stare. She looked at me as if she was trying to see every corner of my face and said, "I shouldn't have done that, but I have wanted to ever since we first met at the reunion."

Why couldn't I have started off my conversation like that rather than "The Love Boat?" Jordan got right to it. This was not going to be easy. I already knew I was going to have problems pulling away from her tonight. *I should just drop her off at the hotel and go home. Fat chance of that happening. Good luck with that one, Max,* I thought.

She knew she was reeling me in but she let me know through that kiss that the rules could be broken. I wondered if that's where the boundaries were, or was that an appetizer to no boundaries? Maybe Jordan was letting me know there could be a free for all between us with no limitations. This was a guy's dream, but at what cost? I thought about the moral bill I would have to pay if I went for the possible payoff tonight. Jordan was great, but my sex meter had measured zero since the shooting.

"Max, you have some really soft lips, and you kiss very well. A girl could get used to that, yum-yum," Jordan said with a seductive innocence.

I sat in the hotel's swanky sea shell and chandelier-filled lobby. The coral and sand color scheme was gorgeous. I walked outside to the upper deck and looked out over the ocean. The view was spectacular. Jordan called my cell telling me her room number and to come right up. The door would be open so I could just walk in.

Anxiety bubbled up inside of me. I was asking for trouble. I needed to back out and leave now because as soon as I enter her room I am at the point of no return. I told her that I was on my way up. I couldn't believe this was happening. My inner voice got louder— *Leave now!*

As I walked into the room, Jordan said, "I am just checking my voicemail at work, and I'll be finished in a few minutes."

The room was definitely very upscale with all its amenities. The mini bar was stocked with the usual overpriced snacks for your late night food desperation. I think hotels shut down room service early so they increase their mini bar revenue. Then you go into cardiac arrest at checkout when you see how hard you got hit for late night snack binges.

I looked around Jordan's room while she checked her voicemail. The hotel lived up to its reputation as a luxury hotel with first class apportionments. Her room had a balcony that overlooked the ocean. She must have paid a grip for this room. I wondered what I was going to have to do so that Jordan would feel the expense was worth it.

I picked up the bottle of wine I secretly brought to celebrate Jordan's visit. Ferrari Carano is an exceptionally great Chardonnay. It's a wonderfully smooth white wine that isn't too sweet, not too dry, with a little oak flavor and a hint of cinnamon and caramel.

Ferrari is worthy of custom wine flukes and not standard hotel glasses or plastic bathroom cups, so I brought a couple of wine flukes that had character. I wanted to make her trip a little memorable. I brought them up to the room in a small black leather-carrying bag, like I was a doctor making a house call. I was making a house call alright. I was calling up trouble for myself.

"Jordan, please join me out here on the balcony," I said, holding the glass of wine I poured for her.

She accepted the gesture and with an approving smile on her face, "I am impressed, Max."

We sat on the balcony sipping our wine. For a while we uttered nothing—just slouched back in the patio chairs taking in the sights and sounds of the Atlantic Ocean's surf hitting the beach about a hundred yards away. We smiled at each other trying to figure out where this was going. I hadn't intended it to go anywhere, but now I wasn't sure what I wanted. Jordan made the first move with a kiss. I guess the wine could have been considered my "yes" move.

Little Max hadn't moved a muscle so I was pretty sure I didn't want anything. Jordan may have thought the wine was the introduction to a seductive dance between us, or that I was trying to lower her inhibitions so she would lower her clothes. What signal was I really sending? I didn't know what I was doing.

"This wine is really good, and where did you get these glasses, because they are beautiful?" Jordan asked.

"Oh, I just picked them up from this little specialty shop I know on Ocean Drive in Delray Beach," I answered matter of factly.

Out of nowhere Jordan said, "I'm not having sex with you, Max."

"That's fine. Remember what we said about how this would go?" I said reluctantly.

"Yeah, I do, so let's toast to whatever, as long as it's having a nice time."

We sat there talking for what seemed like hours. We touched upon everything except our respective relationships. The wine was definitely adding to a heightened state of relaxation. We began looking at each other a little deeper and gazing into trouble on the horizon.

Jordan took off her ring and earrings. She set them on the balcony table. "Max come over here."

Jordan motioned her finger for me to come closer. She kissed me again and repeated, "Max I told you that I was not going to have sex with you."

With a small bit of agitation, I fired back, "I thought we already discussed that and put it away in the done column?"

"I know some people who know of you ...,"

Was she going to tell me about some dirt she dug up on me?

"And?" I said, wondering where this was going.

"I heard something quite disturbing," Jordan said with an inquisitive look on her face.

This line of questioning came out of nowhere. It threw me for a loop. Where was she going with this? My mind went in a hundred different directions.

"I heard you got shot really bad. They said you almost died. Is that true?"

"Yeah, but I don't like talking about it much if you don't mind," I said, completely surprised that she knew.

"Oh—my—God!" Slowly dragging out the words, she put her hand over her mouth while tearing up.

"When we first met, that was the first time I had really been out in over a year," not really wanting to go into it any further.

Jordan stared at me as though she was trying to see my wounds. Curiosity was all over her face even though she was respectful enough not to ask to see them.

I asked, "Do you want to see my wounds?" I don't know what made me do that. I had never done that with anyone before. If you didn't see them when I was in the hospital in a coma, then you lost out. I was never going to allow myself to be on display like that. The wine had me so relaxed I just thought, *what the hell.* Maybe it would gross Jordan out so much that it would kill any of her sexual desire for me.

"I don't know, Max, do you mind? I don't want to unearth any pain you want to remain buried," Jordan replied with great hesitancy.

I unbuttoned my shirt. I couldn't believe I was doing this. Why now, and why her? I slipped off my shirt. I pulled my white, wife-beater t-shirt over my head as Jordan watched me motionless. I stood in front of her, bare chested. I was exposed emotionally as I was physically. I started opening up in a way I never thought I would.

"Jordan, these two young boys shot me up like I was a dog in the street. Marcus and I were leaving a charity event together when the boys attempted to carjack us. He was also wounded. I literally died in the attack, but was revived in the emergency room. I was in a coma for weeks. The shooting jacked me up mentally. I haven't really been myself every since. I have to be honest with you; I haven't been with a woman in almost two years, not even my wife. Until I met you at homecoming, I had no interest in being with anyone on any level, let alone like this."

"I can understand your feelings. I am so sorry to hear what happened to you. I can't believe you were shot. I'm glad they revived you in the ER. If they hadn't, you wouldn't be here with me right now."

I tried to say something, but Jordan said, "Sshhhhhh."

She grabbed my hand and walked me back into the room and pulled me to her. Then sat on the edge of the bed and opened her legs so I could get closer. She hugged me as if she was trying to take on my pain. Jordan started weeping. As the tears rolled down her face, she began kissing my wounds. The first touch of her lips on my scars made me jump like I was in pain. It felt like some of the pain of the past was leaving me with each tear-drenched kiss. I wanted more, but I also wanted her to stop. I had no idea where I would be at the end. Jordan ran her hands down my back, lifting the burdens of my past. She gripped my back firmly, kissed my scars again, and said in a soft whisper, "I want to remove your pain."

Jordan stopped and said, "Max, tell me why I am getting ready to take off my clothes? Tell me why I am so attracted to you?"

I looked at her now frozen in my own thoughts. I was in new territory, powerless to stop anything from happening. "What about what you said about not sleeping with me? I don't think this is a good idea. Don't make me a pity party or your charity case," I said not really sure what I was saying.

"Who could do such a thing to you? You are such a beautiful man, both inside and out. I know you must still have a lot of pain inside of you. I want to love it away on this very night." Jordan took her sweater off over her head. Her red laced bra made her breasts look soft with her nipples peaking through the lace. Although Jordan is 32-years old, her body's initial unveiling revealed a more youthful body. The fountain of youth surely paid her a visit. She unzipped her pants and pealed her pants off her hips like she was stripping a banana's peel from its tasty fruit inside. That's when I saw the first hint of her red-laced panties. The red lace seemed woven into her skin and went smoothly around her tiny waist and a perfectly flat stomach. Her abs had no bulge of fat anywhere.

A slow wiggle excavated Jordan from her jeans. There was no denying it now; the inevitable was on the way. A terrorizing fear engulfed me. Little Max hadn't worked in a long time. I would be mortified if he didn't work now. One part of me thought it would be better if little Max didn't work, while the other part said "please" work. You cannot get a more physically sexy woman than Jordan. I needed to maximize her. I needed to be maximized for that matter. I wanted my body to work again. It might as well be with her. Jordan kissed another scar, and suddenly I felt physical excitement for the first time in almost two years. Little max was waking up, showing signs of life.

Jordan saw the look on my face, "Are you going to join me?"

"It's been almost two years since I've been intimate with anyone. I don't know if I can do this," I ashamedly confessed.

"Don't worry about performing, baby. Just let me take on some of your pain and sorrow. Whatever happens or doesn't happen is alright with me. Okay?"

I took off my black shoes followed by my black jeans. We were both down to skivvies. How long could I hold out without having her? I felt a gradual increasing arousal.

Jordan unhooked her bra from the back, as I pulled her shoulders forward, and lifted the straps off. Her arms came together and she let her bra slowly slide down her arms. Her woman's pride was exposed. Perky and fresh without disappointment, her pride revealed a body that wanted attention. She wanted me in all my brokenness.

I could have exploded by just looking at her seemingly perfect body, but I was not going out like that. She needed to be maximized in grand fashion tonight, but would my busted up body fail me like Gina claimed it would?

I knew where this was heading—destination I didn't want, but a place very much needed. I set myself up for this moment. This romantic serenade began back at homecoming weekend. Who was this woman who was getting little Max to respond? Jordan's gentle kisses and attention to my wounds unblocked the log jam in my manhood. I told myself, *Max don't do this.* Every pain of the past two years said I needed it. If Mason and Marcus were here, they'd be waving pompoms and cheering me on. With my confidence building I said, "Do you want to be maximized tonight?"

Looking puzzled Jordan asked, "What is maximized?"

"It's laying down the loving to the point where you want to walk backwards down the highway," I responded playfully, trying to buy more time before the inevitable happened.

"Boy, you are silly."

"No, really, it's maximizing the fulfillment of everything you want to feel physically, emotionally, and sexually. It's taking you to a place of intimacy much higher and more complete than simply penetration. The end release is just the manifestation of the journey."

"You are either cocky, or extremely confident. I wonder which one of them you are," she fired back.

Her slightly bowed-legs left a space outlining the fullness of her secret place. I was thinking, I didn't want to be one of those buster brothers who gets some new loving and loses his mind, and is done in less than five minutes. There is a lot of pressure on men. If we don't perform up to expectation, or not at all, women will tell all of their girls, or at least the close ones, that you were a worthless five-minute man.

Many women think there isn't anything worse than a man who gets them all worked up and can't last long enough to let them release. Worse yet, if he cannot last past five minutes, he becomes a real loser. They will tell you it is okay, but man, let me tell you, your standing with her gets flushed down the toilet.

A woman can hide herself if she isn't stimulated behind all kinds of reasons that you won't know, but for men it's right there in plain sight. Your action is either standing up or it's not. Men need to know where she is on the satisfaction scale before you derail her impending satisfaction. Women have no idea what kind of pressure men are under. Many a man and their pleasure tool have fallen under this pressure, literally.

I lifted her chin and kissed her neck. I was behind her spooning. I was taking great care not to neglect any part of her body. I was in no hurry. We intertwined our warm bodies together as if we were trying to braid ourselves together. I ran my hands down her outer thighs contouring her wonderfully small frame. Putting my hands on both sides of her face, I gently pulled her face into mine. I kissed her lips, not like I was in a hurry to get some place, but like I wanted to take her there on a joyful ride.

Sliding one hand behind her neck, I tilted her head up and to the side. Exposing the sensuous nape of her neck, I kissed under her jaw bone just below the ear. My kisses were communicating to Jordan. I wanted my kisses and gentle strokes to speak of my desire for her. I hadn't felt like this in a long time. I wanted to savor every moment. I wasn't going to hurry through our intimacy. I wanted to marinate in every kiss, every hug, and every softly spoken word. I wanted to soak up all that she had to give me.

Initially I didn't want to be here, but this movement was good enough for me. We loved on each other for what seemed like hours. When we finally consumed each other's secret it was natural as taking the next step while walking. We both sighed as though we were gasping for air after swimming under water in a pool. Maybe we both needed this moment. I know I sure did, no matter how forbidden this dance was. In the final moments before eclipsing in pleasure, neither of us could have stopped even if we wanted to. I know I didn't and her body confirmed the same.

Afterwards we just quietly snuggled. The moment was complete. Mere words would have only served to degrade the fulfillment.

Jordan finally spoke, "You are dangerous. That level of love we just did can make some women do crazy things. Take me for instance; I've never come close to getting what you just gave me. I'm thinking that I need some of that more often. A woman would start thinking, how can I ever leave the most incredible lover ever? We are already thinking about the next encounter. Boy, you had better watch who you give it to like that, because some woman might go psycho on you if you attempt to cut her off."

I interrupted, "Is that what you are doing, Ms. Anders?"

With a serious look about her face and demeanor to match, Jordan said, "Max, let me finish. I am trying to be serious for a minute. Some woman might get a little too emotional over how maximizing makes her feel and become downright possessive. That is why I called you dangerous."

"What about you?"

"What about me?" she said as if she didn't know what I was asking her.

"You know. What are you doing?" as I fired it back to her.

Jordan replied with this serious but playful smirk on her face, "Okay, you asked so don't get mad at what you get from me! I am looking at you, not just for what happened, but you as a whole. I didn't think about Kyle once. I don't even feel bad, so how can I even think about marrying him? I wish I had met you sooner. On top of that, I have been thinking about you ever since we first met in the hospitality suite. Then, you maximized me. There was something about those perfect lips, that beautiful smile, and those deep mysterious eyes of yours that pulled me in and made me drop my guard and everything else. I'm wondering what it would be like to be with you all the time. I'm fantasizing about when I'm going to see "The Great Maxwell Dean" again. You're charting a course to a place you might not want to go. You may not be ready to go there either. You cannot un-ring my bell. You asked Max!"

Naively and perhaps stupidly I replied, "Jordan, I was hoping you would want to do this again, because I don't want to cheapen tonight by making it a one night stand. I went to a place with you tonight that I didn't think I'd ever see again. You and I have some serious issues facing us. We shouldn't have done this, but we did. There are consequences for these moral hazards we're navigating."

"Slow down cowboy—let's just try to work on the next time for now. I cannot even imagine what Max is like when he is fully healed," Jordan shivered and shook her head like she shuttered to find out.

"So the venerable Ms. Jordan Anders, there will be a next time for us, huh?"

"Did you hear anything I said about you maximizing me, dangerous boy? That applied to me too!" Jordan said with a look of serious calm on her face.

I didn't know what to make of Jordan's post event pronouncement. I just felt like she liberated me from the emotional bondage triggered by the shooting. How could I let that go? She accomplished in less than 24 hours what I or no other woman had been able to do in nearly two years. Sure, what she said made sense for down the road, but I wanted to live in the now. I felt dead for way too long. I want today, right now—I don't know how to spell tomorrow! I'd deal with tomorrow later.

The weekend was over. We were back at PBI airport. We had a couple of great days under our belt. I handed Jordan a note, kissed her, and said, "Have a nice flight." She grinned from ear to ear as I turned to leave. The note to her said:

Jordan,

Thanks for caring enough to set me free. I know neither one of us wanted it to happen, but I'm glad it did. You brought life back to my stalled out existence.

Always, Max-imizing Max.

As Jordan went through the double doors into the terminal, I asked myself, *What now, Max?*

Chapter 6

SHANGHAI SURPRISE

Should I call Marcus and tell him about Jordan's visit? Maybe I should just call Mason instead. Knowing his crazy butt, he'll try to three-way me in with Marcus and rib me for hours. I should tell Mason that I got some and I didn't even need a lady of the night as he suggested at the reunion. Man, Jordan was great. My little men were so backed up. The girl has got some skills.

The phone rang interrupting my midday reflection. "Hello, this is Maxwell Dean."

"Are you busy?" Daria asked in her ever-so-sweet tone.

"I'm always busy at work, but never too busy for Ms. Ross," I replied playfully.

"Max, I just wanted to tell you that I love you." How could she say that to me right now? I was just thinking about my weekend of getting busy with Jordan, and now Daria was throwing the love word at me. In that short weekend jaunt with Jordan, I forgot about Daria. Those three little words formed a dagger of guilt driven into my heart. Even though Daria and I weren't sleeping together, I now felt like I cheated on her. I tried to conjure up a lie for whatever question she'd ask me about Jordan. But how could she know anything about Jordan? I'm trippin'.

I hesitated my response to the biggest three little words that could ever be uttered to a person. Before I could uncomfortably respond with the obvious answer that I loved her too, she offered me a pass. I loved her for who she was, a true friend.

"Max, you don't have to say it back because I know you do. I know things have been hard on you since the shooting. Just know that the Dar is now and will always be here for you."

"Thanks baby, I said as my phone started ringing.

"I know you have to get that, talk to you later, bye." bailing me out of an uncomfortable conversation.

If ever there was a truer cliché, I was saved by the bell, literally. The caller ID on my phone showed Marcus' satellite phone. His boss provided him with a satellite phone so he could be reached in the cockpit while he was flying. That boy did have it good. I should have hooked myself up with his job instead of giving it to him. Oh yeah, I don't know how to fly a plane.

"Marcusssssss," I answered sounding out his name.

"Somebody's in a good mood. What happened? Either Gina gave you some, or she left you. So, which is it? Did she remove the dust from little Max or are you free from purgatory?" Marcus questioned with his dry sarcastic humor.

"You got jokes."

"Well punk, why are you so happy? If it isn't that, then you must have got some more money from your job. Like you need any more," Marcus said.

"Do you ever stop hating sky cap?" I said firing back.

"I got your sky cap, cap din punk," Marcus retorted as though I stepped on his nerve.

"Anyway, neither happened. If I was telling you anything involving Gina, it definitely wouldn't be happy. Jordan came up and dusted off little Max," I said as if I was surprised.

"WHAT!" Marcus screamed.

"Bruh, my action works. Well, it worked for her anyway," I said in a hurry, getting that revelation out before the avalanche of Marcus' questions that would surely follow.

"Wait a minute, I gotta put this plane on autopilot so I can run around the cockpit and not crash."

"You are too stupid," I said laughing and shaking my head.

I heard Marcus scream again. At least I knew there wouldn't be a three-way call with Mason. His satellite didn't have three-way capabilities. Part of me wanted to puff out my chest to my boy and let my testosterone take over. The other part of me wondered what I just got myself into. Daria had been there for me through thick and thin, and I brushed her off the phone over Jordan. Who does that?

"Give up the details punk. What are you waiting for? I got to hear what this woman did to wake up your tool. Me and Mase thought you were going to be the only guy we ever knew who goes back to being a virgin. We worried about you son," Marcus excitedly said.

"Mannnnnnn, her body is smoke'n. Even though seeing that would make a normal man lose himself, that didn't do the trick for me. She asked me about the shooting and I actually opened up and told her about it."

"Whaaat?"

"Yeah bruh, I even showed her the scars. Jordan started kissing my wounds. When she did that little Max started waking up. I can't explain it. The more she kissed the remnants of my injuries, the more alert little Max became. Man, Jordan even licked my scars like she was trying to heal me or something."

"Max, why does everything have to be so deep with you? Why couldn't you get there just because Jordan's body was banging and you wanted to launch her into the fetal position?" Marcus interrupted.

"Why? I'll tell you why, because I'm not a cookie-robbing caveman like you, that's why."

"She was licking you like she was trying to get to the center of a tootsie pop or something. Your girl is a freak. She was acting like she was hungry. You should have given her a baloney sandwich," Marcus said, laughing in the phone.

"Can I finish my story, funny man?"

"That's why you have so many problems with women. You attract all of these deep types of women who are trying to be the next Max love story. You should be like me. I only want shallow women who know it's about hit it and quit it. Hell, they don't even have to be smart as long as she can throw down when we take it to the mat. You should try it sometimes, less drama," Marcus said, conveying his relationship theories.

"Marcus, I didn't want to do that with Jordan. Most of it was fear that I couldn't perform. I know this sounds weird, but when she licked my scars, something happened. It was as if I was letting go of something that had been holding me back ever since we got shot. Something was drawing me to her. I wasn't thinking or acting. I was just being. I felt every part of her womanhood. And brother when I released, it felt like it was coming down from every part of my body. It was like a warm tickling sensation traveling down all of my limbs from head to toe. When I reached the pinnacle of pleasure, that climatic moment was virtually paralyzing. I think everything that was holding me back came out all at once. Man, it was almost spiritual. I don't know how to explain it in words, but afterwards I felt free, like I was released from me," trying to make sense of it myself.

"On the real Max, I'm not in to all of that emotional stuff like you, but if it worked to get my boy back, I'm down with it. All I know is Jordan has some skills. Sounds to me like Max got turned out. I hope she has some friends just like her. Birds of a feather…"

"Turned out, turned in, whatever," I said just as Marcus interrupted.

"Hold on Max, air traffic control is changing my course."

"Miami ATC, Falcon November 8608 Bravo turning right heading 240 and climbing to 35 thousand."

"Okay, Max, I'm back."

"How did they let someone like you who dropped math four times in college fly a sophisticated jet? I bet you didn't tell them about you're A.D.D. did you?"

"There you go hatin' again, Minwell Dean."

"Marcus, I have to get ready for this 10:00 a.m. meeting. See you when you get back, later."

I'd been on the phone almost nonstop since the end of my morning meeting. It felt like I had calluses on my ear. Managing manufacturing operations on three continents is tough even in the best of conditions. Man, the work pace has been fierce since I returned to the office among the polite stares and distant inquiries. I appreciated people not coming up to me anymore to ask me what it felt like to get shot. It was now 3:15 p.m. and I hadn't even had lunch. Time was at a premium and I didn't have much of it. It was exhausting me just knowing that I had to write a briefing document for my boss to take to New York.

The executives meet quarterly in New York to prepare the next quarter's financial expectations for Wall Street. Then they report on the trends, expansions, or decrease in any Business or Product Group.

My boss is an Ivy League graduate with more degrees than a thermometer. He was the president of some student think tank of pocket-protector wearing intellectual introverts. He became the youngest Senior Executive Vice-President of the International Business Group. He is probably the smartest guy I've ever met, but his oral briefings could make sleep itself pass out from boredom. Man, watching paint dry is infinitely livelier than sitting through his presentations, but his boss, the CEO, and the Board, sure listen to him.

My phone rang. I saw that it was Jordan's name on the caller ID.

"Hello, Ms Anders."

"How did you know it was me, Mr. Dean?"

"Caller ID of course. Don't they use technology over there at your company?" I sarcastically fired back.

"Oh, I see. Somebody's got a smart mouth today," Jordan said as though she was checking me.

"Well, Ms. Anders, smart is why they hired me to manage a billion dollar product operations business."

"Whatever man! How did you get that job anyway?"

"I was recruited to the company years ago to add some strength to our U.S. major client negotiation team. Then one day I was asked for my opinion regarding a poor quality and failed performance problem at a plant in China. After hearing a few of the details I told them my theory of the problem and suggested a solution."

"I'm impressed. I guess you really are a smarty pants aren't you?"

"No, not really. I just fake it till I make it," I said attempting humility.

"Can you speak Chinese? Now that would be really impressive in addition to the other skills that you demonstrate in hotel rooms," Jordan said with a coy seductive voice.

"I might be good, but I'm not a magician. Anyway getting back to answering your question…"

"Okay then, continue giving it to me, Max."

I liked what Jordan was saying. She was beyond making subtle innuendos by letting me know she was ready to play some more. Although I was acting like I was unfazed by her comments, I wanted them. I wanted to know if lightning could strike twice.

"Getting back to the story. When I went to the office the next day, I was being sent to China. The International Business Group's VP said my opinion about the manufacturing problems in China was on point. With that, I was on loan to the International Business Group and off to China."

"Just like that? Boy you must have some skills."

"Jordan, like my grandmother always said, I'm blessed."

"After spending three weeks in China implementing operational changes, quality and production both rose. My twenty-hour flight back home produced jet lag that could kill a bull. At the conclusion of my debriefing the VP announced that he was making me the new Director of International Business Operations. The VP took me into his office and showed me the new organizational chart with my name already in the new position and presented me with 2000 shares of stock options. My mouth nearly hit the floor. I couldn't show my emotions, so I hollered inside of my head."

"So you a big baller, huh?" Jordan asked.

"Now I'm not saying all that. I'm fortunate that I was even given that opportunity."

"Don't be modest boy, claim your place in the world!"

"As I was about to leave the VP told me I'd notice a slight adjustment in my next paycheck. I was wondering what kind of adjustment? Maybe it will be a two or three thousand dollar per year raise. My teeth almost fell out of my mouth when the VP told me that my current salary was forty percent below the minimum salary for the position. He also explained that they raised my salary by fifty percent. They added an extra ten percent just to show how much they value my leadership."

"Just what did you do over there? That's unheard of. They must love you," Jordan said as though she was in disbelief.

"I know, I had to pinch myself. I didn't even know this sort of thing was even possible, but I saved them millions when I improved the operations in China," I said as if I apologetically needed to prove I was worthy of the big raise.

"So you're hitting the big six figures, Mr. Big Baller? You have stock options and all of that fat back compensation, don't you?"

"I'm doing alright. I can afford to buy a new book. Why are we talking about salary anyway, you planning on trying to part me from some of it?"

"You parted my legs didn't you?" Jordan came back sarcastically.

"Don't go there, Ms. Anders."

"Why not Max? You didn't like my openness, or did I scare you?"

"Jordan, should I tell you how I kept my negotiator face on while my company was filling my pocket, or do you want to bypass all of that and get into you and me?"

"Oh no, Max, why spoil your record of evading the subject?" Jordan was using that approach to bait me into talking about it.

"Have you ever been to China?"

"Yes, I went to Hong Kong once. Where do you normally stay? And, don't think that I missed you changing the subject again, buster."

"We normally stay at the JW Marriott Hotel at Tomorrow Square in Shanghai. It's located in the Pudong District. We stay there because we do business right outside of Shanghai and get a corporate rate. I love it because it's downtown and has great views at night. The hotel is in the heart of everything—the Shanghai Museum, the theater, and the shopping. The hotel amenities are first class having the familiarity of American hotels and the charm of the Asian culture," remembering my nice memories.

"In other words, it's upscale."

"Hold on Jordan, I have to take this call."

"Sure."

"Okay, I'm back. We must have talked up China. That was my boss telling me that we had a fire last night which destroyed part of the manufacturing area. He needs me to go there and run point on the recovery. I'm on a plane tomorrow morning. I have to get ready for this 20-hour trip."

"Well, they have the best man for the job. Call me when you get back. I'll talk to you then, okay. We'll pick up playing our conversational dodge ball then, Mr. Evasive," getting her last dig.

"Okay, later," somewhat happy to get out of a conversation I knew I wasn't ready to have.

I had to run home and pack for this long flight I dreaded taking. Sitting in a last minute cramped coach seat would torture my knees on the long flight to China. Thank God Gina was visiting her parents so I didn't have to go home to another verbal bloodbath. There was no telling how long this trip would last. I'd pack for a week and have the hotel launder my clothes. I didn't want to call Gina and tell her about the trip, but I guess it was the right thing to do.

"Hi, Gina."

"What do you want, Max?" she responded hatefully.

"I have to leave for China tomorrow because the plant caught on fire," feeling I had to quickly get it in before she spit out some vile hatred.

"And this would be my problem...why?" she sarcastically said.

"Gina, I don't want to..." she cut me off before I could finish my statement.

"I don't give a shit what you want. I am not your wife any more. I just still have your funky ass last name for now, so take your tail to the moon for all I care. You can stay there if you like. Just don't call me and report your itinerary like I care or even want to know. I'll be notified if your plane crashes. Then I'll know where you are," plunging her hatred ever so deeply into my heart just before I heard the click of her hanging up in my face.

Gina was slowly killing any guilt I had about my past rendezvous with Jordan. I didn't understand what I had done that was so bad to merit her hope for my plane to crash. I needed to put Gina out of my mind and get some rest for my long flight tomorrow.

"Welcome back, Mr. Dean. We have a nice suite for you overlooking Nanjing West Road," the JW Marriott Hotel Shanghai Front Desk Manager Xao said with his patented smile that oozed five star service.

"Thanks, Xao, this trip will be intense. We had some major problems at the plant," I replied exhaustingly from the long flight.

"No worry. Mr. Dean will fix like new, you always do. You know if there is anything we can do to make your stay more comfortable, call me personally," in his strong Chinese accent as he signaled to another man to come over to get my luggage.

Xao said something to his staff in Chinese, and they all bustled about like a carefully choreographed band of accommodators. We spent tens of thousands of dollars each hotel stay and were definitely the hotel's preferred guest. After I would get back to the hotel late after long meetings, Xao would often make sure I had dinner waiting for me in my room. Their service was excellent.

I had been in China for a week already. We worked sixteen hours per day trying to recover the operation to one hundred percent. We were subcontracting out some operations. I was bringing quality people from the U.S. to help with qualifying new vendors. I was whooped.

It was 8:00 p.m. on Friday night. I was tired and hungry when Xao walked up to me with one of his bellmen.

"Mr. Dean, let us take your briefcase up to your room for you," reaching for my bag to pass it to his bellman.

"Thanks, Xao."

Xao motioned towards the restaurant, "Your party is already in the restaurant."

As I walked across the hotel's lobby, all I thought about was who scheduled a dinner meeting when I just wanted to go to my room and pass out? The only reason I didn't skip the business dinner was because I was hungry. I thought it was going to be a short dinner with hardly any talking, followed by my hasty exit to bed.

As soon as I turned the corner, I heard, "Hello, Mr. Dean."

My eyes practically popped out of my head in surprise. "Hi, what are you doing here, Jordan? How in the world did you find me in all of China," blown away at seeing her in Shanghai.

"I should be evasive like you? I decided to be better than that. I remembered where you told me you always stay when you travel to China. All I had to do was call the hotel when I knew you would be here. If I could leave a message for you, then I knew you were here," Jordan explained.

"I don't know whether to be flattered or scared that you're stalking me," I said playfully.

"Do you want me to leave?"

"What made you come all this way? I know you didn't fly all the way to China just to finish our discussion that was interrupted over a week ago?"

"Max, for someone who is so smart, your intellect isn't impressive right now."

"What do you mean, Ms. Anders?"

"Remember what I told you about that 'maximizing' thing. Well, I traveled half way around the world because we connected on so many levels, and I want a second helping of that. Now, I said it. Can you handle a woman who speaks her mind and spent $2,300 to get another piece of the great Maxwell Dean?"

"Alright then with your bad self," I said laughing.

"Does that make me sprung, paying that much to come to you? Is your head swollen knowing that you can make a woman shell out that much money to chase the Maximizer?" Jordan sarcastically said trying to blow my head up, or at least see if I would take the bait.

"Neither." I was completely surprised to see Jordan. She was inflating my ego, so much so that I forgot how tired I was. She was completely sexy in her fitted pencil leg jeans and black pumps. Her royal blue shirt with the white collar and white cuffs contoured her breast and small waistline. It marked a dash of formal and a tinge of sportiness. As we talked over dinner the happier I got that she was with me in Shanghai.

"Max, I made a reservation for a room, but honestly I was hoping you'd invite me to share your room? Not really thinking that I would say no, her face had a look of uncertainty.

"I'll have them bring your bags up to my room that can easily accommodate two. I have a suite."

"Whew, I thought maybe you might say no."

"You knew in your gut that you'd be swizzling your way into my room, didn't you?" I asked, smiling and waiting for her to confirm it.

"Silly Max, a woman never tells all of her secrets."

As we walked from the restaurant, I looked at Jordan's body and marveled at her hour glass figure. I'm sure she knew I was looking. This girl was fine. I thought how crazy it would be if Gina had done this. I could only imagine the scene Gina would create. I'd probably have to contact the American Embassy because she'd create an international incident. Once they heard her mouth they'd probably pay me to take her back to the U.S.

"What floor are we on, Max? Jordan asked with a devilish smile on her face.

"I'm on the 58th floor on the concierge level."

"Go ahead baller man. My baby only does the best," Jordan playfully said.

"As much money as I spend here with the army of folks traveling with me—that should buy me a few perks."

"Max, we have fifty-eight floors to go up. I would like to do you right here in this elevator. I bet I could get in a quickie. Have you ever been done in an elevator?" Jordan asked as if she was testing me to see if I was game.

"Girl, you're nuts. That would have to be a real quick quickie," I said, smiling at her probing suggestion.

The elevator had nice white marble and a rose accented tiled floor. The walls were dark walnut wood with royal red tapestry trim. But as nice as it was, I wasn't doing Jordan in it. I can't believe that I was actually debating that in my mind. I guess I was so starved for affection I would almost consider anything. Gina beat me down so much that Jordan was a refreshing change even if she was talking about doing me in the elevator.

"Baby, I just flew half way around the world to be with a man who belongs to another woman. I paid an exorbitant amount of money just to get another taste of our first incredible weekend experience. Don't think for one minute that it is beyond me to drop these jeans and present you with my womanly glory for the taking. What, you gonna turn me down?"

"Jordan Anders, where is this side coming from. You have a little freaky streak in you."

"Come over here and I'll show you just how much."

It wasn't that I didn't want to. I could not afford to take a chance that someone from my team would open the elevator door and see us rolling around on the floor like two hamsters playing in their cage. The truth of the matter was I wanted her too. I was looking forward to making it to the room. I wanted to bust through her jeans on the elevator, but I had to be strong. Why did I always have to be strong? Why can't I throw caution to the wind and jump her little tightness right here in this elevator? Then this little voice spoke inside my head saying, *you're Maxwell Dean, that's why.*

I answered that voice with a question of my own, *"Who is Maxwell Dean?" Just a few months ago I was virtually afraid of my own shadow. I couldn't bring myself around to wanting an intimate relationship with a woman—now Jordan's in my room in China. I live with a woman who hates me and doesn't want me. I have Daria who wants me, but respects the boundaries of my dysfunctional marriage. Now I'm not respecting anyone. Who in the world am I?*

My thoughts were interrupted by the elevator's bell signaling that we had arrived at my floor. Good, I escaped Jordan's elevator friskiness. As we walked into my room, I saw Jordan's eyes light up.

"Max, this is a nice suite. It is huge. I love the Chinese accents," as she walked around the room looking amazed at all of the beautiful artifacts.

I didn't say anything. I just let her take it all in as she continued checking out the room. I felt like a realtor who was showing his client a condo. I stood back unobtrusively watching her open the curtains to take in the view. I had the same response when Xao first brought me here. He told me they upgrade guests like me to the Presidential Suite at no extra cost. It was the finest in luxury with spectacular views of the Shanghai skyline.

A spacious marble foyer led into the living area. The Presidential Suite had the opulence of China's culture, featuring polished timber flooring and rich furnishings. The separate office/study room was great for my work without feeling claustrophobic. Xao told me the suite brought balance to busy important people like me. Busy right, important—wrong.

"This view is spectacular. Wow!" Jordan exclaimed, leaving her mouth slightly gaped open with her hands on her hips as she stared out the window overlooking Nanjing Road.

"Nothing but the best for you, baby," I said, playing as if I knew she was coming to China all along.

"You are such a big fat liar, but in this palace, you can lie to me all night long. Max, are you trying to…how did you say it…swizzle—that's it, swizzle your way into my pants?" she said, looking at me and cracking a smile as she turned towards the bedroom.

"I'm not trying to do anything, Ms. Anders."

"We'll see about that."

"Oh my God!" she exclaimed as she stepped into the huge bedroom.

As Jordan walked past the sand colored marble wall and floored bathroom, she was in awe.

"If you wanted to seduce me, this room just did it. I love all of the little Bonsai trees. Max, you can take me now. I'm yours."

"Girl, you are crazy," I fired back.

Jordan finished sightseeing the suite. We both changed out of our clothes and sat back on the couch watching the BBC on TV for a while. Jordan's shorts showcased her athletic legs, while her thin white-laced top revealed her headlights. I tried not to be phased by her indirect invitation.

It was getting darker. Shanghai's night lights were waking up to a fabulous skyline. Jordan made some wise crack about my making love to her standing in front of the window overlooking the night lights of the art district. We joked about that scene for a while and opted for the couch instead. We were both getting tired.

We lounged back on the couch for a while, making it past Jordan's early hormonal excitement. I enjoyed lying around talking. I was still trying to make sense of what was happening between us. When Gina accused me of cheating, now it would be true even though I would have to deny it. Why should I have to lie? We don't have anything and haven't had anything for a while. Jordan was resting on her side facing me, talking and rubbing the hair on my chest. It was calm and peaceful. This was so much different than what I have at home with Gina. I could get used to this peace.

"I'll be back in a minute," I said abruptly getting up without warning.

"Where are you going?"

"Just to the bathroom."

"Do you need to go to the man throne, baby?" Jordan intrusively asked.

"Dag woman, is there anything off limits to you?" As I walked to the bathroom I said, "Ms. Nosey Rosey, I don't think I need to answer that question."

I lit the candles that came with the suite to scent the room while I handled my manification. Looking at the bathtub, I thought, this thing is huge. I decided to make a hot, relaxing bath to help further my wind down. There were some floral-scented bath gels among the hotel soap and lotion. I dropped them in. Why not go all out, I deserved it, they smelled great.

"Max what are you doing? Are you OK?" Jordan shouted.

"Yeah, I'll be out shortly," I yelled through the door.

The tub was full. The lights were off. The room was only lit by the jasmine-scented candles. I slid my work-weary body into the hot water to relax. Soaking was just what the doctor ordered. There were his and hers bathrobes hanging beside the tub waiting for me when I got out.

Jordan opened the door slowly and peaked around like she was trying to sneak up on me. When she saw me sitting back relaxing in the tub, she just pushed the door open and walked in unashamedly.

She stood there smiling, "Oooh! Max, you are so wrong for this."

"Can't a guy get his manification on?" I replied.

"What the hell is manification?" she asked, puzzled by my uncommon word.

"Women have beautification, so we guys have magnification."

"You are so silly. May I come aboard, captain? And while you're thinking you have a choice, I'll be getting in this miniature swimming pool."

She took her panties off faster than I could process what was happening and muster up a response. She stood there naked and asked, "Is this the appropriate swimming attire?"

I paused for a moment thinking this woman was fine as all get out. She had an out of this world body and was standing right in front of me innocent looking. Her womanhood was uncovered and beautiful. Jordan unabashedly put herself out there and offered her most intimate attributes before me.

"Your birthday suit is perfect," I replied, meaning that in every sense of the word.

She slowly submerged herself into the water with me. She didn't take the position beside me, or sit on the opposite end of the tub. Using her leg, Jordan motioned for me to open my legs. She wanted to lie between my legs, a move I was very happy to oblige.

"Oooh! This is nice and hot."

"I'm glad you like it, Ms. Anders."

She didn't immediately respond. Jordan lay on her side almost exactly like we were on the couch. She gently pushed the hot water up onto my chest and she played with the wet hair on my chest. She looked so peaceful and comfortable. It was just right. I started to say something but decided not to. I just thought we'd enjoy this moment a little longer. Sometimes there's beauty of no conversation.

We probably stayed in that comfortable position for 20 minutes or so before we uttered anything—just holding each other and watching the candles burn.

Jordan broke the silence when she said, "Max, you are something else."

"I think you're sorta special yourself," I replied, when I was actually asking myself what am I doing?

"I'm so comfortable being with you. I was sitting here thinking the weekend isn't even over and I've already had the best weekend in years. You're fun to be with and have a great sense of humor. You are romantic, very handsome, and well educated—shit, the complete package, basically. You made love to me beyond words. During our first weekend together, I had the big "O" for the first time in my life. The only reason I knew it was the big "O" was because it felt so good I was ready to pay you for it. You have taken me to a whole new level, mentally, emotionally, and without a doubt physically," Jordan proclaimed with a look of complete sincerity.

"Jordan..."

"Wait Max, please let me get this all out. What I'm feeling with you is so far beyond great. I think today just confirmed to me that I am not in love with my fiance Kyle. How could I be in love with him and be here with you like this? Kyle and I have had this discussion many times before I even met you. He and I were good friends before we became involved. He was there when I was down. Instead of being a true friend and waiting until I got out of my funk, he pushed me into a relationship. I was devastated by the breakup of a previous relationship. My self-esteem was in the basement. I needed someone to validate I was still worthy of a man's affection. Are you following me so far?" She asked.

"Yeah."

"Being with you made me realize what it is that Kyle and I lack. There's no passion. The passion that you and I shared in this short time never existed with Kyle and me. It's been a long time since he and I have been intimate. It was probably the emptiness of passion that put this emotional chasm between him and me. When I met you at homecoming, I wanted to end my relationship with Kyle. In fact, I told Casey I had to find a way to get out without hurting him. So don't think you have anything to do with the situation between Kyle and me, because you don't."

"Baby, I got to interrupt this one time, I promise," I pleaded with Jordan.

"Why?'

"You haven't noticed the water has gotten cold? I'm gonna empty most of the cold and replace it with hot."

We were silent while the tub was filling. I was thinking about what Jordan said. It sounded like she was getting in deep. I'm not sure if I'm ready for that. A few minutes later the tub was nice and steamy again.

"Isn't that better?" I asked.

"Much."

"Now you can continue," I said.

"You and Kyle are diametric opposites in the passion column. I have been awakened to what passion really feels like. The presence of it with you confirmed that I don't have it with him. You've allowed my emotions time to develop. Kyle publicly ambushed my feelings and hijacked my time to grow into him. He smothered the fire I could've had for him. But there is another part to this."

"What is it?"

"Uhh, oh my God! I can't say this," Jordan said, gasping as though she was drawing her last breath.

Puzzled by her "oh my God" I said, "Can't say what, Jordan Anders?"

"I'm falling for you, Maxwell Dean."

"Before I didn't think I was capable of feeling anything romantically for anyone. My marriage has been in the toilet for years. I don't know why I've stayed with it this long. You are the only person that my body has responded to since I got shot. I have feelings for you. I'm confused by all of my sudden emotional cravings for this sassy little woman named Jordan Anders. I don't know about this...I want to continue seeing you. Are you okay with my confusion?" I asked, trying to explain myself and not turn her off.

"I know I shouldn't try to get with you right now. Our lives are complicated enough at the moment. I've tried to stop it and pull back, but the fact of the matter is, I can't stop. Even if I could, I wouldn't want to," she said.

"Yeah, I know what you mean."

"Max, sweetie, take me to bed and make love to me."

"Come on, Geisha girl, let's get out before the water gets cold again."

Chapter 7

THE SECRET

"Here we are, Mr. Dean, Shanghai Pudong Airport," the hotel's shuttle driver announced. It was Monday morning and the end of Jordan's surprise visit. We had a great time. I learned more things about her. We enjoyed the hotel's five star service and amenities and Shanghai's landscape.

"It's 7:15 a.m. You have about two hours before your flight leaves. You have plenty of time to check in and clear customs. You can casually stroll to your gate. Not like me. Usually I sprint to my plane like I'm running from the law. I get there all sweaty and out of breath. It always seems like my flight is departing from the last gate on the concourse farthest away," I said of her early morning departure as we left the shuttle.

"Baby, I had a wonderful time hanging out with you. I hate that I have to leave. The Presidential Suite won't be the same without me. Don't you have any geisha girls up there in our tub," Jordan warned, breaking up the somber mood of her impending departure.

I came to enjoy Jordan's presence. It was so nice being able to talk to a woman who wasn't hoping I'd die. This trip confirmed what we felt from our first time together. She brought me out of my deep despair from the shooting and had an uncanny ability to open me up. Also, her ability to wake up little Max at will wasn't half bad either. Her visit flew by. It ended way too soon.

In the awkwardness of forced good-byes, we stood on the curb in front of the terminal. We kissed, gesturing the typical farewell salute.

When we hugged, she held me a little tighter and squeezed me like she didn't want to let go.

"You'd better go so you won't have to run to your gate. I need to leave so I can make my morning briefing," I said, pulling back from her embrace.

"I guess you're right," she said as if it was hurting her to agree with me.

Jordan grabbed her roller board suitcase and started for the door. I was about to get in the shuttle when I heard her yell, "Max!"

Holding the door open, I turned around, looked at her and said, "Yeah."

"I can't do it," she said standing just outside of the automatic opening doors to the terminal.

"You can't do what?" I yelled puzzled by her statement.

She started walking back towards me as if she was coming to give me another hug or kiss. I stood there beside the car. I really didn't have time to prolong her departure as if we were some sort of movie scene cliché, running back to each other like Bo Derek in the movie 10. I could see that Jordan's eyes were tearing up.

"My stomach is in knots. I'm sick at the thought of leaving you, I can't do it. I'm not leaving. My mind is telling me to leave, but my heart just won't let me walk into the terminal. You have got me all torn up. I need more time with you to explore what we're about," she said, looking at me and starting to cry.

"Jordan," I replied as she started talking again.

"Unless you say you don't want me to stay, I'm getting back in that shuttle with you. I don't care if you have to work all week. You won't have to entertain me. I just want to be with you longer. Plus, I need more time to see Shanghai," Jordan said, pleading her case then ending on a humorous note.

I wasn't expecting this. I really didn't know what to expect by this surprise turn of events. At first I didn't mind because we had great chemistry, but now this felt like we were moving in together—like a couple. I'm not sure how living with Jordan for an extended amount of time would be. My mind was telling me that since she had been so kind and affectionate to me I should let her stay.

"What about your job?" I asked.

I was thinking that she shouldn't jeopardize her job. If she got fired, she would be a stay-at-home housewife. I kept thinking, *girl you're gonna get fired.*

"I'll call and tell them that something personal came up and I need to be off this week. That is if I can stay with you for another week. I can work online from your laptop if that's okay with you. I'm not worried about the job. I'm worried about you rejecting me," she said, looking into my eyes waiting on my response.

"Come on. I hope you have an understanding boss," I said, grabbing her suitcase to put it back in the shuttle.

"Boy, look at what the hell you got me doing. It feels like I'm strung out on some Max crack. But that's all right cause I'm gonna be waiting to rock your world when you get home from work tonight," she said, getting in the shuttle, making purring and hissing sounds with a deviant smile on her face.

Jordan got back in the shuttle wearing her black spandex riding pants and black leather riding boots. Her turquoise derriere-fitting sweater provided me the anticipation of things to come. I hoped she still had this outfit on when I returned from the plant. I wanted to show her that I appreciated how meticulously she took pride in her appearance.

"Here's my room key. I'll see you this evening. If you want anything to eat, just order it and charge it to the room. I have to go to the plant. See ya later," I said as I got out of the shuttle.

"Have a good day, baby, and I'll be waiting for you when you get off," Jordan replied.

I headed for my rental car. It was a 45-minute to an hour commute to the plant just outside Shanghai. I tried to stay focused on the crowded Chinese roads. I was so distracted by what just happened with Jordan. What was I getting myself into? My marriage was a disaster and now I was taking on another woman before I resolved my current situation. Jordan was technically single, but she had already promised herself to another man.

90

I couldn't help thinking that I was creating more problems for myself. How can Jordan be this controversial? She is beautiful in so many ways. Before I met her, I was in such a dark place. No one had been able to extract me from the shades of despair that had circled me like buzzards hovering above a dead carcass.

God, why did you send me help with so many strings attached? I reasoned with the Most High in my mind. *Did you deliver me from darkness into the hands of a woman who would only plunge me back into the abyss later when she would marry Kyle? My mother and especially y grandmother raised me well enough to know you are not cruel like that,* I continued my debate with the Lord.

But that wouldn't be your doing would it? That debacle would be of my own making, I asked and answered, daring to mirror my conscience.

"Oh shhhh….!"

My heart hit the floor of my rental car as a little boy ran out in front of me. My Toyota's tires screeched as I tried to push the brake pedal through the car's floorboard. I stopped about three feet in front of the boy who couldn't have been more than nine years old. Our eyes locked onto each other as if we could read each other's mind. I know he was thinking in Chinese, and I didn't speak any. His eyes said it all—you almost killed me! I have got to focus, and not on Jordan Anders.

Perhaps that was the message His Greatness was trying to tell me. I had bigger things to focus on that were not Jordan. Maybe the Lord was telling me I shouldn't be questioning Him. I had this startling revelation that my life was paralleling me and this car. I can wreck my life in an instant when I question God and try to do things my way. I had my hands full trying to navigate my own life. Let me get my mind right and think about what is waiting for me at the plant.

When I walked through the plant doors George was there waiting for me. George was the plant manager who reminded me of a nerdy engineer who wore a pocket protector in his shirt pocket. He probably had 15 advanced degrees from the best engineering schools in the country, but failed business politics and social graces. I felt for George because he now reported to me. That had to feel like a slap in the face. I came from the states to take over this crisis and basically—his job.

"Max, the truck carrying our replacement machines was in an accident. The truck turned over and rolled down an embankment. Our equipment was a total loss. This is going to cost us millions of dollars. I've already spoken with the manufacturer. They said it will be a month before we could get a replacement," George said, looking exhausted from the entire ordeal.

After I heard George say a month, I went numb. I didn't hear another sound. I was here now and this was happening on my watch.

I thought, *God, is this a continuation of my misery for questioning you?*

I spent all day dealing with this crisis. When the day was finally over, I was mentally exhausted. I called Xao and asked him to arrange for something nice and relaxing for me and Jordan. I needed to put today behind me. I knew if anyone could make it happen, it was Xao. I liked Xao as both a person and an effective hotel manager. The long drive back to the hotel was almost over. I could see the tall Marriott hotel with its distinctive pointed top on the horizon.

I walked in and saw Xao standing over at the concierge desk. Their concierge service was phenomenal. I strolled across the shiny beige marble floor to where Xao stood.

"Hello, Mr Dean," Xao said.

"Hi, Xao. This has been a crazy day. It seems like everything went wrong. It started this morning and continued throughout the day," I said, exhaling from the day finally ending.

"When I received your call earlier, I heard the distress in your voice. No worry now Mr. Dean, Xao arranged something very special for you and your companion," he said, smiling from ear to ear.

"Okay, whatcha got for me?"

"Do you trust Xao?"

"Yes, I do. You've never let me down before," I replied.

"Okay then, you go and freshen up. Come back down to the lobby in thirty minutes. I have everything taken care of for you. Dress for the theater," Xao said like he was confident in his plan.

"Okay, you're my man Xao," I said, parting for the elevators.

I got to the room where Jordan was waiting for me. She had on my white dress shirt and a blue and gold striped tie around her neck.

"Hey there working man," Jordan said smiling.

Despite looking at this beautiful woman standing in front of me half naked, I said, "Today has been crazy. Everything went wrong."

"Well, Jordan is here to fix that," she said, putting her hand on her hips and shifting her stand so the shirt raised a little higher, revealing more thigh.

"As tempting as you are right now, I had Xao arrange something special for us tonight. So what's behind that look will have to wait for a while. We have to be down stairs in the lobby in thirty minutes."

Looking at Jordan standing there in my shirt and a tie with what appeared like nothing on underneath made me want to call Xao and cancel whatever he had planned. But I knew Xao always came through for me so I didn't want to miss it.

"What do I wear, Max?"

"Xao said to dress for the theater," I said.

"How long do I have?"

"He said be down in the lobby in thirty minutes."

"Okay, then give me twenty-five minutes," Jordan said, wanting to take it down to the wire.

True to her word, we were out the door in exactly twenty five minutes. She was stunning in her curve-hugging, black mid-thigh-length dress. The v-line front of the dress showed just enough cleavage to tastefully turn heads. I don't know what perfume she had on, but it was intoxicating. We exited the elevator, turning the corner towards the lobby. I saw Xao waiting for me just as he said. "Ah, Mr. Dean, you and your companion look fantastic together," Xao said, smiling as always.

"Xao, this is my friend Jordan Anders. Jordan, this is the finest hotel manager in all of China, my friend Xao," I said, watching Xao smile even bigger.

"Oh, Mr. Dean, you are too kind," Xao replied.

"It is very nice to meet you, Xao," Jordan said.

"I have a car outside waiting to drive you to the theater where you will be seeing the Chinese Taiko Drummers. Here are your tickets for the first row on the balcony center stage. They are the best seats in the house. The driver knows what time the show ends. He will be waiting outside for you at the same place that he drops you off. He'll bring you back here where I'll have something else for my very special guests," Xao said not missing any details.

Jordan was smiling like a little school girl. I know she was feeling special because she grabbed my hand and held it tight. We left the hotel on our way to the show which I have always wanted to see. I wasn't thinking much about the troubles of work. I wasn't even thinking about my apprehension with Jordan.

At the show we witnessed two hours of soul-rousing drummers. They were synchronized and amazing. They did things with their drums that I didn't know was possible. I felt like a VIP and Jordan looked like she was the queen bee. Our ride back to the hotel was a quick one.

"Welcome back, Mr. Dean. Did you two enjoy the show? Xao asked.

"It was extraordinary," I said.

"It certainly was. Thank you so much," Jordan chimed in.

"You're very welcome. I have arranged for another very special surprise waiting for you in your room," Xao said smiling as if he was going to receive the surprise.

It seemed like Jordan was pulling away to the elevators before Xao even finished speaking. I'm sure Xao knew I was married from our conversations during past trips. Even though he had never met Gina, I'm pretty sure Xao knew Jordan wasn't my wife. He never inquired. Xao didn't judge me. I felt like he was my Far East friend.

After the sometimes ear popping ride to the 58th floor, I opened my room's door to two ladies standing in the room. The living room was set up like a spa. They were both standing behind two parallel massage tables. One lady spoke up, "Mr. Dean, we are here to provide you and the misses with an in-room personal spa service."

"Max, you are the man. How much money do you spend in this joint?" Jordan said, amazed by the personal service orchestrated by Xao.

"Sir, everything you need is in the bathroom. We'll be waiting here for your return. Take your time," the other woman said.

Jordan and I looked at each other and talked as we received our in room massage. Lying on our stomachs with white towels covering the lower half of our bodies she asked, "What do you want out of life? How is it that I'm here with you? I know that your marriage is over, but why haven't you found the right, Mrs. Dean? I look at you and all of this, and wonder how you got to this point," Jordan said.

I can't believe she started this conversation in front of these ladies. What is she trying to say? Is she crazy?

" I'm not going to have that conversation right now in this forum. Are you trying to talk yourself out of China?" I asked.

"No, I'm not trying to leave you anywhere. I'm just wondering. You are such a wonderful guy. How could a woman ever want to leave this?" she said, trying to clean it up.

Just as the two ladies finished with our massage, room service rolled in a catered meal. Xao really outdid himself this time. Jordan was going to think ol' Max was the man. I tipped everyone 35% for this wonderful evening. I would have to let Xao know he is the man. The food was to die for. Jordan put on my shirt and tie after dinner. I knew the night was going to be "on" sooner or later. After the night Xao orchestrated for us, it would be sooner rather than later.

Jordan went to the shower. I decided to check my email while I was waiting on her to finish. She forgot to close her email. I should have just closed it and opened my email. That would have been too simple. Curiosity got the better of me. I saw a message from a guy named Ivan, saying, "You know I still love you. I will always be yours. I'm sorry for what's happened between us."

I read on and saw Jordan's response, "I'm not discussing this now. I'll talk to you when I get back."

I know about Kyle, but why is Ivan still sending her emails like that? I felt like Jordan was sneaking behind my back. I had this eerie feeling going through the pit of my stomach. I wondered if I was being played. Was this guy so important that she had to reach out to him while I was wining and dining her in China? This was going to put a damper on an otherwise sensational night.

When I heard the shower stop, I shut the computer off without even checking my email. Should I question Jordan about Ivan or let it go like I didn't see anything? Do I even feel like getting into that potential drama tonight?

Jordan came out of the bathroom saying, "The water is hot and feels magnificent, your turn, buster. Ms. Anders will be waiting for you."

As I showered, I deliberated what to do about Mr. Ivan. Man what a day! Is it even possible for any other drama to fit within this day? No, I am not going to be jacked up all night. I'm gonna own the moment.

As I lay down across the bed, Jordan moved in and started to massage my neck. I interrupted her massage, "Jordan, I got online to check my email. You forgot to close your email and I saw the message from Ivan professing his love for you. Is there something you need to tell me?" I questioned.

"I'm sorry you had to see that because it's nothing. You know that Ivan was my boyfriend before Kyle. Every once in a while he resurfaces to try to rekindle something between us. I saw his email and wanted to shut down communication immediately," Jordan explained.

I thought about her response. If she wanted to shut down communication, she didn't have to enter into communication. My senses should have been more alert than my passive acceptance of her answer. It sounded somewhat logical and I didn't have the energy left to pursue the matter any further.

"Max, Ivan was two people ago. I want to end this night saying your name and no one else's. This is our night. I belong to no other man other than Maxwell Dean. Will you have me?" Jordan pleaded by changing the focus.

That did it! When Max showed up, Ivan was history. The ambiance of the better part of the night took over. Jordan hugged me passionately and whispered in my ear the sweetest things. Governments have toppled behind words like that uttered into the ear of the powerful. We commingled our passion and released our tension into the night.

The Far East sun rose and fell many more times during this trip to China. The problems here didn't dissipate much. Jordan and I clicked together very well. Her presence made time gracefully melt away. I was there for another two weeks after Jordan returned to the states.

The day before I was to return to the U.S., Xao introduced me to his brother. "Mr. Dean, this is my brother Chang Si Wong. He is a monk and lives outside of Bangkok," Xao said, refusing to call me Max publicly even though we considered ourselves friends.

Chang Si Wong was dressed in a mustard yellow robe garment. He wore plain sandals. His hair was cut so low that it was almost bald. We used to call that a bur cut.

Chang had a very humbling expression on his face when he said, "It is very nice to meet you, Mr. Dean."

"In the U.S. we address men of your stature by using their title with their name, like reverend, pastor, or father. Do I call you Monk Chang Si Wong?" I asked not wanting to show any disrespect.

"No, such formalities are less important. You may call me Chang if you like. I find little value in the substance of such designations. I seek to be at the heart of truth," Chang said with such a calming tone.

"Chang, in that case can I get you to do what your brother won't do, and that is to call me Max?" I asked, smiling by the comfortable exchange.

"As you wish Max," He said ever so politely.

I was completely engaged seeing a monk in person for the first time. I was awed by this man who appeared not to have a rude cell in his entire DNA. Xao told him that I had very important business in China that kept me stressed. Xao told Chang that I was leaving tomorrow. Chang looked at me as though he was trying to see through me. Chang spoke so unobtrusively when he asked me, "Max, does this life fulfill you? I feel a spirit in you that is in conflict. Forgive me if you feel that I have spoken harshly, I only seek to bring harmony to your spirit."

Okay, what was I going to do with that analysis? I was thinking, No I'm not fulfilled. My life is a disaster. I must be completely jacked up if you can see that in less than three minutes after meeting me. I must stink of internal chaos. Chang's feeling was accurate, but how did he know that? I never told Xao anything about my personal troubles. Xao looked at me like he didn't know anything.

"Chang, how did you know that? No, my life isn't what I want. I was shot a while back, and I've been trying to find my way back to the real me ever since," I replied with relief that I said it to a stranger, and a Far East monk at that.

"The next time you return to China, come to Bangkok and I'll show you one of the most beautiful places in the world," Chang graciously invited.

Chang and Xao had to leave. Although we parted ways, Chang's words left me thinking—*What was that all about?*

Chapter 8

MISS NINE

It was Monday morning and our quarterly earning reports were due to Wall Street. My boss Dan reviewed them last night and then again first thing this morning. He sent me an email message saying, "Looks good Max, and good job with China and all of the OPS leadership meetings last week." The rest of the week moved in a normal way.

I wasn't even going to call Jordan for my last weekend of freedom before Gina was due to come back. I needed some rest this week, so I just sat around watching DVD movies.

Friday in the office I sent Jordan an email that Gina was coming back about 8:45 p.m.

Jordan said, "Try to keep the peace and don't argue."

I replied to her, "One could only hope."

A long day finally ended. I had time to think about my China excursion with Jordan before the hellion came back home. While eating my baked chicken, broccoli, and mashed sweet potatoes, I thought of it as the last super before Gina got home and verbally crucified me. I put on a jazz CD and enjoyed my meal.

I had just sat down when I heard the front door of the house open. It was obviously Gina. Hell on wheels was back. I knew she threw me under the bus with her parents. I could only guess what she said and how evil she made me appear. Luckily her parents were pretty even tempered and never took sides. "Hey Gina, how was your trip?" I asked.

"Hearing your voice lets me know that your plane didn't crash or get hijacked is how I'm doing," Gina replied, spitting her venom at me like a cobra.

"Do you have to be so cruel all of the time? Can you take a break just for one day?" I asked, taking a deep breath in exhaustion from her constant digs.

"Oh, I see. You thought we were going to return and get all warm and cozy? You better walk back towards the light and get it from Jesus, cause you ain't getting jack from me," Gina said, defying compassion like it was the plague.

I have had enough. I wasn't going to say anything. Saying anything else would have brought on further reprisals from Gina's hatefulness. I thought, *I should get back on a plane to China.* I wanted to call Jordan and tell her to come get me. I did neither. I just went to another part of our polar ice cap house.

Our house had six bedrooms, four and a half bathrooms. We had a three-car garage, a huge master bedroom, home office, and a media room. The house had 5,900 square feet of living hell and it was beautifully landscaped with an in-ground pool to put out the fire breathed out of Gina's dragon mouth. We had all of the space and luxury, but no love. Our house was professionally appointed with the finest furniture and accessories, but it was still empty and cold. The house was as full of bitterness as it was decorated. It was a house, but not a home. We ceased being husband and wife and became roommates. We lived in a beautiful house in an upscale neighborhood with a broken down condemned marriage. I used to drive by homes as big as ours thinking how lucky the people were who lived there. I now wonder if they lived as unhappily as we did. There was no curb appeal here.

Later, I heard Gina yell, "Max!"

"Yeah," I responded not thinking anything was wrong.

I was in my home office when she called, so I got up and walked into the bedroom.

"Yeah, what's wrong?"

"Did you have company over to the house last week?"

"No one other then Chris and Marcus." I gave a puzzled look.

"Max, I know you didn't bring some tramp bitch over to this house, in my bedroom and bathroom!"

"You're right! I wouldn't do something like that. I know we are shaky, but I wouldn't disrespect you like that. Why are you thinking that Gina?"

"There's a wine glass sitting on the tub, and it smells like a woman was in here."

"Come on, don't start with this paranoia. I relaxed in the tub with a glass of wine. And this house smells like it always smells. The only new scent in here is the stench of all your hostility towards me. Now that really stinks," I said, pointing my finger towards her as I walked out of the room.

"I'm still here now and until I move out, I don't want you bringing any of your skank, ho, tramps in my house."

My home life had returned to the normal hell since Gina came back. As usual, this little sparring session went on far too long with no resolution at the end.

I got through another exhausting week at the office. My boss was increasing my responsibilities, trying to make up for all of the time I was in China. I reared back in my high back leather chair and folded my hands behind my head. I took about ten minutes just to unwind. My phone started ringing. I looked at my watch and it was 6:45 p.m. I started to answer it, but something inside of me said; *If you do you'll be here another two hours.* Since I had projects going on all over the world in multiple time zones, someone could just be getting to work in China. They'd be fresh and raring to go, while I'm half dead.

I waited till I cleared the parking lot to call Marcus from my cell phone. "Hey man, I've just taken my brain out of my head and put it in my glove box," I exhaustingly said to Marcus.

"Man you're trippin'. You should have just said "no" to the drugs. I'll get you to rehab quick."

"Naw, Marcus! Man, work just beat me down this week. I just want to turn off my brain and have some mindless conversation with some clueless little twit where my intellect could be on sleep, and she would still be impressed."

"Boy you're crazy. What cha got in mind?"

"Let's go over to Sidekicks down at the beach. It should be pretty live right now with other Friday evening corporate refugees like us."

"Cool man, I'm wit it, when?"

"What the hell do you mean when? Dang it man, now! I'm rolling there now. I should be there in about 45."

"Max, man you are ill. I don't even know why I allow myself to be seen out in public with you, but you are my boy and I gotta have your back to keep your tail from getting into trouble. I'm in my car now, just leaving LAX, it'll take me about an hour."

"Damn straight, fly boy. You know you ma boy, but it's your butt that's a trouble magnet that's always in need of rescuing. Cool man, I'll see you there then. Holla."

"Bet. Peace out!"

I made it to Sidekicks ahead of Marcus. A very stressful week ended when I turned into the parking lot. Now all I needed was my boy to show up, and that would complete the week. I didn't even want to talk to Jordan. This was all about the fellas. "I'll take a Kettle-One and cranberry."

"Coming right up," replies the bartender at Sidekicks.

The music was banging and the crowd wasn't too thick right now. There were some fine looking women in there. I called Gina to let her know I was hooking up with Marcus for happy hour.

Gina just said, "Huh!" and hung up in my face.

I knew there wasn't anything but drama waiting for me at home. My stress momentarily returned and I needed an extra dose of something to get rid of Gina's mess.

This beautiful, caramel brown-skinned woman with a banging body walked past me with her girlfriend and gave me a seductive smile. She was probably about 5 foot 6 inches tall, well built and wore a sexy, cream-colored pantsuit.

She was definitely in the 9 range. One is the lowest and ten is the highest, and she wasn't far from the perfect 10. That look begged me to speak to her.

"How are you doing this evening?"

"I'm fine and you?" Ms. Sexy 9 replied with a picture perfect smile.

She had a very pretty smile. Her makeup, not over stated, was just right, which is little to none for ol' Max's taste. She had that short-tight Halle Berry style haircut seen on the cover of just about every magazine.

I said to her with an optimistic smile, "TGIF."

Ms. 9 then faded off through the light crowd heading towards the ladies room. And she didn't look too bad from the back either. I assessed that she was a size six or eight.

"Sir, here's your Kettle-One and Cranberry. That will be $6.50 please," said the bartender as I sat in my relatively comfortable bar chair.

I handed him my credit card and said, "Go ahead and start me a tab please. By the way, what's your name bruh?"

"Mike"

"Alright Mike."

"She's pretty fine isn't she?" Mike the bartender said out of the blue.

"Who?"

"Kristi," he replied.

"Who is Kristi?"

"The girl in the cream-colored pantsuit who you were looking at, "Mike replied with a mischievous smile on his face.

"Yeah man! She is cold. Was I that obvious?"

"Yeah, but so was she. She comes in here sometimes on Fridays. She is a real nice lady and rarely does what she just did with you," Mike replied, keeping that same smile and raising his one eyebrow as if to say 'what cha gonna do'?

"Mike, she is bodied up and fine."

"Quite fine and her personality is as nice her looks and never gives anyone play like she just gave you, bruh. She usually hangs with her girl for a couple of hours and then leaves. They don't dance or anything, just sit at the bar or one of those tables, talk and then leave.

"My kind of woman!"

"She's single too," Mike said with that I'm gonna hook you up voice.

"Mike, you gonna get me in trouble."

"You look like a pretty tight cat. I bet that kind of trouble won't hurt too much. Let me ring this up and I'll be right back," Mike replied as he headed for the center island of the large circular mahogany wooden bar to run my credit card.

Mike walked back just as Kristi emerged from the ladies room.

"Hey by the way, what's your name, Bruh?" Mike asked.

"Max."

Kristi walked back towards me looking absolutely delicious. Most women who are trying to look sexy wear their clothes too tight and reveal way too much. Not everybody's shape should be wearing skin-tight clothes. Many women don't understand they can be extremely sexy without their girls popping out of the bras like hot air balloons. Kristi was obviously well schooled by her mom or grandmother. She was simply stunning! Our eyes connected and out came her award-winning smile again.

"Kristi, now how are you going to walk past me and not come holla at me?" Mike said to Ms. 9.

"Oh, Mike! My bad, you know how it is after a long week?" Kristi replied playfully to Mike, as she moved in my direction.

"How are you doing, Carmen?" Mike asked her girlfriend who went to the ladies room with her. She was a little heavier than Kristi, but equally as put together. She looked very curvy and cute. "Fine Mike," Carmen replied.

"You still over there fashion buying for Whilham's?" Mike asked Kristi.

"Mike, you know how a sistah's gotta do it. I'm putting it down and handling ma business."

"Kristi and Carmen, I'd like to introduce my boy, Max. Max, this is the fashion power broker Kristi and her girl Carmen," Mike said out of nowhere.

I didn't mind Mike introducing me because it saved me from the sometimes desperate look of a cold call introduction. Plus, this was a semi-controlled setting with no awkward pressure and that gorgeous specimen of a woman was up close and personal. I might have to upgrade her to a 10. "Can I buy you two ladies a drink?" I asked.

Mike said, "He's cool, and he's a pretty down brother."

"Well, if Mike vouches for you, I suppose that would be fine," Kristi spoke up.

"Sure Max, ladies what can I get you?"

Both ladies ordered a Chardonnay wine. As I started conversing with Kristi, I saw Mike standing behind them giving me that smile and wink to say, there you go Bruh, now it's up to you.

"Is Max you real name or a nickname?" asked Kristi.

"It's actually Maxwell Dean, but people who know me just call me Max. And what about you two, what else goes with Kristi and Carmen?"

"It's Kristi Wade."

"It's Carmen Turner."

This was one of those awkward moments where the smoke is cleared and it became clear that Kristi and I made a connection. Was I feeling something for Kristi?

"Here you go ladies and that's $8.00 on your tab, Max," says Mike.

"Well, why don't—," I started saying just as Marcus arrived.

"Hey, man, sorry I'm a little late; there was an accident on the freeway. The nosey rubberneckers turned both sides of the freeway into a parking lot. And the accident wasn't even on my side," blurts out Marcus.

"A day late and a dollar short as usual," I replied to Marcus's long response.

"Kristi and Carmen this is my long-time boy, Marcus."

Marcus is a good-looking brother and Carmen is very attractive as well, so they should have at least some conversation dynamics. "How are you doing tonight?" Marcus asked.

Carmen came right out and said, "About to have a toast and a drink before you came up and interrupted."

"Ma bad!" Marcus quipped with a smile.

"Well Mr.rrr—,"

"Harris."

"Well, Mr. Harris, since you interrupted our toast, the least you could do is join us!" Carmen responded.

"Don't mind if I do Mssssssss?"

"Turner."

"Mike go ahead and add a drink for Marcus to my tab. I guess I can buy his crusty tail a drink," I said.

"Max, you know I'm your boy and I keep you from getting into trouble. So this is the least you could do!" Marcus replied with his quick wit.

"Kristi, he is such a smart ass isn't he?" I said.

"That's your boy and I'm not touching that one!" Kristi replied, elevating her eyebrows and cracking a half playful smile.

When Marcus got his drink, Carmen raised her glass and said, "Are we going to toast or talk?" Carmen said wanting to get to it.

"Yeah, Carmen, I'm with you. Are you going to talk or toast, Max?" Marcus chimed in.

"Kristi, they're double teaming me," I said just to get that cute smile of hers coming at me again.

Without disappointing me with her smile, Kristi said, "Then I guess you better toast, baby."

No, she did not just called me baby! She broke the rules by calling me baby. Now she was winding up my interest and letting me know that she had some level of interest. The rule was you don't do that unless you want Max. I hate it when they break the rules. I saw her comfort level increasing and so was Mike's tip. She was as nice as she was beautiful, just like Mike said.

"To TGIF and a welcomed relief from a hard-work week," I proclaimed in the toast.

"You got that right!" said Kristi.

Kristi and I turned to click glasses with Marcus and Carmen, but they had moved to a table.

"Oh well, they left us, Max," says Kristi.

"They're savages without manners. We're better off without them," I wittingly came back. We both laughed. I asked Kristi to please sit and join me and I pulled out a bar stool for her.

"I guess I can since my girl just left me," Kristi said in a thank you kind of way.

"It's all good because I want to unlock the mysteries inside of the wonderful Ms. Wade."

"You're funny, Max, but what makes you think I am a mystery?"

"Since I know very little about Kristi Wade, you are very much a mystery to me."

"Well, Mr. Dean, are you getting fresh with this southern lady?" she asked imitating a deep southern accent.

"Well, Ma'am please forgive the appearance of this southern gentlemen's question. I would never seek to defile such a very, very, beautiful gal with being fresh or too forward. I'm only seeking to gain some knowledge," I replied with my fake southern accent.

"Well, Mr. Dean, I should hope not because I'm enjoying the fine and proper etiquette and company of a southern gentleman such as you."

Like a scratched record from an old turntable interrupting a beautiful love ballad, Marcus intrudes our playful serenade. "Oh boy! What the hell are ya'll trippin off of back there?"

"Yo Marcus we got this over here, thank you!" Kristi triumphantly asserted.

"You may continue, sir," Kristi said with that academy award-winning smile.

"Why thank you very much, Ms. Wade, I will graciously accept your compliment. I would not dare deny the words spoken to me by a lady with such perfect lips. Furthermore, I shall duel with any man who insults me lady," with my bad southern accent still intact.

We both burst out laughing about our little side conversation. There was definitely some chemistry brewing in here tonight. I was coming here to hook up with Marcus and tell him about Jordan and me, but judging by how well he and Carmen were getting along and how great my conversation was going with Kristi, there was a slight deviation in the plan. Kristi was definitely upgraded to a 10.

"How does Max earn his living?" asked Kristi.

"I car jack people."

"Boy, no you don't."

"Alright then I am a Major in the Air Force and I am the senior tire checker for Air Force One. I kick all the tires to make sure they have enough air."

"You are so silly. And the real answer would be?"

"Okay I surrender, I will confess everything. I have no shame left. I am your boyfriend."

"Not yet, but you are going to be a dead friend if you don't quit playing with me!"

Did I just hear what I thought I heard? Yes I did, she said 'not yet.' If that isn't the quintessential statement of interest in me, I don't know what is. She may not have even realized what she just said, but it let me know that she was thinking in that direction and I could see it. Not yet meant she wanted it. Maybe not now, but she wants it. You're in the money now Max, but play it off as though you did not hear it.

"I work for a very large high tech company. I am the Director of International Operations. Basically I oversee all of the international companies to make sure they are producing what they should and keeping delivery schedules. Occasionally, I have to roll up my sleeves and get in there to help the process along." Telling her the truth.

"So you travel a lot?" Kristi questioned.

"At times quite a bit, and at times no, but I travel at least once a month. Up until about a month ago I was going to another country seemingly almost as soon as the wheels of the plane touched down back at PBI."

"Wow! How do you do it? I bet you have a lot of frequent flyer miles," she said in amazement.

"I just do it and I like what I do. Also, I can see the results. That makes the effort feel rewarding. Yes, I have more miles than I can humanly use. I will probably hit one million miles within the next three months."

"Man, that's a lot of miles!"

"And what about you missy?"

"I'm the District Manager of retail merchandizing for Nordstrom."

"Listen to who's talking. I bet you travel a lot too!"

"Not nearly as much as you. My travels are mostly within a 200-mile radius. I take about two trips per year to Paris and Milan to preview and buy new clothing lines for the stores in my district."

"I am sitting in the presence of a fashion power player of greatness."

"Boy, you had better stop, look who's talking!"

The place was crowded earlier but thinned out as the evening came to a close. We had such a great time talking that the time just flew past and it was now 2:00 a.m. Marcus and I walked them to their cars because they drove separate cars. Kristi was driving a sporty little import car. "Max, I really enjoyed the evening. I had fun and I hope we can do it again," Kristi said as she unlocked her car door.

"I thoroughly enjoyed my evening with you as well, Ms. Kristi Wade."

"You are a fool, boy. You had me laughing so hard I thought I would have an accident in my suit."

"Well, I'm glad that you didn't. I would have had to cut you lose if you started smelling like the alley pee corner. But since you didn't, I'd like to call you sometime to do this again over lunch, dinner, barrel rolling, or something like that."

"I would have been upset it you didn't ask me because I had a marvelous time with you tonight. I can only imagine about our future encounters," she replied with that dreamy, 'I'm happy we are past that awkward part of the evening' smile.

"Do you have a business card?" I questioned knowing that she did, but was polite to ask.

"Yeah, here," as she handed me her card.

"Okay, well have a good night," I said purposely attempting to part abruptly.

"Not so quick, forget something did you?"

She held her hand out for my card.

"Oh yeah, I need to give you my card, don't I?" I said humorously.

I pulled out my card and gave it to her. Our eyes locked in that puppy love stare. Kristi's hazel green eyes were reeling me in like a big ol' fish hooked on a line.

"Thanks Max, and let's get together soon and do lunch."

"Bet," I said enthusiastically.

As I started to turn, Kristi said, "Max, before you leave I need to give you one more thing."

Now I was thrown for a loss. Then I thought maybe she was going to give me her home number, so I took about four steps towards her.

Kristi took a step forward and kissed me on the cheek and said, "Thanks for the great time and for being the perfect gentleman."

"My pleasure," as I processed those soft lips that touched my cheek.

She got in her car. I closed the door for her. As she backed out of her parking space, she put her thumb and pinky finger to the side of her face symbolizing the telephone. With words I couldn't hear, there was no mistake that her lips were moving saying, 'call me.' Also, there was no mistake that being together talking all night plus the little peck on the cheek she was saying, 'I want to get something started with you, Max.' I nodded my head yes, then she drove off.

By this time I saw Marcus walking across the parking lot with a Cheshire-cat smile on his face. We both briefly confirmed how nice both women were and that we had traded numbers. I told Marcus I was tired and about to drop on my face so I'd holla at him tomorrow.

When I got home at about 2:45 a.m., Gina was standing by the couch staring at me. She didn't say a word and just turned around and walked into the bedroom. I went into my home office and set my briefcase on the floor and keys on my desk and headed to the bedroom for another hour of questions and accusations. In other words, back to my sentence of turmoil at home.

I walked into the bedroom avoiding immediate eye contact with Gina. I went straight for the walk-in closet so she couldn't see me take off my clothes and put on my sleeping atire. True to form, as soon as I got into bed, Gina said, "What trollop's polluted pit were you in tonight, you muddaf#ck'r!" Gina screamed out.

"I didn't sleep with anyone. I didn't go to any woman's house or anything like that Gina," I said with my back to her in absolute frustration of having to do this again tonight.

"You're a lying ass dog!"

"Marcus and I went out and had some drinks, talked, and now I'm at home trying to go to sleep if you don't mind. Why do you have to curse like a sailor all of the time?"

I dared not even mention who we were talking to or that would set off a continuous verbal explosion until daylight.

The next thing I heard was Gina exploding, "You lying ass whore monger. I hate your punk ass!"

Gina got up and stormed out of the room to sleep in a guest room, which I was happy about. I don't know why she cared who I was with since she and I were over. It was just a matter of paperwork. It would be a quick divorce as soon as we reached an agreement on the division of assets. I already knew that it was a fight in the making since she was so spiteful. I mentally left that chaos and recanted my evening with Ms. Kristi Wade. I smiled as I thought about our playful evening, then I turned over to go to sleep and enjoy this peace while it lasted.

Chapter 9

FREEWAY

"Fore!" I shouted as I hit a wicked hook shot on the 11th hole.

"Boy, Max, you can knock the hell out of a golf ball. You'd probably hit a 400 yard drive if you could make it go straight!" Marcus cracked while he shook his head in disbelief.

"Alright, Tiger Woods, let's see your drive."

"Ping!" was the sound that came off his driver as Marcus took his shot.

"Going, going, gone, ladies and gentleman it's a home run for Captain Harris! He drove that ball a ton right over the brown monster."

The brown monster was this huge tree that must have been there since the beginning of time. The brown trunk of the tree was as wide as a large SUV. "Man, the way your ball flew into the woods is sheer beauty."

"Something flew in my eyes just as I started my swing."

"Right! Your bad game got in your eye," I said as we both found our bad golf game amusing.

We'd both finished the hole with a double bogie which wasn't anything unusual for us—every once in a while golfers. We put our golf clubs into our bags, got in the golf cart, and drove down the beautiful landscaped green golf course.

Winding Ledge Golf Course was is a magnificently well-maintained course that was moderately difficult. It was tranquility at its best when we were playing with no cell phones on, under perfectly clear blue skies shining down on meticulously well cut and very green grass. It was a spectacular day with the temperature in the mid seventies. The Atlantic Ocean sent a gentle breeze streaming across our faces.

The fairway looked like a green carpet. There was a slight hill sloping to the right with a sand trap on the left. There was also a little stream splitting the 485-yard, par 5, 12th hole.

There was a little backup on the 12th hole—a threesome on the tee box and two foursomes behind them and then and me and Marcus. So we just sat under the shade of the tree just to the left of the cart path, sitting about ten yards behind the tee box.

"Tell me about this Jordan woman I keep hearing so much about," Marcus broke the silence of our wait.

"Boy! She woke up the maximizer in a major way. Man, she's got skills!"

"Are you gett'in whooped?"

"Come on, Marcus, who do you think you are talking to? I'm no poor butt brother who couldn't find his way out of a paper bag with a flashlight and razor blades."

"You are a Little House-on-the-Prairie type serial monogamist with a busted man tool, that's who you are! You're taking advantage of this poor defenseless woman."

"I'm not that wholesome, and she's definitely not defenseless, but look who's talking. You are a stalker of defenseless women and a woman-cookie kleptomaniac," I jabbed him in the back.

"True dat, true dat," Marcus quipped.

"The last time I saw Jordan, Gina was in New York visiting some old friends."

"Oh yeah?"

"I picked Jordan up from the airport and she started changing clothes in the truck. She got completely naked on the way to the hotel from the airport. Jordan is definitely no prude. She wasn't the least bit timid about revealing her glory to me. Her body is so slammin' it could wake up the dead."

Raising his voice in excitement, Marcus shouted, "Hell naw Max! Jordan opened it up like that?"

"I kid you not. I've seen her naked before, but there was something to seeing it like that while driving. That thing startled me. Man my action went right up like a hot air balloon."

"Jordan sounds like my kind of girl. Max, are you sure you don't want to give her to me? She sounds too insane for you. You know you like women who embrace chastity and all that nonsense. Jordan is a freak who belongs with a freak like me who hates sane chastity. You should have pulled over and hit that. I know you didn't, did you?"

"No freak boy. We went to dinner and to a club. We kicked it for a little and then we left," I replied.

Incensed by my freakless behavior, Marcus agitatedly replied, "Man, how's she gonna put it in your face like that and you not wear her stuff out? Forget going to the club, I would've given her my club. See that's your problem, you're too cultured and romantic. I go for it whenever, wherever. I can't believe you. You just wasted that golden opportunity to knock her stuff out."

"Before I could even respond to her show and tell, she said, not now," I said defending myself.

"And you let it go like that? Max, you're slippin'." Marcus scorned.

"Hold on Hoss, there's more to come. Don't be a caveman all your life."

"Alright man, then bring it. Stop playing with me, boy. I want to hear the nasty. You can save anything romantic for the chics. I want to know about the sweat," Marcus urged.

"Calm yourself before you burst a blood vessel or something. You're getting yourself all worked up. We left the club about 11:30 p.m. that night. When we got in the truck, she took off her clothes again and got completely butterball naked. She said she wanted me right then, while I was driving. She worked me over for what seemed like a 100 miles. But you know it was only a couple of miles. Bruh, she's got insane skills. She told me to take the freeway so I wouldn't have to stop. Good thing my SUV had tinted windows or someone would have seen her going to town on me. Man, I had to pull over before I hit something. That was a first for me. When Jordan finally stopped, I was left wondering what just happened. She was in complete control and I was powerless to even want to stop." I said, looking off into the distance like I was reliving the moment.

"Man, she's a freak! Max, I told you she's a freak. If she only knew how she was wasting all of that sexual freak-a-thon on Maxwell boring Dean."

"Why does she have to be a freak?"

"Cause that ain't normal. You need to give her to me. That's not romantic and sentimental. That was raw and crude the way I like it. Forget about the boring bedroom; give it to me in a freeway toll booth, I always say. Is Jordan too much for you? She's a freeway freak," Marcus replied, shaking his head in disbelief.

"Jordan is my rescuer. Maybe it's because she is that way that she was able to bring me back from the sexually dead! But where did you come up with a freeway toll booth? You need medication."

"Max, you are definitely back, and I'm glad about that, but you're whooped. That's yo problem. She done brought down the great Maxwell Dean! Just turn in your playa card to me," Marcus insisted.

"Ain't nobody whooped, so don't get ahead of yo self my friend."

"So what's next?" Marcus asked.

"I don't know. By the way what was up with you and Carmen last night?"

"Man she was fly and a sweet girl."

"Yeah, Yeah, Yeah! Get to the point!"

"She gave me the numbers for us to hook up again, so I'm gonna have to put her on the roster."

"Any spit swapping?"

"Just a little peck on the lips," Marcus replied sounding disappointed.

Alright! You in there Bruh," I told him.

"What about you and Ms. Green Eyes, Casanova?"

"Man, Kristi is a beautiful person and we just connected naturally."

"Yeah, I know cause when I turned around ya'll were deep into look lock. Gina could have come in and stood right beside you and you wouldn't have even noticed."

"Marcus man, she is fine! She's a real nice down-to-earth person, single, and not one of those broke babes trying to be a capitalist with my money. She doesn't strike me as a baby mama drama babe either. It's refreshing talking to a woman who is not looking for a sponsor."

"I hear ya, Bruh."

"That body! It was off the chain. She had a great haircut, nice hair, and she had that natural beauty. You know how I can't stand a woman wearing too much makeup. That's a real turn-off."

"She was fine, Max!"

"So was Carmen, but you know Kristi's eyes got me right off the jump," I said, smiling as I recalled Kristi's mesmerizing eyes.

"Yep, you do go for those high class, model-type women. Those are high maintenance honeys. That's why they look at you to be a sponsor. I don't need those high dollar babes who don't ever want to eat at Mickey Dees. Carmen is fine and she probably grew up as a hood rat. That's my style."

"Marcus, you're ill. You're attracted to women who probably knocked over convenience stores in their youth."

"That's right Bruh. They're more grounded and more appreciative because day bin thru da struggle," Marcus proudly retorted, boosting his tendency for borderline classless women.

"You have a point my Brotha of Wisdom," I sided with Marcus' off-color logic.

"So now what about you and that fine, red bone, Kristi?" Marcus inquired as though he was baiting me for something.

"She is amazing! We exchanged info then she called me back to give me a kiss on the cheek. Then told me with that let's get together look, to call her later."

"Max last night reminds me of when we use to pull babes together in college."

"Yeah, you know how we did it." I said, recalling our college glory days.

"Alright, let's review your current stable. There is Gina on the way out, Jordan Freeway Freak-a-thon, Daria College Sweetheart, and now Kristi. Do you think you have enough trouble or are you looking for more?" Marcus fired out, leading to an inevitable point he was going to make.

"With Daria, you know how that goes. We just somehow can't walk away from each other. She is my rock. Jordan works me over and then some. She keeps me from losing my mind behind Gina's madness. Jordan is an excellent stress reliever. I don't think I need to say anything about Gina that's self-explanatory. And Kristi, man, there's something special about her. Can't put my finger on it, but I got this good feeling about her. I'm not even thinking about getting physical, I just love her personality."

"Feeling my butt, Jordan woke up little Max, and now you're getting keyed up to other women. You've got ground to make up from your long hiatus, so that's the only feeling you're getting. Man, if she's like that, don't maximize Kristi until you get your house in order."

"Don't hate Marcus," I fired back surprised by Marcus' conscience.

"Max, you know you're ma dog," Marcus responded just letting me know that he was keeping it real and nonjudgmental.

"Great, finally we're up on the tee box," I said as we departed our golf cart grabbing our clubs.

Marcus teed off first and hit a pretty good shot right down the middle of the fairway. I stepped up and hit a shot to about the same place. We walked back to our golf cart, and tucked away our drivers, drove to our golf balls, but had to wait on the group in front of us.

"This is going to be a slow 18 holes today," Marcus said, taking it all in stride.

"Yeah man, you right on the money there," I replied equally not pressed.

"So Max, you and this Jordan are having gymnastic sex, and she is engaged to be married, huh?"

"Yeah man, the sex is off the chain. Plus, she is a really nice person from what I can tell so far."

"You don't even know her yet. You only know about getting ya freak on. What I know is that you are getting whooped by Ms. Freeway."

"Marcus, man, I ain't gonna front, her stuff is on hit, but I'm not whooped," I replied, defending my control of the situation.

"Bull, you're not whooped! Freeway has brought the great Maxwell Dean down to his knees!" shouted Marcus.

"Ssh, man, don't mess up that shot. Have some proper golf etiquette!" I whispered.

"No, what you really want is for me not to let the world know that Max himself has been Max-imized!"

"Hold on there sport. Na, I ain't gonna say all that! She is definitely the one being Max-imized and getting wrung out. I'm just saying that I definitely like the recipe for her cookies," I countered.

"Whooped!" Marcus shouted again.

Sarcastically, I responded, "Whatever punk!"

"No Max, on the real tip, what is she after? I mean, Bruh, you are pulling down some mean bank. She might be out prospecting for gold? Don't overlook the fact that she is engaged to another guy and boning you. I'm not judging her, but what does that say about her morals. Plus, y'all are playing a dangerous game."

"Naw man she has her own corporate gig, which I know has to be paying her some serious bank. You speak about her morals—well mine aren't exactly stellar right now either," I said, confessing my own failings as well.

"Look at your package—job, ride, crib, bank, plus traveling the world on somebody else's money. You got to admit it Max, your program is what most women want, so don't think that your package ain't a part of the calling card!"

Thoughtfully looking at Marcus I said, "Point taken."

"I'm not trying to do the whole romance thing like you. Dinner, drinks, a movie, and then I'm trying to hit it. You see I know that I'm a ho, but you are trying to be the complete package. Babes are into the whole Max presentation."

"I'm a diehard romantic. What can I say?" I replied, trying to justify myself to Marcus even though he could see right past my façade.

"What little world are you trying to create? Maybe that little world that you create is too much for women like Gina to handle. Is that why you currently have Gina, Daria, Jordan, and now you are migrating towards Kristi? Is it that no one woman can measure up? Do you need four different women to equal one whole woman? And poor Daria, you are hanging on to her like she is your safety valve of last hope. It's not fair that you won't release her from chasing after you," Marcus said blasting me.

I stared at Marcus, pausing before I sarcastically said, "Damn, Marcus, that was almost deep. Who are you Sigmund Freud?"

"On the real, Max, all these women aren't you. I'm the male skeezer up in this camp. So what are you doing and what are you looking for? What can't you find in one woman? Actually, I admire the one woman ethic about you. I will never be who you are, but I don't want you to become who I am either. You are the only example I have for what I should become. You are my moral measuring stick. So you see boy, I need you to get your life together if I am ever to have any hope of reform," Marcus said, surprising me with that startling revelation.

"I'm not looking for anything specific, but..."

Marcus interrupted me mid-sentence, "But nothing. You need to reconnect with your big head again so you'll open your eyes and not get blinded by Freak Freeway, is all I'm saying," Marcus chastised.

"Why you gots ta keep callin' her Freak Freeway?"

"Cause, I'm yo boy and I'm gonna keep it real like none of those other shallow pie-back pseudo brothers would! Plus, you know I'm gonna be ya boy no matter what!"

"Man, if I didn't love you like a brother, I would run over you with this golf cart for calling her Freak Freeway!"

We both started laughing because it was funny and I'd do the same thing with him and his women. Finally, the group in front of us cleared the green so we got out of our cart to take our second shot.

Marcus walked up to his ball to take his second shot and said, "Man, be careful with Freeway. I don't trust her. She either is, or was, in love enough with this guy to get engaged to him and she is still wearing his ring, but yet she is boning you like there's no tomorrow. You my cat and all and I think any woman would be lucky to have you cause you have a good heart. So you know I'm not going to hate on you, but Max, please keep your eyes open because Jordan was getting married before she met you, and now she's in bed with you, that's all I'm sayin'."

As usual, Marcus was right. We had been friends for so long that he could shoot it straight with me. His last words shot an arrow of reality straight into my mind.

I might be something, but I didn't think that I was all that. My ego wasn't so far out of check that I believed I could change a woman's mind that was on the verge of marrying the man she loved. That is something that most men would illusion themselves to believe. My mother always told me that a woman's emotional connection can't be so easily broken, whether she gets mad at her man or not. Men's emotions are like shallow weeds that can be easily pulled up, but a woman's emotions are like tree roots that are grounded and go very deep. My mom also told me it takes a lot for a woman's emotional roots to be unearthed. We men are the ones who can become emotionally detached so easily from our homes by the other women's stimulation of our genitalia. Man, are we really that shallow? I guess so, but is Jordan the same as us, or is she sowing her pre-marital wild oats with me?

I refused to believe that I was being played like that, but Marcus was right. What did I really know about her outside of bed? Oh crap! Now Marcus and my mom had my mind screwed up over Jordan.

"Wakeup Max, your shot!" Marcus shouted.

"Alright! I didn't see your shot, where is your ball?"

"Only right up on the green!" Marcus proudly replied.

Looking cross at Marcus, I sarcastically cracked, "Smug punk!"

"I heard that Mr. Lover Man!" My club made an awful sound as I drove my ball into the trees and I sliced the heck out of another ball.

"Shoot! I just pissed away a great first shot. See what you made me do!" I said as I usually blame Marcus for my bad golf shots.

"The problem isn't me. Your mind is on Freeway's aerobics instead of on this game. I told you, you are whooped!" he sarcastically fired at me.

"We'll see who is whooped at the end of 18 holes fly boy!"

As we proceeded down the golf course, I couldn't help but think about what he said. I would never actually come right out and admit that I really liked Jordan. The important questions were—Did I like her, or did I just like the sex? Or, was I simply hanging onto her because she brought me out of post traumatic stress disorder from the shooting? Maybe Jordan was simply my escape from Gina.

I just kept hearing Marcus' words say that I really didn't know her. Then his and my Mom's words were double teaming me with the reality that this woman was in the process of getting married. Even if she didn't marry her fiancé, would this be the kind of woman I'd want to marry?

Talking to myself, I said, *Now you said the "marriage" word and you barely know Jordan. Man you couldn't go out like that. If Marcus could read my mind right now, you'd never hear the end of it. Max, you have got to get a grip and and get a grip quick.*

Jordan told me that she and her fiancé weren't living together, was she really not having sex with him? Did I care since I was still looking at other woman? I didn't know why, but I did care. Dag Marcus, now you've got me really thinking. What the heck kind of morals did I have, and if it was okay for me to grove with someone else's woman and yet trip out thinking that she might actually be sleeping with her man? *Max 'ol boy, you got some serious issues,* I thought. I must be feeling something or I wouldn't be taking myself through these mental gymnastics.

"Max, when is the last time that you talked to Pike?" Marcus asked, giving me a much needed reprieve from the Jordan conversation.

"Not since the reunion, why?"

"The last time I hollered at him, he said he was trying to get with you about some business idea that he had," Marcus replied.

"Oh! Alright, I'll give him a call next week."

"No, I have a better idea if your weakness is up to a challenge."

"What challenge?"

"I have to fly up to Jacksonville next Friday, so why don't you come with me? You, me, and Pike can hook up and do dinner and drinks."

"Bet, but what's the challenge?" I asked again.

"I did the score, and your Freeway on the brain butt has me by one stroke going to the 18th hole. If you lose, then the tab for our night in

Jacksonville is on you. If you win, it's on me," Marcus said, engaging his over competitive nature.

"Why are you trying to do that to yourself when you know your game is weak?"

"Deal?" Marcus asked again.

"Deal Skycap!"

Chapter 10

THE SENTINEL

My phone rang. The caller Id said Kristi Wade, much to my surprise.

"Hello, Ms. Wade," I answered with a smile on my face that she obviously couldn't see.

"How's Mr. Dean doing today?"

"He's doing very well, and you?"

"I'm doing hungry, you want to join me?"

"Funny you should ask. Your timing is perfect. I'm going to meet one of my best friends for dinner. Why don't you join us? Mel and I are going to the Copper Kettle. Do you know where that's located?" I asked, hoping she would join us.

"Yeah, I know where it is. I've been there before with a client. Great food. What time?"

"We'll be there about 7:30 p.m. We are dressed in jeans. Is that alright with you?" I asked but slightly telling her about our dress so she wouldn't be overdressed for the occasion.

Melonee is my sailor-mouthed home-girl and friend. We are very close and have been for many years. Mel and I often get together for lunch or dinner. She is so cool and keeps me grounded. She will check me if she thinks I'm getting out of hand.

As we were having our dinner, Kristi asked Mel why she and I never dated. I overheard the question while I was turned away talking to a guy I knew in the restaurant.

"Girl, me and Max have never got down like that. He is like a brother to me. Yeah, my boy is fine and all that, but we don't look at each other like that," Mel said.

I pretended to be caught up in the conversation with my partner, Duane. Duane's mouth was moving, but my ears were tuned into Kristi and Mel's conversation. I even stood up to talk so I appeared even more detached from them.

"I mean no offense, but I'm just trying to learn more about Max. I know not everyone breaks up, gets mad, and never speaks again. I wondered if you and he broke up once and are still friends," Kristi probed as if she was trying to figure out what she was walking into.

"Nope, nothing like that. When I first met Max, I thought he was one of those light-skinned, obnoxious pretty boys stuck on himself. When I got to know him, I found out that he is stupid funny and sort of corny," I heard Mel say.

"I can definitely see that in him. Max has a great sense of humor. He's actually downright funny. It's good to know that he is genuine that way and not turning it on to manipulate a woman," Kristi replied, sounding more at ease.

"Girlfriend, Max is the real thing. You have no idea. You seem like a good person so I'm going to share something with you about my boy that I rarely speak about, but I feel something in my spirit about you. You seem so down to earth. I love Max so much and I'm going to tell why. He is the truest male friend I've ever had or will likely ever have," Mel said, buckling down for a seemingly long story.

"I have got to hear this. You have me on the edge of my chair. Do I need to order a drink for this?"

Mel took a deep breath to compose herself before she began. Duane walked away so I had to rejoin our table. I hoped the conversation wouldn't go quiet like most female conversations do because the man walked back into the room. Kristi smiled as she licked her chops waiting to find out some startling revelation about me.

Mel started, "This guy named Rodney who I began seeing was trying to rape my ass. Because I wouldn't let him take it, he started giving me a beat down. We were at my house. He got pissed and started breaking up my shit, and then started in on me. Rodney is about 6 foot, 1 inch tall, 240 lbs, and solidly built. He might be weak by a man's standard, but he threw my ass around like he was Hercules. I ain't but 5 feet nothing, and about 130 lbs soaking wet, so it didn't take much to sling ma ass around like a wet dish rag."

I was surprised that Mel went there with this story. She didn't usually talk about that day. Kristi looked like this was not what she expected to hear. Thinking Mel would talk about an attempted rape must have been the furthest thing from her mind.

"Girl, Rodney was whooping my ass. He was beating me like a dusty rug, hanging on a country clothesline. I was thinking how in the hell was I going to get out of this. I thought that his ass was going kill me and there wasn't anything I was going to be able to do to stop him. He had just picked me up by my neck and punched me in the face for what seemed like about the 100th time, when I heard an explosion downstairs."

Kristi was on the edge of her chair as if she were in a movie theater looking at the scene that made everyone jump in their seat.

"That must have been right after I saw that punch to your face. The explosion sound was me busting through your wooden front door," I interjected.

"Yo ass must have come through that door like Genghis Khan or some shit cause it sounded like a bomb went off. When I saw my door later, it looked my door was broken into splinters," Mel retorted.

"I came up the walkway to your house and I heard a crash. I looked up to your second floor bedroom window and saw Rodney punch you in the face. I lost it then. I kicked the door down and ran upstairs, I chimed in again.

"Kristi, Max was stopping by to tell me about his new promotion. He was going to pick me up and take me out for drinks to celebrate. When he busted through my bedroom door, I was halfway knocked the frick out. I saw the silhouette of this big man then figured out it was Max only after I heard his voice cursing at Rodney."

"I thought Max doesn't curse," Kristi questioned in surprise.

"He doesn't but surprisingly he did that day!" Mel responded.

125

Mel looked at me as if to say I know you don't like me cursing like a drunken sailor, but she's earned the right to tell this story however she wants to. She was right. That event had to be so painful that talking about it had to be somewhat therapeutic.

"Max came through the door swinging at Rodney. He went down after Max's first punch and never got back up. Max beat Rodney down. I never saw Max as mad as he was that day. He beat Rodney. He kicked Rodney. He cursed Rodney out as he was whooping his ass. Girrl, Max jacked Rodney up."

"Max, did you really do that?" Kristi questioned.

"Yep!" I curtly replied.

"Do you have a violent temper?" Kristi asked.

"When a man is beating the crap out of one of my female friends or family, absolutely."

"I'm feeling safer already," Kristi coyly replied.

"Getting back to my story you two—after Rodney beat my ass like Mike Tyson, and then Max beat Rodney's ass like he stole something, Max called Marcus and Mason to come take his beat up ass away. Max wouldn't let them see me because my shit was all tore up. One of my tits was hanging out and that muddafu*#a Rodney tore the panties completely off my ass. My left eye was almost swollen shut from a couple of encounters with Rodney's fist."

"Mel, I can't even imagine something like that happening to me," Kristi said with amazement.

"Shit, that isn't the half of it. My mouth was busted open. I could hardly breathe because that maniac had kicked me in the ribs. I cut my legs on the broken blue smoked vase. I think if Max hadn't stopped by that day, I'd probably be dead."

"If the Lord wasn't with me that day, I might have killed Rodney because I lost it when I saw what he did to you," I quickly responded to what Mel said.

Mel continued, "Max cleaned my wounds. I was so tired from getting my ass kicked that I couldn't even cover up my naked ass. All my shit was on display to Max. I was too busted up to even have shame about that. I was more ashamed of getting a beat down. Max picked

126

me up off the floor and carried my naked busted up body to bed. He covered me up and stayed with me all night. He slept in a chair in my room and guarded me like he was a secret service or something. I guess he was worried that stupid boy might come back."

"If he came back, that might have been his last day on earth," I said.

"The next day I was too sore to get up and make it to the bathroom. I knew that the only thing that would help ease the pain was soaking in a hot bath. Max ran my bath water for me. He had to help me into the tub. He even had to help me get out of the tub and dry off. During that entire time that Max saw me naked, he never stared or looked at me in a sexual way. I loved that about him," Mel said adoringly looking at me.

"You mean my man has morals and integrity?" Kristi said proudly and smiled in approval.

"He gets mad props from me on that tip girl! For the next three days Max never left my side. He cooked for me, got my medicine, and never asked me anything about what happened. When I finally broke down and told him what happened, he just listened and said nothing."

Kristi listened to Mel tell the story with great interest. She learned something about me and at the same time quelled her fears about my relationship with Mel. I remembered that day all too well, but I learned for the first time how Mel really felt about me for that day. I knew we were close, but I never heard her talk about it this way. It was as though I was eavesdropping on someone else's conversation about me. Usually, these kinds of conversations happened when you were not around. I had a ringside seat, as Mel continued.

Mel looked a little down as she continued, "I was crying and slinging snot recounting the ordeal. After I finished, Max said nothing and just hugged me. Although I was in my red and white heart pajama pants and a white tank top, I felt raw and exposed. Max's head was to the side of my face looking behind me as we hugged. I felt his tear drops fall to my shoulder. In the moment of his silent embrace, that tear drop said everything. If there was ever such a thing called love, that was it."

Kristi started to choke up with tears in her eyes. She had been intermittently joking with me during the earlier parts of Mel's story, but now she was quiet and still. It was as if she were frozen in time and became a part of the story. I knew she was holding back a full-fledged rain of tears. It was starting to touch that emotional nerve in me too.

Looking at me with tears rolling down her twitching cheeks, Mel said, "I knew Max loved me that day and I fell in love with him right back. Most people will never understand what that means. When Max had his face on the side of mine, it was as though it was the face of God. I know that Max isn't God, but I felt God's presence and spirit through him. Max's tear drops washed me of my shame and cleansed me of Rodney's filth."

There was no hiding it now. Kristi was crying and so was Mel. I was on my way to letting go some tears hearing how Mel internalized what I did for her not just on a physical level, but a spiritual one as well. I tried to remain man hard emotionally. Mel needed to end this story soon or I was gonna go soft and break an eye sweat drop.

Mel grabbed my hand and held it underneath the table while looking at Kristi and continued, "That is why I love my boy Max. He is my boy and I will hurt any bitch that tries to hurt him. He has the biggest heart in the world, and Kristi yo ass betta not break it. And that's on the real tip! I know I have the mouth of a sailor and Max gets on me about that all the time, but Maxwell Dean is my angel sent by God."

"What happened to Rodney?" Kristi asked.

"We don't speak about that, but Max assured me they didn't kill him. All I know is that he hasn't been seen in town since then."

Wiping tears from her eyes and sounding all choked up, Kristi said, "That is some deep stuff girl. I understand now. Your boy is in good hands with me, and I will never do anything to hurt your best friend," Kristi said with conviction.

"Kristi, I thank God all the time that Max didn't kill Rodney. I couldn't have stopped him that day. As much as I hated Rodney for what he did and loved Max for rescuing me, I wouldn't have wanted Max in jail for trying to protect my honor. Rodney is not worth paying that price. Thank you Jesus," Mel said, gasping as she looked up towards the ceiling.

A silence came over all of us as we reflected on that note. I suppose God was watching over not only me, but Mason and Marcus too for helping me. We never again spoke about what happened to Rodney. I think Kristi was smart enough to respect that boundary and not cross it.

"So Mel, is Max this good with everyone or does this side only come out for his close friends in distress?" Kristi questioned, opening the door for Mel to tell more.

"No, surprisingly he is like that all the time," Mel replied.

"Okay then, describe Max's character like I was interviewing him for a magazine man of the year award," Kristi asked as if she wanted to know about everything down to my childhood dog.

"I can't believe you two are going to do this right here in my face. Have either of you no shame?"

"Now, now, Max, this is girls' night out time. You can sit here quiet and hear what we are saying about you, or you can leave with the knowledge that we are talking about you behind your back. Either way we are going to talk about you. You decide," Kristi said.

"When you put it like that, what choice do I have?" I replied.

"None!" Kristi fired back.

"Okay, Mel, who is Maxwell Dean?" Kristi began her interview.

Mel started, "Max is a gentle giant with a heart of gold. Looking at him you could easily think he played for some NFL team. Listening to him for as little as three minutes would convince you that he was no dumb jock. Max is perhaps one of the smartest men I've ever known."

"An intellectual, huh?" Kristi interjected.

"Max is a well educated man with an uncanny knowledge of so many different things. You feel like there is no subject matter that he cannot speak on. His mind is like some super computer. No matter what you ask, it seems like Max's brain always has the answer," Mel said.

Okay, that wasn't so bad. I could sit here through this. I was trying to hold back my smiling approval and not puff out my chest like I was all that. Kristi and Mel were getting into this. I couldn't help feeling like they were setting me up for the kill later.

Mel looked at me curiously and said, "Max's thick black eyebrows accent his dark brown eyes. His eyes are deep and mysterious. When he looks at you a certain way, you feel as though he sees you all the way to your soul. However, his eyes conceal a part of him that you desperately want to know, but that part of him is locked in the vault behind those penetrating eyes," Mel contended.

"Please continue, I really want to hear this," Kristi said.

Mel continued, "His deep baritone voice resonates through a woman's body producing intimate vibrations that shake loose their inhibitions to open up to him. Max has the ability to seduce women without even knowing he's doing it. His strong presence can often appear intimidating to some, but yet his beautiful smile melts away any feeling of intimidation and it reveals a down home quality that you want to love. He just has this magnetic aura about him. There is a secret within him that you are drawn to, and you are challenged to see if you can be the woman who can unlock the vault to the secrets that lay inside."

"Mel, you make it seem like I'm dungeons and dragons or something," I said, fearing that I was being portrayed as some draconian fetish master.

Kristi quickly turned towards me and affirmed, "Max you almost shook something loose from me the first night I met you, so I'd say she's about right on point so far, so be quiet and take it. Guys aren't usually invited to this party," Kristi said, loving every minute of this.

"He loves watches. Not just any watch—Panerai and Breitlings. They are very expensive. His prized possessions are two watches passed down to him by his late grandfather who was a jeweler for almost 60 years. One is a solid gold Vacheron Constantin, and the others are a Girard-Perregaux and a Petek something. Both of them cost as much as a car. Watches aren't an ego thing to Max; it's a part of what his grandfather passed down to him, which he honors. I know a lot about them because every time we go shopping he drags me into a watch store," Mel continued.

"One of the best things about Max is his ability to talk to anyone from the corporate world to a guy in the projects. Behind all of his high powered education and intelligence is a pretty funny guy who laughs, has fun, and gets as silly and playful as a little boy. That's why those little bastards who shot him need to be wiped off the face of the earth," Mel said, heating up in anger.

"Mel, we're not going into that," I said, trying to calm her down.

"Yeah, Mel, it's okay, they'll get theirs I'm sure. Continue telling me about Mr. Man of the Year," Kristi said, trying to assist me in changing the subject.

"Okay, okay! I was having flashbacks." Mel continued. "You get the impression there isn't anything that Max can't do. He was cut from the Can Do cloth. People, especially his job, marvel at his ability to solve any business problem. Things come to him effortlessly. There isn't anything out of his reach."

"What's Saint Max's downside?" Kristi questioned.

"Max, this part might sting a little bit, but you know I call it like I see it, and I love you to death," Mel said before she was about to lower the boom on me.

I couldn't wait to hear this one. Maybe I didn't want to hear it. Whatever Mel said, I knew it wasn't being done to break me down. Whether I wanted it or not, it was coming and I was staying around to hear it.

"Alright, I'm going to bring it home now about my boy, Maxwell Dean," Mel said followed by a big exhale.

"Come on wih it then," Kristi egged her on.

"Oh boy!" I replied.

"Be quiet, take it like a man and be a good sport about it," Kristi directed.

"He is so smart that it's scary. That's why we call him Beautiful Mind from the character in that movie. He can do anything which sometimes causes him to have a mental traffic jam, and he questions which road he should travel. He stands atop 'Jack of all Trades and Master of None.' It is this dilemma that can be his Achilles heel.

"For all his talent and ability, it would appear that Max is straddling the fence to greatness. Once his energies are no longer divided, he will be something to behold. You would know this about him, only if he chooses to let you in. There has to be a great deal of loneliness for him to exist in his world. The number of people who excel at his level must be very small. It would be easy to label Max as arrogant because of his genius level IQ, but that would only mean that you don't know him. Because if you did, you would know that he is anything but arrogant."

"When Max unlocks the block on what will define him, watch out world because there will be no stopping him. Therefore, the woman who can unlock the vault containing his inner spirit will have herself a great man, mate, friend, lover, and most likely a great husband. He is a great work in progress and a diamond in the rough. Even in the rough he is still better that 90% of the weak-ass men walking the earth right now," Mel concluded.

"Is there a pill that we can give him, or a school we can send him to so he can complete himself?" Kristi playfully asked.

"I'm right here so you two can stop talking about me now," I replied.

Looking at me with approval craving eyes, Mel said, "You know I think you are all that, but that doesn't mean you are perfect. You are perfect to me just the way you are, but I know there is an even better Max locked up inside my most precious friend. Am I still your girl, Max?" Mel asked.

"Absolutely baby, nothing's changed and never will. You keep it real with me and I love you for that," I replied, smiling affectionately.

"You two really are very good friends. Everyone should have a friend like the both of you," Kristi said.

The food arrived like it was planned to come right on time after Mel and Kristi finished roasting me. The food looked so delicious.

"Will there be anything else?" the waiter asked.

"Are you two done with me now or should we ask Danny the waiter to join in?" I jokingly questioned.

I held Kristi and Mel's hand and said the blessing over our meal. When I finished Kristi paused and looked at me as though she was trying to figure something out. Mel didn't pay her any attention, she just began eating.

I looked at Kristi and said, "What?"

Kristi paused and continued looking at me in almost a stare. She pressed the white linen napkin in her lap and said, "Max, you are a praying man. Your stock just went way up. You can tell a lot from a man who prays. My mother always told me the best way to begin anything is on your knees. She said a man who doesn't have a relationship with God is a dangerous man. Now I don't have to worry about your soul because I see that you know Christ."

Mel jumped in saying, "Girl, Max prays all of the time. This ain't anything new. I am the heathen who needs Jesus with my potty mouth."

I looked at Kristi and smiled without saying a word. She looked back into my eyes, shook her head and whispered, "You are something else Mr. Dean."

We ate our dinner and continued talking about trivial things. Every now and then I'd catch Kristi looking at me, trying to look through me like Mel discussed. I was a stone wall. I refused to acknowledge her probing eyes.

After we finished our dinner, all of us walked to the valet booth. Kristi's car came first. Mel and I gave her a friend hug and said good-bye. Kristi gave me that deep look without words as she got into her car. After she drove off, Mel quickly turned to me and asked, "Are you trying to kick it with her?"

The question wasn't entirely a surprise, but the speed in which Mel spun her head around to me was like an attack. I said, "No. I am actually kicking it with someone named Jordan. Kristi is just someone I recently met who appears to be a pretty down-to-earth sister."

Mel huffed, "I heard about Jordan from homecoming and I don't like her. It's your business, Max, but I don't like her. I think she is bad news, and I don't like her. I like Kristi, but I don't like Jordan."

Looking at Mel wondering what she knew of and heard about Jordan, I said, "I got the point Mel. You don't even know Jordan."

Mel looked at me turning up her nose and said, "You are right Max, I don't know her, and I don't like her."

The valet arrived with Mel's car. I told the valet that I got her tip. Mel looked at me as she got into her car and said, "Jordan isn't good for you Max, and I don't like her."

Mel pulled off and there I stood wondering why Mel was so adamant in her dislike of Jordan. I wondered what she heard about Jordan and what did she know that I didn't? I wondered if Marcus talked to her. Did Daria say something, but Daria didn't know anything other than she saw me talking to her at homecoming. Oh well, my car came and I decided to take the long scenic way home along Ocean Boulevard.

Chapter 11

MEETING INTERRUPTED

"Max, I can't believe we've been together almost a year. It seems like I've traveled around the world with you, even though it's been just some weekend getaways. I've been to China so many times with you I should be speaking Chinese, or they should make me an honorary citizen. But this trip is special. Do you know why?" Jordan asked in her cryptic way of baiting me into her conversational trap.

"No, why?" I replied, playing along with the beginning of her cloche and dagger conversation.

"All the other times I flew to you whereever you were, but this is the first time we're flying together. I'm not used to being in the seat beside you. It feels like we're a couple. Since we are going to be over there through the holiday, do you know if the Chinese celebrate Thanksgiving?"

"No baby, I think the whole Pilgrims' scenario is only an American thing," I replied in somewhat disbelief that she even asked me that question.

"You know Christmas is just around the corner, so while you are off saving the world, I am going to shop until I drop. I might even find your Christmas gift. I'm going to spare no expense on finding you the perfect key chain," Jordan said, snickering at her predictably corny key chain crack.

"Oh, I'm going to chain you alright," I said, turning to Jordan lifting my one eye and turning up one corner of my mouth.

"Oooh baby, that sounds tantalizing. I didn't know you were into the whole bondage thing. In that case, I'm going to have to put some other items on the Christmas list. Hmmm…maybe Chinese handcuffs? Would Maxi Max like to be cuffed and spanked?" Jordan said laughing.

"Oh, you are too funny. You had to laugh at that one yourself."

The guy sitting across from us in first class looked over and smirked. He resembled Ronald Reagan. He heard some of Jordan's sullied remarks and I wondered if he was smirking because he was turned on by Jordan's naughtiness. I bet this dirty old man wished Jordan would spank him too. But, no dice! Three's a crowd. Max may be a lot of things, but he is definitely a solo act.

"Max, where did your mind go? I bet you want to spank me now don't you?" Jordan continued with her deviant banter.

"No, my mind is on sleeping during this eighteen hour flight. You are so bad. Forget about any idea you have about joining the mile high club on this fight. Goodnight, Mistress Jordan, I'll see you in China."

Giving Jordan her membership into the mile high club sounded great in my mind for about ten seconds, but I was so exhausted. I put my brief thoughts of an altitude excursion to bed.

"Jordan, if you even think of trying to touch me down there or get frisky while I'm asleep, I'll have the flight attendants put you in the cargo hole with the luggage for the rest of the flight," I said, trying to act serious while fighting to keep my eyes open long enough to finish my sentence. I was so tired I could fall asleep mid-sentence.

"Okay, okay, go ahead and get your rest. But when we land it's on! We might even begin our trip in the cab on the way to the hotel," Jordan exclaimed like she was fiending for crack. I fell asleep thinking I had created a monster.

My time in China went by so fast that it seemed like I left as soon as I arrived. We continued to enjoy the Chinese food and culture. It seemed like Xao hated seeing me leave. As usual, Jordan and I had a great time in China. Relationships like ours worked up to the holidays, and then we had to return to reality. Gina hated me, so getting away was no big deal. I don't know how Jordan pulled it off. I can only imagine what she said to Kyle to not only be apart on Thanksgiving, but not talk to him since we were in China.

Jordan and I took so many trips together. I met her on some of her business trips, and she met me on many of mine. Our frequent flyer miles were becoming enormous. Some of our trips had nothing to do with business at all. We just told whoever needed to know that we were on business. Both of our jobs required so much travel that nothing seemed out of the ordinary.

Jordan booked us into some very exotic hotel resorts in Naples, Florida; Brussels Belgium; Montreal, Canada; Houston, Texas, and so many other little quaint bed and breakfast spots. At times I migrated from being cautious and discrete to not caring and letting it all hang out.

Marcus called it being whooped. Mason said I was sprung. I didn't have a colorful name for this new Jordan odyssey—it just felt good. Jordan made me feel alive. Even though the physical moments with her were nothing less than cosmic events, I can't say that was the main attraction. It wasn't even just her body. It was all of those things put together. At times I felt Jordan was too good to be true. It has all been said, "When something is too good to be true—it usually is."

In the back of my mind I was so caught up in the moment that I knew we had been careless about something. While I wasn't ready to feel the wrath of Gina, I convinced myself I didn't really care. Yet, I still tried to backtrack and recall if I had been careful. Living the life of a lie is difficult, I must admit. I wanted to just get busted so things could become simple.

Marcus' call interrupted my thoughts, "When did you get back?"

"Monday afternoon. I called you, but I guess you were in the air." I responded.

"Max, what's going on with you and Jordan? She is making you do some things that are definitely uncharacteristic of you. I know that I joke with you about being whooped—but on the real, are you?" Marcus asked seriously.

"No. How could you even ask me such a question, playa? Where is this coming from?" I asked half serious, half joking.

"Man, you disappear a lot. You are always traveling with her. I don't see you as much and you have kicked Daria to the curb. At first I thought Jordan was a play thing. I was even happy that you met her because she brought you back from your self-imposed exile after the shooting. Now it seems like she has her hook in your mouth trying to become Mrs. Dean," Marcus said firmly.

"What? Is this an intervention or something coming from the chief babe bandit himself?"

"No, this ain't no intervention or prevention. I'm your boy and I'm just telling you what I see. I know things with you and Gina are jacked up, but this is a dangerous situation the way you are going about it. I don't want you to survive a shooting only to get shot by your estranged wife for a piece of tail. I can tell you that Jordan may be all that in the sack, but she's not worth it," Marcus continued in his mother hen role.

I couldn't get mad at Marcus even if I didn't like what he was saying. He always had my back—and he made sense more times than not.

"I have everything under control. Don't worry, I got this.

"Do you Max? Do you really?" Marcus pressed.

I looked down at my phone and saw it was Daria on call waiting.

"Marcus, I'll catch you later. This is Daria calling and I have to grab her call." "Go ahead. Max, you are beginning to dog Daria for your new piece. Don't do Daria dirty. We go back well beyond Jordan's tenure in your life," Marcus pleaded.

"Alright, I hear you. I'm out," I said, pressing the button to click over to Daria's call.

"Hey Dar," I answered playfully.

I thought about what Marcus said just before we hung up. He was right. I had been putting not only Daria down since I began my escapades with Jordan, but I had stepped back from many of my friends. I knew I could pass the distance off by blaming my job's traveling demands, but the truth of the matter was that I allowed Jordan to reel me into her world like I was a fish on a hook. Daria had been there with me through everything and Jordan rescued my dead desire for anything. Who was I kidding? Jordan resuscitated my ailing manhood. Keep it real Max! I hate it when junior Socrates Marcus makes me question myself. He makes me see the truth even when I want to lie to myself. I said to myself, *The next time Marcus the philosopher opens his mouth I'm going to hit him in the throat.*

"Hey baby. It seems like it's been forever and a day since I've seen you—let alone spoken to you," Daria said in a nonchalant way.

"I know it's been a good minute. Every time I turn around I am going back to China. That plant over there is a disaster. I live in a constant state of jet lag." I tried to figure out why I was lying to Daria. She and I were not in a sexual relationship. I was trying to bring myself around to telling her that I met someone and that was the real reason I had been missing in action. I knew that Daria would be hurt when she found out the truth. And they always find out the truth. All I was doing was delaying her pain. I wasn't ready to lose Daria. She has always been my emotional safety net. Keeping Daria around meant that I always had someone to fall back on. Daria would make a great wife if I couldn't find that toe-curling woman I wanted. Secretly, I hated myself for feeling that way. But I've always needed Daria, and she's always been there for me.

There was a brief silence on the phone before Daria said, "Max, I have something to ask you."

"What?"

"Promise me you won't get mad."

"Maybe I will. Maybe I won't. But I can assure you that I will get mad if you don't stop with the smoke and mirror caveat, and just ask me the question," I said egging her on to a question I wasn't quite sure I wanted asked.

There was a second silent pause. This wasn't like her to hem and haw like this. Over the course of our friendship Daria has asked me some whopper questions without flinching. I wondered what this was about.

"Max, baby," Daria dragged out the "baby" like she was begging for candy. "Why haven't you ever asked me to go to China with you? Have you met some Geisha Girl over there that you're keeping on the down low? Or are you taking some other woman?" That question caught me by complete surprise. Daria asked it as if she knew something. If she hadn't mentioned the Geisha Girl, I would have thought she knew about Jordan. Then again, maybe she threw that in there to throw me off.

"Where did that come from?" I asked Daria, stalling for time to figure out how I was going to answer her question.

"Stop negotiating with me boy, and answer the question. Don't lie. You know I'm just your girl and you can tell me the truth."

"No, I am not doing any Geisha Girls. I think most people over there are afraid of me because I am so tall. I don't think they're used to seeing a guy who looks like me and this tall," I replied, avoiding the other question as if she wouldn't remember asking it.

"Stop avoiding the question, big head. Who are you spending the long weeks and months with in China? Max, don't think that I don't know you well enough to know that you are avoiding the question. Be honest and I'll still love you, boy."

Part of my inner self was telling me to come clean. The other part of me knew that my honesty would devastate Daria. She would surely remember Jordan from homecoming. I wasn't ready to part with Daria. Jordan technically still belonged to someone else. Why should I make a statement to Daria as if Jordan and I were in a relationship? Gina already hated my guts. *I couldn't afford to add Daria to that list. No Max, keep it quiet for now,* I told myself.

I thought, *Max you are going to hell for this one.* I paused for a moment, reared back in my chair and said, "No, Daria Ross, none of the above to both of your questions." Then I pushed my lie deeper into Daria's hopeful heart and said, "Between trying to keep the China operation afloat and going through mental gymnastics with Gina, my plate can't handle anything else."

I hoped that my disgusting lie would end Daria's inquiry. I didn't know how many more lies I had in me. Although I managed to convince myself of the greater good, my dishonesty was self serving—I didn't want to have to keep track of too many more lies.

"Max, everything is going to be fine. The situation with you and Gina will work itself out, and you will save the day at work like you always do. Even though I would love to be there for you, I understand.

You don't need me over there adding to your mix. Just remember, big head boy, that I am always here for you—always have and always will be," Daria said, indicating that she was dropping this line of questioning.

I had a sigh of relief. This was the first real test of my deception with Jordan. It was close. What if she had just showed up in China when Jordan was with me? What if Gina did that? I would have a real mess on my hands. For the first time I looked at a mess in the making. I wondered why my first marriage with Jillian really failed. Why couldn't Gina love me past our child conceiving difficulties? Wasn't I worthy enough of her love even without a baby? I thought when Gina and I married; it was going to be for life. Why did I continue pushing Daria to the back of my love lifeline when I knew she would adore me through anything? And now look at me—smitten over a woman who was cheating on the man who she was about to marry. Daria was talking to me and I wasn't paying attention to her. I was too busy previewing my ever complicated life. I kept faintly hearing something. "Max, Max, are you listening to a word I'm saying," I finally heard Daria shout.

"Yeah, I heard you," I said, lying through my teeth.

"Okay, what did I just say then?"

"I heard you. I'm not a lab rat that needs to be tested," I said laughing.

"Right, lab rat," she said sarcastically, followed by her sucking her teeth.

Daria was right on the money. My mind was off trying to get my arm around what I was doing. I was trying to figure out how I got myself in this impossible situation. If all that wasn't bad enough, I met Kristi, who was wonderful. I had four women in my life and I'm only sleeping with one. Mason would tell me I'm stupid for not doing all of them. Truth be told, I shouldn't be in bed with any of them. *That would be too much like right*, I told myself. *Max you are a lunatic.*

Just then I heard the beeping in my ear piece indicating that I had another call coming in on call waiting. The number for Collette appeared on my phone's screen. "Daria, I have to take this call. It is the Assistant District Attorney, Collette Hawthorne. I'll talk with you later," I said, rushing Daria off the phone.

"Alright. Handle your business—bye bye," Daria said, parting as I clicked over to take the call.

"Hello, Ms. Hawthorne," I said, answering the call.

"Hi, Max. I thought we agreed that you'd call me Collette."

"You're right. What can I do for the finest ADA in all of Florida?" I said playfully.

"I see someone's in a good mood today. There are a few things that I want to speak with you about. Are you free to meet me for lunch today?"

"Sure. Where do you want to meet?"

"There is a little restaurant called Antonio's on South Clematis Street about a block west of Flagler Drive. It's right near the little park where they have the free outdoor concerts. Do you know where that is?"

"I've never been to Antonio's, but I know exactly where you are talking about. I can be there about 12:45 p.m. this afternoon, is that okay? Is there any problem with the case or the sentencing?" I asked, wondering why she called for a face to face meeting.

"Don't worry Max, everything is fine. There are just some things that I want to speak with you about. Some things are better discussed on a full stomach, so I'll see you there at 12:45 p.m. Bye." Collette hung up the phone leaving me with questions regarding the need for this meeting today.

When I walked up to Antonio's, Collette was surprisingly already there. All throughout my interactions with her, I was usually early and Collette made her grand entrance.

Collette stood and gave me a friendly light hug and said, "Hi, Max. Thanks for meeting me on such short notice."

"How could I refuse the most beautiful woman who could lock a brotha up?" I replied, pulling back from her.

Collette was as gorgeous as ever. She had on her blue power suit and conservative black pumps. It's hard to imagine Collette as a public servant. She had the body and looks of a Hollywood actress.

We sat for a while enjoying some small talk. After a few minutes Collette asked, "Max, do you regret your decision about your assailants?"

"No, not at all," I replied wondering why she had to bring me here to ask that question.

"Good. How have things been going with you since the trial?"

"I'm not going to lie. Things were rough. I withdrew from life. My marriage is over. I am just starting to see the light of day again," I said, not really sure why I didn't just say I was fine.

"Do you think your marriage is salvageable?" Collette pressed.

"No, that bad boy is more than over. There is no hope for us. I won't even waste your time with the details," I said, tossing my head and rolling my face towards the sky in frustration with the entire Gina mess.

"I don't do divorces, but I'm a pretty good lawyer if you need one," Collette gestured innocently.

I smiled at her and said, "I know how good you are."

"Do you really, Max? This may come across as opportunistic or even horrible timing, but I don't think you know me as well I would like you to," she said, looking at me and biting her bottom lip.

"What are you talking about?" I asked, seeking confirmation from her about what I thought she meant.

"You are far from stupid so don't try playing dumb. In the interest of cutting to the chase, I am interested in exploring a personal relationship with you. I haven't been oblivious to how you've looked at me. You were married while I was prosecuting your case, so I had to keep things square. Now the case is over. I just did my victim follow up which closes our official relationship. Technically, you aren't married anymore, and I am a single woman with needs that not many men could fill—present company excluded of course," Collette spoke as if it was her opening statement in court.

"You saw that huh? I guess I didn't fare so well with my attempts to be discrete," I replied, trying to salvage some face from getting busted.

"You might have gotten away with it if I weren't checking you out as well. You men always get caught which is why you shouldn't become criminals. We women are so discrete you all have no clue. We pick you all apart with our eyes and you don't even think we noticed you at all." She continued, "You forget it's my job to be observant."

I couldn't believe what I was hearing. During the trial I often wondered what she would be like if I got with her. Now, that opportunity was knocking on my door. *This was crazy*, I thought. I didn't know whether to be excited or lose my mind. I was smart enough to know I couldn't play with a woman who could put me behind bars.

"Collette, I had no idea," I said, surprised by what I now thought was the whole purpose of this meeting.

"And if your marriage was fine, you still wouldn't have any idea." I get hit on all the time. A woman in my position can't respond to every guy. I'm not a snob, but I can't get with a man who isn't on the same intellectual level as I am. I want a man who isn't looking at me for my income so he can be a stay-at-home dad. You are definitely a smart guy who has his own and doesn't need mine."

"Well, Collette, I have to be honest with you. My marriage is over, but I'm not yet divorced. We haven't even filed anything yet. She is still at the extreme hate-for-me stage right now," I said, not sure why I didn't just squelch her advance outright.

"That's fine. I appreciate your honesty," Collette coolly said, unphased by the apparent technicality of my still being legally married.

Collette's phone rang. She answered it and someone was obviously talking to her about her work. What in the world was going on? For a quick second I wondered if Collette would make a good Mrs. Dean. Just as quickly, I thought Collette was an addition to my current problems that I needed to let go right on past me. Gina, well maybe not Gina, but Daria, Jordan, Kristi, and now Collette were most guys' idea of a wet dream. They would love to have so many beautiful women for possibilities. This was the furthest thing from a wet dream for me. This scene was as confusing as my trying to read Chinese writing. Perhaps even if I got with Collette, that relationship would end up just as my others did—in disaster.

Collette hung up the phone and said, "Max, I'm going to have to cut this short. Two officers were just shot and killed in the line of duty. They caught the shooter and I have to get back immediately." She continued, "I hope we can get together soon when things calm down. Think about what I said," as she got up to rush out of the restaurant.

"I'm back on my way to China for work. I'll call you when I return," I said.

Collette gave me a friendly peck on the cheek as she departed. I didn't really have to go to China right now. I just needed some time to process this hole I continued digging deeper for myself. *Why didn't I just say something that would have let Collette know that I was unavailable? What's wrong with you Max?* I asked myself.

I had to call my boy. I had to talk with somebody because this was getting crazy.

"Hey, Max, what's up punk?" Marcus answered in his usual familiarity towards me.

"Mayday, mayday, mayday! Marcus, Max is in trouble!" I screamed into the phone.

"What's wrong with you? What have you done now? Is Gina chasing you around the house with a fireplace tool?" Marcus said laughing.

"No stupid, I just had lunch with Collette and she wants to start seeing me. Daria suspects that I'm with someone. I'm grooving with Jordan more and more, and then there is Gina the viper. I didn't cut Collette off. I let her walk away thinking there is a possibility for her and me," I said frantically without stopping between sentences to breathe.

"I told you to stop trying to be like me. I am the dog not you, Mr. Relationship Man. You need to leave the women player stuff to me," Marcus said, trying to be funny. "On the real, Max, what are you doing? Why did you go to lunch with Collette?"

"I had no idea she was going to come at me like that. I went to lunch with her because I thought she was going to discuss something about the case with me. Dude, she was looking as fine as ever though."

"You are a serial relationship kind of guy who is always in search of the perfect Mrs. Dean. I can't for the life of me figure out why you haven't found her. Lord knows, you have always had some fine women. They have all been superstars by most men's standards. For some reason you always find their faults so you can continue your endless relationship search. You have Gina "the Sybil" Dean, who could easily become a serial killer of one—you. There is Daria who is waiting on you to become hers like you are the second coming. Then there is

Jordan 'the nymphomaniac' Anders, who may not have a moral bone in her body. Then you met Kristi and got all gooey over her. And, as if you didn't have enough psychosis of your own making, you are entertaining ADA Collette Hawthorne," Marcus said, painting the disaster of my life like he was painting one of those picture by numbers.

"Wow! That was so insightfully unhelpful Plato."

"What do you need me to tell you that you don't already know? You can't straddle the fence. You have to pick one horse and ride it. Be with Daria or release her from her self imposed relationship exile waiting on you, who's likely to never show up. You are out there with Jordan like you are stupid. You are doing stuff that can get you killed. Kristi is a nice girl, but I can tell you she isn't about to let you dog her out like Jordan. She would be your challenge. You can't figure out if you want easy, hard, faithful, or psychotic." Marcus stopped for a brief minute and asked, "So why didn't you shut Collette down right from the start?"

"I don't know."

"Max, you know we go back a long way. I love you like a brother and you know that. Why can't you get your love life together? You are relationship dyslexic. If you don't get a handle on what you want to do with these different women, I see trouble brewing on the horizon. The only good thing is, you haven't slept with any of them except Freeway," Marcus said, still trying to have my back like the loyal friend he's always been.

"There you go with that Freeway mess again. But, I hear you boy," I said, conceding Marcus' point.

That's why I always turned to Marcus. He always kept it real with me even through my misdeeds. I hated it when he was right. Even though he was my boy, it felt like he was a smug punk when he was right.

"Max, am I going to have to fly you out of town in the middle of the night to keep these women from killing you?" Marcus said, trying to lighten up the desperation of my call. "Okay, Mr. Dean, that will be $500 for my 15-minute counseling session."

"Funny. Deduct it from the $100 million dollars you already owe me for getting you your skycap job," I replied, laughing at Marcus over the phone.

"I see you still have your sense of humor. Good, you'll need it when these women are chasing your ass down the street when you get busted as a playa with no game. Ha ha that, Laxwell Dean," Marcus said, not letting me one up him.

Even though Marcus was playing, I seriously thought about what he said. I needed some time to sort this entire thing out. I wasn't trying to be a player. I simply didn't know what I wanted to do or how to go about it.

"Max, are you all right?" Marcus asked.

"Yeah man. Thanks."

"Okay. I gotta go now. I'll keep the plane fueled and ready just in case you have to be on the run." Marcus hung up the phone so I couldn't fire back.

I thought again, *This was most men's dream, but it was becoming my nightmare.*

Chapter 12

DINNER NIGHT

Gina and I sat down at La Tratatorio's on the river to have dinner. La Tratatorio's was a swanky Italian restaurant known for sophistication and intimate ambiance. This was a perfect place for Gina and me to begin our reconciliation, if that's what she had in mind. Gina said we needed to talk and resolve our issues. She smiled seductively as she convinced me of her sincerity by saying we could talk in public and told me that choosing La Tratatorio's should assure me that she wouldn't create a scene.

"Max, I don't like where we are now. I want to be able to put our troubles behind us," Gina said, appearing sincere while displaying a little smile.

"I would like that too," I cautiously replied.

"Tonight will be a special night for us, I promise. It's going to be good for us, honey."

We had been sitting there for a while chitchatting about everything. I thought the evening was progressing nicely until I saw Jordan walk into the restaurant with Kyle. I knew it was Kyle from the pictures that Jordan showed me. Oh my God! What were they doing here? I hoped that if Jordan saw me, she'd do an about face out of here. I had to play this very cool so Gina wouldn't suspect anything. Inside, my blood pressure was rising like the mercury on a thermometer in hell. This was the nightmare scenario that everyone feared, bumping into your extracurricular partner when you were with your spouse. I couldn't focus on anything but coming up with an escape plan without being obvious. Maybe if I pretended to go to the restroom, I could call Marcus and tell him it was time to fire up the plane!

"Max, where is your mind? Look at the menu please," Gina said, unaware of this developing disaster with Jordan and me.

I struggled to mutter out a vaguely coherent response, "Oh, I was just taking in the ambiance of this place."

"It is really romantic and intimate, but look at the menu please. I want this to be a special dinner for us, okay?"

It seemed as though Gina's lips kept moving but made no sound. All I heard was my mind telling me different options to flee from this moment. I wondered if Jordan saw us yet. I didn't have to wait any longer. Our eyes met. My heart did a double beat. I wasn't sure if I should act like I didn't know her. I wondered what was going through Jordan's mind. Would she walk over and speak to Gina and me? What would I say if she did? My internal stress meter was in the red zone.

Jordan looked great. Her outfit was in full regalia. Her usual sex appeal was in full bloom despite the awkwardness of the moment. I needed to keep my mind on this potentially explosive encounter, but Jordan's seductive look kept reeling me in. I thought, *Max, this has the makings of a disaster written all over it.* Of all the restaurants in South Florida, why did they have to show up at this restaurant?

Oh no! Just when I thought it couldn't get worse, Jordan and Kyle started walking towards us with the Maitre d'. Gina looked up at them just as another couple was seated at their table. I was desperately trying to keep my composure.

Gina looked away for a moment, "Max, do you know what you're going to order?" she asked so matter of fact.

Jordan and Kyle continued walking towards us. I was cool, calm, and collected outwardly, but inward, my heart was seriously pounding. It felt like it was beating so hard the valet parking cars outside could hear it. My mouth dried like the great salt flats and any taste on my tongue left me. I took that big nervous swallow of infamous guilt. It felt like I was sending sawdust down my throat. I just knew that anyone watching me would have thought my adam's apple poked out six inches as I swallowed a single drop of saliva. Jordan and Kyle walked down our isle towards the left rear of the restaurant. Their table must be behind ours. I hope so, that way I wouldn't have to look right into their mugs, although it would have been better if their table was in Zimbabwe rather than in our restaurant. They were going to walk past us. I tried not to look at Jordan. I put my head down and pretended to be looking at my menu.

"Hi, Kyle," I heard Gina say.

My mind was trying to process what I just heard. *No, I did not hear what I just thought I heard. No way!*

"Hey, Gina," Kyle replied as I looked up.

No way, this was not happening to me, I thought. Gina and Kyle couldn't really know each other. This wasn't possible. What is the likelihood? There couldn't be a worse situation than your wife knowing the fiancé of your mistress. I told myself, *Max you couldn't have screwed this one up any more if you tried.* I asked myself again, *How in the entire world did they know each other?* I looked up at Jordan and she too looked dumbfounded by Kyle and Gina's familiarity.

"Kyle, this is my husband, Max," Gina said, cordially introducing me.

"Nice to meet you," I replied as I stood to shake his hand.

I gripped Kyle's hand strongly. A firm handshake was required by a man of any substance. Kyle's handshake back to me was lackluster at best. A wet roll of Charmin would have been more rigid. I must admit, somewhere in the recesses of my mind I would have much rather broken Kyle's hand than shake it. That way, Jordan would have to rush him to the hospital and out of this restaurant.

"This is my fiancé Jordan Anders," Kyle replied, introducing Jordan to us.

"Kyle, why don't you and Jordan join us for dinner? We have this table for four and it's just the two of us. Besides, we need to catch up," Gina politely offered.

"We don't want to intrude," Jordan spoke up, trying to avoid this unpleasant moment as much as me.

"No intrusion. Please join us, I insist," Gina said with a level of kindness that I hadn't seen come from her mouth lately.

This was the apocalypse. Marcus won't believe me when I tell him about this one. Who would? I surely don't and I'm living it right now. I don't want to know this dude. I have been sleeping with his woman so the last thing in the world I wanted to do was be his friend or have any prolonged conversation with him. I was not ordering any appetizers or dessert. I wanted dinner to be over faster than it began. They could even skip the water if they want to—that would be more than okay by me. What could they have to catch up on? They needed to worry about catching me when I run outta here.

Kyle's average height, fair skin, curly hair, and his nonathletic build reminded me of a kid named Tommy from back in the neighborhood. I bet just like Tommy, Kyle got picked on, beat up, and had his lunch money taken from him when he was young. He reminded me of the guy who was pocket protector smart in school, but couldn't get a girl to acknowledge that he was even alive. Momentarily I had deviant thoughts of him being whipped by a dominatrix. I could see that Jordan ran him—henpecked!

The waiter came by and took the drink orders. I wanted to tell him we didn't want anything to drink; in fact, we would take everything to go. But our Gomer-Pyle looking waiter was trying to work on getting a big tip. For such a classy restaurant, Pyle looked as out of place as a single golden tulip sprouting up in the middle of red roses. He didn't know his tip would be huge if he'd just pull the fire alarm so I could escape this uncomfortable night.

There was a momentary silence as Pyle brought the water out. Pyle started giving us his rendition of the specials, slow and deliberate, like he was giving the State of the Union Speech. When he finished his painful menu diatribe, Kyle said, "Give us a minute."

I thought, *What do you mean give us a minute, you indecisive moron? You need to get into speed mode with the order so you and Jordan can get out of my face.*

Gina perched up in her chair and engaged Jordan in polite small talk. "So, Jordan, what do you do for a living?"

"I'm an IT manager," Jordan replied innocently.

I pretended to listen intently because I didn't want to talk to Kyle. I didn't want to fake any interest. Where was Marcus when I needed him? He was my boy and he was supposed to be here running interference. I hoped by some miraculous event Marcus would parachute into the restaurant like one of those idiots who lands in the middle of a football stadium during the game.

Gina looked interested in what Jordan said. She continued with a follow-up comment, "Jordan that sounds like an exciting job. I bet it's not nearly as exciting as your occupation of screwing my husband."

Jordan's mouth dropped open as she stared at Gina, not knowing what to say. I thought, *O' Lord.* My mouth went from parched to as dry as the Mojave Desert. A nervous jitter traversed down my arms to my legs. I felt like a staggering boxer after he was pelted by a surprise right hook.

This was not a coincidence. This was a well planned ambush. My brain scurried to figure out what to say. It wasn't really about what to say as much as it was which lie would work. Jordan and I were caught completely off guard. We didn't have a chance to synchronize our "alilies"—that is, alibi and lie combined together to be utterly and completely untruthful. That is the worst kind of lie, and we weren't prepared to invoke it.

Kyle and Gina obviously came together and colluded on the facts before they launched their well orchestrated sneak attack. I thought about going to the restroom and pulling the fire alarm myself. Kyle was too calm for the situation so I had to keep my eye on him. I wasn't sure if he was going to punch me in the face or attempt to strangle me. I just wanted him to do something, get mad, curse me out, leap across the table, or something. *Don't just continue sitting there like someone stole your puppy. Have some outrage,* I thought.

Gina continued, "Don't look so surprised. You two weren't very discrete with your raggedy affair. I would expect this from Max because of where we are, but Jordan you're engaged to be married, you nasty skank. Max, the least you could do is act like you have some shame about your mess," Gina said, increasing the bitter contempt in her voice.

"I...," I started to say... when Gina cut me off.

"Shut up, Max! I don't want to hear any more of your lies come out of your mouth. If you even look like you're going to get up from this table, I will stab you in the throat with this fork. Since you and that tramp decided to humiliate us, both of you are going to sit here and hear me and Kyle out," raising her voice to a level that made an older couple turn and look at us. It felt like the whole restaurant got quiet.

I had no idea what was going through Kyle's mind, but I knew I had to be on the lookout for a punch because that's what I'd do if I were him. Instead, Kyle looked at me for a minute or two without saying anything. I actually wanted him to swing at me so they'd throw us out of the restaurant and this nightmare would end. Kyle must not have been able to hold his feelings any longer when he asked, "Max, didn't you know she was engaged to be married, or didn't you care because of the troubles in your marriage?"

Is that it? I thought. If it was the other way around, I would have leaped across the table and already started giving him some free dental work by way of my fist. I would have been wrong to attack the guy, because a man can only do what a woman allows him to do. We men want to hit something and displace our anger in hopes of salvaging some semblance of pride, neither of which ever happens. We just end up in jail, beat up, or worse, but still we are left with the nauseating fact that our woman chose to enjoy the company of another man at the mere cost of our overblown ego. Of course, we adamantly feel—that could never happen to me.

If the situation were reversed, Kyle and I would be going at it right now whether Jordan was worth it or not. Kyle getting beat down would be in full effect. Good thing for me that Kyle didn't have the typical alpha male mentality.

Kyle turned to Jordan, "All of this time you weren't having sex with me because you said you wanted to wait until we got married. I had to find out from Gina that what you were holding back from me, you were giving to Max. You and Max disgust me. I can hardly stand to look at you."

"Disgust hell, you need to flex your balls and hit his ass in the mouth," Gina interjected with cold steel, black eyes and the hatred swelling up in her voice.

"Gina as much as I want to, that's not my nature," Kyle responded defensively with an eerie sense of calm.

"Then you need to change your nature," Gina said, actually wanting Kyle to hit me. She continued, "What? Do I need to give you the pictorial of Max spreading Jordan's legs from east to west and pounding her like ground beef? Maybe you need to visualize her hissing like a cat from climaxing or panting like a dog from being worked out for hours. I guess he'll need to throw her up on this table, knocking over plates and forks and drill her like a power tool before you will become even agitated. What will it take for you to man up and bust Max's ass in the mouth like the junkyard dog he is? I don't understand you. I'm pissed at what Max did and I don't even want him anymore."

Gina looked like she was getting more upset that Kyle wasn't resorting to violence. I don't know how he stood her relentless berating of his manhood. He should have told her to shut up. Gina was deliberately pouring salt on Kyle's wound.

Kyle looked to Jordan, "How long has this been going on?"

Jordan pleaded, "I can't remember. I didn't plan any of this, it just happened. We just started talking and our friendship grew into something neither of us intended. You ambushed me into an engagement I wasn't ready for, and the pressures mounted. I met Max at the end of a bitter argument between us. I have fallen for him. Kyle, I am so sorry. I never meant to hurt you."

"Sorry isn't going to cut it Jordan," Kyle replied, sounding like he was trying to mount some semblance of outrage.

"Cut it, you need to cut her ass," Gina said, spewing her continuing call to violence.

Gina was getting louder. The maitre'd came over and said, "Is everything alright?"

"Yes, everything is alright. We are just having an excited discussion," I replied.

"Lies just roll off your tongue so easily just like you are fluently speaking another language. Max, you are such a dog. You are a habitual liar. You and that troll sitting across the table from you," Gina said, gritting her teeth like she was holding back her desire to hit me in the mouth.

Gina continued, "Jordan, I found your number and a note you wrote on Max's boarding pass. The 'You got me tingling' part was cute. I called your house to curse your trifling tail out, but Kyle answered the phone. After I grilled him like salmon about who he was and why his woman was tingling from my husband, we started putting this plan in motion to expose both of you before you all had time to coordinate your lies."

Kyle chimed in, "We know all about the affair, so lying is useless and an insult to our intelligence."

"Jordan, you just don't know. I'm doing everything in my power not to reach across this table and gouge your damn eyes out. I dare you to say something back to me, I'm not like your weak ass man—I will come across this table and slap the leftover taste from this afternoon's lunch out of your mouth!" Gina said, biting her bottom lip.

"Gina, maybe we should leave now and finish this discussion at home," I said, acting like I was trying to calm the tension, but really trying to run out of there.

"Home, home! Boy, you ain't got no home. If you even think about coming in the house where I sleep, you'd better not go to sleep. If you do, I can't guarantee you'll wake up with all of your body parts. No, you blew home. You made yourself a new home in between that tramp's legs. I'm filing for a divorce. I'm taking all of your shit, at least all that I don't destroy or sell while you are locked out between tonight and tomorrow. If you even think about flexing and coming home anyway, you'll find yourself on the wrong side of a domestic violence episode.

"Maybe after Kyle kicks her to the curb, you can stay with your tingling Jordan. You'd better be careful because that tingling might be something you can't get rid of. Dogs usually carry fleas or worse. Max, if for some strange reason Kyle decides to keep Jordan, you can call your dysfunctional 'co-patna in crime' Marcus and move in with him."

155

"Gina, I know that I've given you every reason to hate me, but let's talk about this. There's a better way to handle this situation," I said, knowing that I was talking to a stone cold wall.

"Max, did you ever bring her up into my house—into my bed? Tell me that you didn't stoop that low. Please tell me that you didn't have that thing secreting her scent into the mattress I sleep on. Tell me that you didn't strip me of all of my dignity," Gina said, fighting back the tears because she wasn't going to give Jordan the satisfaction of seeing her break down.

"No, Gina, we never did anything in our house or theirs. We wouldn't do you all like that. Kyle, I can assure you that Jordan and I never crossed that line," I said as if that would make what we did better.

Jordan and I tried very hard not to make eye contact. I felt like people in the restaurant knew what was going on. I could swear they could hear every word spoken at our table.

Our waiter, oblivious to what was going on, came out and asked, "Are we ready to order, or would you like me to repeat the specials?"

"Gina, I am so sorry about this. I…I just got swept away by Max's gentleness and the solitude he was in from his tragedy," Jordan said, trying to atone her misdeeds to Gina.

"Bitch, does it look like I care about your reasons. As far as I'm concerned they should have shot his sterile ass dead. He isn't anything but a half of a man and you're a piece of a woman. I'm glad we never had children so I wouldn't have to worry that his seed would continue contaminating the earth. I'm sure that the only life your polluted hole can bear is a disease. How dare you even speak to me," Gina said raising her voice to the drawing stares from many restaurant patrons. "I'm not like your spineless man; I will whoop your ass."

Gina started pushing back from the table, "Girrlll, you just don't know," Gina said, fighting back her obvious urge to pounce on Jordan as she sat back down.

Gina obviously forgot Gomer Pyle was standing there until he said, "Ma'am you will have to calm down or I'll have to get my manager to ask you to leave."

I wanted Gina to get irate again so they would put us out. I was ready to leave a long time ago. I was so embarrassed; I wanted to crawl underneath the table. Kyle was frighteningly silent. I didn't understand him at all. Jordan told me before that he was soft, but I never imagined he'd be almost afraid to stand up for himself or Jordan. Jordan said he lacked a backbone. I was seeing firsthand what she meant. His restraint made me almost want to punch myself for him.

"Go get the manager. Tell him that he needs to throw this stank tramp and her spineless piece of trash man out of his establishment," Gina said to Pyle while looking right at Kyle and Jordan. "Why don't you bring back some nuts for appetizers? It appears that Kyle is starving for some."

"Ma'am, that's unacceptable behavior for our restaurant. I will get the manager for you," Gomer said as he walked away seemingly frustrated by it all.

"Don't come back here getting in my face or you can be dealt with too!" Gina yelled, not to be outdone by the waiter's attempt at having the last word.

"I thought we would escape these kinds of people at this restaurant." I heard a woman say that was two tables away.

I looked in the direction of the voice to observe an older woman who reminded me of Aunt Bee from the Andy Griffith show, dressed in a red Laura Bush-like dress suit. The woman looked like she came from old money. The man she was with looked like he just emerged from a brandy and cigar room from the nineteen fifties.

"What do you mean these kinds of people, you old battle ax?" Gina fired back.

"You need to take that ghetto behavior back to where it's accepted and appreciated. The other patrons and I didn't come here to listen to it," Aunt Bee said.

My embarrassment took a back seat to my offense to Aunt Bee's outdated attempts to stereotype us. I assumed her husband looked mortified because of her comment.

"This isn't the sixties and we don't eat back in the kitchen. You can take your smug suburban never-had-to-work-a-day in your life kept ass home," Gina shouted back.

Some people got up to leave while others stared. Gina's exchange made the restaurant's hectic pace come to a halt. The manager came over to our table after stopping by Aunt Bee's table to apologize for the commotion.

"I'm going to have to ask you all to leave," the restaurant manager said.

"Why? Is it because we stand up to racist old geezers?" Gina said.

"No, because you are insulting other guests, my staff, as well as causing a scene," he said while showing us the way out.

Jordan and Kyle looked completely taken back by Gina's conduct. I thought they were happy to go. I knew I sure was. In this case the humiliation of Gina's restaurant episode was worth it to end this evening. *I'll never show my face in this place ever again,* I thought.

Outside we handed the valet our ticket. Jordan and Kyle stayed several feet away, trying not to associate with me and the Tasmanian devil standing beside me. The affects of the Kyle and Gina ambush were disintegrating.

"Here you go, sir," the valet said as he gestured to hand me my car keys.

"I'll take those," Gina said to the valet as she snatched the keys from his hand.

The valet guy looked at us like he knew there was some drama going on. I gave him a tip that compensated for Gina's rude key snatching.

"Get away from the car door. Walk home!" Gina commanded.

"Come on, Gina. This is taking things a little too far. I'm not walking home," I replied frustrated and tired of the ordeal.

"Walk home, fly home, or catch a cab, I don't care which one you pick, but you aren't getting in this car with me. I don't want to be in the same car as you; after all, you don't have a good track record with cars. I don't want to be in the car with you and get shot up like Sonny, in *The Godfather.* I'm sure the boys that you sent away have their homeboys out looking for you. Besides, as I told you inside, you no longer live in our house. Get used to being homeless."

As I stood there alone, I saw Kyle and Jordan get in their car and drive off. Gina took off right behind them. Like the music stopped and

I was the only one left without a chair; there I stood, feeling like a man without a country.

About 25 minutes passed after I called Marcus before he pulled up to the restaurant—the scene of the crime. It seemed as if he were a coroner coming to do the chalk outline of what was left over from my now dead marriage.

"Thanks, Marcus, for coming to get me," I said, getting into his grey SUV.

"When you called me and told me what happened in the restaurant, I couldn't believe it. Man, based on what you told me, it sounded like it was crazy in there. I can't believe Kyle didn't hit you. I would have given you a beat down."

"Can you not rub it in?" I snarled.

Marcus was my boy and I knew I wasn't going to get off that easy. True to form, Marcus fired another shot at me, "I told you I am the lady's man, not you. Max, you are a good guy. You tried but failed to have game with the ladies, now look what happened, good guys gone wild," Marcus joked, laughing so hard he sounded like one of the hyenas from the animal channel.

Tears began rolling down his face as he couldn't stop laughing at my expense. Only from Marcus would I accept this kind of blatant disregard for my predicament. Truth be told, it is kinda funny now that it was over. He continued, "You need to stick to that old boring, romantic madness and leave dealing with multiple women to experts like me. You are a miserable failure at it, Max ol' boy."

I looked at Marcus like I wanted to give him a beat down. He was right; I failed with Gina and Jordan miserably. This went so wrong for me. If Kyle wasn't different and a better man than me, I could have been killed. Although I wasn't trying to be a player, I suppose the outcome was the same. That wasn't who I am; I just wanted to find that one true love. *Why is this so doggone hard?* I silently quizzed myself.

"Max, I'm glad you're alright. As usual, I'm always going to be here to bail you out of your insanity. I suppose you're bunking at my place tonight. Let me warn you that I don't have any food in the house. All I have that's good in the fridge is Corn Flakes and Pepsi. Anything else in the fridge is already or becoming a science experiment."

"Just drive and shut up. Let me morn in peace, punk," I snapped jokingly.

Marcus turned up the music and we continued driving to his house. Reality was starting to set in during our drive. I asked myself what I was going to do now. My entire life was locked up in a house that I was just barred from entering.

"Max, I have to take a jet out next week to get an upgraded navigation unit installed, fly with me and we'll go see Pike. It'll do you some good."

Chapter 13

SCALES OF JUSTICE

"Max! Max! Max!" Marcus yelled.

"What?" I snapped wondering why he was yelling at me.

"Max, where is your head? I called you three or four times and you acted like you didn't hear me. Where's your mind?" he pressed.

I was frozen in my thoughts. *I know I looked like the Poltergeist kid staring into the snow filled TV. I reached the end of my marriage and I felt like a complete failure. It was like New Year's Eve on Times Square—only this countdown was for the ball to drop on my marriage. The only difference was there would be no kazoos, kisses, or celebration. There would only be the sound of the judge's gavel signaling yet another Max relationship failure.*

"Marcus, it feels like I'm on my way to an execution—the hangman's noose. This drive feels like a funeral precession rather than you driving me to court," I replied with a slow solemn cadence of sadness.

Looking at me strangely, Marcus said, "You're kidding me right?" He continued before I could even mount a sorrowful response. "You need to pick your butt up out of this feel sorry woe-is-me moment and realize that in the two years since the shooting, Psycho Suzie Gina has put you through hell. She's tried to humiliate you at every turn. And, need I mention the restaurant incident with Kyle and Jordan, or when you went back home to get your clothes and she had already turned Edward Scissor Hands on your wardrobe?"

Trying to defend Gina I said, "I know Gina has had difficulties with our marriage, but I can't say she has been raised to the level of being called Psycho Suzie."

Marcus was losing his patience with me. I had every reason to condemn Gina, but I took no pleasure in our break up. By many people's account, I was more than justified in hating her. He was ready for me to throw Gina under the bus. I think he wanted me to move on and forget about her. I think he feared the relationship cliché of so many broken marriages that end up in a second marriage, and more often than not, a second divorce. What Marcus didn't realize was Gina Dean's door was closed, nailed shut, and encased in cement.

"Soft for Psycho Suzie, Maxwell Dean, you've given Gina more chances than people get appeals on death row. Now you need to be put out of your misery. Go into that courtroom and close this chapter of your life. Dude, life will go on. It just has to go on without Suzie Scissor Hands," he pleaded.

When Marcus pulled up to the front of the white stone courthouse, I knew that for all of his grand standing machismo, he wasn't going to enter the courtroom with me. I didn't blame him. Truth be told, I didn't want anyone to see my marital ship sink. I wanted our relationship to sink under the judge's gavel like a ship doomed on a cold night, slipping below the ocean's surface heading for the quiet darkness at the bottom of the sea. I wanted complete anonymity in the shame of my divorce.

"Max, you know I'm not staying to experience Mrs. Gina Hell on Wheels again. Call me after it's over if you need a ride. Now go in there and end this thing!" he demanded as he drove off steering into traffic.

While I was shuffling through my legal papers, I saw Gina heading into the courtroom. Her eyes looked a little bloodshot red and crazed. The stoic seriousness of the moment was broken by Gina's usual barrage of hatred hurling towards me.

"Where are your little tramps? Why isn't your sidekick here to see me take all of your prized possessions? What, you didn't want to be embarrassed in front of your dysfunctional friends? Max, you are so pathetic. You have a surprise coming when we see the judge," Gina shouted trailing behind her attorney into the courtroom.

My attorney, on his cell phone with his office, didn't witness Gina's spectacle. After about an hour, the court clerk called our case. Gina and her attorney approached the wooden table and chairs on the right side of the court. My attorney, John Polk, and I went to the table on the left. Dozens of spectators sitting in the galley looked like on lookers in the coliseum, waiting to see who'll bleed. I tried not to make eye contact with Gina. Marcus was right—she was acting just like a Psycho Suzie.

The court bailiff swore us in. The judge came in a couple of minutes later. The judge was a medium height man with salt and pepper hair, albeit mostly salt, and looked like he didn't take crap from anyone. The name plate in front of his bench read, Judge Roy Billington.

Judge Billington read a file in front of him and then looked up at both of our attorneys, "I see there are no children, and this is a relatively short marriage. Why don't we have an agreement over the division of marital assets? Have the parties tried to work out a settlement?"

John stood erect and was the first to speak, "Judge my client Mr. Dean has very generously offered Mrs. Dean more than the statute requires under the community property provisions of the Florida Statutes. Yet, Mrs. Dean has rejected every offer."

The judge looked towards Gina's attorney puzzled, "Mr. Adams is this correct?"

Mr. Adams shuffled some papers as if he was trying to find an acceptable answer, "Your Honor, my client feels there are extenuating circumstances to consider that are much more than just the law."

"Mr. Adams, in Florida there is only the law. Why don't we take a short recess? We will take a pause to see if counsel and their clients can work to settle this today. You don't want me to settle this. I'm not clogging up my court docket with this simple matter. If you make me rule on this matter for you, then I will consider that I've done a good job if I make both parties equally unhappy, you get my drift?" the Judge sternly replied.

Replying in unison, "Yes, Your Honor."

"It's 10:40 a.m., the court is in recess until 1:00 p.m.," the Judge said as he hit his gavel on the wooden plate and stood up.

"All rise." The deep voiced bailiff yelled as the Judge got up and walked out his private exit behind his bench.

"Max, I'm going to try this one more time with Gina's attorney. I will meet you back here after lunch."

"Okay John, good luck."

I had a sickening feeling in my stomach the results would be the same with Gina if the judge gave us another year to work it out. Gina hated me and wanted to stick her knife in me as far as she could. Her new instrument of death was the court. I thought, *God, if this could just be over already. I cannot believe that things have sunken to this abysmal place with a woman that I once loved more than anything.*

After an uneventful lunch of uselessly pining over my abominable failure rate at finding love with the right woman, I was back in court to face Gina again. My attorney came in about five minutes after me with Gina's lawyer in tow. I looked at John in hopes that he would flash me the settlement thumbs up. Instead, he twisted his lips to the side and shook his head "no." John looked almost as deflated as I felt.

Seconds passed before the bailiff stood and yelled, "All rise, court is now in session."

Judge Billington looked at both of our attorneys, "Well counselors, do we have an agreement?"

John spoke first, "Judge we have tried everything, but we cannot get them to agree to anything."

The Judge's face changed from jovial to extremely annoyed, "Mr. Adams is that true?"

Mr. Adams dipped his face down in apparent frustration and solemnly replied, "Yes Judge."

"This is not rocket science and I'm not going to spend a lot of time on this matter. What is the problem Mr. Adams?" the Judge sternly questioned.

I looked over at Gina; she turned her head to the side full of attitude as if she could care less. She almost looked happy that no one could force her to settle. It was like this courtroom moment was her stage. She was the star attraction and no one was going to make her do anything she didn't want to do. I think Gina felt she was in total control.

"Judge, my client has rejected every offer proposed by opposing counsel. She insists on having Your Honor decide the case. So here we are Judge," Mr. Adams replied.

The judge increased his face's frustration wrinkles. I could tell that he was trying to hold his composure regarding our case. I thought, *Welcome to my world Judge.*

"Mrs. Dean is the statement made by both attorneys correct?"

Gina's attorney motioned for her to stand, "Yes, Your Honor."

"Why? What is preventing you from settling this matter? I've looked over the file and nothing suggests Mr. Dean is being unreasonable," the judge asked, looking as if he was begging Gina to make sense of why we were not done with this charade.

"Because it's not half of everything," Gina defiantly replied.

I looked at Gina and shook my head and thought, *Oh Lawd! Don't do this to the judge too.*

The Judge looked back through the court papers and raised his eyebrow curiously, "Mrs. Dean by my account and the stated property values, Mr. Dean is giving you 79% of the assets. Am I missing something?"

Gina rolled her eyes and shifted her hip posture and erupted, "It's not half of everything. I want it all. I want all of the money and half of everything. Saw the damn dog's bowl in half and give me my half of it. Take the bed and saw it in half. The law says that I am entitled to half of all of the community assets. I don't want half of the value. I literally want half of everything, and all of the money. Since Maxwell Dean is half of a man and was woefully deficient in giving me a child, then he should be consistent with being half. So unless Max and his pathetic lawyer could give me literally half of everything, I refuse to settle. I've already had to settle for an empty womb and I won't settle anymore."

I was mortified. I couldn't believe Gina just said that to the judge. She has lost her mind. If she isn't careful, the judge might not give her anything. I thought, *This courtroom has seen a true spectacle—Gina in rare form.*

Everyone in the courtroom looked stunned. I was used to Gina talking to me like that, but I couldn't believe she was talking to the judge like that. I thought to myself, *You all have no idea.* I watched everyone from the court reporter to the bailiff look at Gina like she was insane.

Completely dumbfounded, John leaned over to me and whispered, "Is she serious?"

Equally clueless, I whispered, "What you see is what you get. I cannot believe that is why we are still stuck in this courtroom, but Gina has been losing it lately, so it doesn't surprise me."

"Mr. Adams, is your client joking? Did you know about this before we returned from lunch?" the Judge questioned.

Looking embarrassed, "No, Your Honor. I have been unsuccessful in moving my client to a different position."

The judge looked at Gina in utter disbelief, "I can sympathize with your emotional pain in not being able to conceive and will extend you some latitude in this proceeding, however, this is not an actionable cause for this court. You will watch your mouth and conduct yourself with the proper courtroom decorum. My courtroom is not the Jerry Springer Show. I am not King Solomon and we do not saw things in half. Now, I could order you all to take a fifteen minute recess and come back with a more sensible resolution, or I can rule. As I said before, if you force me to decide, a good ruling would be one that makes both parties equally unhappy. Which do you want?"

Before Gina could answer, John spoke up, "Your Honor, my client has bent over backwards to appease Mrs. Dean as evidenced by him offering to give her 79% of the marital assets. That is considerably more than the statutory 50%. Mrs. Dean has been totally unreasonable. Mr. Dean offered both community property and premarital assets. My client should not have to suffer any additional discomfort because of Mrs. Dean's irrational actions."

"Point well taken, Mr. Polk," Judge Billington replied.

The Judge turned back to Gina, "Well, Mrs. Dean, the ball is in your court. What is your pleasure?"

I could see that Tasmanian look in Gina's eyes. I could tell she wasn't going down without a fight. Where most women would break down and cry, Gina gets fired up.

Gina put her head down and looked at the table for a couple of seconds. Then looking up at the Judge, shaking her head she said, "I knew it. You are one of them aren't you? You are in the same frat pack as Max and his other degenerate misfit friends, aren't you? You need to excuse yourself from this case. I knew I wouldn't get a fair result from a man judge. This is bullcrap! The law says I get half. You need to obey the law and give me half. Don't abuse me just cause I'm not in the boy's club."

I couldn't believe that Gina uncorked on the judge like that. She was fuming. Her attorney better shut her up. If she isn't careful, she could piss off the judge and end up getting executed. Gina might get both her and her attorney thrown in jail for contempt of court. The bailiff moved closer to the Judge in case Gina completely lost her mind and went for the Judge. I thought, *I'm going to tell Marcus that Gina got electrocuted for clowning on the Judge.*

The Judge's eyebrows scrunched together, his anger mounted. Outraged by the accusation, he turned to Gina's attorney, "Mrs. Dean, you are out of order. Mr. Adams get your client under control before she sees the proceedings from a jail cell on closed circuit TV."

The judge's threat made the entire courtroom come to a silent halt. I imagine it was hard for the court reporter to focus on typing while Gina launched her verbal assault against the Judge. *It's over now. You are going to get it. The Judge is going to nail you,* I thought.

Gina's attorney leaned over to her and softly told her, "This is highly inappropriate, you need to calm down. The Judge is not going to do what you asked. We need to settle this so you can move on with your life."

The Judge looked at Gina and her attorney, "We are not going on another recess. Mrs. Dean; you will control your outbursts. We are concluding this right here, right now, and in the next 92 seconds."

Mr. Adams tried to say something else to Gina, but before he could finish, Gina stood straight up and screamed, "You men sicken me!

Your whole life is spent trying to get between a woman's legs. Then when you make it there, you don't even know what to do. You men are as dumb as your penises. If you could manage to do something constructive with that thing, you might actually contribute to the world."

"Mrs. Dean I urge you not to say another word and listen to your attorney. You are stretching my patience. You are a nanosecond away from contempt." The Judge's tolerance was all but gone.

Tearing up and reddening with anger, Gina raised her voice, "I have contempt for the entire self-serving male species. I am tired of being empty. I have no place to go after this. I am so tired of Max, you, and every other man-dog," she stubbornly persisted.

As she continued verbally assaulting the Judge, all I could think of was a scene from the movie *The Green Mile*, "Walking the mile, walking *The Green Mile*." The judge is going to put Gina on death row. When she gets like this, even the Pope would have her walking *The Green Mile*.

Hammering his gavel on the bench, "Mrs. Dean, I find you in contempt," the now frowning Judge charged.

Defiantly standing her ground, "I don't care. You men just band together and destroy women. You get us all emotionally open, and then you take a dump on us like dogs crapping on the lawn. Judge, you are in contempt right along with all of the other male misfits. Max broke me, and you're finishing me off. Are you happy now? All of you men need to be neutered!"

I could tell the judge was pissed. I don't imagine he gets talked to like that very often. The bailiff went over and stood next to Gina. I saw the bailiff turn his head and speak into the radio microphone clipped on his shoulder. Two more bailiffs and a sheriff deputy entered the courtroom. Then two more plain clothes officers entered the courtroom from the door behind the judge's bench and stood on both sides of the judge. Gina was imploding. I don't know why, but despite everything that Gina put me through, my heart was breaking as I watched her melt down. I sensed that she was at her emotional end. I choked up and said a silent prayer for her. *Lord, help her through her pain and anger.*

The judge was seething, "Mrs. Dean, you've worn my patience beyond thin. I was going to send you to the closed circuit cell, but I'm not going to prolong your discomfort any longer. The facts in this case are clear. I am going to issue my ruling and close this case."

I thought, *Thank you Judge, otherwise you all are going to have to put the K-9 dogs on her.* John and I just stood silently and watched while Gina's actions killed her case and made ours.

Judge Billington turned to me, "Mr. Dean, I am going to grant you your entire premarital assets. You will give Mrs. Dean her car and all of her personal property. Mr. Dean will retain all rights and sole ownership to the home. Lastly, Mr. Dean will give Mrs. Dean some walking money. I order you to give Mrs. Dean 50% of all cash, and 50% of the value of your current stock and investment portfolio."

I can't believe it. She actually got less than what I was going to give her. I guess it doesn't pay to piss off the judge. I felt like the judge could have given it all to her. I wasn't going to allow myself to be defined by "stuff."

Undeterred by Gina's tirades the judge looked at Gina sharply, "Mrs. Dean that is my ruling. Now, we have one other piece of business to attend to. I found you in contempt of court. Bailiff, take Mrs. Dean into custody."

I watched in horror and disbelief as the officers handcuffed Gina. She didn't break out into tears as most people would getting handcuffed heading to jail. Oh no, not Gina. I saw her anger boiling over into combustion level. I hoped she wouldn't try to fight the court officers and end up getting tased. *Lord, please don't let Gina take it to that level,* I silently prayed again.

Unmoved by the judge's decision that meant she was going to jail, Gina looked at the judge, taking one last parting shot, "I don't know how you sleep at night, you sell-out sexist!"

Gina tried to stop them from taking her out so she could continue verbally berating the judge. She resisted the bailiff's attempt to lead her away. A female deputy ran over to help take Gina out of the courtroom.

"Stop resisting," the deputy ordered.

"I'm leaving. I just want to say a few more things to that arrogant misogynistic judge sitting up there in his batman cape like he's God," Gina spouted, as more officers entered the courtroom.

"Ma'am that is not an option at this point. It's over. It's time to go either willingly or forcibly," the bigger male deputy said as he unholstered his taser. After a few more bailiffs and deputies joined in the fray, Gina was taken out of the court's rear door.

The judge hit his gavel on the round gavel block and went on to his next case as though nothing happened. That gavel ended my marriage and Gina's freedom in one pounding thud. As I departed the court free from my wife, Gina was handcuffed and led to a jail cell. I never expected this ending, and I knew Marcus was going to tell me I should be happy for both, the end of the nightmare and a better financial outcome. All I thought about was how I felt Gina's heart and soul disintegrating in the end. Her words saying that she was empty circled my mind like buzzards flying over a dead carcus. Maybe going into custody would provide her an emotional pause. Maybe it would prevent Gina from hurting herself. I headed out of the court taking the long walk down the white marble stairs. I walked to the curb with my head up even though my heart was sinking.

My friend to the end, Marcus, was back to pick me up from court. I didn't even have to call for him, he was already outside waiting. As we rode home, I told him about Gina's Oscar winning performance in court. Marcus listened with his mouth wide open through most of my story.

Marcus covered his mouth with his fist and blurted, "Damn man, she clowned the judge like that?"

I just looked at him, "Come on, you better than anyone know how Gina gets. Of course she went completely left on the judge."

Laughing and hitting his steering wheel, "Damn, Gina is a fugitive. She shouldn't have missed the *Scared Straight Show.*"

"Boy—you are stupid," I replied, grinning at Marcus' sharp wit.

"Are you going to take her and Mr. Jingles some cornbread?" he joked about my *Green Mile* comment. He looked at me with a straight face, "Do women have to worry about dropping the soap too?"

Marcus was on a roll now. He was going to tell one joke after another all the way home. I must admit he is a funny guy. Gina gave him comedic material like he was doing standup.

After nearly an hour of Marcus' gut-busting comedy during our ride home, I wanted to be alone, but yet I needed a distraction from obsessively mourning over the death of my marriage. I thought about calling up Jordan, but I didn't want or need sex. I didn't want to call up Daria and drag her into another one of my tragic relationship moments. I knew Marcus would be flying in a few hours. In my miserable hour of selfimposed confusion, I summoned up a brilliant solution.

I swiftly punched up the number before I could change my mind. I let the phone ring for what seemed like forever. *Don't you have voicemail or do you sentence people to endlessly listen to your phone ring?* I thought.

I was just about to throw in the towel and hang up when I heard, "Hello."

Smiling from ear to ear, I said, "Hi Kristi, this is Max. Did I catch you at a bad time?"

"No Max, I just got out of the shower. I worked out a little earlier and needed to get this sweat off me. What's up, dude?" sounding happy to hear from me.

"Well Kristi, I could use a friend," I solemnly pronounced.

"Sure, what's wrong?" her voice changed to serious concern.

I wondered where to begin, or if I should say anything at all. I was still exhausted by the entire court ordeal. Kristi was one of the sweetest people I'd ever met. We always had great conversations in the past. I wasn't sure which way I was going with this conversation, but for the moment I was just enjoying the sweetest voice of my new friend. I was just content to hear a calm woman's voice. It was more than alright with me to let her voice take me to the end of today—tomorrow will be better—I just know it!

Chapter 14

BOYS WILL BE BOYS

"Falcon Jet November 8608 Bravo, you are cleared on runway 5L," I heard the air traffic controller tower say in my headset as we were about to land in Jacksonville.

"Roger 5L," Marcus replied to the tower.

As we taxied to where corporate jets park, I saw Pike in the window of the corporate jetport terminal. I wasn't sure if I was allowed to ride in the cockpit with Marcus, so I thought about running back to the main cabin before someone saw me. I guess he knew what he was doing, so I remained in the co-pilot's seat as we taxied to a stop. This jet was so sleek looking with its burgundy and tan color lines sweeping the underbelly of the plane from the nose to the tail of the aircraft. The cream-colored leather seats were huge and comfortable like home recliners. Except for the cockpit, the entire plane was one big first class cabin where the seats all swivel and recline. The cabin and the service bar were all accented in rich-looking burl wood. Man, this plane was swanky. I can see why Marcus loves flying this thing. Who wouldn't? As we entered the terminal, Pike greeted us with his patented big ole Kool-aide smile beaming across his face.

"Whazzzzzzzz ahhhhhhhhhhhh!" Pike sang out his what's up greeting sounding like he had turrets.

"What up though dog?" Marcus replied.

"Pike the snake oil man salesman," I hollered back to him.

"Ya'll two are ill, but I'm glad to see ya," Pike said, smiling from ear to ear as though he just won the lottery.

"Where are we off to Pike, because I'm starving?" I asked.

"We're gonna hit this new spot in North Jacksonville called Windows Café. I heard the food there is slammin," he replied.

"Cool, let's do it," Marcus confirmed.

"How's Sarae?" I questioned.

"Awe man, she's good."

"Did she give you a hall pass to hang out with the fellas tonight?" Marcus sarcastically questioned.

"Marcus, don't hate on his loving marriage. Just because you're the tramp of the friendly skies," I shot back.

"I know you not talking Mr. Freeway!" he snapped.

"Hey, hey boys, you behave now, my wife loves both of you and told me just to tell you all hi, and have a good time out with the fellas," Pike chimed in.

"Pike, your butt hit the gold mine with Sarae. I still don't see what she sees in your old crusty tail," I said, joining Marcus double teaming digs at Pike.

"You had a good wife too Max, so what the hell happened there?" Pike questioned me like he didn't know the story.

"Pike, that's a long story that you already know. I'm not ruining this night with that story. It's over and done now. Our divorce was finalized last month. Man, Gina clowned the judge. She went off in court. I thought they were gonna tase her," shaking my head still in disbelief.

"Whaaat?" Pike sang drawing out the word as though he was holding a chorus note.

Marcus couldn't wait to jump in on that. I knew he was going to start up the commentary and he wouldn't be able stop, "Pike, Gina went off on the Judge and they sent out the 'calling all cars' distress signal to all of the other officers. She was doing the Gina in rare form. I know they were outside the courtroom suiting up with riot gear," Marcus said laughing.

Pike started laughing, "Whaaat, you're lying."

Getting egged on by Pike even more, Marcus continued, "She told the judge that he was a dysfunctional frat-pack boy. Then she told him he was in contempt of his own court like she was the judge. She saw that backfire when the real judge had Gina handcuffed and toted off to jail."

In disbelief Pike turned to me, "Max say it ain't so. Tell me that Marcus is lying. No, Gina did not go there."

Looking at Pike, I sighed, and rolled my eyes up towards the sky, "Man, I wish Marcus was lying. Gina went all the way there. She went off on the judge so hard that I thought her head was going to do a 360, her voice got deep, and she spit that green demon stuff at the judge. Dude, it was crazy."

"Pike, I told Max about getting these women all strung out on him. These women aren't ready to fit in Max's little love story. He needs to hit it and quit it. Psycho Suzie is a prime example why I'm going to stay single. I don't want any woman to love me, that way she has no expectations and it's easier to dump her," Marcus said, puffing himself up again as usual.

"You are a caveman from the romantic dark ages. Your love tactics breed female serial killers," I fired back.

Pike joined in smiling, "Max, I don't know why I'm encouraging this Neanderthal, but he does have a point. You did make Gina go crazy."

Marcus' face lit up as Pike cosigned, "See Max, I told you so."

I thought, *That's all I need, Pike agreeing with Marcus. Cosigning with Marcus would be all that he needs, and then we will never hear the end of this all weekend long.*

"Hold on, Marcus, not so fast," Pike said raising his finger to indicate he had another point to make.

Pike continued, "Marcus, you are a caveman. At least Max tries, but gets it wrong, whereas you are wrong from the beginning and don't even think about getting it right."

Interjecting on Pike's point, "No Pike, Marcus actually believes in his wrong prehistoric approach to women."

Surprised, Marcus looked at Pike, "Oh, oh, I know you're not talking. At least we are in the game on opposite ends of the spectrum. You on the other hand gave up and let Sarae milk the manhood out of you like a cow back in college."

174

"I knew you would go there. Go ahead skycap and hate on my good thing. Max, give Marcus your baggage tags so he can get the luggage," Pike cracked back.

"I'm a pilot, not a baggage boy or a cabbie, dammit," Marcus said laughing like Pike got him back.

I knew it would not be the end of this conversation. I'd catch it from both Pike and Marcus while we were hanging out, but I would also get it from Sarae when we made it to Pike's house. I wasn't too concerned though because these were my best friends who never judged me.

"Alright, alright," Pike huffed, "Sarae got a new job and fat pay increase!" "That's great man, where is she working now?" Marcus asked.

"She works for this big consulting firm called Zane Bock."

"You're kidding me! Max isn't that where Jordan works?" Marcus excitedly asked.

"Yeah!"

"What's your girl Freeway's whole name and I'll ask Sarae if she knows her?" Pike spoke up.

"I see Marcus has already gotten to you with that Freeway stuff. Her name is Jordan Anders. That company is so big, I doubt Sarae knows her. I'll remind you later because I know you won't remember anything after you start getting on your liquid libation."

Thirsty for nosey details, Pike said, "Alright but you're going to have to give up the details about the freeway ordeal."

"Man, Sarae works for a sistah who she said is down as hell!" Pike immediately chimed.

"That's tight," Marcus replied.

The three of us rolled out in Pike's SUV headed for another boys night out that was sure to be side-busting funny. Admittedly, we become silly and stupid when we get together. I don't think Sarae worries about Pike going out with us because she knows from our college days that we just get stupid together and really don't even think about getting with women then. If anything, we trip out on them.

Pike and Sarae have been married since we all graduated from college over 15 years ago. He is still in love with her like they just got married. He has never stepped out on her. I admire that about him.

Because we've been close for so many years, we love Sarae just as much as we love Pike. She's really a sweet person who didn't judge me for my breakup with Gina. Sarae just told me that she and Pike were there for me if I needed anything. We are more like family than anything else.

When we got back to Pike's house at 2:30a.m., Pike was two sheets to the wind, but then again so were we all. Pike was a tad bit more well done though. I drove to Pike's house because he wasn't in the best shape to drive. I knew Marcus needed to relax from flying, plus I have the highest tolerance for alcohol and was fine.

Sarae greeted us as we came in, shaking her head," Look what you two did to my poor baby."

Sarae smiled about it knowing that we'd never let anything happen to Pike. She had the guest rooms of their three-bedroom ranch style house already made for me and Marcus to spend the night. I was too tired to say anything more to Sarae other than hello and goodnight. Immediately after Marcus and I greeted Sarae with a hug, goodnight is exactly what came next. Sarae put Pike to bed and said goodnight to us. Everyone retired to their respective rooms for the night.

The morning sunshine streamed in through the soft Caribbean Aqua colored lace curtains of the guest room window. Sarae had the room elegantly decorated. There were thought provoking abstract paintings on the cream colored walls. She had an antique dresser and night stand that looked like they came from 17th century royalty.

The room smelled so fresh from the pear-scented potpourri. It was sprinkled in the bottom of a clear glass vase that had clear marbles holding up a tropical flower arrangement. This room was decorated in vintage Sarae style and taste. The girl has decorating skills.

The most amazing thing about Sarae was she decorated mostly from things that she picked up at garage and yard sales. Sarae wasn't one of those sit at home and wait-on-her-man's-payday to empty his wallet women. She had an artistic eye and could have easily been an interior decorator. Sarae was good for Pike in that way. If it was left up to Pike, they would still be using milk crates as furniture like we did as struggling college students.

The digital clock sitting on the nightstand read 9:41 a.m. I got out of bed and started regaining my senses from last night. I detected the scent of Sarae's award winning breakfast-fresh blueberry pecan waffles and Canadian bacon. Breakfast has been her specialty since college. Her blueberry pecan waffles are to die for.

I was the first of us three amigos to arrive in the kitchen. Sarae was there doing her thing for her three favorite men.

"Good morning troublemaker!" Sarae greeted me squinting the skin between her eyebrows and sucking her teeth.

"No matter what Pike said, it wasn't me! It was Marcus. He's the ring leader," I replied, waving my hand from side to side—quickly defending her half hearted attack.

"Pike said you'd say that."

"Is there anything that little snitch doesn't tell you?"

"Nope!"

"Where is playback Pike anyway?"

"He rolled out of bed with a hangover. The last time I saw my baby, he was on his way to sit on the throne!"

"Okay Sarae, that's a visual I don't need, TMI," I said laughing at that disgusting image.

We both laughed as she said it's too much for her sometimes too. Pike's butt on a toilet seat isn't on my breakfast menu. Sarae already had the table set and started pouring me a glass of cranapple juice. Just as I said thank you, she said, "Sooo Max, I heard the great Max is being sexually slayed by someone called Freeway Freak?"

Sitting at the table in my jean shorts, a burgundy t-shirt and sandals, "Oh Lordy, not you too with the Freeway madness!"

She paused from preparing breakfast, smiling, "Max you know you and Marcus are just like my brothers... and you know playback, as you call him, can't keep anything from me."

"Of course, I should have known. What was I thinking?"

"And yes I know Ms. Jordan Anders. And now I know what all of the hush, hush, buzz was all about. I overheard my new boss and Jordan talking about this new guy she met that has been, as she puts it, 'Blowing her back out sexually.' I thought she was engaged to be married? You know me Max; I don't play that, so I thought she was a tramp."

I know it's easy to think Sarae was judging Jordan. I knew she wasn't. She was judging the act against her values on the institution of marriage. Sarae is a traditional woman with concrete values. She believes in one woman for one man, and vice versa. She not only respects the institution of marriage, she honors it. Sarae always says that she didn't say her vows to Pike; instead she said her vows to God about Pike in Pike's presence. Now that's a woman. Calling Jordan a tramp most likely reflected Sarae's dislike of her actions.

"You know how the Maxi-Max has to do it," I replied defensively, trying to camouflage my inner guilt.

"You know I love you, and always will, but you were a freak back in college, you are a freak now, and you will always be a freak!" Sarae grinned.

"Not again with the freak stuff. I am a respected member of corporate America."

"Corporate Freak is more like it! We've all been down since college and you are our boy, so we'll ride with you no matter what, and you know this...freak! I guess I am just glad you are back to you since the shooting. That hurt me so bad," she responded as if she was allowing the shooting recovery to excuse my behavior.

Sarae got a serious look on her face, "You know you are family to me and I'm gonna love you without ever judging you. I need to know if you divorced Gina because of Jordan. Did another women cause you to leave your wife?"

"No. Nobody other than Gina caused our marriage to fall apart. Perhaps there was something else I could have done to save it, but I just don't know what that could have been. If Gina had stayed the way she was when we got married, I would still be with her," I replied unsure I was ready for such a serious conversation.

Still serious, "Are you sure? Do you swear Max?"

Not certain where she was going with this, "You know I don't swear anything on my God, but I promise you it was all about the two of us. Gina could never recover from her inability to conceive. Our entire life and marriage was about Gina not being able to get pregnant. Plus, she couldn't understand or accept the college bond you and I have."

"Maxwell Dean, I can't figure it out. I know you, so I know you are a great guy, but why can't you hold on to a relationship? I know you aren't a womanizer like Marcus. I see it all over your face. You want something like what Pike and I have, but you never seem to get it, and when you get it, you can't hold on to it. You are very handsome and women always ask me about you when we all go out together. So I know you are a desirable catch for any woman. So, I asked myself what in the world are you doing with Jordan? She is so not you. Is she a rebound to Gina or a confidence booster from the shooting? Either way, I don't see it."

I sat there listening to Sarae talk to me and raise some great points for which I had no real answers. I listened to her act like a caring, concerned sister. For all of our joking around and making wise cracks at each other, Sarae still worried about my happiness.

I looked at her go there with me, "Okay Socrates, is this an intervention? You're right; I don't want a revolving door of women. I do want a relationship that is stable and long lasting. I can't seem to get that and I don't know why. Every time I think I'm there, it crumbles. It's like some sick joke that continues making me the punchline."

"When we almost lost you after the shooting, it nearly killed Pike and me thinking that we would lose you. It would have been a shame for you to leave this world without ever loving that special person. Now you have a second chance. Don't blow it. You have everything that a woman would love. You just haven't found out who Maxwell Dean really is. I know you can do it. I'm rooting for you."

Just then, Pike and Marcus walked into the kitchen right on time like they had staged my toasting the night before. Both of them chimed in, "King Freeeeeeak!"

"Baby, don't waste your time on Max. He ain't nothing. He wouldn't know a good woman even if she came up to him and bit him on the nose. Max loves chaos and nutty women. Don't be fooled by slick Willie, Max is a freak," Pike proclaimed.

"Now I'm getting triple teamed."

Pike spoke up, "Hey Baby!"

"Yes, Boo Sweetie!"

"Oh, I'll just vomit now with all of this Baby, Boo, and Sweetie, crap! Give me a break," I said, shaking my head.

Sarae turned up her lip, "Don't hate, Max. Just because it ain't, 'Oh Max blow ma back out daddy, pound me Max, hump me harder Max, oh drill me Max until I can't walk, Freeway madness!' Our situation is real love—something you and flyboy don't know anything about."

We all burst out laughing, as she panted hard, pumped, and gyrated her hips—imitating Jordan, pretty well I might add. Even though Jordan's hair was shorter, Sarae's shoulder length straight hair flopped around adding to the humor.

"Ya'll two should take your act on the road. It's so funny that it's not," I fired back.

Sarae was like that, very real and down to earth. Pike acted like Marcus and me. That's why they made the picture perfect couple and also why we had been great friends since we all first met in college.

I remember about five years ago when Pike called Marcus and me to tell us that Sarae's dad was in a car accident and was in critical condition and not expected to live through the night. Marcus called me immediately saying we'll fly the jet up to Jacksonville to pick up Pike and Sarae and take them to Cleveland to be with her dad. Marcus' boss was on vacation in Switzerland, and Marcus took the jet without even thinking that it wasn't his plane to fly for his own personal reasons.

While Pike was in the plane's cabin consoling Sarae, Marcus was flying like someone possessed. I was lining up a limo to meet us at the airport to drive us directly to the hospital. During that trip Sarae was hurting and we did everything possible to comfort her. Even though she was our partner's wife, we felt her pain as if she was our wife too.

Marcus and I made sure that she and Pike didn't have to worry about a thing. We took care of everything. Although we had all been close since college, I think it was at that moment our bond was sealed in compassion for Sarae's pain. Her dad died nine hours after she arrived at the hospital without ever regaining consciousness. We all cried together. Sarae was like our family which made us co-owners of her sorrow.

Sarae is an only child and very much a daddy's girl. Marcus, and Pike, and I stepped in and relieved a lot of the burden from Sarae and her mom. Marcus, Mason, and I were pallbearers at her father's funeral. That is what you do for friends you love.

We've been household names in her folk's house since college. They would always ask about Max, Marcus, and Mason. That's why no matter what Marcus and I do, Sarae and Pike will never turn their back on us. The smell of Sarae's breakfast ended my stroll down memory lane.

After about 45 minutes of woofing down Sarae's world famous blueberry pecan waffle breakfast, Marcus quizzed Sarae, "Who is your new boss? Is she fine? Is she single and still have her own teeth?"

"Not that she would be interested in you, she is single and about a size 14 or 16. She is extremely smart and professional."

"Girl, you know that is just right for me. I'm not like Max who is attracted only to petite women who all turn into super-sized problems. You know I like women who aren't demanding and don't act like they are entitled. You just need to introduce me to her and let me work my magic," he replied over confidently as usual.

Shaking her head in disbelief, "Oh good grief."

Pike jumped in, "Baby, what's her name?"

"Pasha Grant."

When Sarae said her boss's name was Pasha Grant, my teeth almost fell out. I was thinking, *Oh hell naw! I have a cousin named Pasha Grant; can this be?* Good God! I have to ask Sarae where her boss if from. This would be too bizarre if she was my cousin. *How many women out there could be named Pasha Grant,* I reasoned with myself.

"Where is your boss from?" I asked.

181

"Chicago, I think I remember her saying."

"Oh hell naw!"

Sarae widened her eyes and questioned, "What's wrong?"

"Oh crap! Hell naw!" I repeated.

Everyone looked at me asking, "What is it? What's wrong?"

I didn't answer anyone. I just sat there looking like I saw a ghost. I was processing what just happened in disbelief. I didn't know what to say, what to do, or what to think.

Chapter 15

TWEEBEE

I couldn't believe this. I dialed the number—it was ringing but I didn't know what to expect. I thought, *Maybe I should hang up before anyone answers, but then again—I had to know.*

"Hello."

"Is this Aunt Cookie's Pasha Grant?" I timidly inquired.

"Who is this and how do you know my mother?"

"I know many things about you, Tweebee."

"This has to be my cousin Maxwell Dean, because he is the only one who has ever called me Tweebee," Pasha replied excitedly, guessing it was me on the phone.

"The one and only."

"Boy, how did you find me?" Pasha curiously inquired as though she knew I tracked her down through the family.

I wanted to get right to it and ask Pasha about Jordan. What a small world. What are the odds that Sarae worked for my cousin and that she and Sarae both worked with Jordan? I wanted to hear some of Jordan's confidential girl talk, but first I had to do the family catch up thing with Pasha, or Tweebee, as I called her when we were little. I called her Tweebee because when she was little she had a small body and a big head like the yellow cartoon character *Tweety Bird.* I really didn't mind the telephone family reunion. We had a close family. It was that closeness that I was counting on to get the true skivvy on Jordan.

"Pash, I got your number from my boy's wife Sarae who works for you," I said revealing my source and answering what I'm sure was one of Tweebee's nagging questions.

Sounding surprised, "Oh really? I just hired her. She's a nice person and great at her job."

"Yeah, so you'd better treat her right because she is as much family to me as you are; the only difference is, you are blood."

"Looking out for Sarae won't be hard. I got you cuz," she replied, sounding like she sucked her teeth before saying it.

We switched our conversation to family matters and getting caught up on relatives. It seemed like we hadn't spoken to each other in years. She was always one of those quiet introspective people. She never wasted her words. There was a moment while she was talking that my mind strayed from the conversation. I thought, *How I am going to have the Jordan talk? I know with Pasha I could just come straight out with it, but I was pressuring myself to find a crafty way to introduce the subject. Pasha isn't the judgmental type and wouldn't look down on me about Jordan, but the last she knew I was married and had to know that I was aware Jordan was engaged. Now she was about to learn that I was sleeping with her colleague. What a mess.*

"Max, do you remember Uncle Junebug?"

"Yeah, what has his old slushy butt done now?"

"Did you know that Uncle Junebug got so drunk one night that he drove the car through the front door into their house?" she asked, raising the pitch in her voice. "Can you believe that?"

Raising my voice, "Whaaat?"

Like getting to the punch line of a funny joke she replied, "When the police got to the house, Uncle Junebug said that he thought someone was breaking into the house. He thought they would hurt Aunt May and he had to protect her. He told the police that he rammed the burglar with the car to stop him because that's all he had. Trying to compose herself she paused…

"Max, it was a goat!"

"You have got to be kidding me!" I shouted laughing.

"No, Max, I kid you not. I cannot figure out how in the world he thought a goat looked like a grown man. After the police told him that it was a goat and not a man, Uncle June slurred, 'It looked like a man, a short, fat hairy man. I am an old man you know my eyesight ain't the best.'

"You know it was Billy who came to the house?"

Surprised, "The Billy Hargrove? You mean to tell me that he is still the police down there?"

"Yeap, the same Billy who has been a cop so long people think he came out of his momma's womb wearing a gun and a badge."

Shaking my head in disbelief, "How old is Billy now–700?"

As Pasha laughed, I continued, "I think Billy was the traffic cop for Noah when he was loading the animals into the Ark, still wearing his too short pants, showing off his dingy white tube socks."

She continued, "When Billy pressed Uncle Junebug about the incident, Uncle June said, "You are too stupid, boy. Why do you keep asking me stuff? The dang thing had two round eyes that were looking at me so I thought it was a man. Aw hell, Billy, go ahead and take me to jail cause I'm drunk–you know I'm drunk–hell, even I know I'm drunk, so what are you waiting on. I'll just go over to your squad car and wait for you—take your time, I'm not going anywhere."

"Uncle Junebug has always been a happy, honest drunk."

"That's not the end of the story."

"Girl, what now?"

"As Billy put Uncle Junebug into the back of his squad car, Aunt May came outside in her granny gown calling him an old fool. Uncle Junebug yelled to Aunt May, 'Cut up the goat, that's good eating,'" Pasha laughed uncontrollably.

Laughing with her, I pictured my 86 year old Uncle June, the happy drunk farmer, saying that about the goat. He didn't like wasting anything on his farm. It wasn't as if he didn't eat goat, but it was the first time he killed one by a 1976 Buick. Uncle Junebug used to justify his drinking by saying that a man has to have a drink every now and then to stay happy. The only problem with Uncle Junebug's drinking was the now and then became daily."

Uncle June called Aunt May 'Doll Baby.' He said, "If I stop sipping, I'll start cheating." Uncle Junebug used to brag saying that he had been faithful to Aunt May for 62 years because of Fred. He held up his bottle of Old Grand Dad, pointing to the picture of the man on the label, calling him Fred.

"Max, after Billy got him in the back of the squad car, Uncle Junebug yelled through the rolled down rear window, 'Doll Baby, forget about bail, just bring me and Fred a goat sandwich, and don't forget to put hot sauce on it.'"

Struggling to catch her breath from the constant laugher of yet another one of Uncle June's comedic moments, "It was crazy that night."

Pasha and I continued recalling funny stories about Fred as we laughed about our favorite Uncle. As she told another story, my thoughts transitioned back to the looming discussion about Jordan. I kept telling myself, *Just come out with it*. I was cowering in part under my guilt for sleeping with Jordan when I should have been trying to save my marriage from becoming a fatality. I was cowering under my thought, *Maybe I am becoming a home wrecker*. I told myself, *Man up and do this*. Oh well, here goes nothing.

"Tweebee…"

"What's up cuz?"

Unbeknownst to Pasha, I was trembling when I took my big saliva swallowing gulp, "Sarae isn't the only person I know in your office. I just learned from Sarae that a friend of mine works with you."

"Who is it Max, maybe I know him?"

"Her name is Jordan Anders."

I looked up at the ceiling in my room waiting for Pasha to say something. I didn't know how she would respond to my new revelation. I'm sure this was the last thing she expected to hear after all these years.

There was a short pause…"Oh really? How do you know her?"

Now I found myself pausing. Now that it was out there I wasn't sure where to go with it next. I felt the sweat beading up on my forehead and I thought to myself, *If I don't say something she will figure out Jordan and me from my cryptic pauses*.

Finally after a few seconds of pauses that felt like hours, "I met Jordan in the hospitality suite at a hotel where my college had home-coming. At first she didn't have the outward appearance that would make me ooh and ah, but I was feeling somewhat animated that night, so I struck up a conversation with her. I learned we had a great deal in common because we both traveled the world. Although there were other people around us, we got lost in our own conversation recalling our joint stories of traveling abroad. We formed a friendship and have been kicking it since then."

She huffed, "So…, what does 'kicking it' mean?"

Before I could get another word in, she blurted out, "Jordan has been telling us about this guy she has been getting with, but she only calls him 'A'." "Max, isn't your middle name Aristotle?"

"You know it is, Tweebee."

Sounding like she had her ah ha moment, "It makes sense. You Maxwell Aristotle Dean are in fact the mystery man—A."

Blowing off her big dramatic moment, I said, "Spare me the histrionics."

Sounding like a kid, Pasha sang, "I'm tellllllllinnng Aunt Dee."

"No, you are not going there. Why are you gonna tell my momma on me?"

"Oh boy, you know I'm not telling Auntie on you. Did you know Jordan is engaged?"

"Yes, Jordan told me about her engagement, and she was on hold with it—on the way to calling it off. Pash, I didn't know she was engaged when we first met, she told me later. She told me that she couldn't go forward with it and told her fiancé she needed some time," I replied trying to justify my indiscretion with Jordan.

"Maxwell, is this a booty call or do you like Jordan in a deeper way? Jordan has been telling some girls in the office about this guy she only identifies as "A" who she has been pining all over. She talks about "A," as though she is in love with him. We've heard everything. She even told us about how spineless she thinks her fiancé Kyle is, but she has not called off their wedding. Not too long ago she had her wedding dress delivered to work and tried it on in front of us. She wasn't acting

187

like her wedding was called off," Pasha said, revealing some new information about Jordan.

Internally reeling from the wedding dress issue, I barely questioned, "Really?"

She continued, "Max, tell me you haven't fallen for this charlatan. I know Jordan isn't married, and maybe she does really like you, but I think she is playing you, cuz. Jordan still sees her previous boyfriend Ivan. She comes in and tells us when he comes over. Ivan isn't really studding Jordan. He doesn't put up with her nonsense and only comes around when he wants to. She is still very much into Ivan, even if it is only once a quarter."

Now I was getting pissed, "I knew about Ivan, but she only told me about how abusive he was to her. She made it seem like Ivan still pursues her. She said they run into each other at social events only."

"Nope, they have attended events together. You are the third leg to her three legged stool. The other girls and I listen to her exploits, but we just think she is nasty and shallow."

Feeling like the sucker of the month, I admitted, "Wow Pash, I am seeing a mountain of lies that flow out of her mouth like diarrhea and every bit as disgusting."

"Max, Jordan is alright as a person as long as you aren't interested in sleeping with her. I don't dislike her. She and I have gone to lunch on many occasions, but I think her man life is over the top. What do you see in her?"

Feeling deceived and wanting to crawl underneath the carpet to hide in shame, I reluctantly replied, "Pash after the shooting I was a wreck mentally and physically. My marriage was crumbling and I was afraid to even come out of the house. I couldn't get back in the saddle. All the confidence I used to possess about everything including my career was gone. I went an entire year without even *wanting* sex, let alone *having* it. I don't think I had an erection for a whole year!"

"Okay Max, I love you as a brother, but that was TMI. I do not want to have any pictorial images about your *thing!*"

"Yeah, yeah, yeah." Continuing my justification, "I met Jordan after my boys dragged me to homecoming. At first I just had a mild curiosity in the humorous girl who I enjoyed talking to about traveling. Then we continued talking and ..."

Pasha chimed in interrupting, blowing in the phone, "Blah, blah, blah, get to the point before I collect my pension Mr. 'A' Dean."

"Okay, Tweebee, big head little bird."

"Max, you are my favorite cousin and all, but if you call me that again, I will have you killed."

"Okay, Jordan was tender and gentle when I didn't even feel like much of a man. She loved on me like I was a virgin. She brought me out of my emotional prison after the shooting. Then once I recovered, she made love to me like an Olympic champion. Jordan's got skills."

"Okay boy, I get the point. I do not need to hear any more. Your last detail gives me the hebee geebies. Knowing both of you and all that getting busy makes my skin crawl, yuk!"

"You asked. Don't ask questions you don't want to know the answer to," all the while I was happy to have embarrassed my favorite cousin.

"Max, hold on while I go take an alcohol bath and disinfect myself."

"Funny."

Although I was enjoying this bantering back and forth, I was still disgusted and hurt about a dishonest betrayal of the girl I thought was my emotional savior. Marcus warned me about her when we golfed. I hate it when he's right. My mind played out various scenarios of what I was going to do now that I knew about Jordan's lies. I wondered if I should tell her that I know or keep it in my back pocket for some future use. I wanted Pasha to dig deeper and tell me everything, yet I wasn't sure if I wanted to feel like I just got played for a fool. Here marks yet another milestone of Max and female failure. *Are there any good women out there for a fellow*, I wondered? Finding the right woman to love seems impossible. *Is there anyone out there who is up for a serious relationship with a man who wants to love just one woman?* I continued interrogating myself.

"Max, why did you get so quiet?"

I was trying to come to grips with my thoughts and feelings. "I'm thinking about how you have just blown me away with all of this information."

"Not what you wanted to hear, huh?"

"Since you are family, and my allegiance is to you and not Jordan, let me tell you what I think about her. This is how I read Ms. Jordan Anders."

I wasn't sure I could handle this. I didn't know if this new revelation about Jordan would be so devastating to my ego that I would consider having a sex change rather than a breakdown over the disappointment of yet another woman. This was starting to feel like an epidemic. Maybe I should call the Center for Disease Control and report this. I could ask them if there was a way to control my female failure epidemic. That's it; I can name it the FFE, discovered by Maxwell "Stupid" Dean. Boy, did my parents miss the mark when they gave me the middle name of Aristotle. He was smart and insightful, whereas I am woman stupid and see nothing.

"Max, I've figured out your girl and here is who I think Jordan Anders is at her core. She has a great job and it makes her feel important. Her appealing figure makes her feel desired by every man. Her form-fitting clothes market her as being sexy. Her attire usually leaves very little to the imagination. Her outward appearance screams to be noticed and recognized. Inside she is hollow, empty, and desolate. She attempts to give the illusion that her inner spirit is inherently deep and abundantly sincere. I think when she tells a man that she loves him, I'm sure she believes it, as she is able to marginally define what true love entails."

I listened as Pasha painted an unflattering picture. She was revealing a different person than I thought I had been seeing. I thought maybe Ivan should have been brought to Gina and Kyle's little surprise party. As raggedy as our little secret was, I was learning it wasn't everything. At least it was all that I was supposed to know. I felt like such a fool.

She continued, "Jordan's life is a theatrical production where she is always in character, so much so that her life seems like a collection of personalities and roles. I think her true self is lost. I don't know when she lost herself or what caused it, but I think her life's true light was extinguished long ago. It's really a sad tale too often told where someone tries so hard to be a person of importance so they can be accepted and valued. That makes them lose their identity. Jordan is really a nice person imprisoned within the stage play of her many characters."

"Pash, you make her sound like a multiple personality who is bordering on schizophrenia. Is she going to turn into Chucky one day or what?"

"You're stupid," Pasha said laughing. "Are you concerned that you really didn't know what sauce you were dipping into? I don't think she will go all Lizzie Borden on you, but she isn't a *Leave it to Beaver* wifely type either."

"Well, that's a relief."

"Let me get back to giving you my complete assessment of Jordan so that you will be well informed to do whatever you are going to do with her. You asked, I'm telling you—girlfriend is a real piece of work. I'm not sure what either one of you three victims see in her, but here is my opinion."

I suspect that Pasha was trying in her own way to protect me. It isn't often that you get the inside track about a woman who you are seeing. I wished Pasha could have been there to forewarn me about Gina, but I was getting the real deal about Jordan. Pasha was taking the cover off of Jordan's lies and dropping the floor beneath her very feet.

Reluctantly, I asked for her to lower the boom on me, "Give it to me Pash."

"Okay, but let me get a glass of wine first. I need to relax before I continue," and she put the phone down.

I paused to think while she was off of the phone, *Oh Lawdy, Jordan is driving my cousin to drink, or maybe the rest is because what she has to say is so rough that even she needs some liquid assistance to help her get through Jordan's mania. I guess if she was telling me this in person maybe she would need some crack.*

After a few minutes Pasha picked up the phone, "There, I'm back."

"Continue with your story, Socrates," I sarcastically said, wanting her to continue her psychological analysis of Jordan.

"Jordan is a freak, not in a particularly bad way, but she will never be able to have enough sex to make her feel whole in the way that she wants or needs. Her body will never be great enough to keep men from leaving her once they see her for the scared, insecure, and shallow woman that she is. They will come to the same conclusion as any man of substance will—that body and clothing are a distant second to an inner quality. Her life is marketing a product that hasn't yet been produced. Deep down inside her conscience she knows what she must do to attract a man because of her lack of self-confidence. She has tasted the bitter fruit of rejection time and time again to know something is wrong with her, but she lives in a state of denial. That causes her to have this continuous revolving door of men."

I listened in disbelief about Jordan—so beautiful, but so screwed up.

"She must besiege men like you with a barrage of superficial pleasures to keep him entangled in her emotional abyss. Unsuspecting men are kept back on their heels so they will only be consumed by her sexual psychosis and never be allowed to stand on solid footing. Her experience has shown her on many different occasions that once a man realizes who she is at her foundation; the demise of the relationship lay just around the corner."

"I think that is why she has to keep more than one male suitor in the pipeline at all times. That way she's guaranteed herself, she won't have to be alone. She settled on the number of three men as the appropriate staple of insurance. This life of men has become her three-legged stool that has held up her fragile existence. I think it borders on self-enabling emotional destitution. Somewhere in her brief moments of reality, she knew this was the order of the day for her life. This was a stage that she was powerless to leave. She's relegated to changing man props, like her own characters.

"Jordan is a one-dimensional woman who is confused and dangerous to herself and to the others that she is able to unsuspectingly lure into her webbed theatrics. She hasn't accepted that she has a need to tap into a higher power to bring order to her internal chaos."

I interrupted, "It sounds like she needs Jesus."

"Max, I'm not sure what you saw in her, past her body. I'll be surprised if you're still attracted to her once you see past the sex. Cuz, you are slipping to get caught up by her. I thought you were smarter than that."

"Jordan has an uncanny ability to make you erase boundaries you once held sacred. She knew what I wanted and she was more than obliged to give it to me—however, whenever, and as much as I could stand, and then some. She sent my rational thoughts into the twilight zone by catering fully to my frail ego. She propelled me forward on this intimate odyssey that crippled my desire to reject her. She loved me into oblivion until I wanted to stay blind to what we were doing. Marcus warned me that a woman like Jordan used her body and personality to compensate for her lack of depth as a real woman of substance. He told me that I was whooped and sold on her superficial package. He said as long as she was doing the 'freaky deaky' I wouldn't look deeper into who she really was."

"You should have listened to him. Jordan's road leads to nowhere."

Wanting to hear something that would give me the ammunition to tell her that she was wrong I asked, "How can you tell all of this about her?"

"I am a woman, Max, and we know other women. We can smell their tricks and schemes. Where were you when Aunt Dee was saying that women are scheming when men are dreaming?"

"I got lost somewhere between that and her saying that castor oil was good for you."

"Pash, Jordan is starting to sound a little like she's interning to become a serial killer! Someone must have hurt her bad to make her this scandalous. "

"Whatever that past was, it made her insecure with herself today. Whatever pain she experienced, she seems determined to embrace all that is unholy to prevent it from reoccurring again. A man who can't give Jordan his all seems perfect for her as long as he gives as much as she wants. She doesn't have a problem sharing a guy with another woman; as long as he can't give his all, she won't have to commit her all. I think she feels it will keep her from getting hurt. With the three-legged stool she will never be fully invested in anyone. It's clear to me that somebody hurt her deeply by leaving her. That kept her living her life with the three-legged stool approach with men, so she would never be left completely alone. Her men will always be interchangeable with another. Each change takes away a part of the pain of her inner self. Even though she designed this process as a means to protect her emotional core—it serves as a bitter and painful confirmation that she is still very much flawed."

I continued listening to Pasha deconstruct the woman I thought highly of. I never would have of gleaned so much insight about Jordan on my own. In his own way Marcus was trying to tell me the same thing. His version was filled with more Marcus-isms and considerably more abbreviated. I asked myself, *How do I get out of this thing with Jordan?* Then I thought, *Maybe I could stay and get what I wanted now that I know the truth about her.* All I have to do is not fall in love and get burned—after all the sex is great. *Do you hear yourself stupid?* I asked myself.

"Pasha, how could I be so stupid and miss all of this? If you can see it, then why can't I?" I asked as if I were dying of thirst and begging for a drink of water.

"I can answer that question in four words."

"This isn't funny, but humor me anyway."

She spoke straight to the point, "You are a man! I'm telling you this so you won't continue getting blindsided. Let me wrap this up for you because I need to get to bed. Jordan's whole existence is built on a lie. She has no idea of who she really is. She only knows that her body makes men want to buy what she is selling, hook, line, and sinker. I think Jordan targets married or involved men because they are the ones most willing to see only what she wants them to see. When a man is cheating on his wife or significant other, sex is the main attraction. You all get caught up in that and ignore everything else. This is the perfect scenario for a woman like Jordan—you won't be focused on her quality as a woman, but rather her physical assets. I guess the theatrical stage that is her life is more comfortable than reality. Now you have it, Jordan Anders in a nutshell. So what are you going to do now, Max?"

Just then my phone beeped letting me know I had a call. I took the phone away from my ear and saw that it was Jordan. I thought, *What are you going to do now? Do I take the call and bust her with all of my newly acquired intelligence?*

"Pash, speak of the devil. Hold on a second, this is Jordan on the other line."

"Take her call because I have to get some sleep. Go ahead, cuz, and handle your business. I'm interested in knowing how you are going to handle her, but not tonight. I am exhausted. I love you, cuz, go get'em. Bye bye," with that Pasha brought the Jordan revelation to a merciful end.

Now I wondered what I was going to do with Jordan. The timing couldn't have been better. I turned my attention back to Jordan's call.

"Hello."

"Hey baby, this is Jordan."

Chapter 16

CONFESSIONS

After a hectic night of speaking to Pasha and then Jordan, the morning greeted me with a call from Daria. "Hi Max. Boy where have you been? No one has seen you since homecoming. What's up with that?" Daria asked after I answered the phone.

"Hey Dar. Why are you calling and harassing me with the interrogation? Who are you—the post homecoming hall monitor? I'm just kidding. I have been working a lot. One of our factories in China has been having a lot of problems, so I've been there often managing that crisis," I explained with only a half truth.

I lied to my best friend Daria. I knew she wasn't stupid. She suspected something, I could feel it. Now that my marriage was over and Daria and I were free to hang out more, we still didn't. Normally we would have, but my free time was absorbed by Jordan. I knew I should have been open and honest with Daria, but I couldn't. I rationalized that it would hurt Daria more to tell her that I was seeing Jordan. I was lying to myself. The truth was—I didn't know how things would work out with Jordan and I didn't want to close the door with Daria. I knew that when all else fails, I could count on Daria to love me unconditionally. I knew it was wrong, but what else could I do? Was I treating Daria like one of Marcus' 7-11 babes, or did I need a three-legged stool like Jordan? I was going from mess to messy. The last thing I wanted to do was hurt Daria.

Daria was as understanding as ever, "That's a shame, but if anyone can straighten it out, you can."

"Oh, you think I got it like that?"

"Max, you have some mad business skills. I don't understand it, but God knows, everything you touch in business turns to gold. Boy, you are blessed beyond measure. I am your biggest fan and always will be. The world needs Maxwell Dean in order to work, and so do I."

I felt really bad brushing her off in favor of Jordan. I thought about what Pasha told me about Jordan's lies and double life. I should just dump Jordan and get with Daria. I know we would have a great life together, but as close as we are, I just don't have the love and passion that I should have in order to take us to the next level. I often question myself on whether such a thing even exists. As a friend, they don't make them any better than Daria, but as a Max-mate, I am less certain.

My thoughts produced a silence, prompting Daria to call my name several times to revive me from my curious silence, "Max, Max, did you hear me?"

"Dar, baby I'm sorry. I was thinking about work. What did you say?"

"Work my foot. What I said scared your butt. Don't worry Maxwell, I am not asking you to marry me or whisk me away to some far away romantic island. Take it easy boy, I was just kidding you. But you are very talented."

"Thanks Dar, I really appreciate your support and confidence," I sighed in relief.

"You know that's how we get down. We are there for each other. We support one another."

"You know that's right."

Before she could take us down that uncomfortable road again, I preempted her, "Dar, I will have to go back to China within the next day or so. Things are so messed up that I might be over there for a while. The company is looking into getting me an apartment this time instead of my usual hotel stay. That is a clear sign that I will be there for the duration of the crisis."

"Alright then, go ahead and do your thing. Save the world, superman."

Even though I was just trying to change the subject, there was a lot of truth to what I told Daria. China operations are in trouble. I was going to be there for a while, but I was saying that to prevent Daria from pushing her agenda of us making a go of something more than just friendship.

Just then my phone beeped let me know I had an incoming call. I looked at the caller ID and saw that it was Marcus.

"Hey, Dar, that is the Skycap. Let me take the call and I'll call you back."

"Tell Marcus I said hello. Max, please call me back because there is something I want to talk with you about," she said ominously, withholding the subject of a conversation I feared was coming.

"Okay, I will." I clicked over answering the call, "What's up, Skycap? Can you get my bags and don't scuff up the handles this time?"

"Oh, you got jokes. It wasn't funny Min-well Dean. I am a pilot and not a baggage handler I told you, punk."

After I laughed for a minute, "I was talking to Daria when you called. She said to tell you hi."

"Daria is cool people. Max, how long are you going to keep her in prison?"

"Where is that coming from? Are you suffering from oxygen deprivation? What are you talking about? I am not doing anything to Daria."

"That is exactly what I'm talking about. You know that Daria is looking for her shot with you. Why, I don't know, but she is nonetheless. I'm sure almost losing you to the shooting and your divorce from Gina are probably making her more anxious about getting with you. If she knew how much of a punk you are like I do, she'd run away and not look back, but somehow you have the poor girl caught up in a Maxwell Dean trance."

"Ha, ha, ha, that's not funny. Keep your day job, fly boy. I think Daria is starting to drop subtle hints about her and me. I'm not ready for that right now. Just before I took your call, she said that she wanted to talk to me about something. I don't want to hurt Daria. I don't want to let her put her heart out there and then hurt her by saying I'm not interested."

"Boy, you have got yourself into a real jam. You know Daria loves you. She has been patiently waiting on you to run out of dysfunctional relationships and end up with her. I personally don't know how she does it. Max, Daria is our long time friend. On the real, you cannot hurt her. You need to cut her loose so she is not hanging onto the hope of something that will never come. Daria is great, but she is not for you. Man, don't lose Daria's friendship. Tell her the truth about you and Jordan."

Hearing what Marcus said, but not ready to concede to his completely valid points, I admitted, "I really don't know what I want, so how can I tell Daria about Jordan? What if things don't work out with Jordan? I talked to my cousin Pasha who told me that Jordan has been lying to me about her relationship with her ex."

"What! You needed Pasha to tell you that Freeway is a no good lying babe that you would do better without. I told you that she was trouble when you told me that she was getting with you and she is engaged." I wasn't confused before, but now I was. I thought to myself, *This girl who I knew was wrong for me made me feel so good. She was all wrong, but yet she was right. She brought me out of my mental hell. Why would God give me someone like this if I wasn't meant to be with her? Daria was so perfect as long as I didn't need any passion. How could she be so right for me on paper, but feel so wrong for me in my heart? Maybe she was the kind that people say you grow to love.*

"You just had to go there, didn't you? You had to say I told you so, didn't you?"

"No, I didn't, but I'm saying it now. Don't get mad at me now because the sandwich that you made doesn't taste good anymore."

"Man, you are right. I don't want to hurt Daria like that. She has always been there for me. I owe her better than what I'm doing."

Marcus sensed my trepidation, "Max, don't punk out, you need to tell Daria, I'm serious."

For some reason this was hard for me. Even though Pasha gave me the inside tip on Jordan's lies, deep down inside I still wanted her. I wondered if I was whooped. I asked myself, *Why I am on this road? What was it about this state of madness that I felt powerless to escape?* Jordan was not so beautiful that it would make me stay with her. Collette and Daria were both more attractive than Jordan. How did Jordan bring me out of my slump when nothing or no one else was able to free me? That has to mean something. I feel so stupid for letting a collection of women drive me crazy. Now I know why Marcus only wants 7-11 women. There is no headache, no decisions, and no drama. Realizing that Marcus called me and not the other way around, I asked, "Marcus, what were you calling me about in the first place? I know it wasn't about this situation."

"No real reason, just calling to holler at you."

"Alright, cool man. I gotta run. I have to get ready for another big meeting on the mess happening in China. Later."

I thought about this situation and what Marcus said. I knew if I didn't say anything to Daria, it would fuel her hopes for having a relationship. That would give her false hopes that would make telling her later hurt like it was a break up. If I tell her before then it would seem like the same old scenario—a confused Max. In my state of confusion and uncertainty, honesty would be saying nothing.

I felt I needed to talk to Kristi but wasn't sure where to go with the call, but I made the call anyway. "Hey, Kristi, this is Max. How are you doing?"

Sounding as nice as she always does, she answered, "Hey dude, I was just thinking about you, if you can believe that. I know you think I'm giving you a line of bull, but I was literally about to pick up my phone and call you."

"And what did I do to merit the honor of your thoughts?"

"Stop it, boy. This is not a negotiation where you have to prime me up. I just called to see what you are doing tonight. I want to treat you to dinner."

"Well then, let me check my schedule. I see that I might have a few time conflicts. There is the meeting with the President and Congress to negotiate an end to the partisan gridlock on Capitol Hill. Right after that meeting, I have to fly to the Middle East to negotiate peace in the region. Then I take the space shuttle to China to meet with the Premier to negotiate reducing the trade deficit between the U.S. and China. After doing all of that, in the next eight hours, I should be able to fit you in for dinner if the secret service clears you and I'm not summoned to the White House."

"Wow Max, did I ever tell you that you are so full of crap? You may be charming and all, but you aren't all that? Come back down to earth now. If you can make it I would love to have a dining experience with you later on. Listen to me, now you have me talking crap. I have something to tell you." Kristi covertly asserted.

Puzzled by Kristi's cryptic message needing to tell me something, I asked, "What is it? Is everything alright?"

"I guess you will have to show up to find out. Besides, this is my treat and I have a little gift for you."

"Why didn't you say that first? In that case I will be there. I'll blow off the Premier because he's cross-eyed and it freaks me out when I think he's looking at the ceiling, when in actuality he is staring me in my face. I'm just joking, I'll be there."

She laughed, "You are so silly. I'll text you with the details, bye boy."

I was thinking about what gift Kristi might be giving me. Given my propensity for jokes, I thought it might be a gag gift. I also wondered what she wanted to tell me. Maybe she got promoted or was relocating. Whatever it was, it brought me back to my current reality. I needed to talk to Daria. I couldn't figure out how to tell her.

I finished showering and got dressed. I quickly brushed my teeth and dabbed on some cologne. I was just about to walk out of the house when my phone rang. I picked up the phone. "Hello."

It took me a minute to recognize the familiar voice, "Hi Max. Do you have a minute?"

"Oh hi, Collette. How is it going?"

Collette paused a minute..., "Well, Mr. Dean, things aren't going so well at this moment in time."

Uncertain of what the problem was and why she was calling me, I asked, "What's wrong?"

"Max, I'm sorry I had to leave you at lunch that day. I have been so busy with work and bogged down in an endless supply of violence to prosecute. Today is one of those days that I hate my work. I hate that my existence is nothing but work. I have no real life. I've had a few glasses of wine and I'm thinking about you in an unprofessional way. To put it bluntly, I'm sitting at home all alone in a Miami Dolphins' jersey—horny and wanting you to come visit me. There doesn't have to be any expectations or weirdness, just a night where you can take advantage of me."

I was speechless. This was the last thing I expected to hear. Trouble was coming my way in bunches. I was dumbfounded by not only Collette's bold invitation, but also by her candid solicitation for a sexual encounter without commitment. First, Daria wanted to talk, and then Kristi wanted to have dinner and talk. Now Collette was calling and inviting me over for some loving with an extremely beautiful woman. There was no pretense about her intensions. She made her desires very clear. *What do I do?* I thought.

Still speechless I said, "Collette I don't know what to say. I am so ready to run right over there and comfort you. However, I feel like I would be taking advantage of you in your semi-depressed state. It seems like you would have regrets the next morning that would make things weird between us."

"Max, I am not the kind of woman who has some wine and loses control. My desire for you is definitely not alcohol induced. This is the conversation that I wanted to have with you at lunch, but we couldn't finish that talk. I am one of the top prosecutors in the city. I graduated at the top of my class in law school, and I work in a career field that demands toughness. Right now, at this very moment, I have let my hair down and am talking to a fellow career powerhouse, who I think knows how to handle my forwardness. Did I read you wrong, Mr. Dean?" she asked with remarkable candor.

This night was turning out to be something else. Do I call Kristi up and lie to her by telling her that something came up? Should I go to Collette's house and fulfill the fantasy I had about her the first day we met in her office. I thought about how she would look peeled away from her courtroom power suit. *What am I going to do?* I asked myself.

I'm going to hate myself for making this decision. I collected myself and lied, "Collette, I was trying every which way to figure out how I could pull off coming over to your house tonight, but I have to get ready for an early morning meeting before I catch my flight to China. We are having a crisis at one of our operations over there. I have to burn the midnight oil to prepare for an early morning meeting with the executives, and then I'm on a flight right after. I am afraid that we will have to table this for the moment."

Right after I turned down Collette's invitation I asked myself, *Why did I lie?* I should have told her "no." I should have been honest and told her that I had some prior plans. This was a prime example of how I would dig myself into holes with women and wonder why or how I got there.

Sounding very disappointed, Collette said, "I understand having to prepare. I'll give you a rain check for when you return. Wine or no wine, I'll keep my jersey warmed up and ready. I guess I will just retire to bed early then. Max, have a safe trip and call me when you get back."

Sighing with relief as to how well she took my rejection, I confirmed, "Okay, I will call you when I get back. Goodnight."

I hung up the phone and made a dash for dinner with Kristi before anyone else could call me. As I drove to the restaurant, I thought about what was happening. It was becoming a serious mess. Many guys would love being in my shoes, especially Marcus, but I didn't. Kristi has always been a nice, sweet girl. I was looking forward to having a quiet dinner with her that was sure to be enjoyable.

When I entered the restaurant, I looked around for Kristi. Seeing that I was looking for someone, the hostess asked, "Are you here for Ms. Wade?"

I looked at her a little surprised, "Yes."

"Right this way, sir."

The hostess escorted me to a booth in the dimly lit restaurant. The ambiance was pleasant. Kristi looked ravishing as usual. She and I exchanged greetings, cheek pecks– then we sat down across from each other. Her burnt orange short outfit showed her wonderfully sculpted athletic legs. We talked before and after we ate. Dinner at the Ritz Carlton is always fantastic. The service was impeccable. After dinner we walked outside towards the back of the hotel grounds that overlooked the Atlantic Ocean. We stood outside in the warm night air laughing and talking about everything from A to Z. We went back to the outside deck and sat around the fire pit.

Kristi got quiet and pulled out a small flat box from her purse and handed it to me, "Go ahead and open it. It won't bite."

I shook the box and looked up at her. "What is it?"

"Open it and find out."

I opened the box and was quite surprised by what I saw. I was a little dazed by the implication of the gift. I looked up at Kristi in amazement as if to say, "What is this?" For the second time tonight I was speechless.

Kristi broke the silence. "These are two hearts that are broken in half. One half has my name on it, and the other yours. I am attracted to you Maxwell Dean, and would like to have a relationship with you. As you can see, I am not your average girl. We will each keep the hearts with our names on it. When you are ready to give me your heart, hand me the half with your name on it and I will do the same."

Not knowing exactly what to say, I blurted out, "I had no idea."

"I see some things in you that I very much admire and are attracted to. I feel your spirit. Judging by the ease by which you talk to me, I think you have a similar feeling. I would like to start seeing you. I am not a loose woman so I will warn you from the start—my panties will not be forthcoming. Do you understand what I'm saying?"

I had planned on telling Kristi about my dilemma with Daria. I was comfortable with our friendship and felt I could ask for her honest opinion on how I should handle that situation. Now that went right out the window. I would love to date Kristi, but doing so seemed insane right now. What was going on? I just left a call with Collette about her interest. This was madness. I started wondering if Marcus was setting this all up to have me get *Punked*.

Collette was ready to get intimate. Jordan was a borderline nymphomaniac. Daria was looking to take her shot with a relationship, at least that's what Marcus thought. I hate to admit it, but he was seldom wrong in these matters with women. And now Kristi has thrown her hat into the ring. What else could happen? I have to go to China to escape all of these women. Is all of this happening because I got shot?

Did that release some kind of endorphin that's making me irresistible to women? I have no idea why all of this is occurring at the same time. My mind was racing with all kinds of thoughts and questions.

I knew I had to say something to Kristi. I wanted to say something to her—I just wasn't sure what that should be. "Kristi, the gift is amazing and a first for me. I am honored to accept it. Even though I didn't know you felt this way, I have on occasion thought what it would be like to date you. I would very much like to get to know you better and see you. I have to tell you that I will be out of the country a lot, managing a crisis in China, so much of our relationship will start out long distance. Do you still want to do this with me?"

Kristi looked at me smiling, pivoted her body in her chair to face me, and hugged me. As she pulled back from the hug, she said, "Long distance is fine with me. In fact it will allow us to get to know each other and not be compromised by awkward situations."

I was thinking the long distance would provide me time and distance to put my house in order. I could not be around any of them physically while I was figuring out how not to bury myself in women problems.

I smiled at Kristi and said, "You're amazing. I have never started out a relationship like this. There is something amazing about you that I can't quite put my finger on."

Kristi's quick wit kicked in. "That feeling is me already working on your heart. You know that I am a one man woman. I don't mess around. I take my relationship with the Lord very seriously and treat my body as a temple in every way. Do you understand what I'm saying?" she asked looking into my eyes, wondering if I understood sex would not be on the menu.

Actually, I was thinking that is a good idea, so if I stay with Jordan or decide to see Collette, Kristi won't feel like I used her for sex and left after I got what I wanted. If things didn't work out, we wouldn't have invested everything.

Seizing the opportunity to project moral strength, I replied, "I'm glad you feel the way you do. I just ended a very toxic marriage, and I'm not ready to jump into anyone's bed. In fact, suggesting that right now would have turned me off. When and if we ever do that, I want it to be based on something other than the desires of our loins. I would want something so much deeper."

"I am so glad you feel that way. I've never done anything like this before. Asking you that I want to see you is way out of character for me. Honestly, I wasn't sure what you were going to say. I wasn't really prepared for your answer. I was just following my heart. I want to do it right though."

We talked for a while longer before realizing it was late. I walked her to the door where the valet brought her car up quickly. We hugged again and she drove off. My car came up next. On my way home I wondered more about what just happened than being thrilled that it did happen. Normally I would be happy about dating a woman like Kristi, but I had to deal with Daria, Collette, and Jordan. Marcus' words haunted me. *Why wasn't I happy with one woman? Why hadn't I found the right one yet?* This new development had all of the right ingredients to blow up in my face, leaving me with nothing other than a very soiled reputation. I only had a couple of days at best to try to put my life in order before I left for China. I told myself, *Max, ole boy, you are going to be a very busy dude.*

After a crazy night of all sorts of dreams, I woke up to the same issues I had the night before. First on my agenda today was to call Daria. I needed to preempt her conversation by telling her about Jordan and me. Then, I needed to deal with Jordan's lies. This was going to be a rough day.

I thought about going to see Daria to have our talk, but decided against it. It was going to be hard enough without complicating it with face to face dynamics—right now I cannot face her. I thought it would allow Daria the opportunity to save face and not have to deal with me looking at her while rejecting her again. Marcus would call me a coward, but I thought in this case it was the smarter path to take in helping manage Daria's dignity.

I paused before dialing up Daria to think about this. I had to erase all of my second thoughts about doing this. I punched in her number and was partially hoping she wasn't home.

"Hello Maxi Max," Daria enthusiastically answered.

Knowing that she saw my name pop up on her caller ID, I asked, "What's up Dar?"

"Nothing much," she replied, unsuspecting this was anything other than our normal chit chat call.

Not wanting to dilly dally around, I got straight to the point. "Do you have a minute because I need to talk to you about something?"

"Yeah, what's up?"

Here goes nothing, I thought, "Dar, I started seeing the girl from homecoming named Jordan. I don't really understand how things unfolded this way, but she brought me out of my dark place. I'm not completely convinced that she is right for me, but I have to explore why she was able to bring me out of my depressed state when no one else could."

I paused for her reaction. There was a deafening silence for a minute. Knowing Daria as I do, she was disappointed and trying to pick her words so she wouldn't say something that she'd regret. Daria always believed that people shouldn't say things out of anger that they can't take back. She always looked at the long term rather than getting caught up in the moment.

She broke the silence. "How long has that been going on? Did you get with her at homecoming?"

"Dar, you know I was only with you and the crew at homecoming. Jordan and I started talking shortly after homecoming. We only recently took it to another level. She woke me up and brought me out of my semi-catatonic existence that I lived in way too long after the shooting."

"Max, do you love her?"

"Oh no, not at all. I do enjoy her company and want to see if this is just a phase or something more."

"What phase—like me. Is that what I am to you, a phase? Or am I just the rebound that you fall back on after you learn that none of these women are what they seem?"

I could hear the tension mounting in her voice and dreaded where this was going. "Daria Ross, you aren't my rebound—nor are you a phase. You are still a very special friend to me who has been with me through thick and thin, all of my ups and downs. I value that about you."

"I know this may come across as jealous hating on Jordan, but I am going to say it anyway. Jordan is not good for you. As a woman I know this. There is something wrong with that girl," Daria protested.

Perplexed by her opinion, I asked, "How do you know that when you don't really know her?"

She fired back, "Woman's intuition."

Before I could say something else, Daria asked, "Max, are you ever going to give you and me a shot? We've known each other so long and shared enough moments together that I think we could succeed as a couple where you have struck out so many times with those other bimbos. I have seen them fall by the wayside one by one, but I am still here. Have you ever thought about why that is? How many women are you going to have to go through before you realize "The Dar" is where you need to be!"

"Daria, it is because I have failed so many times with so many different women that I'm not sure what I want. I can't bring you into my madness and do you that way. If we get into a relationship, it will eventually migrate into sex. If we don't work out as a couple, I'll always have that on my mind. It would make things weird between us and it could ruin our friendship. That would be the greatest tragedy. Baby, we may end up together some day, but I have to be right, and at this point in time I am definitely not there. You mean a lot to me and I am not ready to jeopardize that with sex. I may be confused, but some of my boundaries are still intact, and I'm not ready to cross this one."

Daria seemed like she understood and accepted that answer for now. "Okay."

Sensing this had turned into a successful conversation, I asked, "Are we alright? You still my girl?"

With a lighter tone in her voice, she replied, "We are good Max, but you won't find anyone better for you than me. I think in time you will come to realize that all on your own. Our history is too deep. I don't think any of your girl Fridays will be able to compete with that in the long run." She added, "I gotta run, but do me a favor, will you?"

"Sure, what is it?"

"Protect yourself and don't get anyone pregnant."

I laughed at that preposterous thought. "Girl, you are nuts. I am not ready for that. I'm not even thinking that way."

Daria took her parting shot before hanging up. "You're laughing and not thinking along those lines, but it doesn't mean they're not. Bye dude."

With that dangling thought, Daria hung up. That went better than I thought it would. Now that I have successfully arrested one problem, I am left with Jordan, horny Collette, and sweetie pie Kristi. I told myself, *Don't rest Max, you're not out of the woods yet. Now what about Jordan and her lies?*

I wasn't able to sulk too much because I had a crisis to deal with. As I was running around doing errands, I got a call from Dan McCarther, the group president for my part of the company.

"Hello this is Max."

"Hi, Max, this is Dan McCarther. Do you have a minute to talk?" Dan asked ever so calmly.

I was surprised by his call because Dan had never skipped over my boss and called me directly. "Hi Dan, yes I'm free. What can I do for you?"

I wondered if this was going to be a "carrot and stick" conversation. Dan started with the carrot first. "I hear that you are the master of turning around broken businesses. I know that you have worked with our plant in China before. They are having some major problems down there. We are on the cusp of launching a major business campaign and China is the critical path to that effort. I heard you are the miracle worker and that's about what we need down there."

"Do you know what all of the issues are?"

He took a deep breath and admitted, "That is the problem, I don't know, and I don't trust what information I am getting. That's why I want you on the red-eye flight tonight. Everything has been arranged.

This is highly unusual which is why I asked Steve for your cell number to call you directly."

That was the stick. I had to be on a plane that night. Turning around a problem of this magnitude was the thing that huge performance bonuses were made from or careers ended. The fact that a group president was calling me personally meant this project was highly visible.

Sounding like I was fully on board, I responded, "Dan, I will go there and give it everything I've got. I will hit the ground running and immediately assess the problem, root causes, and then map a path to recovery. Will Steve be my lead back here? Will there be others on the team here in the U.S.?"

Bringing it back to normal corporate decorum, he said, "For now, run everything through Steve while we assemble all of the appropriate people. However, I will never be far away from this project. This is the number one priority of this business unit. I appreciate your sacrifice. I have another call I have to take—you take care and have a safe flight. Bye."

All I wanted to do was call Kristi and see her before I had to leave. I hoped she was home. I didn't have long to process things with her before I had to leave.

Kristi answered the phone. "Hi, Max."

"Hi beautiful! Our plant in China is collapsing, and they booked me on the red-eye to China tonight. I was wondering if I could come by and see you for a few minutes."

Sarcastically she replied, "Of all the people in your company, they have to send you like they are sneaking you out of town in the middle of the night? If you have another woman that you want to go see, couldn't you come up with a better excuse than the old China story?" She laughed, "Of course you can come by big head."

When I got there, Kristi was as beautiful as ever in her jeans and high fashion t-shirt. There was truly something special about her. We talked for a while and had some iced tea. An hour flew by before I left. I went home and finished packing. Before I knew it, I was being asked what I wanted to drink before takeoff. For the time being, I was trying not to think about what catastrophe I was flying into. I couldn't help thinking about the mess I left behind. A funny thought surfaced, *I wonder what Gina is doing right now.* Why did I even go there? I had my hands full enough with Daria, Jordan, Kristi, and Collette. What have I done and how do I get out of it? Work in China definitely was the short term answer. My thoughts of home went out with the cabin lights.

Chapter 17

UNCHARTED WATERS

Xao greeted me at the front check-in desk smiling so hospitably, "Welcome back, Mr. Dean. How long will you be staying with us this time?"

Fatigue ridden from the long flight to Shanghai, I exhaled deeply in anticipation of what I knew was to come, "Xao, my friend, this is going to be a long one. I have no idea, but it will be a while."

"Well, I have no doubt that you are the best man for the task. Please allow Xao to upgrade you at no extra cost to the executive suite. Mr. Dean, don't worry about checking in, I'll take care of it for you. Just leave your passport with me and head directly to your suite and get some rest." He motioned for the bellman to get my bags.

I was exhausted. Without my usual time to prepare for the trip, I was just whisked away seemingly in the middle of the night to face a disaster at the plant. Xao is a really great guy who works his hospitality business like a maestro. I know Xao must have looked at my jet-lagged face and said Maxwell Dean is done. Let me get him in bed lying down before he falls down. He wouldn't be wrong because I was beat.

After a good sleep that was not long enough, I arrived at the plant. I didn't waste any time getting brought up to speed on the situation. I met with the plant manager, the head of quality, the production manager, and the materials manager. Somewhere between the last briefing and my arrival I learned the wave soldering machine was down, the air handlers were inadequate for insuring no contamination in the clean rooms, and the inspector lied on his employment application and didn't have the training or education as a quality control inspector. In short, all manufacturing had come to a complete halt. Production was shut down and they had no clear cut plan for recovery. The plant manager was completely over his head. As much as he wanted to fix the problem, it just wasn't within his capability. I rubbed my head in frustration and thought, *This is far worse than we ever imagined.*

It was 10:00 a.m. on Thursday, which made it about 2:00 p.m. on Wednesday back at the office. The time zones always get me confused. I am a day ahead of Florida, which always makes me feel like I am in the future for them because technically today hasn't happened yet in the United States. But, then again, I thought, *I age faster every time I come to China.* I had to get on the phone with the people back at the office and deliver the unsettling news.

"Global Operations, Connie Langford," my assistant answered the phone.

"Hi, Connie, this is Max. Are Dan and Steve around?" I asked getting right to business.

Connie sensed the urgency in my voice and decided to forgo the usual casual pleasantries, "Max, I will see right now, please hold." Connie returned, "Max, they are getting them right now. Dan was in with the CFO, and Steve was on an international call. I heard your tone and told them it was urgent. How bad is it?"

Acknowledging her talent for insight, I replied, "That's why I can't live without the best assistant in the entire western hemisphere—you read me. I don't have to spell everything out; you read, analyze, and act. See, if you weren't married to your Hercules strong husband and didn't have a bus load of kids, I would have married you by now."

"Thank you, but I am way too old for you, but we do make a great team."

"Connie, it's bad. Production is shut down. I probably won't be coming back any time soon. My stress level is already climbing."

Knowing exactly what to do, Connie said, "I will get with corporate security and all the appropriate people to handle all of your affairs back here. I will get your spare house key out of your desk and get going on that. I'll tell Steve I'm handling it. Oh, Max, they just walked in. I'll transfer the call to your desk. Hold on, and take care boss."

"Hi Max, this is Dan and I have Steve here. What's going on? How bad is it?"

Preparing to deliver some horrible news that would surely cost some people their jobs, I got right to the point. "Dan, Steve, it is far worse than we could have imagined. All production, manufacturing, and quality control have stopped."

I heard Steve utter the first words, "My God."

I reported to Steve, but Dan spoke up asking me for a complete briefing as I heard him tell Connie to get the CFO and conference him on this call. After a short pause, the CFO joined the call and I briefed them on all of the problems. After about an hour of going over every gruesome detail, Dan asked, "Max, what do you need?"

I hated what I was going to say because it meant being away from home for a long time. "I am going to have to assume complete operational control of the plant."

Dan replied, "Then, do it right now. Connie will have a memo to that effect there before we get off the phone." Dan paused and then said, "Max, we have a $100 million contract for that product booked, and another $200 million being stoked on the fire that we anticipate getting realized this fiscal year. Consider yourself relocated to China. We will handle all of the paperwork, visas, and securing your home. I know I don't have to tell you how important your success is over there. We will look to move you from the hotel to a home, but that may take some time. In the meantime, you have the green light to do whatever you think is necessary to turn that operation around."

We ended our call and I got to work. I knew that I was going to push, challenge, and become very demanding of everyone in the plant. I knew I would be working over the weekend, but I was still tired from the trip and stressed out to the maximum.

When I got back to the hotel, Xao ventured over to me, "Max, you look like you need a break. Would you like to come with me to visit my brother up in monk country? I think the peace and harmony could do you some good."

Happy to take my mind off the plant for a while, I accepted. "That is so kind of you to offer, I would love to."

Xao smiled, "Very well, go freshen up, pack some things, and we'll leave in an hour."

Xao and I talked during our journey to see his brother, monk Chang Si Wong. I learned some fascinating things about the Chinese people and their culture. I saw so many beautiful temples with gold pointed roofs. The ornately handcrafted buildings were spectacular. Although Chang's village was in a rural area, he was from Bangkok— the "City of Angels." When we arrived at Chang's little village, it was magnificent. Everything looked so simple as if time and progress had skipped right past this place. Xao allowed me to spend a lot of time with Chang. Chang was a delightful humble monk that seemed to have this wonderful spiritual aura about him. I felt completely at ease. We talked a lot. Chang read me down to my soul. It was amazing. Chang sensed my inner troubles. Not the work related ones, but as he put it, "The one life within my inner spirit—my center." The time passed by so quickly. Although Chang didn't give me a lot of answers, he did leave me with a lot to think about.

The weekend was so restful and enjoyable until we entered the lobby of the hotel. I looked across the beautiful marble floor and saw Jordan sitting there waiting. I couldn't help but think, *She is going to ruin the entire chi that I received from my meeting with Chang.* I knew Jordan brought some drama that I didn't feel like dealing with.

I stopped and stared at Jordan as she looked sad and desperate. I walked over to her and said nothing. The disgust on my face spoke volumes enough. I am sure that my hugless silence signaled to Jordan that she was in for a cold reception.

"Max, I know you probably don't want to see me and won't believe a word I have to say, but I couldn't leave things the way they were. I tried to call you, but you wouldn't take my call."

I refused to respond to her comment. I just looked at her as if to say, "So what."

Jordan tried eliciting some sympathy, "I got here yesterday. They told me you were gone for the weekend. I hoped to talk to you Saturday and Sunday then leave on the red-eye Sunday night. Since you are just getting back, I need to stay a day or two longer so that we can talk."

I broke my silence, "I never told you to come here. You should have stayed at home. I know you must have paid a pretty penny for your airfare, but that is not my problem." Raising my voice, I added, "What do you want from me Jordan? Why do I even matter to you? You have Ivan and Kyle. Do you have some sort of sick obsession to have every man that you want? We were already lying to our mates—did you have to lie to me too? Do you ever tell the truth to anyone?"

Jordan looked as if she were going to cry, "I know this place is where you stay for work. I don't want to make a spectacle by crying and begging you to talk to me out here in this public lobby. Can we go to your room and talk there?"

Still cold and unmoved, I asked, "What about your room?"

"I checked out already. I only had it for Saturday and Sunday."

"Okay."

I hated that Jordan had this habit of just flying down here unannounced like she was going from Florida to North Carolina. Because of the 20-plus hour flight from China to the U.S., flights to and from are not that easy. As we rode the elevator up to my room, I thought, *This was probably not a good idea.* I looked at Jordan's body and momentarily got that spark back. Jordan was amazing that way. I thought about where I'd be if it weren't for Jordan. Because of that, I decided to let that count for something and give her some time to talk.

After we entered my room, she tried to lighten up the moment. "They love giving you these big ole luxury suites don't they? Which suite is this one?"

"Executive." Wanting to get back on point, I bluntly asked, "Okay Jordan, we're here. What do you want to discuss?"

"Can I have something to drink first? My mouth is so dry."

"Sure, help yourself. There's water and soda in the refrigerator."

She got herself a ginger ale and sat down on the couch. I was sitting in the gold colored high back chair across from her. I sat there waiting for her to take a drink from her glass of non-alcoholic courage and utter some pathetic excuse or another out and out lie.

216

After Jordan took her drink, she hit the couch. "Why don't you come sit over here?"

"I'll pass."

"Max, I'm sorry that I hurt you. Given what you went through before you met me, the last thing you needed was drama from me. I did lie to you. I had been still holding on to Ivan while I was with you and Kyle. I'm not proud of that, but I had my reasons."

"You had your reasons, what reasons? We already knew that we had someone else in each of our lives. I had Gina and you had Kyle. If you wanted to keep Kyle, then why start something with me?"

Jordan hesitated, trying to catch her emotions. "All of my life I have been objectified by men, sexed, and then they left. Men have always left me. I never want to be alone. Kyle is such a good guy, perhaps too good for someone as damaged as me. Ivan tolerates me but isn't going to be the kind of guy who will settle down with me or anyone else. My relationship with him is one of convenience for both of us."

As Jordan told me about Ivan and her, I thought, *Frightening similarities to me and Daria.* The big difference was—I was not sleeping with Daria. As much as I didn't want to, I could relate to Jordan on the Ivan issue, but I still was not going to tell her that about Daria.

She continued, "Then there is you Max. You have a beautiful spirit, but look at when I met you, at the end of a marriage. That wouldn't inspire a girl to think there is a strong chance for longevity with you. Since we have been kicking it, I have lived in a constant state of fear that you will leave me. So, holding on to Ivan and Kyle keeps me from getting too vested in you, or so I thought. The truth of the matter is, I am already vested in you. I think you and I could work. I know I have made a mess of things, but I don't know how to fix it. I thought you left hating me. Max, please say that you will give us another shot."

Ignoring her last question, I wanted some answers. "How did you know I was here in China and at this hotel?"

"I called your office and they said you were out of the office. I remember all of the issues you had with China, so I figured you were here. Plus, I probed your assistant telling her I was a classmate who was trying to set up a dinner with you while I was in town. She told me that you would be out of the office for a while. I know how much you like this hotel, so I put two and two together and hoped it equaled you being here. Otherwise, I spent $3,000 on a ticket for nothing," recanting her dogged determination.

Admiring her tenacity, I said, "You might be a liar, but no one can call you stupid."

I wanted to believe that her hurt could make her do something stupid and emotionally self preserving. I suppose to some degree I was just like her. After all, I was not telling her about Kristi, Collette, and very little about Daria. There was one big distinction, I am not having sex with either of them, and I am not promised to anyone for marriage. In my mind that distinction kept me separate and apart from Jordan. Somewhere in the deep recesses of my mind, I knew there was a smidgen of moral superiority floating around back there.

Looking directly into her eyes, I raised my voice. "I don't trust you. I just don't know about you. The way you go about things I might have a guy gunning for me that I won't even know about because of your lies and deceptions. With you there isn't even any honor among thieves, sorta speaking."

Walking across the room to sit in the second high back chair next to me, she said, "I would never jeopardize you like that. I know what you've been through. That thought is unconscionable to me."

I quickly snapped back, "That's the problem with your lies. You may unknowingly compromise me. Men will kill another man if his pride is wounded enough by some other man bedding down with his woman. That is a dangerous game."

Jordan conceded, "I get it now. This will never happen again."

After discussing things back and forth for over two hours, I was tired and needed to get to bed. I already knew that Jordan would be spending the night in my room. As good as Jordan looked, I wasn't going to sleep with her. She took a shower and came out in something skimpy. Her body was simply a thing of beauty.

"Jordan what time does your flight leave tomorrow," I asked, wanting her to leave while I still had the strength to resist her.

"I catch the red-eye tomorrow."

As I started closing the door to my bedroom, I offered, "The sofa pulls out into a bed where you can sleep. Goodnight."

I heard Jordan mutter, "You have got to be kidding me. A 20-hour flight and I get the rollout sofa?"

The night went off pretty much without a hitch except for the one time Jordan tried to sneak into my room later that night, only to find the door locked. The next morning she asked me why I locked the door. I was kind of feeling for Jordan, but I kept it tight and didn't let her know it. Finally, I took her to her flight.

Three months had gone by and I was finally seeing some signs of hope for the plant. My stress was still as high as ever. I had regular briefings with the executives back in the U.S. We produced our first part since the manufacturing shut down. It seemed like our greatest waste of valuable time was getting new manufacturing machines cleared past customs. Our new air handling machines were quarantined in Chinese customs for six weeks. The week after we went back on line was Kristi's birthday. We talked a few times, but the time difference killed us. I managed to cook up a little surprise for her birthday that took some real ingenuity.

As I stood there impatiently like an expecting father waiting for news about the delivery of his child, I had no idea how this would turn out since I hadn't spoken to Kristi since I started planning my sneak attack. After clearing security, Kristi came out the doors towards me. She didn't immediately see me. When she did, her eyes lit up and a big smile spread across her face. That smile let me know all was good. I moved towards her still smiling myself, hugged her and then pulled back, "Welcome to Shanghai, China."

Kristi kissed me on the cheek. "Max, boy, I don't know what to say about you."

"Well, you start by saying hello."

We talked some small talk when we picked up her bags. She kept asking me how I pulled this off and kept it a surprise from her until the last minute. I told her don't be mad at her, but her friend Carmen was complicit in my caper.

As we got into the taxi, Kristi gently elbowed me in the side. "What is this all about? I want details. I know this must have cost you a fortune since I haven't paid a dime for anything, and I flew in first class."

I cryptically responded, "All in due time."

When we arrived at the hotel, she exited the cab and stood outside looking at the hotel and everything around it. "This is simply beautiful."

She loved the lobby of the hotel. Xao came over and introduced himself. Without waiting for her response, Xao said, "Ms. Wade we have your room and everything ready. The bellman will take the bags to your room."

Looking at Xao hesitantly, she said, "Thank you. How did you know my name since Max did not introduce us yet?"

Xao smiled, "Max is a very special guest of ours, and you are a special guest of his. Of course I would know who you are."

"Max, what you are trying to do?"

I looked at her intensely peering into her beautiful eyes, "Happy Birthday. Kristi, I got you your own hotel room because I have no expectations. I am hoping that you enjoy your birthday with me. Also, I would greatly appreciate if you would allow me to show you the China that I have gotten to know,"

As she smiled tears came to her eyes, "You are so awesome!"

"Go freshen up. Everything has been arranged, and you are on vacation for the week. It has been cleared by your boss— thanks to the assistance of Carmen."

For days we had dinner, went sightseeing, and took in some Chinese cultural events. I enjoyed her so much. I realized that she was more fun than I had ever thought. The time came and went so fast. The weekend before she was to leave, I took her to meet Chang. She loved that experience. She spent some time talking to Chang alone. I'm sure it was as much of a treat for her as it has always been for me.

When we got back to Shanghai, we had dinner in my suite. It was such a special moment. She became really quiet and introspective. She looked at me as if she were trying to figure me out, while at the same time she was contemplating on what she wanted to say to me. I went with the silence and didn't disturb her.

Moments later she broke the silence, "Max, I could fall for you. If I kiss you as I want to do right now, I might not be able to control my instincts on being a woman with needs."

I didn't know what to say as she moved closer towards me, positioning herself to kiss me. I moved back and said, "No, not now, and not at the price of your promise to God. I have done a lot of things in my life that I not proud of, but this will not be one of them."

I reached out and grabbed her hand and held it, while I took my other hand and gently caressed the side of her face. As I rubbed her cheek, touched her ear, and her faint side burns, Kristi turned into my touch. In this tender moment I looked into her angelic eyes, "I want to take it slow."

As I lightly squeezed her hand so she could feel my passion, she smiled approvingly, "I can do slow Max. I can definitely do slow."

In that moment I think I garnered her respect. I don't think she knew what to do with what I just said. I think it surprised her. I know it certainly surprised me. I wanted her, but yet I didn't want to do anything but get to know her. We talked some more and sat up looking out of my window at the Shanghai skyline at night. Our last night together was beautiful. I found a tender spirit in Kristi. My heart wouldn't let me take her where I had taken so many other women before.

The next morning the time was at hand for her to leave. I had a great time with her. She was such a trooper by not complaining about my leaving her during the week to work. When we arrived at the airport, I had to let her go. She hugged me tightly, and then gave me a quick peck on the lips. "Max thanks for everything. Most of all, thanks for being a gentleman and not taking advantage of my temporary weakness. I need to thank your mom for teaching you how to respect a woman."

With that Kristi's visit came to a conclusion. I enjoyed her and wouldn't mind her coming back. On the drive back I contemplated just how different she was from Jordan. I thought about Jordan too, and the things she said to me during her impromptu visit.

Monday rolled around and I was back to the grindstone. We were slowly gaining ground on restoring full operations. We were in no way out of the woods yet. Another month went by and we were up to 40 percent production capacity. The executives were ecstatic. I had been putting in 16 to 18 hour days. I had been in China for five months now and was beginning to see light at the end of this nightmare.

Friday was here again. I thought about going back to see my friend the monk as I had been doing more frequently. I loved my time with Chang. As I entered the lobby of the hotel, I saw Jordan… again. This time I went over to her and admonished her for just showing up without giving me prior notice.

Despite everything I said, I was happy to see her for some reason. We went up to my room, I freshened up for dinner. After dinner we went for a walk around People's Square when I turned to Jordan, "This is the last time that you will be able to drop in on me like this because they are moving me to a house. I am not going to tell you where that is. For one, I have no idea where it is, and two, we need some boundaries." She looked at me vulnerably and said, "Okay, but when you get your house, please let me know where you are just in case something happens to you."

"We'll see. When do you have to go back?"

"Sunday. This is a quick turnaround trip."

We made it back to my room and talked for a while. I was feeling that I was experiencing a more truthful Jordan. I was enjoying this alter ego. We both took separate showers and met in the living room. We watched a little TV—the international news was all that we could understand. With both of us a little tired, I announced I was going to sleep.

Jordan wasn't sure what to do. "Are you locking the bedroom door again?"

I knew I should have, but regrettably, "No."

"Is that an open invitation?"

"No, it's me too tired to mount a defense to keep you out."

It wasn't long before my five month hiatus in China ended when something romantic took over with Jordan's ever increasing strategic nudges. Just before we crossed that line, I thought about Kristi, and then just like that it was gone. Just as she did when we first met, Jordan managed to transport me from intimate exile to bliss. We comforted each other to a point of euphoria. Exhausted by our energy draining reunion, we just lay there talking like the old Max and Jordan.

Jordan smiled, "The Maximizer is back."

Those words should have been complimentary and enjoyable. Instead they chiseled some doubt into my heart. That doubt was now traversing towards regret. I can't really explain it, but in an instant the entire event went sour. I mean I actually had a sour taste in my mouth like poison. I felt like I was getting physically sick. I wondered where this feeling came from and started thinking it was something I ate.

Jordan rubbed my forearm. "I have something to tell you that is 100 percent the truth."

I wondered what it was this time. Maybe she was going to tell me that she decided to marry Kyle, or that she wasn't going to see Ivan any more. I even had a brief thought that maybe she was going to say that she was getting counseling. None of those proved remotely the case when Jordan hugged me and whispered in my ear, "Max, I want to marry you. Will you marry me?"

I was floored. I didn't see that one coming. What do I do with that question? I stalled, "Aren't I supposed to be the one who says that?"

Jordan quickly countered, "Is that what you want to do? You know that I'm not a traditional girl. It doesn't bother me to ask you. I am ready to give up everything for you. I know that we just got back together and I caught you totally off guard, so if you can't answer me right now, that's fine. At least you know where I am coming from. I am staking my claim."

I thought, *Dear God, what have I done? I am going straight to hell, do not pass go or collect anything.*

Not wanting to do this wrong, I said, "Jordan, it is way too soon for that. We did just get back together. The thread of trust that you broke isn't so easily repaired. I cannot go there right now. Plus, I have no idea how much longer I am going to be here in China. I may end up living here."

Not deterred one iota, she replied, "If you want to marry me, I will follow you whereever you go. Just think about it. I am planting my flag here."

My emotions went running wild. I felt so guilty. I thought about Kristi. I thought about what kind of future I would have with a woman like Jordan. Now I wanted Jordan's trip to end sooner than later. We talked for a few more minutes before a long work week and jet lag got the better of us.

Time seemed to move so slowly towards Jordan's departure. As soon as I got back to the hotel from the airport, I called Marcus. I needed some reinforcements for what just happened. Darkness fell over my spirit like I was going into a hole. I actually felt guilty about what I did to Kristi.

I don't know why I was so frantic to talk to him. "Marcus, I need help man. I just messed up real bad. I am in a hole." I said, so fast I know he must have thought I'd been kidnapped or something.

"Slow down, what's wrong? I almost didn't pick up because I don't know this number. What happened? Are you alright?"

I wasn't thinking about our normal playful nature. I just got into it saying, "I brought Kristi over here to China for a week and it was great. Jordan just showed up here twice. The first time we didn't do anything. The second time we did and she asked me to marry her. I feel so guilty because Kristi is so nice and I really like her. I haven't even kissed Kristi, but I feel as though I should tell her about what happened with me and Jordan. Man, I hate what I did with Jordan. I am sick about it. I feel like I'm having a heart attack," I said in rapid fire again like I spit it all out without breathing in between sentences.

Marcus replied ever so calmly, "Max, you have got to calm down. It will be okay. First of all don't do anything. Don't call Kristi and tell her anything. Are you interested in marrying Jordan?"

"No!"

"Then you need to tell Jordan that flat out. And you need to put more distance between you and her. Do you really like Kristi? I've never heard you speak or act like this about anyone."

Still acting hyper-frantic, I said, "I don't know anything other than my conscience is devouring me right now. I feel the need to tell Kristi what I did. What have I done, Marcus?"

Marcus had an uncharacteristic seriousness in his voice. "It will be alright. Just don't tell Kristi. That is the wrong thing to do right now. You are scaring me dude with how you are acting over this. I've never seen you like this. Are you alright? You're not about to jump out of the window are you? I'm serious, Max."

"No, I am not suicidal, just mad at myself and confused about what to do. Alright Marcus, thanks bruh, but I am gonna get off the phone and work through this, later."

"It will be fine. Call me if you need me, later."

I took Marcus' advice and didn't do anything, at least not talking to any of the women. I went to see Chang. As usual he had some words for me that weren't really answers to my questions. They were words that cut to the heart of my spirit. I returned from Chang's village knowing there was a call that I needed to make. I still had a feeling that I had toxins in my body.

I reached Kristi. She sounded so happy to hear from me. My heart sank. I felt like a low life scoundrel. I was about to break this beautiful person's heart.

Sensing something was wrong by my less than happy tone, she asked, "What's wrong? Are you okay?"

I hesitated and paused before spilling my guts like I was in a catholic confessional.

"Kristi, there is no easy way to say this, so I will just come right out with it. Jordan flew here twice without me knowing it. The first time she spent the night and caught her flight back home. She wanted to get back together with me and I said no. On her second surprise trip a month after you were here, I got with her. I feel terrible. I saw Chang afterwards. I broke your trust and I feel terrible about it, but I can't keep it from you or lie to you about it."

Kristi said nothing. I heard her crying. The sound of her crying gutted me. I heard the anguish in her crying and felt her pain. It hurt me. I felt like I took a pure person and defiled her. I looked at the ceiling in my hotel room and said to myself, *Lord forgive me for destroying your angel.*

I wiped my face, trying to rid myself of the pain I was feeling. Never before had I ever felt this bad for hurting a woman. On the other hand, I'd never been this honest or guilt ridden either.

Ending her teary silence, she asked, "Are you in love with Jordan?"

"Not in the least bit."

Kristi stopped crying and then calm and dignified, she asked, "Then why did you do it, Max? I thought you wanted to explore a relationship with me. After we had such a beautiful week in China, why did you do this to me?"

I struggled to make sense of what I did too. "I have no answers, but I can tell you that I am torn up in my soul over my selfish and dishonest behavior. Right after it happened I became physically sick and spiritually wrecked. I wanted her out immediately."

She calmed a little. "Is this the best you can do? Is this the kind of man that you really are? Were you just lying to me and presenting yourself as a sheep in wolves' clothing? Did you get my boss and my friends involved in helping you orchestrate my trip to China only to humiliate me in front of them? Who does that? Just who are you Maxwell Dean? Who are you really? I am not that kind of woman. I don't deny my God and I don't share my man. You have really hurt me. I'm glad that you were at least man enough to be honest and tell me before I invested anymore emotional capital in you."

I really had no answers, at least none that would soothe the wounds I had just inflicted. All I could do was tell her what was in my heart. "I am not that guy. I am so much better than what my recent behavior dictates. You brought something better out in me, and as soon as it began with Jordan, I knew I had made a grave mistake. I called Marcus panicking and seeking his advice. I called on the Lord and asked him to forgive me for hurting you, one of His angels. What I did tasted real bad to me in every way imaginable."

I heard her voice perk up a little, "You actually prayed to God about what you did? You asked for His forgiveness?"

"Kristi, my heart was destroyed by what I did. I felt like I actually offended God. My prayer felt like it came from every limb in my body. I almost felt out of breath when I finished."

I took it further. "Can you ever forgive me?"

"You have already been forgiven by the one who counts most. I serve Him and don't go against what He does. Of course I forgive you, but as for you and me, that's another story altogether."

She stopped crying, "Max, don't confuse my faith with my heart. I need time to sort things out. How much longer are you going to be in China?"

"I don't know, perhaps another six to eight months. Why?"

"That is about how much time I will need. Your indiscretion will take time, prayer, and meditation. For now, you and I are nowhere. I know I appear calm because I am not one of those women who get angry, curse you out, and want to hurt you. That is not me. I am hurt and very disappointed in you, Maxwell."

Knowing that still waters run deep, as I am sure does her pain, I humbly spoke, "I understand. I am very sorry."

I heard Kristi starting to cry again, "Max, I have to go. You take care of yourself. Good-bye."

"Okay, bye." I hung up the phone feeling like I hung up on the best thing in my life. I crashed and burned with her. I was going to need some more serious conversations with the monk.

Seven more months passed by. The plant was finally 100 percent operational and I was heading back to Florida. I hadn't been home in over a year. I was ready. As the plane lifted off the runway heading westward, I said farewell to Shanghai for now. I nestled into my first class seat and went to sleep for the journey home.

Chapter 18

GOLDEN ANGEL

I was meeting my best friends in the hotel lounge for drinks. I told them that I was buying the drinks tonight. However, I had an ulterior motive for gathering them together. I invited Jordan too, but I wasn't sure she'd show up. Now let's see, that's Pike, Sarae, Jordan, Daria, Mason, Marcus, and Mel. I think that's it. Seven people plus me, that's eight. *Drinks could get rather expensive,* I told myself. Oh well, I don't care, it's worth it.

I had the service manager, Bill Wilks, reserve us a section in the lounge. They had a private party section which was nicer than the open bar area. It had a couple of burgundy leather sofas and some of those big matching leather chairs. The walls were painted pine green with walnut wood panels on the sides and ceiling. With the dark burgundy carpet, the private area looked down right stately. The few circular tables and leather chairs looked like they could have been used for private high stake poker games. Yes, this room was going to do quite nicely.

I told Mr. Wilks this gathering is very important to me and I wanted to make sure that everything was perfect. Bill was more than willing when I told him I'd give his bar staff a 50 percent tip above the bill just for accommodating my group. Having it all together was necessary for what I planned.

Mel was the first person I saw walking up. She had on her jeans and a university t-shirt. She was casually dressed, relaxed, and ready for our little private party. Mel showed up early to get her drink on. She was a girl who could drink most men under the table and was really funny when she got drunk. Some people who can't handle their liquor get violent or worse, stupid. Mel, on the other hand, would have you busting a rib in laughter.

We greeted each other with a casual hug. "Max, are you sure you want to pick up the bar bill?"

"Yeah, Mel, I'm sure. You're my girl so do your thing and don't worry about nothing."

She looked at me widening her eyes, "Boy, they must be paying yo ass some long paper if you can work it like that."

Downplaying my income blessing, I said, "Not really. I just robbed my piggy bank."

Mel fired back as though I had billionaire money, "You mean your paycheck broke the bank, Big Willey."

"Mel, actually I am ready for you to do your drinking comedy show. You know how you get when you get liquored up."

"You know you're wrong for that. You better have my back if I do get twisted in here and not leave my ass laying on the floor drunk and drooling and shit," Mel wisecracked.

"You know I got you. Don't I always?"

"Yeah you do, that's why you are my boy." I think Mel was referring to when I came to her defense with Rodney. I certainly meant it that way. Mel and I exchanged memories, stories, and current events while we waited on the others to join us. I loved Mel. Despite her often dirty mouth, she was real. There was nothing fake about her. She often wore this hard defiant exterior, but inside Mel was this sweet, vulnerable, and a tender-hearted girl. Few people could see the Mel I saw.

Marcus came through the door excited, saying, loudly, "Max, boy I'm gonna put a serious dent in your wallet tonight."

"You see that Mel? Here comes that fool."

"Don't trip. You know that's your boy. Marcus is the boy version of me. That's why you love him too," she said, defending Marcus.

"Yeah, between the both of you, I should either be in detox, nuts, or both."

"There you go hatin' again. Go show your boy some love. You know you want to," Mel countered, pushing me towards Marcus.

"You just think you know me."

Blowing me a kiss as she motioned me towards Marcus' crazy butt, "I do. That's why you love me, baby."

"As always, crazy girl."

"Ain't this a fine picture? Max and Mel in full effect," Marcus said as he pointed to Mel.

"Marcus, if I didn't know any better I would say you're jealous," I said shaking Marcus' hand and giving him our sportsman hug.

"Of what?"

"Whatever flyboy. Now I have both Bonnie and Clyde here."

"Marcus, why don't we just kick his ass now?" Mel fired.

"Mel, when are you going to get anger management counseling?" Marcus said to her with an affectionate smile.

Mel retorted equally playful, "When you gonna stop hat'in on me cause you can't have any of my goodness?"

I interjected, "I thought this was my event, you two?"

"Mel, should we let Max in the party?"

Smiling from ear to ear, Mel said, "I guess so, if he's nice."

"Thank you very much."

"Okay, Max, what's this all about?" Marcus seriously asked.

"In due time, buddy. When everyone gets here," I replied.

Impatiently accepting my surprise Marcus said, "You are so cloak and dagger."

I was pretty tight with all of my good friends, but I was closest with Mel and Marcus. We sat in the bar just laughing and cutting up while we waited on everyone else. We had so much fun that I'm sure they forgot there was a reason for our gathering. They had no idea what was coming. They couldn't have guessed it even if they tried.

I wondered how they would react. I must admit I was a little nervous myself. Not for what I had to tell them, but because I had never done it before. There was no turning back. I had to do it. I tried to anticipate how people were going to react once they found out. I had to put that thought out of my mind and just enjoy my friends.

The rest of the gang started arriving. I invited both Jordan and Daria. I could only imagine what kind of drama that was going to bring. I wondered again, *What in the world was I doing?* I kept convincing myself that I needed everyone here.

"If it isn't Pike and Sarae with Mason in close tow behind," I said, smiling as they came into the room.

Sarae came over and gave me a hug. Pike and Mason gave me the normal testosterone filled dude handshake proceeded by a one arm hug.

I playfully questioned Sarae, "When are you going to leave that unappreciative bum you're married to?"

"And be with who? You, Max?" she shot back.

"What's wrong with me?" I asked, widening my eyes.

"Do you really want me to answer that?" Sarae responded twisting her lips.

Pike started laughing. "Don't look at me. You opened that door playa."

"Yeah Sarae, tell me," I replied as though I would be surprised by her answer.

"Okay, Mr. Dean. I can tell you in one word," she boastfully claimed.

"What word?"

Mel jumped in, "Read him girl!"

Marcus added his peanut gallery input, "Damn, Max is about to get blasted."

Pike looked at me like, I told you so. "Don't look at me. You started this. You know my wife loves you, but you asked for this thumping."

"Alright Sarae, give me the one word," I pleaded.

"Ok, you asked. Freeway."

I heard the oohs and ahs from Marcus, Mason, Mel, and Pike. It seemed like everyone else in the bar knew what she was saying. Even I had to laugh at that one. She got me. I didn't expect her to hit me with it though. Sarae knew about most of my escapades. It wasn't because I told her. Pike couldn't hold water. That's why Pike couldn't ever cheat on Sarae. He'd tell on himself before he would even realize he was doing it.

"Sarae, you know you are wrong for that." I fired back laughing.

"Max, even if you weren't like the brother that I dearly love, and if I weren't married to your best friend, I would still be too boring for you," Sarae protested.

"Too boring?" I asked.

"Yeah, like Gina, Daria, and Jordan. You know I don't get down like that. I don't know any one woman will ever work for you. What's gonna work for you? What are you searching for?" Sarae said, hitting me again.

Sarae was dead on even if she didn't know it. I had been searching. No one ever really did it for me. I had been at it for so long I wasn't even sure I would know the right woman when I found her. I knew this was what Sarae meant and what everyone else thought. Sarae used to say I was a great catch who couldn't be caught.

"Max, she is putting you on blast. I told you don't go there." Pike came back with his second I told you so.

"Pike, get your wife," I said pushing Pike in Sarae's direction.

Pike smartly said, "Dude, I'm not in this. I have to go home with her."

"Max, look at what you did. You talked up your harem. Here comes Jordan and Daria. Somebody's gonna whip your tail tonight if you're not careful," Sarae exclaimed with part love and part woman power.

Mel protectively pronounced, "Sarae, they know the game and the rules of the game. Ain't neither one of them gonna get sideways with Max cause I will regulate up in this bitch."

"Mel, I would be right there with you, girl. You know I love Max too." Sarae added.

I wasn't quite sure if I had lost my mind by inviting both Daria and Jordan to my gathering. Daria knew that I had been with Jordan, but Jordan didn't know that I had still been periodically talking to Daria. Surely it was going to slip out somewhere. I wouldn't have done this any other time, but my reason for doing it was greater than my fear of being exposed. This night could get ugly. My entire reason for this could backfire, but I had to take that chance. Daria has loved me like no one else could. She shelved her pride and celebrated with me and Jordan. Thinking that I might be intimate with Jordan had to be eating her up. *How did they end up coming through the door together?*

Sarae stopped her gang-banging diatribe to ask what was probably on everyone's mind, "Max, where have you been? We've not seen you all year. Are you funding this celebration because you got promoted to president or something?"

Daria and Jordan heard the question as they walked up. People were looking at me like it was the old *EF Hutton* commercial, where everyone stops in their tracks. They froze waiting for my answer. Jordan and Daria wanted to know the answer to that question. They hadn't seen much of me either.

"Yeah, Max, where have you been?" Jordan asked as if she was trying to determine if there was someone new.

I could see a sigh of relief come over Daria's face. I'm sure she thought I was with Jordan. Knowing I wasn't with Jordan was probably the thing that kept her emotions in check while she shared the stage with Jordan tonight. I could only imagine the emotional explosion that was coming later.

"I spent most of last year out of the country."

That was both the truth and part lie. It was not untruthful. It just wasn't the entire story. I guess you could call it a lie by omission. I wasn't about to get into all of those details tonight. Besides, as much as I traveled, it was believable.

Marcus chimed in, "I hardly saw my boy either. I thought someone kidnapped him."

Given how close Marcus and I were, if he hadn't seen me then they knew I must have been busy. Marcus had come in right on queue as if we had rehearsed it.

Mason chimed in as if he was the man in the know, "I knew where he was because all I had to do was have my boys at the U.S. Department of State run his passport history."

"Well why didn't you say something to someone?" Mel asked sternly.

Mason asserted, "Two reasons. First, what I did could have got me fired. Two, if he wanted anyone to know, Max would have told them."

Jordan and Daria sat quietly as if they were trying not to be exposed. That didn't make any sense because everyone knew the deal with me and them. I was happy with their silence. The fewer questions I got the better. I didn't want them to see a lie on my face. Given how close we were, Daria would have been the one to see it.

Marcus flexed, "Mel, we fellas have a code. Mason was honoring the code."

Mel screamed out with a firm emotionally crackling voice, "Code my ass! The last time you two fell off the grid we got a call that you two had been shot and Max almost died. So I don't want to hear nothing about some bullshit code."

Sarae affirmed, "I'm with her on that one."

"Point taken. Now can we talk about something happier?" I said, trying to change the subject.

There was a brief but serious moment of silence. I think we all reflected back to that day. I didn't know Jordan when that happened. She wore an expression that said "left out." Jordan was excluded from our bond about that event. I think she knew better than to cross that line by letting anyone know that she even existed at that moment. My wounds healed, but they didn't know the event still wasn't over. I kissed Mel and Sarae on the cheek and apologized. Then I pinched Mel on the butt which made everyone laugh.

Marcus asked breaking into a momentary somber mood, "Mel, do you ever complete a sentence without profanity?"

"Kiss my ass, Marcus. How bout that sentence?" Mel fired back.

We laughed hard because that was vintage Mel. You had to just love her. Sometimes she and Marcus went at it like Martin and Pam from the *Martin Lawrence Show*. We all knew they loved each other. We cried when Rodney assaulted her. She cried when Marcus and I were shot.

We continued talking, laughing, and joking for hours. The night went on without any incident between Daria and Jordan until...We all hung out like we were all just friends. I wasn't sure how that would go with both Jordan and Daria sharing me at the same time. That was a first. A couple of times I could see the hurt on Daria's face when

Jordan was speaking to me. Jordan had a sense of arrogance that said, "I'm gonna be in your bed tonight after we leave here."

I thought things were going fine until Sarae said with an "I told you so" tone, "Max, trouble is brewing on the horizon."

"What are you talking about, Sarae?"

I was so caught up in our conversation that I hadn't noticed anything. I was thinking what could it be now?

Pointing in the direction of the restroom Sarae informed me, "Jordan headed to the ladies room and Daria was in tow right behind her."

"So, what's wrong with that?" I asked.

Sarae fired back in disgust with my naïveté. "You men are so blind and stupid."

Getting agitated with her elusive response, I asked, "Woman, what are you talking about?"

Intensity building in her voice Sarae said, "Max, Daria has been cringing every time Jordan opened her mouth. Even Stevie Wonder could see the tension building. But, oh no, not Max, you think your program is so tight. Well, your shit stinks and it may erupt in the ladies room."

"Cat fight, cat fight!" Marcus retorted with sarcastic laughter.

This was the last thing I needed. I walked out of our private area after Daria and Jordan. As I entered the other room, I saw Daria and Jordan standing by the bar face to face. They weren't fighting, but it didn't look good.

"Don't try to be all up in here like you got it like that. You're nothing but the flavor of the month," Daria told Jordan condescendingly.

"Is that so? What flavor are you, has been or rocky road?" Jordan fired back with her oratory talons fully extended. Jordan's form fitting clothes were accentuating her point that she was the queen bee now.

"Look, chick, I've known Max for years. Our relationship is long and deep. It transcends a flavor of the month. I've seen many stank ho's push up on Max and fall by the wayside. And I'll watch you fall in line too," Daria said as though she had not only claws but a bite too.

"Who you calling a stank ho?" Jordan stared her down.

I walked up just in time. Sarae might have been right. Given the short but heated verbal exchange I just heard, I'm certain a brawl was brewing. These two were going for broke with their barrage of verbal insults. Daria was protecting her home court advantage. Jordan was trying to assert her new "lioness of the den" title.

"I know you two aren't about to act up in here like that. Come on, ya'll know I'm not about to let you all act like two alley cats fighting in here like hood rats."

"Max, your girl ran up on me. I was on my way to the ladies room," Jordan heatedly defended herself.

"Girlfriend, you needed to be checked. You're trying to come across like you're all that and you just got on the scene. Some of us have been down long before you came about. I'm not going to let you disrespect that," Daria replied, not only defending her place.

"Check this out. This is my celebration and I invited everyone here. If you all don't like each other, fine don't talk to each other then, but don't ruin my celebration. I love both of you as well I love all of the other people here. If you are not down with that, then leave. Have some respect for yourself and me."

They both looked as though they were waiting for me to leave so somebody could get scratched. But they both saw that I meant business and they were wrong for spoiling my celebration. If they were acting like this now, I could only imagine what was in store when I unveiled my true purpose for bringing everyone together.

"Daria, let's allow Jordan to go to the ladies room and we will rejoin the party. Shall we?" I sarcastically chided.

"Sorry, Max." Daria said.

"Jordan, I'll see you back in the room when you return from the ladies room."

"My bad baby," Jordan said as though she was getting in her last jab at Daria.

Man, women are worse than dudes. We would just fight or not fight. We certainly wouldn't come back to the same party. In fact we wouldn't even come if we knew the other guy was going to be there.

Men just aren't built like that. Thank God they are women with some class, despite how classless they just acted.

As Daria and I entered the room, Mel blurted out, "Daria, did you cut that heifer?"

I replied to Mel before she got Daria hot again, "Don't start Mel. Leave it alone."

Sarae chimed in, "Boy, Max yo stuff is raggedy."

"Thanks Sarae. Moving right along." As I tried desperately to change the subject.

Marcus was across the room shaking his head and laughing. He gave me the thumbs up.

Mason said right on cue, "How bout d'em Bears?"

We all laughed. With that comment the ice was broken and we were on our way back to enjoying the evening. The true test was going to come when Jordan came back from the ladies room.

I ordered appetizers and drinks to keep everyone enjoying the moment. The hot wings were great. I bought enough of them that I could have gotten a flock of chickens for less money. I was only drinking cranberry juice spritzers. Jordan came back without incident. It was as though she and Daria's altercation never happened. I wasn't stupid. It was still there. They just kept it inside. That's fine with me. Whatever works!

The bartender informed, "Mr. Dean, we are doing last call in about 15 minutes." Where had the time gone? It was going on 1:00 a.m. in the morning. I still had to do something for tomorrow. I was second guessing how I was going to do it. Was I going to slip things under their hotel room doors? *I better just do it now,* I told myself. This is why you brought everyone to this get together tonight.

"They are about to do last call. Does anyone want anything else?" I asked everyone.

"Yeah, how about some more of those wings," Mason requested.

"How about another order of wings for everyone and another of what each person was drinking?" I asked the bartender.

"No problem, Mr. Dean."

I spoke up, "While we are waiting on the wings and drinks, I'm inviting all of you to Sunday brunch tomorrow—my treat."

"Max, how much money are they paying you now?" Pike asked.

With a cloak and dagger smirk, I answered, "Enough ma brotha."

Everyone said they would attend brunch tomorrow. I could see questions on their faces as they wondered why I was being so generous. Every time someone tried to box me in about our side reunion, I was elusive.

"Please be down in the lobby at 9 a.m. tomorrow. I bought each one of you a gold angel that I want you to wear tomorrow. They are custom made of 18K gold. It is very important for you to wear this over your heart tomorrow. Please dress in your Sunday best. We are going to a very special place."

Marcus asked, "Max, what is this all about, and why all the secrecy?"

"It's just my treat and my surprise." I responded still eluding my covert purpose.

Guessing as though she knew, Daria asked, "Why don't you just tell us they offered you the president position?"

Ignoring Daria's guess, I continued, "I spent a lot of money getting these angels handmade from gold in Bangkok last year. Each one has your initials engraved on the back."

"Boy your money is deep," Mel said smiling while looking at her engraved angel.

As I handed angels to Daria and Jordan, I'm sure everyone wondered what in the hell I was doing and how Daria and Jordan would react. I know the women were wondering why I would give them the same gift if I was going to marry the other one. We finished our drinks and got ready to leave. I paid the $1,793 bill and left the $900 tip as I promised.

I saw Jordan looking at me out of the corner of my eye. I knew she was making contact to suggest hooking up for the night. I wouldn't look directly at her. I knew Daria was staring at Jordan to see if she was going to try to get with me. I told everyone I had to talk with the manager and for them not to be late in the morning. As I parted with Mr. Wilks, I reminded everyone to wear their angel pin. I was not going to be with Daria or Jordan tonight. I gave Mr. Wilks the tip and decided to make it an even $1,000 to distribute among his bar staff.

The night had been long and enjoyable. Tomorrow's brunch would be an even longer day. I was exhausted. I prayed to the Lord to give me strength. As I opened my room's door, I heard the door open from the room next to mine.

I heard the voice ask, "You had an enjoyable evening?"

Exhausted, I replied, "Yes, very nice."

"I take it mission accomplished then," the voice responded.

"I guess so," I answered.

"Good night."

"Good night." I responded back happy that exchange of words ended so I could get into my bed and pass out. Tomorrow was a whole other day. It would be the curtain call for what everyone wanted to know.

Chapter 19

SUNDAY BRUNCH

I was as nervous as a little boy stealing his first candy bar. The door was in sight. The only question was if I could get away with it. The day was here. I had a terrible case of the jitters. No matter how anxious I was, I had to go through with it.

"Mr. Dean, we are all ready for you," the front desk supervisor said as if he was bringing me into the manager's office.

"Ok, thank you so much for allowing me to do this," I said, extending my hand in gratitude.

"Our General Manager told me a little about what you were doing. I think it's great. Behind this glass you can see them, but they can't see you," the supervisor assured me.

"The only problem I see is if they start to stray. It's not like I can go out there and direct anyone," I said like a worrying parent getting his kids off to a prom.

"Mr. Dean, I'll have our concierge standing by ready to redirect anyone who looks lost."

I looked at the supervisor's name tag—Nick Price. He looked just like a Nick Price. A very neatly groomed white guy who seemed like he had been preppy his entire life. He had the personality and demeanor of a service industry professional. I was glad to have Nick helping me pull this off. Nick seemed like a very nice guy who was as interested in the event going off without a glitch as much as I was.

"Thanks, so much Nick. All of my friends can be easily identified—they'll be wearing an engraved golden angel on the left side over their heart."

Nick got swept up by my stage play surprise. "Wow, that's great! What a classy touch for Sunday brunch."

It was almost 9:00 a.m.—just about showtime. Pike and Sarae should be coming down first because they are always punctual. My heartbeat quickened. I kept reminding myself why I was doing this. Months of planning were about to unfold. I had everything choreographed to a tee. My hands were shaking as Nick talked to me. I looked for the first people to make their way down to the lobby. I didn't hear a thing Nick was saying. I just heard this dull rumbling sound coming from his direction.

Those five minutes took what seemed like an hour to pass. Then I saw them. Pike and Sarae entered the lobby right on time. If this one went well then I could relax. *Oh good, both were wearing their angel pins,* I thought.

I was going to identify my friends by name to Nick. He would convey their names to his concierge by radio. The concierge had one of those earpieces like the secret service. He told the limo driver who would in turn direct them to his limo by name. No one had any idea this was coming. Seeing their faces was priceless.

My voice crackled, "Nick, that's Pike and Sarae Mitchell."

Nick spoke into his radio, "Pete, see the couple walking towards you? The woman in the olive dress and the man in the tan suit are Mr. and Mrs. Mitchell."

The concierge walked up to the first driver and whispered the name to him. I couldn't believe this was happening. There was no turning back now. A few hours from now this will be all over or all hell will break loose. *God, give me strength.*

"Mr. and Mrs. Mitchell, I'm Harold. Mr. Dean hired me to be your driver to brunch today. My car is right outside if you follow me."

Pike asked Harold as if he wasn't sure that Harold had the right Mitchell, "Are you talking about Maxwell Dean?"

"Yes sir."

"Baby, what is your boy up to? Last night, and now a limo today, if Max wasn't a man I would think that he was pregnant," Sarae told Pike.

Pike asked, "Harold, where are we going for brunch?"

"Mr. Mitchell, I am not at liberty to say. I am just supposed to drive you there."

"Okay, let's go then. I guess we'll see what Max is up to soon enough," Pike said as though he was convincing himself to play along.

One down, I thought. That went smoothly. Pike and Sarae were the calm ones. I hoped my girl Mel wouldn't curse the driver out when he says that he's not at liberty to say where he is taking her. This felt like I was giving birth and I was only four centimeters dilated. I wanted to hurry up and get there, or did I?

One by one they all came down and followed the same process as Pike and Sarae. The drivers were instructed to drive them around until they received a call on their cell phone. Then they could go to the location. I had to be there before they got there. The last one down was Daria. Off she went. I gave Nick enough cash to tip his concierge and door men for me. Now I was on my way. The calls went out to the drivers. They were told to drive slowly and begin making their way there. I, on the other hand, had my driver act like he was driving in the Indianapolis 500.

It wasn't that I couldn't get there after them. I just wanted to be there so I could see the expressions on their faces. I didn't want them to see me. That way I could avoid all of the probing questions.

At last we arrived just as one of the other limos pulled up. It was Mel. How did she get here so fast? She was one of the last to leave the hotel. I stayed in my limo so she wouldn't see me. The windows were tinted. I cracked the window to hear what she said as I watched her exit her limo.

"What in the hell!" she said as she looked up at the church.

Mel couldn't help her mouth. She even cursed on the steps of the church. She looked like she wasn't sure whether she wanted to go in or get back in the limo.

"I still have part of my damn hangover from last night, and he's gonna have my ass up in church," I heard her say with part dismay. "I don't need nobody's redemption this morning. I need some aspirin," Mel said to the driver as he told her to enjoy the service.

"I'll be here to pick you up when you get out of service, Ms. Ridgeway," the driver advised.

Mel walked across the sidewalk to the entrance of the church just ten feet away. The church greeter was waiting for her. Mel stopped and looked at my limo. She wanted to see if someone was getting out so she wouldn't have to walk into the church alone. I was hoping that Mel wouldn't come to the limo and knock on the window. She might yell to whoever was inside the limo to get out. She wasn't past doing that. She was a girl who would run towards making a scene instead of avoiding it.

"Mel!" I heard a voice sounding like Marcus.

I turned around and saw another limo pulling up. Marcus had his window down.

Marcus blurted out, "Hold up. Wait for me."

I'm sure he didn't want to walk in by himself either. The usher closed the church door as Mel walked towards the curb where Marcus' limo was letting him out. The limo came to a stop. Marcus exited the limo before his driver could make it around to open his door.

Mel defiantly asked, "What's this all about Marcus?"

"I have no idea!"

"What you mean you have no idea? That's yo boy. You're supposed to know what the hell is going on," Mel fired back.

"Mel we're in front of the church. Can't you watch your language?" Marcus said, embarrassed and looking around to see who heard Mel curse.

"Okay, alright, damn! If God's gonna forgive me for ma drunk ass last night, then He can give me a pass for my mouth this morning."

"How you gonna be negotiating with the Lord?" Marcus asked.

Acting like she was going to have a religious experience, Mel replied, "Do you have to rain all over my praise this morning, boy? Damn!"

"Whatever girl! You go ahead and get down like you want to," Marcus said in concession.

"Here comes another limo. Maybe this is Max. Then we can find out what the hell this church thing is about," Mel said with a look of anxiety on her face.

I turned around again. There were two limos turning onto the church grounds. Both limos stopped in front of the church one behind the other. Sarae and Pike got out of the first. Jordan exited the second limo. I breathed a sigh of relief when Jordan and Daria didn't arrive together. What could be worse—Mel the chief instigator or more sparks from last night between Daria and Jordan? Thank God that didn't happen.

Sarae and Pike spoke to Jordan. Marcus said hello to everyone and gave Jordan a plutonic hug like she was one of the inner circle of friends.

Mel said as only she could, "Girl, you have courage. I'll give you that. I wasn't sure I'd see you again after last night."

Jordan smiled politely and kept moving towards the church door.

"Pike, do you have any idea why we are at church when we are supposed to be having brunch?" Marcus inquired.

"Maybe Max wants us to get our praise on before you savages get yo grub on," Sarae replied with a snide grin on her face as she continued walking towards the church usher, "Has anyone seen Max?"

"All of you are with Mr. Dean. Right this way. We have reserved seating for you," said the beautifully dressed usher. She was a modest looking young lady in an earth tone dress with a thick black belt around her waist.

"How did you know who we were?" Jordan asked completely surprised by the familiarity of the church greeter whom she didn't know.

They all looked surprised by the usher's knowledge of them. Even Marcus had to take a moment of pause to hear her answer. They didn't know it, but I had planned everything down to the smallest details. This is one of the moments I hoped I wouldn't miss.

"The angel pin that you all are wearing. I was told to look for you. That's how I knew you were with Mr. Dean," the usher replied so matter of factly. "You all have great seats down front."

"Ya'll can't tell me my boy ain't bad. He had this planned to the hilt. That's what these pins were about, but why the church thing? We could have just blessed the food. It didn't require a full church service to thank the Lord for the brunch," Mel said in mild protest, trying not to curse.

Mildly amused by the look on Mel, Marcus, Jordan, Pike, and Sarae's face when the reason for the angel was revealed to them by the greeter, I returned to my own state of anxiety. I was taking this time to ease my tension while awaiting Daria and Mason's arrival. From here this could either go well or quite badly.

Moments later Daria arrived followed by Mason's limo. They were all here. I felt like the space shuttle count down. It was T minus fifteen minutes and counting. I watched Daria and Mason go through similar episodes as the first group. Then they disappeared into the sanctuary heading towards the others before them. It was too late to do anything now and I hoped for peace between Daria and Jordan.

I finally exited my limo. I saw Pasha walking up. I hadn't seen her in a while. I called her to come and be a part of my Sunday brunch. I wasn't sure she was going to attend. Pasha was in a small measure apportioned to this part of my life.

"Hey cuz!" I greeted Pasha as I have for years. "I'm glad you made it. I wasn't sure you were coming since you hadn't confirmed," I continued.

Pasha explained smiling, "I wasn't sure I was coming either. But I must admit, what you told me about this peaked my curiosity. I had to see this for myself."

Shaking in my shoes, I said, "It's too late to turn back now. You'd better get in and find a seat. I hear the choir starting to sing."

The choir was also my queue as well. I needed to get in there myself. Pastor Larry Coleman and the Restored Life Ministry church choir are awesome. I didn't want to miss a minute of the singing. I needed to quell my nervous stomach.

"Hi, Max," Deacon Eldridge said. "Come this way so you can see everything. Pastor Coleman wants me to bring you back so he can say hello to you before the service." The Deacon led me to the back of the pulpit to the Pastor's office.

Pastor Coleman has been my friend and spiritual advisor for many years. Whenever I am in town I attend his church. That man can preach. Whenever he preached his message, it always seemed like it was just for me. There was no other brunch message that I wanted to hear other than his.

"Hey, Max!" Larry greeted me with a big smile as I opened the door entering his office.

"Hey Pastor," I said shaking hands with him—giving him a hug and pat on the back.

"Max, what did I tell you about that Pastor stuff? We are friends so call me Larry," correcting me to the true place of our friendship.

"Pastor, it's time," Deacon Eldridge reminded him.

"Okay, Deacon." I could see that he wanted to stay and catch up a while. "Max you better take your seat because we are about to start. By the way I am proud of you for everything that you went through to get where you are now. When they told me you had been shot and were in a coma, I prayed. God revealed to me that you would be alright, but I knew that I had to come and lay hands on you in prayer. You are a favorite son of this church, and I'm glad you came here even though I'm not your home church." Larry spoke words straight from the heart.

"Ok, see you later," I replied as he walked out the door.

I took a minute to reflect on what Larry said. It hit me again. Not just the shooting, but also where I had been in my personal life.

I left Larry's office and looked through the window into the sanctuary. The choir was rocking. I saw my friends across the sanctuary in the first two rows getting into the music. There were three sections of pews in this medium sized church. My friends were on the left side. I think the church seats about three thousand people. Every seat looked occupied this Sunday. It was as if they knew.

My friends were so into the music I think they were oblivious to my absence. They were certainly going to know I was with them very shortly. I had a knot in my stomach that felt like it was the size of Texas. I made billion dollar deals, but I questioned whether I could do this little thing. Business is impersonal, but this was going to be very personal.

The choir sang about four songs. Their performance was coming to an end. I saw Larry start to make his way towards the pulpit. That was the signal. I looked over at my crew and saw that a few more people from the reunion joined them. There didn't appear to be any lasting hostility between Jordan and Daria from last night. Deacon Eldridge tapped me on the shoulder, "Max, Pastor left this for you. He wanted you to have this before service."

I replied with surprise and humble gratitude, "Thanks, Deacon Eldridge, I surely wasn't expecting this."

"I think it was his first one," Deacon continued.

I turned back to Larry so I wouldn't miss a minute of his sermon. I saw Jordan looking around a couple of times to see if I was near or had sat somewhere else in fear of her and Daria going at it in church. I'm sure people were beginning to wonder why I hadn't arrived yet. The awesome vocals of the choir kept their worry about me at bay. I was going to join them soon, but not in the middle of Larry speaking.

"It isn't often that you get the privilege of doing something so magnificent that it nearly brings you to tears," Larry said as he started the service.

He continued, "I have performed christenings of the children of members who I have baptized. To see them grow up in the church and then bring their children to the Lord is one of the most incredible feelings I have as a pastor. The honor that I have today is at the top of my list of achievements as a pastor."

I could see the congregation moving to the edge of their seats in anticipation for where Larry was going. They were eager to know what it was. Larry was almost in tears as he continued. He had me too. He was reeling me in right along with everyone else.

"I was surprised when this came to me. It's one of the things that you never think would happen. Not because it wasn't possible, but just because you never thought that was the direction of God," Larry continued building the drama and suspense.

If Larry didn't get on with it, I, right along with everyone else was going to burst at the seams. He was winding the church up like he was about to deliver a potent spiritual punch line in his sermon. I was so caught up that it felt like I was ready to explode.

Joyously exclaiming God's will to the congregation, Larry said, "Church, if it is alright with you all, I am going to submit to the will of God and let the Holy Spirit have his was up in here today. I know that this may be a little different service than usual, but I am not in control."

"Come on Pastor!" someone from the congregation yelled.

"Choir please hit that last song's melody," Larry requested.

The choir got up and picked up at that last emotionally rousing song. I didn't know the name of the song, but I recognized it was one that I loved by Donnie McClurkin. Although it was clearly impromptu, the choir cranked it up just like they had rehearsed the song. The church erupted in joy and celebration just like they do when bands come out for encores at concerts. I was starting to get goose bumps on my arms. Larry had the congregation ready to come out of their seats and ignite.

I looked at my friends and I think they had all but forgotten about me. Mel's face was streaming tears. Daria had her head down and swinging from side to side. Pike had his arms stretched out towards the ceiling with his eyes closed and shaking his head. Larry touched everybody.

Larry stood up while the choir was singing and said, "If you have ever been beaten, broken, down, broke, hungry, I'm here to tell you that it's not over. God can bring you back from the doorway of death. You are not alone. No need to be lonely," Larry belted out as the choir brought the roof down.

It seemed like the choir just kicked it into a higher gear. Suddenly the significance of this song came upon me. Larry was talking about me. I was at the doorway of death. A chill ran down my back and permeated sideways towards my ribs. I felt emotions well up in me that I had denied since being shot. I realized that I had fallen down, but God pulled me back up. I had been hiding from that terrible day in the shadows of denial for so long. Larry and the choir shined the spotlight on me. I was out in the open and exposed. I felt emotionally naked and didn't know how to feel about it.

A singer rolled up the melody, "It's not too late to get back up again."

Larry exalted to the top of his lungs, "Church, get back up. Get out of that seat right now and proclaim that you are back in the game. We fall down, but we get back up. It's not too late to get back up again."

I looked out and there were hardly any dry eyes left. I think he was secretly tapping into each and every person's individual pain center and giving them permission to fight back.

The singer repeatedly sang, "Get back up again."

I was about to come from the side and go into the main sanctuary and get me some of this Holy Ghost party. I couldn't take it anymore. Something was driving me towards the congregation.

Larry must have seen me out of the corner of his eye and signaled for me to hold up and not to come into the main sanctuary yet. I was asking myself, *What do you mean no?* I can't stop myself. It was like I had to pee really badly and couldn't get my zipper down. If something didn't give soon, it wouldn't be pretty.

Larry shouted, "Church, I tell you that the Lord has something special about to move in His house this morning."

Screams of joy were now echoing out from all corners of the church. Amen's and hallelujahs were flowing harder in the church than the Mississippi river.

Larry signaled for the choir to wind it down. It was clear that he had worked the church up into a spiritual frenzy. They were ready to receive whatever he had. It was time.

Larry started setting up his message as the choir was winding down and the church members were at an emotional critical mass.

"I have a good friend who was at the brink of death and God snatched him back from the clutches of the devil. He had seen the doorstep to God's house before God told him to get back up again. He said it's not too late," Larry said to the emotionally charged group.

They erupted even more. "Thank you Jesus," one lady yelled.

People were crying and on the edge of their seats hanging on to every word that was being uttered. So was I for that matter. I looked down at my friends standing in the first row of the pews to see if they were as moved as I was. Pike was clutching Sarae's hand and had tears streaming down his face. Sarae was comforting him and looking like she was barely hanging on herself.

Jordan's eyes were closed as she rocked from side to side. It seemed like everyone was standing. You could see most of the deep red cushions of the church benches. Everyone was standing atop the royal blue carpet ready to launch at the sound of any word of praise coming from the pulpit. The hard exterior of Mel melted away and I saw the emotional sensitivity of the true Mel. I'm not even sure she was aware that she had opened up to the Spirit.

I peered in from the side of the sanctuary. I traversed my own emotional spectrum. Larry brought back memories that I had tucked away in denial. I was overjoyed to see my friends moved by the word in church. I wanted to get into the sanctuary and be a part of the spiritual revival. I was scared to move. I didn't know where Larry was going with me in the introduction of his sermon. *Oh, God help me,* I thought.

Larry continued, "One night this brother called me in the early morning and said, 'Larry I need you.' He also said, 'I have a ticket for you at the airport if you can please make it. It's a matter of life or death.'"

"I didn't know what he was talking about, but I knew what life or death meant. I asked him, "Where are you?"

He told me, "overseas." Larry continued with his story. The sanctuary looked at Larry like they were frozen in time. I kept wondering where he was going with his story. Larry continued, "I asked him when do you need me there? He said, 'Immediately.' I asked him if it was that serious."

"I love this guy. He is a really good dude. I prayed and prayed that my wife wouldn't kill me for even bringing such a—let's just say unusual request to her. Now most women would look at you like you are a scheming two-headed snake, but my wife loves him too and said, 'Give him my love and tell him I said take care.'" Larry continued as he had the church hanging on every word. You could see they were waiting on the next word to come out of his mouth.

"Six hours later the wheels were up on this huge 747 plane, and I was on my way to what, I had no idea. I can't explain it, but God said go.

"This guy said, 'If you don't have time to pack, we'll get you anything you need. Help me Larry, I am terrified.'" Larry told the congregation, his voice choked up and broken.

The church was so quiet that I don't think anyone was breathing. No one moved. My crew was at full attention. The Deacon's mouth was half open as he continued listening.

"Church, when I got there I saw my friend—he just broke down. He looked half dead. He fell to the ground and thanked me for coming. He literally grabbed me around my ankles and cried. When I asked him what was wrong, he said something got into him, he was dying. There was a local religious man who had been praying for him. He told me what it was and we both started crying. Church, I prayed to God and said, "Oh my God for the first time in my many years of pastoral service, I felt small and helpless." His voice still breaking.

Some eyes were watering. I think the ushers were so caught up in the story they wouldn't have even known if someone had gotten up and left.

Larry wiped the sweat mixed with emotions, "I told this brother, I am here and we'll face this together even if there is nothing that I can do for you. I asked him if he was afraid this would be a painful death."

"He said, 'I know where I am going and how much of a better place I've been told it is, but I don't know if I'm ready.'"

A lady gasped, "Oh my God" as she covered her mouth. "My Lord," she said. The church seemed to have its collective mouth open ready to receive the carnage from the story. People felt the pain and desperation of it all.

With a climaxing outburst Larry said, "Here he is back from death. He was clinically dead on an emergency room gurney—fallen, broken, shot, and left for dead. He got back up again and was resurrected into a new life. He is brand new and God delivered him to you!"

The church erupted. It seemed like everyone came to their feet. Hands were clapping and people were shouting. The older saints of the church were crying. I could see the eyes watering of younger people who looked like they were near death and despair. Larry's story touched a nerve of hope in them. That would be a tough act for anyone to follow.

"Oh my God!" Daria bellowed out.

"Oh shit!" Mel screamed and covered her mouth as she struggled to catch her profanity in church.

Marcus' eyes got as big as billiard balls. He looked as if he had seen a ghost. If I didn't know any better, I could have swore that hardcore Marcus himself was getting choked up.

"I'll be," Marcus said as if to stop short of saying the word damned.

Jordan looked like she was about to faint. Her vision was pinpointed to one place on the raised pulpit. Her expression was like someone had just stolen her puppy. I could see that she was struggling to say anything.

I read Pike's lips silently ask, "What the hell?"

Sarae said, "Oh my God." The tears were rolling down her face. Her hands were near her mouth and shaking. She couldn't take her eyes off the pulpit.

"Thank you, Jesus." Sarae said as she continued to tremble. She grabbed Pike's hand and held it tight.

Sarae started jumping in jubilation which seemed to be the powder keg that ignited the rest of the church. The church's already excited mood intensified. People I knew who attended this church for years were shaking in joyful tears. They had expressions on their face as if Jesus himself was being introduced to the pulpit. I think people were shocked. It was as though Larry introduced a rock star at a concert. The congregation clapped and screamed as if a star had walked down the red carpet at the Oscar's.

I was a bit overwhelmed by it all. I needed to get from the back and be a part of the excitement. I was feeling the emotion as well. I felt if I didn't get out there now, I was going to implode.

I saw Mel look at Jordan. Jordan looked up at the altar saying, "Oh my God, Oooooh my God!"

Everyone was stunned and so was I. I gotta get out there NOW!

Chapter 20

HATS OFF

All eyes were on Larry standing in front of the Altar looking towards the side of the pulpit. He started singing, "Get Back Up Again."

"Here he comes, back up again," Larry excitedly shouted.

The band joined in playing the instrumental to "We Fall Down." When the first note came out of the choir's mouth, the church exploded again. This church was on fire. I thought, *People aren't going to forget this church service.* Larry blurted out from what seemed like pure emotion as if it was an uncontrollable utterance, "Holy Spirit have your way."

"Have your way in here," Deacon yelled.

People were dancing, moving, and fully caught up in the moment as the choir churned up an emotional hailstorm by repeating the melodic bridge of the song, "Get Back Up Again."

Larry shouted, "Welcome, my brother, my friend, and now my colleague, the Reverend Maxwell Dean."

My friends were shaking their heads in disbelief. I'm sure this was the last thing they thought would be my surprise. They didn't even know the half of it yet.

The choir sang, "It's not too late to get back up again."

What a fitting song for the occasion. I couldn't believe that I was actually standing in church in a pastor's robe. Is this what happens when you get shot, die, and are brought back to life? Before I couldn't wait to get out there and be with the church. Now my legs didn't want to move. I thought, *Devil don't do this to me right now. Help me, Jesus.*

I came out in Larry's first minister's robe. Deacon gave it to me just before service started. Wearing it was such an honor. It was like a father passing something precious down to his son.

The time was here. I continued walking towards Larry. It was like I was crossing a desert alone and all eyes were on me. I told myself, *Don't trip and fall.* My walk felt awkward, but I knew that was just in my mind. It felt like the longest most desolate walk in the history of mankind. I wanted to sprint across the stage just so I could have company. A minute ago I was confident, but now I felt like a nervous little boy about to say his lines in his first school play.

I've spoken to big and important crowds before, so what's the big deal, I told myself. Reality told me that I've never done this. The stakes were never this high. Larry and the choir had the church so spiritually combustible. Was this the set up for failure? Doubt spun in my mind like a merry-go-round. I didn't think I could say anything to top this mood or equal Larry's introduction.

Jordan looked at me not knowing what to say or think. I know she'd give me a mouth full after church. The expression on my face told Jordan, "What can I say?" I'm sure she had no idea what was coming next or what my being a pastor would do to our relationship. Last night Jordan was smug and arrogant to Daria. Today it's backfiring. At last, the secret that I kept from everyone for a year was finally out. I was happy to have that weight off my shoulders. It was hard keeping my secret from everyone except Marcus. After my call to him about Kristi, he was scared for my safety and flew over. I told him everything and swore him to secrecy.

I heard Pike ask Marcus, "We are like brothers and I had no idea. Did you know about this?"

"Yeah, but he swore me to secrecy. As much as I wanted to tell you, I had to respect Max on this, Pike."

Pike looked at me and gestured with his lips saying, "I'm gonna kick yo ass."

That was his way of admonishing me for not telling him. I knew he would tell me that he is my boy. You can keep things from other people, but not me. We go way back too far. You could have told me about this. I knew I was going to have to mend some fences with Pike and Mason.

Some of my crew turned their attention to Daria. They looked for her reaction. She just stood there looking straight at me in shock. Daria's feelings for me had taken many blows over the years with women that I put before her. I'm certain she is more than confused about how this latest development will affect us. It's pretty hard to argue with the Lord, but she just may find a way. The fact that I didn't tell her was pissing her off. In her mind it wasn't about the Lord, it was a matter of courtesy and respect.

My eyes traversed the crowd and found Pasha. She looked at me. She put both of her hands to her mouth and blew me a kiss. I read her lips as she smiled and silently said, "I love you, cuz."

I turned back to my best friends in the world. They were visibly happy but each resembled someone in shock. I'm sure each one of them contemplated how my new life as a minister would change our friendships. Mel would probably worry about cursing in front of me now and having to apologize incessantly for her foul mouth. I knew Marcus would worry the most. He would wonder if we could hang out and still be boys. I knew we would. It wouldn't change anything except our woman chasing.

Daria would probably take it the hardest. Not just because of my new role, but because I never told her what I was doing. I knew she wouldn't have a problem with me becoming a pastor. She would consider my secrecy about accepting the calling as a personal betrayal of our friendship.

Pike and Sarae would just be in wow mode and accept it. Mason would more likely tell me that more women would be after me now. He would say, "Women love them some preachers." His mind works like that even though I know he'd just be joking.

This will be as big of an adjustment for them as it is for me. Each of my friends looked confused in their own right. They looked like someone just hit them in the gut and gasped to catch their breath. As if Jordan and Daria weren't already confused enough about why I had both of them here for this, I know they were wondering how this would change my relationship with each of them. If my new role as Reverend Dean wasn't obvious, I'd be making the answer real plain very soon.

"Good morning, church and friends," I started.

The Church started quieting down a little.

"I am as surprised to be standing here as you are to have me here. Be patient while the Lord takes me where He wants me to go. I know I gotta get there," I continued.

"Take your time pastor." The lady in the big tangerine colored church lady hat said, smiling in approval.

"I brought some friends with me who didn't know this was coming. They are my best friends. I kept this from them for almost a year until now. They are over there on the left side in the front row looking like they just saw a ghost." I said as I pointed to them.

I thought this surprise would be sinking in, but they still looked like they walked into their own surprise birthday party. I asked them to stand and be recognized. The Church applauded.

Mel looked at Jordan and smirked. It was as if her look said, "Your shit is cut off now skank." Mel and I were so close that I could read her thoughts of profanity. I could feel Mel laughing at Jordan. She was never a fan of Jordan.

I turned to Larry and thanked him and his wife for allowing me to publicly accept my calling in his church. Larry's wife came over and hugged me. She whispered in my ear, "Welcome to the family Max."

I whispered back, "I'm scared."

As she parted towards the section of the church where I just came from, "I know. That's why I sent my husband to you when you called. I didn't know what it was, but my spirit knew he had to go to you."

Larry put his arm around me. "Max called me to Bangkok because God called him while he was there. He was doing his company's business and then God switched his mission to doing God's business."

The Deacon shouted, "That's right, that's right."

The woman in the tangerine hat shouted, "Yes, Lord!"

"Church, God told my spirit that Max is the service today. I'm gonna sit down and let the Holy Spirit have his way if that's alright with you all," Larry said, backing away and not waiting for an answer.

Being the service was a complete surprise. My anxiety ratcheted up tenfold. I stood behind the pastor's podium. I felt alone. It was like standing in front of the whole world. People waited for me to deliver some words that would affect their lives and faith.

My pastor's robe got heavier, not by the weight of the material, but rather from the weight of expectation. My legs trembled underneath the robe. Perspiration gathered on my forehead and started rolling down my temples. My hands were shaking. *Hold it together, Max,* I told myself.

The congregation was still amped up. I was glad because that gave me time to gain my composure. I started my address to the congregation: "Over a year ago my friend Marcus who is sitting right there in the second row and I were shot by two youngsters in an apparent carjacking. At one point I actually died in the emergency room."

"Oh, Jesus," tangerine hat lady shouted.

Not really knowing where I was actually going with this, I continued, "Unbeknownst to me at the time, I was revived into a new life and a different purpose. God resurrected me for this day."

"My God," Deacon shouted as the rest of the church echoed in other spiritual outbursts.

My friends knew about the shooting. They were as captivated as the other church members. They never heard me say it like this. They had no clue what was coming next, but first I had to get past the next part.

"For the last year my friends hardly saw me. I was in China most of the year on business. I was also gone for another reason too. I was in Bangkok where I met an older holy man. He's a monk named Chang Si Wong. The monk was an unassuming man who you could easily overlook. He wore traditional monk clothing. He wore an earth tone robe with one of his shoulders out and basic sandals on his feet. Asian with a bald head, Chang Si Wong is a simple man."

I saw the looks on some people's face trying to picture Chang. I bet some people were picturing a man looking like the Dalai Lama. That picture wouldn't be half wrong.

"We initially met through his brother who was the manager at the JW Marriott Shanghai Hotel where I stayed while on business in China.

We talked for only a couple of minutes. In that short time Chang Si Wong sensed some unrest in my spirit. He later invited me up to his monastery in Bangkok where we talked for hours. That lead me to several more trips where he quieted my spirit and I heard the voice of God calling me. I just couldn't get enough of what he was saying to me."

The Church silently hung onto my every word. They looked like they were wondering where this was going. I was actually not sure where I was going, but it was my story.

This was all new for my friends. Boy, were they about to get the shock of their lives. They were learning why no one saw me for almost a year. Max's mystery was unfolding one surprise after another.

"Day after day, I couldn't wait to talk to Monk Chang.

I continued sharing my thoughts with the congregation. "I thought to myself what could I have in common with a monk when I was raised Baptist. God's language is universal. Chang Si Wong put the pieces of the puzzle together for me. He shared higher wisdom and purpose about getting shot, dying and being revived. With a calm and reassuring voice, Chang Si Wong shared the impact of western culture to my spiritual center. I was fascinated by his culture where monks journeyed to find their spiritual center."

I continued, "I loved our conversations so much that I went back to Bangkok during my off time and for vacations. Our conversations became one of the most important things in my life. It wasn't until later that I realized that I was sort of in seminary school."

"My Lord, my Lord," Deacon shouted.

"Thank you, Jesus," The tangerine hat lady blurted out.

Without knowing it, I realized I was preaching my first sermon. "One day this feeling came over me that was so strong it took my breath away. I was with Chang Si Wong. We were in his home. It was a small modest bungalow scarcely appointed with only a bed, eating table, and two benches for seating. His couch as we would call it was a pad that looked like a thin-folded mattress sitting against the wall with an array of pillows on it. He was making his usual herbal tea on the small stove that looked like it had only two burners. I was preparing for another one of our great conversations when cold chill ran down my back, piercing my body, radiating around my ribcage as if it was circling me and wrapping me like a cocoon. It wasn't painful, but I was frozen in that spot. I stretched my head upward towards the sky as if trying to free myself. Chang Si Wong moved about as if he was oblivious to what was happening. Maybe he was, since all this was going on inside my body. He lit some incense and poured some water into a white porcelain bowl with faint blue specks. I wanted to tell him, I was in distress, but I couldn't seem to speak. I wondered if I was having a heart attack."

I paused to gain my emotional composure. Tears ran down Sarae's face as if she knew what was coming next. Pike was on his way to choking up. The usually tough acting Mel was caught up in the story like she was living the moment. Clearly she had forgotten that Jordan even existed. Jordan looked like she was still trying to come to grips with me as a pastor. Daria looked like she still had a thousand questions for me. Marcus looked like he wanted to know what happened to his boy. I was giving them the first shot, but the second blow was soon to follow.

I picked up with my story again, "I was about to be full of fear when I heard, 'Fear not. It's time. I told you I would see you again later.'" I remembered the man in the white robe saying that to me when I was shot. I was going into the white light when I saw Him. I later realized that happened when my heart stopped and I was clinically dead at that moment. This time I didn't see Him, but the sound of his voice was unmistakable. His voice was calming and clear—not deep or mysterious, but gentle, regal, and reassuring. I knew I heard a voice, but the sound wasn't coming into my ears. It was as if someone took off the top of my head and pressed the sound into my brain. I realized I saw Jesus when I died, but he wasn't ready for me so He said, 'I will see you again later.' Jesus sent me back about the same time they shocked my heart and revived me."

"Whoa Lord, my God, my God," the lady in the tangerine hat said.

I heard a string of hallelujahs ring out across the church. *Was I preaching or telling a story? I wondered if there was a difference.* My thoughts were interrupted by a familiar voice.

"Preach, Max," Marcus shouted from nowhere.

Oh my God, that was a first from Marcus. I looked at him beaming with joy. What got into him? This was something he had never done as long as I knew him. If I reached him, then I could reach anybody.

Continuing with my story, I said, "Church, I screamed an unrecognizable sound. I don't know what I yelled. My mouth opened and sounds came out from every corner of my body like water flowing through a strainer. My mouth stayed open as the steady sound continued exiting my body. It felt as if I was running out of air like a singer trying to hold a long note. Although my yell lasted only seconds, it felt like thirty minutes. I can tell you now that I was giving up my soul to God."

Mel's hands covered her mouth as tears streamed down her face. Marcus put his arms around her as tears welled up in his eyes. Mason grabbed Daria's hand as she showed signs of softening.

"Oh, Max, thank you Lord," Sarae said, crying and jumping in place as she raised her hand towards the ceiling.

The church was suspended in time as I shared with them the intimate way of how the Lord called me to the ministry. As the church became emotionally raw, I continued, "Chang Si Wong never even turned around. I wondered if he heard me or was I day dreaming?

"I blinked my eyes to what seemed like a camera flash. I thought I saw the man in the white robe in the light's bright white flash. The voice was pressed into my head again saying, 'It is done. Walk with me, lead for me, fear not, help is on the way.' In his departure I knew it was Christ and he called me by name."

A lady in a lime colored dress stood up in tears. Her arms were stretched towards the ceiling as she said, "Thank you, Jesus."

Mason was in shock. Pike was crying. Marcus had his head down and was swinging it from side to side muttering softly. Daria was in tears. Mel was crying, fully exposing her soft side. I saw a very cold side of Jordan as she wore no emotions on her face. The entire church was pouring out their souls except for Jordan. Was she worried?

I continued taking this somewhere, even I wasn't sure where. "Chang turned around and sprinkled water in my face like he was blessing me with holy water. He knew what just happened, but we didn't speak about it. He said, 'I must go now. I won't see you anymore on this trip.' That is when I called Larry. I was scared. I thought I knew what happened, but I needed help figuring it out. My heart raced like it was trying to jump out of my chest. I thought I was dying. I called Larry and another close friend. Larry and my friend came without hesitation."

Jordan looked over at Daria as if she knew she flew over to Bangkok to be with me. Jordan knew she didn't go, so it had to be Daria. Daria was too emotional to acknowledge Jordan was even still in the church. At that point, Daria assumed it was Jordan. Both of them assumed incorrectly. "The Lord said He would send me help. He did. You know Larry was one. Let me introduce you to my other friend who is here to support me in my first service as a pastor," as I signaled for my friend to come to the stage.

Mel's eyes looked like they were going to leap out of their sockets. She was completely surprised. Marcus's mouth hung wide open. I think Daria was relieved it wasn't Jordan. Jordan didn't know my friend. She just looked happy it wasn't Daria. People were wiping their faces clear of the tears.

"Here she is church, the other half of my helper tag team sent by God," I excitedly announced her arrival.

She came to join me at the pulpit. She looked marvelous in her burnt orange/brown colored dress tapered and high at the waist. It was cut just above the knee. Her brownish colored hair was meticulously cut in that short Halle Berry style. She exuded class as usual.

"Here is my friend and helper, Kristi. I suppose I should say my help-mate and new wife, Mrs. Kristi Dean." The church shocked, but happy, were congratulatory in their response. They stood up and clapped as they greeted her. Kristi didn't look nervous at all. She looked right into my eyes with love in hers. She walked up to me and gave me a quick peck on the lips and stood right beside me. We both knew my friends were freaking out.

I turned to my friends to see the fireworks. This was the gut punch for Daria and Jordan. I knew mayhem would ensue with Daria and Jordan. Even though Jordan and I weren't together, she always thought she could get me back. She had done it before by appealing to my flesh with sex. I knew this blow would be emotionally lethal to Daria. She always knew that she and I would still have each other even though we had other people in our lives. I knew both the ministry and Kristi would signal the end of us the way we knew each other for many years. Mel was the first to speak because she met Kristi before. "Daaammm," she uttered not being able to withhold the language.

I'm not sure a lot of the church heard her. Mel covered her mouth quickly as if she was trying to take that word back.

Jordan spoke loud enough for half of the congregation to look in her direction, "This Mothafu#*er!" She was seething.

The ushers walked towards her, expecting a scene. Calling me a M-F in church was going to get her tossed. Jordan hurried out of the row, rudely trying to get past people, stepping on their feet without waiting for them to move. "Let me out of here!" Jordan demanded.

More ushers headed towards Jordan. I hoped she wouldn't ruin my day. Kristi was cool and composed as if un-phased by it all.

"No Max didn't humiliate me like this in here," Jordan grunted as she stepped into the isle followed by some ushers directing her to the door.

"Be gone trick, good riddance wit yo skank ass," Mel said, getting in her parting shot.

I saw the pain on Daria's face and felt sorry for my dear friend. I wished she didn't have to find out about my marriage like this. I had no choice, this was God's plan, not mine. Accepting your calling to the ministry must be done publically. I'm hurting because she's hurting. It was gut wrenching to know I'd be hurting Daria. I agonized for nights about this day. Inside I was broken and conflicted. I didn't know or understand why God wanted me to do it this way. I had no choice but to be obedient to Him.

Sarae's bright smile of approval provided me momentary comfort. I'm not sure if her joy was for me or that I had finally settled down. She looked at Pike. Before she could ask him anything, Pike said, "I had no idea!"

Mason looked much the same way as Sarae did with Pike. Each wanted to know if the other knew about me getting married.

Rejoining my sermon, I said, "I dated Kristi last year. We started out as really good friends and became closer. She took a leave of absence and joined me in China while God transformed me. I found something more in her that was better than me. She stuck by me as I struggled to let go of some old habits. She asked me if that was the best I had to offer, or did God make me better than that. Kristi wasn't angry, she appealed to my divine purpose. In that moment she took me to a place no other ever did." Daria looked like she didn't want to hear this. Her hurt was turning to anger. For the moment she wasn't going out like Jordan did—maybe that was her pride. Whatever it was, I was happy for her emotional control.

"Girl, you can't argue with God," Sarae the level headed one said to Daria, trying to ease her pain.

The scowled look on Daria's face said she wasn't having it. Marcus knew to leave it alone. Mel, who often says things without inhibition, amazingly also left it alone.

I looked at Daria and said, "We've come a long way, through many ups and downs, but the Lord put me on a new course. What was can no longer be, not because of me, but because of Him that is in me. The old me died in body and was resurrected in the hospital. My old spirit also died and was resurrected in this robe. Larry knew that as soon as he saw me in Bangkok."

Even though the church thought I was still giving my message, I was actually saying good-bye to Daria's hopes of us being together. Only she and I knew that. I don't know if I could have had the same poise as Daria if the situation was reversed. I don't think we men are built to be that emotionally strong.

Daria headed for the same door that Jordan departed through. I couldn't blame her for leaving. It was as though I was rubbing my joy in her sorrow. I wasn't, I was proclaiming my joy with two God ordained weddings—Kristi and the ministry.

"When she arrived in Bangkok, the Lord showed me that Kristi was my soul mate. She said that God revealed the same thing to her on the long flight over. I am going to keep this real," I told the Church as I was about to invite them in to me our private life.

"Tell it, pastor," Deacon shouted in laughter.

"Keep it clean, Max," Larry spoke up.

"Tell it all, pastor," a slightly full figured lady shouted with a sassy smile that said I wanna be all up yo business.

"My wife and I never slept together until after we were married. It wasn't because I was strong enough to resist this beautiful woman. God, just never let us have the opportunity to do it. I am grateful for that because we got to know each other on a different level and God kept our union pure and blessed. Brothas, y'all know what I went through," I said, saying shwooo and wiping my forehead, indicating it was tough.

The church laughed, especially the men. The women laughed too because they knew what it would be like to be in love with your man but not give him any for a year.

"I know, my best friends weren't allowed to attend my wedding. I hope my boys will still remain friends with me even though they didn't get to stand up for me. You have to do what the Lord tells you to do. Larry married us in a small private wedding with him officiating, his wife witnessing, and Monk Chang Si Wong standing in as the best Monk," I said, interjecting some humor with the best Monk comment. Laugher rang out. Even my boys had to laugh at that one. God was playing out my entire new life in Christ before this very church congregation.

I continued with why I did this the way I did, "I know some of my friends will think that I am cruel for letting them find out this way. In their shoes, I'd probably feel the same way. I am not trying to hurt anyone. I have to take you to the scripture to make sense of this, which is from Isaiah 55:8-11 (NRSV)."

The Lord said,

"For My thoughts are not your thoughts, nor are your ways My ways, says the Lord. For as the heavens are higher than the earth, so are My ways higher than your ways and My thoughts than your thoughts. For as the rain and the snow come down from heaven, and do not return there until they have watered the earth, making it bring forth and spout, giving seed to the sower and bread to the eater, so shall My

word be that goes out from my mouth; it shall not return to me empty, but it shall accomplish that which I purpose, and succeed in the thing for which I sent it."

"You're right, pastor," Deacon shouted.

I knew some people would get it and some wouldn't. Some people wouldn't want to get it. They wanted God to fit into their box, rather than the other way around. Following the Lord isn't about what is convenient. It's about accepting His will and walking in our purpose. I didn't know why I had to let everyone find out this way, but God had a reason that wasn't mine to question.

"We got married in Bangkok but made it official in the United States right back there in Larry's office," I said, pointing towards his office.

"Marcus was there for that one because he stalked me and tracked me down. Me and all of my boys are tight, but getting shot together, he and I will always have that special bond. He wanted to tell the others, but I swore him to secrecy. I told him that he was now a part of God's directive."

I needed to tell the church how we came to get married, or the only people this would make sense to was my friends. Even my friends wanted to know how Max the most eligible bachelor got hooked that fast.

"Church, if I could have just five more minutes of your time, I'll explain how this beautiful lady came to be my wife," I said knowing that curiosity was killing the entire congregation right now, not to mention my friends.

"Go head, pastor, preach!" one enthusiastic lady exclaimed.

"Speak, pastor," Marcus demanded sarcastically.

"Brang it on pastor," Deacon yelled proceeded by a huge smile.

I thought that this was already shaping up to be a defining moment in my new life as a pastor. *Lord, give me the right words to be a blessing to you*, I silently prayed.

I began, "At first I was frightened because I was becoming powerless when I tried to resist falling in love with Kristi. She sensed my fear, pressed on, and loved me anyway. She took on my pain and troubles and ministered recovery to me. This woman swallowed up my pain and sought no gain. My love was all she wanted. I was always searching for someone or something. At times I returned to women I felt comfortable with. I tried to find something in other women. I was like the dog that chases his tail but never catches it. Standing up here with Kristi today says I didn't have to chase it, God gave it to me. When I left, she stood by me patiently awaiting my return with unabridged love. You see, God was talking to her long before I heard him talking to me."

Kristi sat down as gracefully as she came to the pulpit. She crossed her legs like a classy lady would. My pride in her was only exceeded by my love. Although she loved me dearly, I wondered what she thought about me airing our life out in front of the church. That's difficult for anyone. If anyone could handle it, she could. She's a true Godly woman.

"Tell it, Max, baby!" Sarae said, smiling and forgetting that she should be addressing me as pastor.

"Uhuh, uhuh," rang out in unisons from the various sections throughout the church.

Kristi sat beside Larry in the pulpit listening and watching the church respond. I could feel her pride. I knew my wife well. Her feelings weren't based on arrogance. She wanted people to know how God affected me and how she stuck by me even when she hated some of the things I did. The Lord didn't make it easy on her to stay by my side. Kristi has a Master's degree and wields a great deal of power in her male dominated industry in corporate America. She is by no means a pushover.

"Y'all stay awake because I'm going somewhere with this," I boasted.

The church laughed. "Come on, pastor. Preach heah!" Deacon screamed in excitement.

I took a big, guilt-gulping swallow and laid my humanity out prostrate before God and the Church in a sin-confessing way. "I cheated on her. I desired worthless trinkets and useless flights of fancy. Worse than admitting my indiscretion to Kristi, was coming back later to tell her that I got the woman pregnant. I destroyed her emotionally. Then

I had to tell her that Jordan lost the baby. I wanted to celebrate being off the hook, but I realized that I just lost a life that was a part of me. I ran from the one who was in my corner, for the one who wanted my corner. I didn't cheat because she did something wrong, I cheated because I was still a boy trying to act like a man when I didn't know how because I didn't know Jesus."

The church erupted by my admission of acting like a boy. I think the women finally felt some vindication from all the pain they endured by men like me who never admitted anything. I still got some grimacing looks that said, 'You dog.' I expected that because to some degree I was just that. It wasn't because I wanted to play women—it was because I was never man enough to resolve my issues before I dragged someone else into my madness. I was never the man that a woman wanted and I didn't know how to tell them I'm not what you need.

The men looked at me with mixed feelings. Some stared at me like I was breaking the man code. Others looked like my admission was hitting them between their eyes. I made the dogs bark, and the boys cry in shame. I must admit that confessing my past before the church was cleansing my shame as well. Mel looked at me with disappointment in her eyes. She wasn't judging me, she simply didn't agree with my conduct.

I picked up my story as the church was completely engrossed in my dirty laundry-airing story. "Kristi sucked up all that hurt and forgave me without judgment. She took me back amid my appalling behavior and just loved me that much more. I was undeserving of love from someone as wonderful as her. She wrapped her arms around me and told me that we'll finish together what we started together."

I wondered if I hurt Kristi by making her relive our pain again in front of the entire church. I knew she accepted me and what happened as a part of my getting where I am now, but even I found it difficult to trudge back through that carnage.

"In closing, I asked the Lord to choose my mate. When I submitted myself to God's will, Kristi called me and said she was still here. I asked the Lord if she was who He wanted me to be with—let her forgive me. Kristi told me that God told her to stay and love me through Him.

With tears streaming down her face, she said, "Max, I am here to stay. I forgive you."

"I realized that God put us together. My friend, that pastor right back there and his wife taught me what marriage vows truly mean. My friend the Monk changed my view of living. God told me that I had to love her through Christ. One night I had a dream that Kristi disappeared. In the dream I awoke to Jesus the next morning. I looked over in amazement that He was there and my wife wasn't. I quickly bellowed out to Jesus, 'I LOVE YOU.'"

"I asked Jesus, where is Kristi? He said, 'She is here because she is in me and I in her. How can you say you love Me if you don't love her. Throughout your sins against her, she loved Me. She endured the pain you inflicted on her. I felt her pain. You must love Me through her and she will love me through you. Where she is, there I will be also.' They both loved me in spite of myself. Kristi understood she and Jesus are one. What I did to her, I also did to Him. Church, look at one another and love each one as if they were Jesus Christ Himself. We cause Him so much pain by the way we hurt each other. Thank you for letting me share that message with you. God bless you."

The church erupted in a thunderous applaud as I walked from the pulpit and gave Kristi a hug and kiss and then hugged Larry and his wife. I just came to surprise my friends with my becoming a pastor, but God surprised me with a sermon from the heart.

I thought, *As it turns out, brunch was my feeding them the Word. Amazing!* I still owe them a meal which will be forthcoming after we leave church.

Chapter 21

REDEMPTION

"Baby, I can't believe a year has gone by since we got married and you accepted your calling into the ministry. As fast as time flies, twelve months doesn't feel long anymore. It kinda feels like by the time you get going, you're celebrating another ball drop in Times Square," Kristi said as she noted the upcoming anniversary of my first sermon.

"I know."

I arranged to have a private shindig with my friends in an intimate gathering over the summer. You could say it was an anniversary of sorts. In grand Max fashion, I had another surprise in store for them. If they thought getting married and becoming a pastor was big, this surprise would send them over the edge.

"Have you confirmed that everyone is coming?" Kristi asked, making sure I didn't forget anyone. She had an expression on her face like, you're asking for trouble.

"Yeah, everyone confirmed except Daria. She's the only one not coming. I understand why Daria isn't coming. She is still having a hard time dealing with our marriage. I do miss my friend, but only God Himself comes before you, baby. I know only time will close the tear in her wounded heart." I felt responsible for Daria's pain. I loved our friendship, but couldn't give her what she wanted. I wanted friendship but she wanted more. In the end, my values cost me our friendship. There's a time when a man has to take a stand against all women for his wife. My vows said, "Forsaking all others," and that is what I committed to when I said, "I Do." I'd heard that Daria was depressed. I wanted to help her, but I knew I couldn't. All I could do was pray and be there when she emerged from her darkness.

Trying to comfort me, Kristi said, "She'll be alright, baby. It just takes time. We women incubate pain and hurt. We can't bounce back like you guys can. Most men's emotional vitality is the same as a flat tire. Our emotions run deep. I don't think I could rebound this fast if I were in her shoes. She'll be back."

That sword cut both ways. I wondered if Kristi was still incubating my indiscretion with Jordan. Kristi was such a spiritual woman that I didn't think she would ever let me know even if she was still hurting. When she said she forgave me, she meant it. To Kristi, "I forgive you," was not some tired, old tawdry cliché. Her forgiveness was meaningful and sincere. Most people say they forgive you, but they remind you of your offense every chance they get, but not my Kristi, forgiven for her means it's done, gone, and don't do it again.

I never met a woman like her who took the worst of me and still loved me. I gave her every reason to write me off as another low life, cheating scoundrel dog. I took her love and spit on it when I got back with Jordan. If that wasn't bad enough, I had to get Jordan pregnant. Kristi is truly everything I ever wanted in a woman. I remembered the day Marcus asked me while we were golfing what I was looking for in a woman. I found it all in Kristi. And what did I do with it? In all my testosterone-filled, egocentric manhood, I went back to open a door that God closed. I promised God that if she stayed with me after all that, I would be faithful and never dog her out again.

When I thought this conversation was going to quickly fade out, she said, "Honey, you are a heck of a man when you can get women to fall in love with you without any intimacy."

I decided to take another conversational road, "Why are you surprised, that's how I got you wasn't it? Once I met you and felt your spirit, I couldn't soil God's gift with the momentary pleasures of my flesh. You were worth waiting for. I made so many mistakes in the past. This time I had to change how I did things if I wanted a different result. I guess you could say I was fasting sex until the Lord ordained you as mine."

Kristi sought conformation in our tender moment, "Was I worth the wait?"

I looked at Kristi and saw the hope and respect in her eyes. Even though she knew that I dearly loved her, she wanted to hear me say "yes." I was going to say "yes," but saying only that word couldn't fully convey my heart. Truthfully, everything about Kristi wowed me. I put my hands on both sides of her face, pulling her towards mine. I kissed her lips tenderly. Then I kissed her forehead and then pulled back to look into her eyes and said, "Waiting until after we got married to make love with you was by far the hardest thing I've ever done. I was never able to do that with anyone else. Every straining moment of patience drew me closer to you, strengthening my love for you. Baby, I love you more than I will ever be able to put into words. I will spend the rest of my life letting you know that you were very much worth the wait." Pulling her closer to me, I hugged her tightly.

Kristi looked at me with puppy eyes. She took a big swallow, trying to get composure, "Maxwell Dean, I love you so much. I am yours until the very end. Thank you for waiting. I wanted to save myself for my husband. I was saving myself for you my king. Your greatest act of manhood was respecting my Christian values and waiting for me." Joyfull tears started rolling down her face.

No other words were necessary. We felt our love. It seemed like months flew by as we were now on the dawn of my new Maxwell unveiling.

What a way to begin a Fourth of July holiday. My friends were all arriving within hours of each other. I had everything lined up and planned with meticulous attention to all of the details. I had the transportation from the airport set. I had everyone's accommodations set. The timing would have to be flawless.

"Honey, are you sure you don't want to be out there to greet everyone when they arrive?" Kristi questioned.

"No, baby, I want to be right here where we can see and hear all of the action. You know how I have a flare for dramatic and exciting surprises."

"Okay, but your surprises are why Daria isn't here today. I'm not taking a dig at you, I'm just saying," she said in a way that asked—Are you sure you know what you're doing?

Each of my friends had a separate cabin all to themselves. Kristi had fruit baskets and snacks in their cabins. Their refrigerators were stocked with water and juices. We placed a note in each cabin instructing them to gather in the shade underneath the big tree that was nearest to the camp firepit. The cabins were situated in a circular pattern with a big white stone-lined firepit in the middle.

I looked at Kristi arranging things in our cabin. I felt so blessed that the Creator of the universe took time from His busy schedule to create such a human masterpiece just for me. She was stunning, forgiving, sexy, and all mine.

What a woman, I gasped in my thoughts. *Lord, I'll do it right this time.* After I said that a cool breeze blew across my body. Just then I remembered that's what Nanna's words were to me while I was in a coma. I don't know why that came to me now, but in my thoughts I remember telling Nanna that I would. I meant it too. Kristi takes my love to heights I never knew existed. She loved me past my faults. She always told me she loved me through Jesus.

Kristi announced, "Max, the vans are pulling up." As people exited the vans, she chided, "The gang is all here! You still have time to back out of your sneak attack."

"Nothing doing, baby cakes, I'm going through with this. They are my best friends and know how I am. I might ruffle a few feathers, but it's all love."

As Mel walked past our cabin window, I heard her cursing about how hot it was. "I could kick Max's ass for bringing us way out here to the middle of freakin' Sherwood Forest. I'm a city girl not Laura Ingalls from *Little House on the Prairie*. What are we going to do, play cards with the damn grizzly bears? Since my boy is a preacher now, I promised him I would try to stop cursing, but bringing me out here like I'm on *Survivor* is pushing it dammit!"

"Kristi, Mel is trying not to curse. I think the devil is trying to get the better of her. She's not swearing like a drunken sailor, but maybe just a slightly annoyed dockworker though."

Kristi smacked her lips and shook her head, "Bless her heart."

"Ah man! I stepped on the roots from hell and rolled my ankle. Now my brand new white sneakers are dirty. I'll probably have to go down to the creek and wash them in the Amazon River, cause I know they don't have a washing machine up here in this place. Do they even have running water? Max is gonna have to buy me a new pair of sneakers," Mel complained.

I heard Mason snap back, "It ain't that serious, vain girl."

Mel shouted back, "You need to shut up, Budda. Nobody was talking to you. Why don't you take your jungle-sandaled, ashy feet and reboard *Amistad*. I heard they freed you."

Not wanting to be bested by Mel, Mason fired back, "You know you want me. Budda means more man to love. I'm the real man you need, Ms. Man-less Mel."

"Mase, if I got with you I'd still be single because you'd die from too much Budda, too many what… let's say…carbs, cholesterol, calories, inches around your waist, and too much meat on that fat head of yours."

This is how it was with my friends. They loved each other dearly, but they ribbed each other like haters. Mason and Marcus always liked to get Mel started. Pike watched and didn't say much because Sarae reminded him that he had to go home with her at night.

"Baby, they are at it all ready. They couldn't last 12 minutes before getting started," I told Kristi smirking.

"Who started it, Mason or Marcus?"

"Guess?"

After thinking for a moment, Kristi said, "Let's see. In the woods, Mr. Jungle love Mason."

"You got it." About thirty minutes or so passed before people started making their way to the chairs we had situated under the shade tree. I think they unpacked and rested for a minute from the long 45-minute trek out to the camp from the airport. The instructions we left in their cabin told them to relax and start making their way to the tree in about 30-45 minutes.

I saw Pike and Sarae, Mason, Marcus, and Mel. They started talking about the resort and why I paid for everyone to come out to the boondocks to help with these kids.

"Where's Daria?" I heard Mel ask.

Sarae spoke up, "I talked to her a while back. I don't think she's coming. She is still torn up about Max and Kristi. She doesn't want to say much about it. She's been through a lot with Max since college, but this one tipped her over reality's scale. I think Daria knows Max is gone for good. Daria will eventually come around. We all go back too far. I can't even hate on Max for what he did. He, Kristi, and the Lord are on some whole other program right now. God knows Max has gone through some women searching for Mrs. Right."

Marcus cosigned, "True dat. He is my boy and all, but Max is different now. It's a good different. One that fits him."

"Oh Lord!" Pike blurted out.

Everyone turned to Pike to see what startled him. He looked like one of those people witnessing an oncoming tsunami approaching the shore trying to figure out where to run. Everyone looked at him and then in the direction he was looking.

Mel was the first person to speak. The rest of them didn't know what to say. "You little troll. What in the HELL are you doing here? Didn't your face get broke enough at church last year? What? Are you here to break up my boy's marriage? Because I can break yo ass if you need something else broken. I told Max I wouldn't curse, but if you're here to git sideways, my mouth may cause me to go straight to hell, but I will be dragging your little strumpet ass right with me."

Jordan interjected, "Wait..."

Marcus started moving towards Mel like he was positioning himself to get between them if Mel started to fight. Mel really didn't like Jordan. Her protective nature for me kicked in. I looked and listened from inside our cabin to make sure things didn't get out of hand.

Kristi cautioned me, "Max, this could get out of control."

"I won't let it," I reassured her, but was not really sure myself.

The last thing the group expected was to see Jordan here. Most were shocked, but Mel was more agitated. This was a surprise that surely wouldn't go over well at first. I just hoped I could keep it together long enough to get through my monster secret.

Mel countered Jordan, "Wait for what? Wait so you can swoop down on your home wreckin' broom and try to destroy my boy's marriage and ministry? He is a man of God now and doesn't get down with yo nasty ass program no more. You got some nerve showing up here with your drama. In fact, let me get out these earrings so I can knock you back into the nasty hole you crawled out of."

Sarae didn't move a muscle. I think deep down inside, she agreed with Mel. She probably thought somehow that Jordan was partially responsible for Daria's absence. Marcus moved closer to Mel and put his arm around her to calm her down. I think he was really holding her back. Mason inched towards Jordan to defend her if Mel broke free from Marcus.

Jordan signaled towards one of the cabins, "I know how you all must feel, but I'm not here for that. Baby, come over here."

"I know you all knew of him but never met Kyle," Jordan announced.

Mel calmed down some and I sighed as I watched everyone take a pause. The temperature went down, but the trouble wasn't over yet. Kristi looked at me like I had better not let this get out of hand. I had her support to a point, but she didn't like "messy." She kept reminding me they were real people with real emotions that ran deep.

Kyle walked out, not sure what to do. On one hand, I'm sure he wanted to come to Jordan's defense, but on the other hand, he would rather sit quietly and not interfere. "Hi, everyone."

People just looked at him and this entire situation like they were looking at some horrific natural disaster flash across the TV screen. Mel looked like she was getting ready for round two.

Jordan painfully exclaimed, "Kyle is the fiancé that I was cheating on with Max."

Pike blurted out as Sarae elbowed him in his side, "Ahh hell. I need a drink."

"Kyle is it?" Mel asked as Kyle nodded his head yes. "You must be truly spineless to come up in here with her knowing that the man who boned your woman behind your back brought us here with his wife. What kind of dude are you? What are you two freaks here for, to see if this is a swinger's resort? Do you think we're going to have some sort of ménage trios or ménage four? It ain't gonna happen homeboy. My boys can dust off your ass while I'm getting in your nasty woman's behind."

Jordan said calmly with reverent respect, "No, Mel, it's not like that. Kyle is my husband. Max was the pastor who officiated our wedding. Kristi was there too. We all went to counseling and reconciled what happened. Max got Kyle's phone number from me to call him and ask for his forgiveness. Max said he had to do that before he could purify his calling. It was beautiful. It made me look at myself and the damage I caused."

Looking like she had just got punched in the stomach, Sarae told Pike, "Honey, get a drink for me too."

Motioning to Kristi, I said, "Come on, baby, now it's time for us to go out there."

Kristi quickly headed for the door. I think she wanted to hurry and lower the temperature outside before anything serious could erupt. Her facial expression was second guessing my Max production. Mel just stood there looking as did everyone else—not knowing what to say. *Our cue to come out and begin unveiling our secret couldn't have been timed more perfectly,* I thought.

As we turned the corner, I smiled at everyone, "Hey everyone, I'm glad you all are here. I see that you have been told about one of our surprises."

I continued, "Mel, I thought you were going to watch your language for me?"

"Max, you know I'm trying, but when you pull something like this, you're lucky I didn't curse out the Pope," Mel said laughing.

I walked over and hugged her, "Okay, I'll give you that one, this time."

Marcus brought more levity to the conversation. "Boy, I had to hold Mel back from turning into the *Karate Kid!*"

Mason chimed in, "What's next? Is Daria about to jump out of a cake in a star spangled thong?"

Mel fired back, "Can you stop being nasty for at least thirty seconds, you over baked Mr. Clean?"

Trying to keep Mason and Mel under control, I replied, "Okay you two, we aren't going there right now."

Sarae got right to the main question, "Max, why are we out here in the middle of nowhere? This is a nice resort and all, but what's up with this? The thing you did with Kyle is why you are a man's man. I've got to give you your props on that one. Why are we here versus meeting where it's cooler?"

I looked at my watch and it was just about time for the surprise to get here. This was going to blow them away unlike any other thing they had experienced with me since college.

Mel turned towards Kristi, "Girl, you know I love Max, but I don't know how you can stand him."

Kristi eyed Mel, "You know with all that we've gone through, if God himself hadn't told me that Max is who He gave me, I would have run out of this situation. My grandmother told me when I was a little girl that I was going to be a preacher's wife. When I fell in love with Max, I said so much for granny's startling revelation. Max was the farthest thing away from the pulpit in every way imaginable. My spirit told me to love him anyway. The night Max called me from Bangkok telling me about his calling, I couldn't believe it. I looked up towards the sky and said, 'Oh my God, granny, it's happening.' "

Kristi continued, "With what Max's Nanna said to him and my granny to me, God had them stitching this quilt together in heaven with an unbreakable thread. Mel, I am so in it with my baby for better or worse!"

Everyone turned towards the place where the airport shuttles dropped them off. Two long, white tour buses pulled onto the grounds. They kicked up a cloud of dust as they traversed the winding dirt road.

When the buses stopped, the dust surrounded the buses like fog on a concert stage waiting for rock stars to exit.

"You all are my best friends in the whole world. I had to have you all here to share in something wonderful with Kristi and me. This isn't a resort—it is a youth camp called Camp Nebo. Remember when we told you all that we purchased a ranch, well, this is it. We purchased this camp to serve at-risk youth according to Christian character principles. Starting this weekend Kristi and I will live here. I resigned from my job to try and make a difference with misguided young people," I said, stunning the group into jaw dropping silence.

Marcus questioned, "Are you sure you want to do this?"

For the moment everyone turned away from the buses and focused on me. The grilling from my friends had just begun.

Mason, crinkling his eyebrows, "Man, tell me you didn't walk away from an over $200,000 a year job to live out here in the animal kingdom for a bunch of juvenile delinquents? People would give their left arm to have a job like yours, and you gave it up for what? Bruh, did you get brain damage when you were shot?"

"Yep, that's right. God moves in mysterious ways. This is now my ministry. I know you think I'm nuts and this sounds crazy. You're still my boy, Mason. Based on the strength of that, I know you are going to support me. I know all of you think I've taken leave of my senses. However, our bond won't let any of you give me anything less than your full support. Will it?" I asked, knowing the answer.

I thought about Daria not being here for this. I was a little sad about that because she was not here to see my life going to a new level. I still hadn't told them the real secret. I suppose I was breaking it to them slowly. The wait wouldn't be much longer.

"When I told my job about what I was planning to do, they fully supported me. The president of the company told me that if I agreed to serve as a consultant for the company on several of my projects, they would pay me a one year salary and match it with a grant to Camp Nebo since we set it up as a non-profit. Kristi and I told them to give it all to Camp Nebo," I replied.

Pike raised the pitch of his voice several octaves, "Are you crazy? You had them give almost a half million dollars of your money to the camp?"

Sarae, smiling in approving adoration, "Max, you have truly been touched by God. I am happy for you. I think it's wonderful."

Mel burst out laughing, "You da man Max. I wouldn't have walked away from that much money for them little bad ass cretins. But that's me. I ain't all religified like you. The only place I'm ever gonna be preaching is at bedside Baptist."

Jordan interjected, "I have to say something that may be a little rough to hear at first, but please let me get it out."

Mel looked at Jordan and motioned that she was reaching for her earrings. Mel was calm, but she clearly still wasn't a Jordan fan. She looked like she was on guard, just waiting for Jordan to get out of line. I wasn't sure what Jordan was going to say, so I was a little apprehensive as well. I hoped she wasn't going to pull the dirt out of the closet that we nailed shut during counseling.

Jordan started saying, "When I first met Max, he said he wanted to maximize me. Maybe some of you know that maximizing was about sexual conquest."

I thought, *Oh Lord! I don't want her to go there. Even though Kristi and I went to counseling to get past this, the wounds were still there even if they weren't hemorrhaging—this was a good way to open them up again.*

Sarae said as Mel started with the earrings, "Girlfriend, we don't need to hear this."

Jordan pleaded, "Let me finish, please!"

Everyone paused for a minute as Jordan continued, "I was devastated when Max announced his marriage in open church. When Max called Kyle to make amends for our sin, he set me on a different course in life. He and Kristi ministered to us. So when he told me and Kyle what their plans were, we wanted to join his cause. It felt so right that both Kyle and I took our savings and gave it to Max and Kristi for Camp Nebo. Not only that, but we agreed to take some time from our jobs to help them get it started. So you see, Pastor Maxwell Dean started out to conquer me one way, but ended up maximizing the spiritual person in me that never existed before. I went from man to man searching for a love they couldn't provide. Max brought that love through a man named Jesus. I will forever be grateful to Max and Kristi for helping me get where I need to be."

Sarae's eyes teared up. Kristi smiled as she seemed touched by Jordan's declaration. She hugged Jordan and said, "God's ways are not our ways, honey."

I was moved to hear something so nice. I never thought about things that way. It touched me. I'm also glad that she didn't take the story any further back than that, I thought.

"Oh my God!" Pike shouted.

"Hell naw!" Mason said following Pike.

Everyone turned to Pike and what he was looking at. Oh boy it's here now. Everyone was looking at all of the two busloads of kids filing out of the buses. It looked like they just kept coming. That wasn't what Pike was screaming about.

Mel crossed her arms in disgust, "What kind of shit is this? Isn't that them? I know somebody is either incompetent as all get out, or they are playing a sick joke. Max, aren't those the two boys that shot you and Marcus?"

I replied unemotionally, "Yep."

"I got my gun. As a federal agent I can bring my fire arm with me on the plane. I brought it because I thought I might have to shoot a snake or something out here in the wild kingdom. But I'm ready to break it out for some two-legged snakes too," Mason said as he started moving towards his cabin to get his gun.

"Stop Mase. You don't need to get your gun. Marcus, are you all right?" I asked.

"No. How did they end up here? Didn't the justice system know they were sending the boys that shot us to your camp? How screwed up is that?" Marcus fired back, trying to keep his composure.

I looked at Kristi to get her ready for what I had to say next. She looked at me hunching her shoulders and tipping her head to the side to signify, okay—do it. I was about to open up a hornet's nest. My palms were sweating. I was thinking, *here goes.*

"I requested them. I went to the court and petitioned to have them released to my camp," I announced as I waited on World War III to break out amongst my friends.

Mason screamed, "You did what?"

Mel jumped in, "You have lost your doggone mind this time, Max. The entire surprise thing is cute, but this is some serious shit. They are junior killers. What if they have flashbacks?" she added.

I grabbed for the radio in my back pocket and turned up the volume. "Ben, send Jason over here," I said to the group leader on the radio.

Pike said uncharacteristically raising his voice, "He is the one who shot you. All of his bullets found their mark in your body. Do I need to remind you that technically they killed you? You were dead until the doctors brought you back to life. And now you are asking him to come over here and want us to stand here for that?"

Everyone was stunned. It didn't seem like any of them were comfortable with the shooters being here, let alone coming over to face us. They just didn't know that isn't the half of it. What was still yet to come would be nothing less than mind blowing.

"There is more to Jason's story than you might think. I want him to tell you like he told me. Give him a chance. It'll be alright," I said, trying to calm everyone's anxiety.

As Jason took the walk over, I couldn't help but remember everything that happened to bring us to this moment. I couldn't help but wonder how long ago God put this course of events in motion. I got to know Jason from a different perspective. Now it was their turn. Jason was a little thinner than the last time I saw this five-foot-eight inch tall kid. I reckon prison food wasn't the best. As he approached, I winked and nodded my head for him to begin.

Greeting a crowd that was definitely not feeling him, Jason said, "Hello, Pastor Dean, and everyone." No one said anything as Jason began speaking, "Pastor Dean told me that he wanted me to come over and speak with you all. Given everything that's happened, this is hard for me to say, but I'll try to say it. When I tried to carjack Pastor Dean and Mr. Harris, I was an angry kid who didn't care about anyone or anything. I grew up without a father. In fact, I never knew my father or ever met him. So, I felt like if my father didn't care about me, why should I care about anyone else. I'm not offering that as an excuse. I'm just saying what was in my stupid head," Jason cried.

For the most part no one seemed particularly moved. I could sense they still hated Jason. I knew Mason wanted to get his gun. I knew they had no idea what was coming. I did. It was life changing.

Jason continued, "One day during the trial our attorney told us that it wasn't looking good for us. He asked the prosecutor to accept our plea deal. He said if they didn't accept the plea deal, I would be getting out of prison just before my seventieth birthday. Those words hit me like a wrecking ball. I thought I was hard, I tried to act tough, but that night I broke down. That sounded a lot like a life sentence to me. When we got back to our cell, the guard said that it looked like we'd be going to a maximum security prison. He said maximum security prisons are like gladiator schools. The guard told us the inmates there looked forward to fresh young meat like me and my accomplice Dequan. I remember him saying that one of three things would happen—we would either become someone's woman, get beat up daily, or get new charges for killing someone for trying to defend ourselves. He topped that off by saying that either way, we were screwed. I felt dead. My life was over and I wasn't even old enough to have a driver's license. I tried to figure out a way I could hang myself in my cell. I cried all night. Exhausted from crying all night without thinking, I said, 'Oh God, help me' and continued crying." Jason choked up again.

Sarae was crying. Mel was quiet, but I knew she was moved too. The guys were not as emotional as the ladies, but I sensed their hearts were softening somewhat as well.

"Pastor Dean is a saint. I wouldn't be here if it wasn't for him. I think my plea went from God's ears to pastor's heart. To have my attorney tell me that pastor had the prosecutor accept our plea deal, and then later find out that he petitioned the court for us to come to this camp was something that I never could have imagined. My only lifeline came from the very man whose life I tried to take," Jason said with tears rolling down his face.

Sarae cried out, "God bless you, Max."

Mel questioned, "What made you do it, Max?"

Okay, ready or not, I was about to tell them something they could not imagine. I was about to tell them how God moved in my life. I was about to give them my own rendition of Moses and the burning bush. I was about to unveil my life changing moment. The man in the robe who visited me after the shooting was Christ. When He saw me and said, "I'll see you again later," later was to give me an assignment. I had no idea it would be this.

I went over and embraced him. "Thanks Jason. Stick around for a minute please."

"Okay, Pastor." Jason replied with red watery eyes that still contained welled up tears.

"I know you all have questions. Why? Each time I tried to tell the prosecutor to send the little bastards straight to hell, I couldn't reach her. Then, I felt sick. Something inside me simply would not let me go there. One day I had this strong feeling that came over me to let it go. When I decided to let it go, I got through to Collette. I told her that I wanted to meet the derelict's parents who raised these monsters before I decided on their attorney's plea offer, even though I had already decided to accept it," I explained.

Mason looked perplexed, "What was the point of that then?"

I continued, "I wanted to tell the parents if I were deciding about their sentences, I would send them to the electric chair for being such horrible parents. Their neglect almost cost me my life. There was nothing in my mind that they could say to excuse what kind of monster they unleashed into society."

I told them the story about the day I was to meet the parents in the courthouse.

"While I was waiting to meet the parents, I ran into this woman who looked familiar. I couldn't place her though. She was wearing a pale blue skirt and jacket. It reminded me of the powder blue tux I wore at my junior prom. The woman looked tired, like life had been kicking her butt. Her tall frame, boxy full figure, and the bags around her eyes resembled a joyless woman who was just hanging onto life. It seemed like once upon a time she was hot, but now she was reminiscent of someone merely existing—waiting on the next crisis.

"The woman saw the puzzled look on my face and said, 'We met once at college. You probably don't remember me. I never saw you again. I dropped out after only one semester.'

"I vaguely remembered her, but nothing stuck in my mind. She could have been anyone. She told me her name was Karen, but still nothing clicked. So, I blew it off and asked her why she was here. 'Are you here for traffic court?'

"Looking down, not making eye contact, she said, 'I wish. I bet I know your name.'

"Surprised by the comment I replied, 'I bet you don't.' And she came up with my name.

"I thought, *How did she know that? Did she hear someone call my name?* She said, no one told her, she remembered me from first semester of freshman year." I was impressed that she remembered me after only one meeting so many years ago.

I paused with my storytelling. Mason seemed a little uninterested. Mason lead with stares of, okay nice story, but why did you let them off. I knew all my friends wanted to know what I said to the parents. I thought, *God does have a strange sense of humor.*

Deciding not to immediately answer the questions that were on everyone's mind, I continued telling them my story. "I asked her why she was here if not for traffic court. She said her son had gotten into some trouble and she had to be there.

"I naively asked if her husband was coming.

"In her words, she said, 'I'm not married and my son's father has never been in his life. He never knew his father. It wasn't his father's fault. One night of passion is all it took. The next morning I slithered out of his place before he even woke up. I wasn't loose or anything, but since my parents held me so tight growing up, I just wanted to break out when I got a taste of college freedom. After I found out I was pregnant, I never even went back to tell the guy. To this day I never told his father he had a son. We were young and I never wanted to ruin his life by saddling him with a kid. I was so stupid. I have caused so much pain with my secret. Now look.'

"I tried to comfort her and said, 'It will be alright. What did your son do?

"Karen's tears attracted the attention of many of the people sitting with us in the waiting room. This unwanted attention was getting uncomfortable for me. I hoped the people didn't think I was with her or causing her to cry. Ashamedly, I was a wee bit embarrassed by the growing spectacle.

"She said crying uncontrollably, that it was attempted murder. I thought this woman was in for a rough ride on that one. I couldn't imagine having a kid who was facing murder charges. Worse yet, she had to face this trial alone. I felt for her. I wanted to tell her about my case, but didn't because she already had enough on her plate.

"Then she said carrying around this secret for all these years had almost destroyed her. She knew who I was because Jason was her son. He was the one who shot me."

As my friends continued listening to my story, everyone, even Jason was stoically quiet. All of Camp Nebo seemed motionless. Jason was crying. All of the girls were crying. Kristi came over and held my hand. I was starting to feel the emotions from everything that happened over the last few years. I knew everyone felt it, that's why I went through with the plea deal. You couldn't be human if you weren't touched by Karen's story. At last it was all coming out. I think they even felt sorry for Jason.

I continued telling them the story. "Karen pleaded with me for forgiveness. And then she admitted that her shame from one night of bliss almost caused the destruction of two intertwined lives who had never met each other."

Pike wiped tears from his eyes. I don't think things immediately resonated with what I just said in telling Karen's story. I think they were still emotionally raw from hearing Karen's heartfelt story and seeing Jason standing there crying. Then, I saw a face light up like Moses when He saw the face of God on Mount Horeb.

"Oh my God! Oh my God! Father Jesus!" Sarae said, gasping and covering her mouth.

Sarae was crying profusely. Everyone looked at her as if she saw a snake. Marcus looked at Sarae trying to figure out why she was falling to pieces. Pike was crying himself as he tried to comfort Sarae. I was trying to hold it together. Kristi held me and whispered into my ear, "It's going to be okay, honey." Big burley Mason looked like he was wounded and looking for someone to hug. Mel grabbed Mason and hugged him just as his eyes started watering.

I struggled to part my lips to say something. I saw Jason crying and shaking like he was releasing all of the emotional pain of his life. I felt like he was coming face to face with all of his demons. Kristi and I walked over to comfort Jason. Jordan sobbed as she held Kyle. She looked at me as if to say, it's alright to let go. Sarae broke away from Pike and joined us. Sarae grabbed Jason's hand and held it tightly but lovingly. Everyone was emotionally exposed, but only Sarae figured it out. My surprise was coming into focus. Life led us to this moment. No one was safe from the work of the Lord.

I shook like I had the chills. Choked up and crying, I managed to squeak out the words in my broken and intermittent voice that no one ever expected me to utter, "Yes, Sarae, you guessed it… everyone, Jason is my *son!*"

The End.

AUTHOR BIOGRAPHY

Lewis Banks is an author, screenwriter, and former radio talk show host, currently living in Florida. For more than twenty-five years, he worked in high-level management positions for companies such as Florida Power and Light, Hewlett Packard, and General Electric.

After leaving the corporate arena, Banks went on to start the non-profit Camp Nebo, dedicated to helping at-risk youth. Now, a sought-after motivational speaker, he has given public talks at a variety of churches, schools, and other community forums.

As a best-selling author Banks has been nominated for various national literary awards and has written for a university newspaper.

Banks is currently pursuing an MDiv and an MFA in script and screenwriting from Regent University.

Made in the USA
Charleston, SC
20 June 2015